About th

Zara Cox writes contemporary and erotic romance. She lives in the Garden of England – aka Kent – with her hubby and two kids. She loves to read and travel. In 2017 she managed to visit her number one bucket list destination – Hawaii – and is now actively pleading with her husband to live there! She loves to hear from her readers, and you can get in touch with her via Twitter @zcoxbooks, on Instagram zaracoxwriter, or Facebook zaracoxwriter.

Dare Me

Dare Me
to Crave You

ZARA COX

MILLS & BOON

First Published in Great Britain 2023
by Mills & Boon, an imprint of HarperCollins*Publishers* Ltd,
1 London Bridge Street, London, SE1 9GF

www.harpercollins.co.uk

HarperCollins*Publishers*
Macken House, 39/40 Mayor Street Upper,
Dublin 1, D01 C9W8, Ireland

ISBN: 978-0-263-31915-6

CLOSE TO THE EDGE

To Grace Thiele,
for being the physical manifestation of Lily Gracen.

CHAPTER ONE

Caleb

THE QUICK GLANCE at my wrist was a bad idea. I knew the moment my gaze dropped to the black-and-azure face of my watch that I'd added another half hour to this circus.

Shit.

"Oh, am I wasting your time? Do you have somewhere *important* to be?" the whiny voice demanded.

I sighed.

The ability to turn circumstances, good or bad, to my advantage was what had earned me my renowned status. But no one starts life thinking they were going to do what I do, be what I am.

A fixer.

I wasn't complaining, though. I was great at my job. Sometimes I wish I wasn't *this* damned good… Oh, who the hell was I kidding? Most days I loved my job. Tonight, not so much. The 2 a.m. calls were the worst. Especially when they interrupted a very promising pre-fuck blowjob.

But hey, what was a small case of blue balls when the siren song of work beckoned? As evading tactics went, it was an effective way to hold the demons at bay.

I shoved my hands into my pockets and glared at the glassy-eyed man-child straddling the banister in front of me. "Yes, actually. I do have somewhere else to be. So if you're going to jump, get it over with so I can get on with my night."

Christ, you've surpassed yourself this time, Steele.

My client's slack-faced shock confirmed my thought. "Are you fucking serious?"

"As Zachary Quinto's eyebrows. This is the fourth time I've had to deal with your...unhappiness this month alone. Normally, I would've washed my hands of you or dragged you to rehab. But I promised your father I'd look out for you. The only thing you're addicted to is laziness—"

"You don't know what you're talking about. The band kicked me out!"

"Because you set your GPS to Cabo instead of your studio in Culver City. Last month it was Vegas. The month before it was Atlantic City, right?"

"I can't just turn up and sing! I need inspiration," Ross Jonas sulked.

"And you think you're going to find that by jumping off this balcony tonight?" I shrugged. "Go ahead, then. I can have you in a nice corner slab in the morgue by sunrise."

His jaw dropped again. "Holy fuck, you're something else."

I closed my eyes and wished those words were coming from a different mouth, preferably the scarlet-painted female one I'd left in my bed. When I opened them again, Ross was still there. Shame.

I wasn't twisted enough to wish my client dead but I wanted this over and done with.

He wasn't going to jump.

We'd been through this dance enough times. He chose this suite because there was a deep pool conveniently situated six floors below. And if by some exceptionally bad luck he didn't make it, I had four guys on the ground floor of the Beverly Hills Hotel ready with a giant inflatable to catch his sorry ass because sadly, this wasn't my first rodeo with a pseudo-suicidal client.

I would've dropped him as a client a long time ago, for his selfish antics for starters, and because I never took on suicidal clients, not even ones who were faking it. I wasn't ashamed to admit suicide was a red-hot button for me. But Ross's father was my first client, the guy who'd given me a break in a cutthroat place like LA, then gone out of his way to recommend my services to others. And when Victor Jonas had all but begged me to look out for his son, I'd agreed unconditionally.

The worst Ross, only child of rich, overindulgent parents, would suffer tonight if he did jump, was having the wind knocked out of him.

Whereas I was destined to suffer a stronger resurgence of the nightmares I fought each night, not to mention the cold shoulder of a pouty redhead if I didn't wrap this up fast. "Yes, I *am* something else. And *you* have ten seconds to shit or get off the pot."

I straightened from my leaning position against the French doors and moved toward him. He glanced furtively behind him and paled. "Fuck," he muttered.

Two feet away I stopped and crossed my arms. "Listen to me. You keep flirting with death like this and one day you'll succeed. Do me a favor, Ross. Put a little bit of the effort you use to jerk me around into doing some *actual* work. You might be surprised at how good it feels to reap the results of your hard work."

The belligerence drained from his face. "But I'm out of the band."

"Call your guys in the morning. Beg if you need to. Humility goes a long way if you truly mean it," I said. I had no clue whether that was true or not. Humility wasn't exactly a strong suit of mine. "And while you're at it, try showing up when you say you will. Deal?"

When he nodded I stepped back, staying alert as he slowly climbed down. Relieved, I followed him back into the suite he'd checked into for the purpose of pulling this shitty, dangerous stunt.

I breathed through the fury and resisted the urge to tear another strip off him. "One of my guys is going to stick around, make sure you get to Culver City nice and early in the morning. Sound good?"

I slapped him on the shoulder and headed for the door. With any luck, my date would still be warming my bed.

"Hey, Caleb."

I turned around. "Yeah?"

"Would you...really have watched me jump?"

My face tightened. "If you wanted to, I couldn't have stopped you." I paused a beat. "Did you?"

He shook his head sheepishly. "No."

My anger spiked another notch. "Pull a stunt like this again and I'll push you myself."

I left him standing in the middle of the living room, shoulders hunched, pondering that.

My jaw tightened as the elevator rushed me to the ground floor. Unfortunately, the memories Ross had triggered weren't as easy to leave behind as I exited the five-star hotel.

For my mother it'd been third time lucky. Or *unlucky*, depending on which side of the fence you stood on. My steps faltered as the acid-sharp pain that always accompanied the memory of her death plowed through me.

Damn Ross Jonas.

With a deep breath I walked out, handed a twenty to the valet attendant holding out the keys to my Bugatti and slid behind the wheel.

Before I could pull away, my phone beeped. Tugging it out of my pocket, I found a centerfold-worthy picture gracing my screen. The accompanying message flashed seconds later.

This is what you could've had tonight. Call me never!

I was torn between a smile and a scowl. A smile because if I chose to call her right then, she would've answered. A scowl because the redhead was the first to tweak my interest in a while, and I'd hoped she would end this uninvited dry spell that had taken over my sex life. But despite my earlier anticipation, the desire to get her back in my bed was dwindling fast. I stared at the picture again and stroked my dying wood a second before I hit the Delete button, erasing her from my contacts altogether.

I gunned the engine onto the Pacific Coast Highway, pointing my car toward Downtown LA. With my bedroom plans now shot to shit, and in no mood to return to an empty bed and dreams filled with memories I didn't cherish, work was the next best option.

Nevertheless, I cursed when my phone rang. "Dammit, doesn't anyone sleep anymore?" I griped.

Maggie, my assistant, answered, "You don't pay me to sleep. You specifically stated during my interview that I wasn't allowed to sleep."

"*You* don't get to sleep. That doesn't mean you can interrupt mine. I'm shocked I need to explain that to you."

"Tell me you're not heading to Fixer HQ right now and I'll hang up."

I didn't bother because she had a GPS tracker on my car. Once or twice that tracker had saved my skin and extricated me from some unsavory situations.

"What do you want, Maggie?" I switched lanes, enjoying the sweet purr of the engine.

"Wow, someone's grumpy," she muttered under her breath, then said briskly, "We have an urgent situation."

I tapped my finger against the wheel. "Aren't they all?"

"This one is less sex, drugs and rock and roll, more... something else."

I suppressed a growl. "By all means, hold the dramatics."

My sarcasm bounced right off her thick skin. It was one of the many reasons she was invaluable. "I'm sending you the address her people sent me. You can be there in fifteen minutes."

The joy in my ride gone, I cursed. "Her *people*? Did you not explain to them that I don't deal with *people*? That it's one-on-one or not at all?"

Maggie sighed. "I know how to do my job, Caleb. Trust me, please, just a little?"

I frowned. I didn't trust blindly because I didn't trust anyone. Maggie knew this. Why she was choosing to tap into a resource not readily available to me wasn't improving my mood. The sizeable monthly paycheck I signed bought me her hard work and loyalty. I didn't expect anything else, and certainly not her request for me to trust her.

My phone buzzed with the incoming address. "I'll be in touch." I hung up, pulled off the road long enough to check out the Mulholland Drive address before I executed a slick U-turn.

High walls and electronic gates greeted me when I reached the property. Everything about this smelled like trust-fund princess with her panties in a twist about her latest flame. Or a chihuahua kidnapping that wasn't worth my time.

Only the assurance that Maggie excelled at her job made me roll down my window and press the intercom.

The cast-iron gate slid back, and I drove up the cobbled driveway of a large stone mansion. In typical Hollywood style, the original property had been remodeled into a grotesque status symbol, with little care for artistic design.

I hid my lip curl as I stepped out and spotted the rent-a-cops stationed on either side of the house.

The front door swung open to reveal a young, sharply dressed man on the threshold. He seemed out of place in this setting but I wasn't here to judge. "Good evening, Mr. Steele. If you'll come with me?" He didn't offer his name and I didn't ask for it. This was LA, where even D-list celebrities were paranoid about revealing their identities to the wrong person.

The inside of the mansion was as gaudy as the outside, the designer having gone to town with an explosion of golds and leafy greens splashed across every surface.

Suppressing a shudder, I went down a hallway into a large living room, growing impatient when a look around didn't produce the *her* Maggie had mentioned.

"Wait here, please."

He left. I paced, silently hoping this trip would be worth my while. I had a dossier full of needy clients but their demands were nothing I couldn't handle in my sleep. Thoughts of sleep, or the woeful lack of it lately, ramped up the disquiet inside me.

I was busy smashing it down when the double doors opened in front of me.

At the first sight of her, my gut clenched tight and my lungs flattened with expelled air I wasn't interested in replenishing.

I wasn't sure whether it was the shock of her roughly chopped white-blond hair that gripped my attention or the wide, full red lips currently getting sucked between her teeth. Maybe it was the bright, oval-shaped green eyes staring directly at me. Or the lush petiteness of the body draped from head to toe in black leather and lace.

Leather and lace.

The combination was lethal enough without the silver-studded leather cuffs encircling both wrists and her slim throat.

Jesus.

She was a cross between a wannabe punk rock star and a BDSM enthusiast's wet dream.

She stared at me, our height disparity forcing her to angle her head and expose her delicate neck to me. Edgy hunger burned through me as I tracked her alabaster-pale face, the lightest flutter of her nostrils, the velvet smoothness of her mouth. The racing pulse beneath her choker.

She inhaled and exhaled slowly. "I hear you're a fixer."

"You heard correctly." I wasn't in the phone book. Referrals were strictly by word of mouth. I sent silent thanks to whichever client had sent her my way.

She gave a brisk nod. "Before we start, we need to discuss an NDA," she said in a sexy voice I wanted in surround sound in my head.

I was used to nondisclosure agreements. No one worth a damn did business these days without first whipping out an NDA. But whether it was the time of night or my general mood lately, I shook my head.

"Before we discuss NDAs I need the broad strokes of the job first." Who was I kidding? This woman, who-ever she was, intrigued me. I was fairly sure I was going to take the job.

Her mouth firmed. "Fair enough. I've picked up a stalker," she said matter-of-factly. "It started off as cyberstalking but in the past three weeks it's escalated to physical stalking."

The bolt of unexpected protectiveness shot through me, unsettling me enough to make me cross my arms. "And you haven't called the cops because…?"

"Because it could be linked with the work I'm doing."

"What work?"

"Extremely sensitive work that I can't discuss with-out you signing the NDA." She held out the document.

My intrigue spiked. "Okay, let's see it."

It was seven pages long, far more detailed than the standard three-page NDA, with her name left blank. I noticed her studying me from the corner of my eye as I read it a second time. When I was done, I shifted my gaze to her, my interest mounting when she met my eye boldly. "It looks good. Pen?"

As if on cue, the door opened, and the young guy who opened the front door walked in. I watched him, then her, looking for signs of a relationship. She nodded her thanks when he produced a pen, but there was nothing else in her gaze that tweaked my senses.

I grimaced at the relief that shot through me, and signed.

She took the pen and inserted her name.

Lily Angela Gracen.

I stared at the name, searched the corners of my mind and came up empty as the guy witnessed the document.

As she walked him to the door I allowed myself a second, more intimate look.

Hell, she was *stunning.*

No one deserved to be stalked, online or in real life, but *fuck*, looking at her, I understood why she could become an object of some psycho's obsession.

The moment the thought crossed my mind, I froze, rejecting the idea of her being in danger, even while my cock stirred to life, excited by the magnificent vision crossing the room toward me.

She moved with understated but sexy awareness, a woman who acknowledged her considerable attributes but didn't need to flaunt them. A woman who knew the power of those curvy hips, her plump lips and generous breasts.

Despite her combat boots adding a couple of inches to her height, she barely came up to my chest. Petite, perfectly proportioned, she was the epitome of a filthy, decadent Pocket Venus.

She probably weighed no more than a hundred and

ten pounds. On a good day I bench-pressed twice her weight. My mind reeled with images of how she would feel in my arms.

Easily pinned against a wall, her naked, delicious weight trapped between my greedy hands.

Easily tied down to a bed with silk ropes if that was her thing, her skin flushed pink as she straddled the fine line between preorgasmic tension and a screaming climax.

Easily subdued and tossed into the back of a van by some unhinged asshole with entitlement issues.

I yanked myself away from lurid sexual scenarios and adjusted my stance to ease the constriction in my pants as the most gorgeous creature I'd seen in a long time stopped before me.

"Who was he?" I nodded at the door.

"He came with the house rental. I asked him to stick around to witness the document."

"Okay, now that I've signed your document, let's start again. I'm Caleb Steele. Fixer."

She stared at the hand I held out. "Lily Gracen, chief coder for Sierra Donovan Media."

Despite what was happening to her, she had more than a little sass. And if she was a coder, she had brains, too. A lethal combination on any given day. Packaged in that body, I got the strongest suspicion I was in for an exhilarating ride.

After several moments she took my hand.

The second I felt the warm sizzle of her flesh, experienced an extra shot of testosterone through my system and watched her eyes widen in mutual acknowledgment of the rush, I accepted my reality. Signed NDA or not, the unholy fire spreading through my bloodstream had only one destination.

I was going to cross a helluva lot of lines, all of which started and ended with one fact.

I was going to fuck Lily Angela Gracen.

CHAPTER TWO

Caleb

WHOA. TAKE IT down a notch or six, cowboy.

Getting involved with Lily Gracen while she was my client had *bad idea* written all over it. I'd learned that lesson the hard way.

Which was why I broke my rules for no one.

A fixer's first and last defense against failure was his neutrality. Starting out I'd disregarded that by getting involved with Kirsten. A young actress on the precarious rise, her cultivated vulnerability had slipped beneath my guard, triggered emotions she'd expertly manipulated to suit her purposes. Emotions that had turned me into a laughingstock and nearly tanked my reputation.

Never again were two words I abided by.

Already, my sexual attraction to Lily Gracen was getting in the way of that neutrality. And that bite of protectiveness the moment I saw her? That needed to go, as well. My task was to find her stalker without messy emotions getting in the way.

But…once that was done, there would be nothing stopping me from rewarding myself with a taste of her.

Yeah, I wasn't perfect. At no point in my life did I try to be. You can't go countless rounds in the boxing ring of life without emerging with a few scars both inside and out.

I'd dragged myself from the rougher parts of South Central LA and into the twenty-thousand square feet of a Malibu mansion via some seriously rocky terrain, experiencing every imaginable facet of human nature along the way.

It was the reason I now lived by three simple rules:

Protect the innocent and vulnerable at all cost. Always.

No sleeping with clients, no matter how tempting.

No sleeping with the fucking clients, no matter how fucking *tempting.*

The foundation of rule one would never waver. I feared for the foundation of rules two and three as I held on to Lily's hand, drifted my thumb across one satin-smooth knuckle. She gratified my touch with a sharp catch of her breath.

God, I wanted to hear that sound louder, preferably preceding a scream as I buried my cock inside her sweet little pussy.

But first, I needed to get down to business.

She beat me to it by tugging her hand out of mine. "Shall we discuss the details?"

As she walked away, I caught the scent of her perfume—earthy, evocative of rain-soaked heather, the kind that invited you to roll around in when the sun came out. I wanted to follow that scent with my nose. And then with my hands and my mouth.

Down boy, I cautioned my cock when it jumped in agreement.

"Sure."

She sat down at one end of the sofa, crossed her legs and waved me to the seat next to her. "Sit down, Mr. Steele."

The take-charge attitude from such a diminutive person was an unexpected turn-on. I let her have the leeway. For now.

I sat, dragging my gaze from her shapely calves and thighs. "One thing you should know—I won't be managed. If you want me to catch this…person, you'll let me do my job."

She stared at me for a moment, then shrugged. "We'll get to that in a moment."

Again, I tried not to react like a horny teenager to the sound of her voice, but God, it was something else. Hell, from the top of those roughly chopped locks to the tips of her boots, she was something else.

"Is Steele really your last name?" she asked abruptly, her slender arms folded.

I raised an eyebrow. "Do you always go out dressed like that?" Okay, not how I'd wanted to start, but it was a pertinent question. I didn't have a problem with the way any woman dressed, but some guys out there were sick enough to form vile opinions about women based on the way they dressed.

Her pointy little chin rose. "What's wrong with the way I dress?"

I laughed, absently noting how the sound scraped my throat. "Nothing to me. But everything to the wrong person."

She inhaled sharply. "What does that mean?"

"That I hope your stalker is the type who's just obsessed with your outer appearance. Those are the easiest to catch because they can't help themselves. They'll slip up and attempt to make physical contact with you sooner rather than later."

A tiny shiver went through her but her gaze didn't waver. "Why are you assuming the stalker's interest is sexual?"

"Because I have eyes. You're a fucking knockout. But if you say it's not, I'm willing to delay a final verdict on the bastard until I hear all the facts."

A light blush bloomed into her cheeks. From the way her lips pressed together I could tell she hated that little evidence of her emotions. I enjoyed it a little too much. "Are you always this blunt?" she asked.

I folded my arms to prevent them from doing something stupid. Like tracing that blush down to her throat. "Always. That going to be problem?"

Her small fingers gripped her biceps. "Only if you don't like having it reciprocated."

"I'm good with blunt. I prefer it, even. And yes, Steele is really my name."

It was one of the few facts my mother blessed me with in the midst of her dark despair; and one of the first things I did when I established solid, reliable contacts through my work was to find the man whose blood coursed through my veins. Turned out I came from a long line of mostly no-good Steeles. A shocking percentage had been criminals. Of those that were alive, including my father, I wanted nothing to do with in this lifetime.

I refocused on her as she recrossed her legs, and I couldn't stop myself from staring. The hem of her black leather skirt had ridden up to midthigh, and she was making no move to pull it down. That tiny bit of exhibitionism ramped up my temperature another hundred notches. My tongue grew thicker and I watched her foot bounce for several seconds before I realized she was waiting for me to speak.

I cleared my throat and forced my brain back on the right track. "You think your stalker isn't interested in you personally. So it's work related?"

"I think so."

"Okay. Tell me about the project you're working on." She hesitated.

"I need to know where to start looking. Who to rule out," I pushed.

She toyed with the tiny spikes on her wrist cuff as she weighed her words. "It's an algorithm that significantly comprises data. On a small scale it can store almost fifteen times as much data as on the ordinary thirty-two-gigabyte chip you use on your phone."

Okay, that blew my mind a little. But I suspected my mind was about to be blown even further. "And on a larger scale?"

"If our planned launch is successful next month, it can render almost all the current data storage algorithms obsolete in under a year." She spoke with quiet but fierce pride.

I gave a low whistle. "And you wrote the code? All of it?"

There was no false modesty. Just a firm nod. "Yes. It's all mine."

"That's impressive."

Her gaze rose from her wrist to mine. The determined fire and pride that burned in her eyes said she knew what she was capable of, and was hell-bent on going after it. I could see how that would piss a few male egos off.

"Thank you," she responded in a low, husky voice.

Impossibly, the evidence of power she held in her small body and that huge brain of hers turned me on even more. I was a greedy enough asshole to admit that I wanted to experience what that power blazing through her felt like. I wanted to see her drunk on it, if only for a moment, so I could feel the intoxicating afterburn of it.

But that urge would have to be curtailed for a while because, unfortunately, her revelation had thrown open several avenues where the threat could be coming from.

I rose, thankful that with the much bigger problem on my mind, my body was calming down a little from its sexual frenzy. Although I still needed to turn away to hide the semi-erection throbbing behind my fly. I was crossing the room when I heard her question.

"Is something wrong?"

I glanced at her over my shoulder. "That depends on how wide your circle of trust is. And how wide *their* circles are. I suggest we get things moving sooner rather than later." I pulled out my phone and was about to hit the first number on my speed dial when it blared to life.

Maggie's uncanny timing was impressive. But not if she was calling with anything that might distract me from Lily Gracen.

"Yes?" My voice was terser than I intended, but what the hell. The night was turning out to be interesting in some ways and extremely frustrating in others.

"Just checking in. On the off chance I blew it, I wanted to know if I should tender my resignation now or get some sleep and do it in the morning," Maggie said with a pinch of sarcasm that straddled the fine line between amusing and insubordinate.

But despite my irritation, I toyed with giving her a bonus for landing me this job.

"We have a new client."

"Yes! Great job, Maggie. I've no idea what I'd do without you, Maggie. I'll even consider giving you that pay raise you've been hinting at for the last six months, Maggie."

"Keep talking about yourself in the third person and your boss will think you're a lunatic and fire your ass."

"I don't want that. At all. What do you need me to do?" she asked, back in my preferred super-efficient mode.

I strolled to the farthest window while I updated Maggie on the assignment. "My first thought was to keep her completely off the radar while I hunted down this creep, but I've changed my mind."

"O…kay."

"I need you to prepare a couple of safe houses. Have the jet on standby, too. We might need to change location quickly."

"Yes, boss. Right away, boss."

"Don't be a smart-ass, Maggie."

"Absolutely not. Safe houses. Private jet. Check."

"Good girl. And if you insist on it, you can go get some sleep after that. But I need you bright and early in the morning. Got it?"

"Of course. I'll text you once it's done."

I hung up, satisfied with taking the direct approach to Lily's problem.

I turned around. She'd stopped messing with her cuff, but her fingers were linked over one knee, and the look in her eyes was mildly censorious.

"You have something to say?"

"Do you treat all your employees like that?"

I pocketed my phone. "Like what?"

"Like they're one level up from chattels."

I retraced my steps back to her. "I don't have a problem cracking the whip, if that's what you mean. I find it works best if it's established clearly who's boss." I didn't add that Maggie often rolled her eyes when I used my dominant voice. Which was pretty much all the time.

"So that's your thing? You like to lord it over people?"

I shoved my hands in my pockets as I stood over her. This time the disparity was even more acute, and her upturned face was even more exposed. Fuck, she was so small, such a delicious morsel wrapped in a bundle of sharp brains and fierce beauty. That feral urge to possess her stormed through me, firing up every cell in my body.

Still, I should probably have curbed the words that slid to the tip of my tongue. But hell, I was never one to back down from speaking my mind. I'd learned the hard way how high the cost of holding my tongue could be.

"Would you like me to lord it over you, sweetheart?"

Her eyes widened into alluring green pools. Her nostrils pinched delicately as she inhaled too quickly. "Excuse me?"

"I will, Lily Gracen, but only if you ask me very, very nicely."

Lily

There were so many things wrong with his statement that I didn't know where to start. I wasn't even sure where shock ended and annoyance started. Which was surprising since for the past three years I'd lived in an environment dominated by the worst type of male ego—one with a half-decent brain and a bottomless bank account.

Silicon Valley wasn't the place for shrinking violets, and while my start at SDM may not have been conventional, I soon learned to find my voice or be flattened by pompous assholes.

That voice was now trapped somewhere between my throat and my tongue as I stared up at the seriously gorgeous man planted before me, watching me with eyes that started saucy little fires in my body.

I cleared my throat. "You're forgetting who hired whom, Mr. Steele. Technically, I'm your boss. If anyone will be *lording* anything, it'll be me."

For some reason that made his piercing blue eyes gleam. "I don't have a problem with a woman calling the shots. Within reason, of course."

Between his eyes and his deep, sexy, gravel-rough voice, I forgot, for a moment, the sinister threats hanging over my head, jeopardizing everything I'd worked hard for. I was so close to living my life on my terms. To being free of the devil's bargain my stepfather had struck with my employer to keep me shackled.

But staring at Caleb Steele, the deep unease I'd been bottling down since my stalker's first contact faded a little, enough for me to experience new, equally unsettling sensations.

The thinly disguised sexual interest in his eyes had lit a fire beneath my skin from the moment our eyes met. I knew the way I chose to dress, the individual statement I made with my hair and clothes, meant I attracted looks that my younger, teenage self would've shied away from. But that was before I was forced to grow a hard shell. Before it became clear that no matter what I did, all I would ever be was a monthly check to my stepfather for the meager attention grudgingly tossed my way through years of bitter, enforced parenting, and a means of harnessing my talent from Chance Donovan, the man I worked for.

But freedom was within my grasp.

Once I got rid of my stalker problem.

Somewhere in a place I refused to visit very often, the sting of rejection resided. But that pain had diminished significantly over time. In fact, I discovered the neat little trick that the more I worked the less I thought about my dismal past.

Except that work was now in jeopardy. The jagged circle of thought brought me back to my solution—Caleb Steele.

The man who stood before me was a tower of raw masculinity and unapologetic dominance.

His dark blue eyes were commanding to the point of hypnotic, and he dripped the kind of sexual assurance that very few men could carry off.

As for the impressive bulge I glimpsed as he strolled across the room a few minutes ago…?

I pressed my suddenly hot thighs together, struggled not to drop my gaze to the part of his anatomy that was unnervingly close to my face and cursed the blush creeping my neck.

You have a stalker, *Lily Angela Gracen. The last thing you should be thinking about is how incredible it would be to give your first blowjob to this drop-dead gorgeous man who's staring at you as if he wants to take a very big, very greedy, bite out of you.*

I stepped back from the edge of insanity as he leaned down, bringing his impressive height and stunning physique closer.

"Lily... Can I call you Lily?" he asked in that insanely sexy voice.

Enough already. My control may be slipping from me in other areas of my life. I wasn't going to let it slip here. "No. You can't. You haven't earned that right."

He raised one sleek, dark eyebrow, and hell, even that small action was crazy-hot. And when he smiled, his eyes gleamed with a new, carnal light that threatened to set me on fire all over again. "I don't usually go in for the brownie points system but if that's what turns you on..." He shrugged.

I frowned. "You misunderstand. Deliberately, I suspect. We're not discussing what turns me on. Or...having you lord...whatever over me." *Thanks, brain, for choosing today to deliver my speech in stupid ellipses!* "That's not going to happen, either, by the way, just so we're clear. *I'm* all about having this problem handled, ASAP, so I can get on with my life. Plus, I'm friendly with people I trust, and I don't trust you." There. Direct and to the point.

"You don't trust me...yet. That's okay. I'm skeptical, too. For instance, I'm not totally convinced that a bodyguard or a private investigator can't handle this job. So, Lily...how are *you* going to convince *me* to get off the fence?"

I hated the ground-shifting sensation that came with the idea that he could walk away. My research had indicated he was the man for the job. I didn't have time to find another. "You want me to pay you double? Is that it?"

The snap of irritation in his eyes indicated I'd caused offense. My stomach knotted harder.

"I turn away three out of five clients. Money isn't an issue for me. If you want me, do better."

"Fine. I was told you're the best of the best. I need the best."

He didn't answer for several drawn-out seconds. His hands returned to his pockets, and he rocked on his feet before he nodded. "Great. You've got me."

Convinced the loaded words were just in my mind, I ignored the heat pooling in my pelvis and pressed on. "It's almost two in the morning. Every second that passes is a second I'm being kept from doing my job. So can we proceed, Mr. Steele?"

"Does anyone else know you're being stalked?"

"Not yet, but if the threats continue I'll have to inform Chance Donovan. He's my boss and CEO of SDM."

Thoughts of Chance cooled my churning jets. As the moneyman behind my project, he was under pressure from his board of directors to deliver the code on time. Over the past month, that pressure had been redirected my way, with hints of the unpleasant consequences should I fail to meet my deadline.

"I'm hoping you'll fix my problem before that becomes necessary."

Caleb nodded, and I caught a different gleam in his

eyes. Respect. Maybe a little admiration. For some absurd reason, pleasure fizzed through me.

"I was going to suggest a safe house but I'm guessing you'll draw attention to your absence if you don't show up at work?"

"Yes. Usually, I can come and go as I please, but I have a team working with me."

His eyes narrowed. "A team?"

"The algorithm I'm building is huge. I have three teams of three working independently on different aspects of the code to minimize leaking of confidential information. They all report to me."

"So they don't know exactly what you're working on?" he fired at me.

"No." That had been Chance's idea. One I disagreed with but had no choice but to accept.

My expression must have given me away because Caleb frowned. "What aren't you telling me?"

My gut told me Caleb was the kind of guy who needed full disclosure or he might walk. "Chance and I have a history."

"What kind?"

"I was fourteen when I…came to his attention."

His gaze stayed fixed on me. "Let me guess. You hacked him. He caught you and convinced you to work for him instead."

A cute anecdote except for the part where I became tied to my so-called savior via a thousand wires made of veiled threats. I tightened the knots of pain and bitterness threatening to unravel. "Something like that," I replied. "Anyway, I can't be away from Sunnyvale for long. Which is why I'm going back tonight. What I want to know is will you be coming with me?"

A hard glint entered his eyes. "I will. On one condition. If we're going into your stalker's territory, you'll agree to do things my way, including letting me step into a situation if I think it's for your own good."

"But—"

"No buts. It says so in the small print of my retainer."

We faced off, a vortex of thunder and lightning swirling around us, eddying us dangerously closer. "It said I had to relinquish reasonable power to you. Not *all* power."

"*'There will be times when the fixer may have to take an* act-first-explain-later *approach to a situation. The client agrees to comply if such a situation arises.'* Did you make a note of that line?" His voice was low but deadly soft.

"Sure, I read that part. And you're probably used to having your every mandate agreed to immediately. Unfortunately, you and I will have a big problem if you insist on being...rigid."

"I can be as flexible as any situation demands. But not in this case. You forget. You *need* me."

I hated my words being thrown back in my face. Almost as much as I'd hated the thought of hiring a bodyguard and waiting the stalker out.

I was weeks from being free of Chance and my stepfather. The thought of adding even an extra hour's delay to that liberating moment was unacceptable. Still, relinquishing control was hard. "Do you find a client taking charge of their own safety a deal breaker for you?"

My question seemed to throw him off. A tiny frown pleated his brow, and then his striking blue gaze left mine to scour my body before returning to my face. As I watched, he reeled himself in. Like the man, his expression was fascinating to watch. It was as if he'd been in danger of overstepping a line and had coldly and ruthlessly corrected his course.

"No, but if you want an obedient thug, feel free to pick one of those rent-a-cops outside."

"All right. If you're up to something more challenging, then I agree to your terms."

The direct taunt to his supposedly flawless record—and yes, to his ego—was one I made with my breath held tight. For reasons I couldn't fathom, I hated the thought of him walking away even more.

With a single step, he closed the gap between us and lowered his lips to my ear. "Be very careful where you throw your little gauntlets, Lily Gracen. One might come back to bite you in your delectable ass."

It was impossible to stop the hot little shiver that raced through me. He saw it, and a bright blue flame lit his eyes.

"Well, be warned. I bite back."

"This is going to be very interesting," he mused. Then without taking his eyes from mine, he reached for his phone. I heard faint ringing in the background before it was answered.

"Maggie, is the primary crew in place?"

"Yes, they'll land in Palo Alto in thirty minutes. They can be at Miss Gracen's house in an hour. Do we have a green light?"

He lowered the phone. "Do I have the green light, Lily?"

"Your team is already in San Francisco. So you intended to take my case all along?"

He shrugged. "I needed to make sure you were fully committed but I saw no reason not to start the ball rolling."

I took a steadying breath. "I don't appreciate being toyed with, Mr. Steele."

All traces of humor left his face. "Then we're in total agreement because this is no fucking joke."

His harsh reply tightened the skin on my nape, warned me there was something else going on here.

"My guys are waiting," he pressed. "All they'll be doing tonight is setting up a few cameras outside the property and scoping out the area. They're experts, trustworthy, handpicked by me. They won't rifle through your underwear drawer or whatever naughty things you keep in your closet if that's what you're worried about. So, do I have the green light, Lily?" That last bit was muttered with a hot little taunt as his gaze raked my face.

I fought to hold on to my irritation and dismiss the tiny lick of embarrassment.

So okay, I wasn't the tidiest person at the best of times. And being neck-deep in my project, I'd let my standards slip a little further and canceled my cleaning service because I hated the disruption. Which meant any number of personal items, including the ones I used to de-stress after a hard day's coding, could be scattered anywhere in my house.

The joy of living alone meant I could pleasure myself anywhere from my bathroom floor to the movie room lounger where I usually crashed when I couldn't be bothered to drag myself to my bed. The thought of Caleb Steele's men reporting my habits back to him made my palms burn with humiliation.

Which was absurd.

I was a grown woman, for heaven's sake. One with healthy needs I wasn't ashamed of satisfying in defiance of the restrictions Chance Donovan had tried to place on me.

Nope, I wasn't going to think about Chance or how he tried to control me through Scott, my ex-boyfriend.

Very soon they'd both be so far in my rearview I'd need a telescope to see them.

"You have the green light," I said, blanking my mind to the possibility of my sex toys being discovered. "You'll need a code to get into the house."

The small cocky smile that curved his lips suggested that he really didn't, but he chose not to vocalize the fact. "Shoot."

I rattled out a long alphanumeric code. He impressed me by not asking me to repeat it and recited it to Maggie without hesitation.

About to hang up, he paused when Maggie called his name. "Yes?"

"The pilot is still on standby. I'm assuming you and the client are returning to Palo Alto, too?"

"Yes, we'll be at the airport in half an hour." He hung up, the blue of his eyes drenching me with the sensation of being swallowed whole. "Come on. Let's go get this bastard out of your life."

I grabbed my things and followed Caleb Steele outside with the distinct feeling he'd left out a vital part of his statement. Something along the lines of... *and then we can get onto more important things*.

Or maybe that was all in *my* dirty imagination.

CHAPTER THREE

Lily

IT WASN'T THE first time I'd ridden in a Bugatti—Silicon Valley was crawling with billionaire tech geeks who collected supercars like they were baseball cards.

But it was the first time I'd ridden in a supercar driven by a man like Caleb Steele. And this, too, was turning out to be a sex-steeped experience.

The man drove his car like he was making love to it. Scratch that. He drove like he was fucking it. Smooth. Sexy. Relentless. Each flick of the gear and flex of his thigh as he switched from gas to brake was a hypnotic symphony. One so absorbing I couldn't look away.

I realized my lip was caught between my teeth, and my fingers were digging into the soft leather, and forced myself to release both. To take a breath unfortunately filled with sandalwood and prime male, in order to get my brain on track.

Caleb Steele was the type of guy who would see my discomfort as a weakness and use it to his advantage.

"Where are we flying from?" He'd been mostly silent since we left the mansion. Admittedly, I found it a little disconcerting, especially since I'd anticipated being peppered with questions.

He changed lanes again before he answered, sending me a sidelong glance that left me with that faint impression of what being electrocuted by a low current would feel like. Even after he looked away, I experienced aftershocks.

"Van Nuys Airport. Don't worry, petal. I'll have you home in no time."

"I don't like pet names, Mr. Steele."

"You don't like pet names and you don't want me to use your first name. The only way I'm calling you *Miss Gracen* is if we're role-playing naughty teacher/ stern principal."

I was gripping the seat again. *Dammit*. I forced myself to uncurl my fingers before I damaged them because I needed them to write code. "Maybe this wasn't such a great idea, after all."

Watchful blue eyes gleamed wickedly in the lights from the dashboard. "Sorry, baby, it's too late to change your mind. You're stuck with me."

Baby. Sweetheart. Petal. He probably had an endless list of pet names he tossed at women.

Short of lowering myself to his level and calling him Big Guy or Sexy Ass or Hot Rod, I had to concede this round. "Fine, you can call me Lily. Because, heaven forbid, you run out of pet names and start calling me *honey cheeks*."

"Thank you, Lily," he said in a low, deep voice that rumbled over me like delicious hot fudge over a sundae. "And by the way, I would never peg you as honey cheeks. Not with that flawless pale skin." That slow-building, insanely sexy smile returned. "Is it deliberate?"

"Is what deliberate?"

"Your paleness. It works well with the Goth vibe but it must be hell to avoid the sun when you live in California."

"What does the paleness of my skin have to do with the case?" *Or anything else that doesn't make me think of sex?*

"Zilch. This is insatiable curiosity on my part. So?"

"So, you'll just have to accept that it won't be satisfied this time."

"Shame," he murmured. "I'll just have to use my imagination."

I averted my gaze, but I was still thinking about that smile, the effortless sensuality he wove into the most innocuous words, when he swung the powerful sports car onto the exit ramp leading to the airport.

After passing through security, Caleb drove into a brightly lit hangar and parked next to a gleaming white jet. Its steps were lowered, the engine humming. The pilot and copilot were talking to two airport officials as we alighted but my attention was drawn to the woman standing at the bottom of the steps.

Her short, sequined silver tube dress, long silver necklaces and rows of hooped earrings ruled her out as an attendant. She was shrugging into a bomber jacket when Caleb stepped out and came around to open my door.

"Do we need to discuss appropriate work attire again?" His tone was bone-dry as he addressed her.

She reached up to free her bun, then gave a resigned grimace. "Not that you'll care but I interrupted my date to return to the office for this assignment."

"A *date*? With an actual guy?" Heavy skepticism laced his voice as he retrieved my overnight bag.

The woman rolled her eyes and turned to me. After a quick once-over, she held out her hand and smiled. "I'm Maggie, Mr. Steele's long-suffering assistant. You must be Lily Gracen?"

At my nod, her face turned serious. "We'll catch the A-hole who's doing this to you. Don't tell my boss I said so, but he's ace at what he does. Our success record is pretty impressive. You're in good hands."

Caleb slammed the door. "Cut the corporate spiel, Maggie. Lily already knows she can trust me."

I ignored him, and smiled at Maggie. "Thanks."

"Did you bring what I needed?" he asked his assistant.

Maggie nodded. "Everything is already on board."

"Are we cleared to fly?" he pressed impatiently.

"Almost." She pointed to where the copilot was talking to the ground crew. "They're not happy that you're flying outside curfew—"

"You told them it was an emergency, right?"

"Yes, boss. They still need to tick their boxes. Give them a minute."

"I don't have a minute," he snapped, turning toward the group.

"Seriously, they're almost done—" Maggie started, but he was already walking away. She stopped talking, looking a little perplexed.

I frowned. "Is he always—?"

"The definition of a bull in a china shop? Surprisingly, no," Maggie answered her own question, her voice contemplative. "Sure, he's impatient and he wants everything done yesterday, but it takes a lot to ruffle his feathers. Although…"

"Although?" I prompted after a throb of silence, telling myself it was just mild curiosity that triggered the desire to know what made the enigmatic fixer tick. What made him give a damn and what bounced off those impressive shoulders?

Maggie's sharp, gray-eyed gaze snapped to me. I suspected the evasive answer before she opened her mouth. "A testy client earlier tonight before he came to see you. That's all."

I suppressed surprisingly sharp disappointment and glanced over to where the man I'd appointed as my fixer was gesturing impatiently to the men. He stood over a head taller, easily the most striking, and the low timbre of his voice rumbled through the large space, sending a decadent shiver to my lady parts.

After a minute the officials handed over papers to the copilot.

Caleb returned and picked up the overnight bag he'd set down next to the car. "We're clear to fly. Shall we?"

I sidestepped him when he reached for my arm, prompting another raised eyebrow I ignored. The lingering tingle between my thighs insisted touching him was a bad idea.

"Great to meet you, Maggie," I said.

The assistant smiled. "Likewise."

I walked up the stairs to the plane, aware that he trailed behind me. Drawn by an undeniable need, I looked over my shoulder. He'd paused with one foot on the bottom step; his eyes were fixed on me. Or rather on my ass. That insane tingle intensified between my legs.

I barely had time to step back before he was towering over me. For a handful of seconds, he stared down at me. Then his gaze flitted past me to the small cabin.

"Go grab a seat, Lily. We need to be wheels up before the stiffs out there find another reason to delay us."

The interior of the plane was as pristine and classy as the outside. Fitted in mahogany and cream tones, the club seats were grouped into two sections, one side with a shiny table separating the seats and the other without.

I chose the seat with a table. Anything for a buffer between Caleb and myself.

He watched me slide into the window seat. He didn't immediately sit down, even though the jet was rolling out of the hangar. Instead, he took his time to shrug off his lightweight jacket. The midnight blue shirt underneath was fitted, lovingly following a streamlined torso.

When he pivoted to hang up his jacket, the muscles in his back rippled with a sleek, edgy synergy that triggered a need to see him minus that shirt. Unlike me, he was perfectly tanned, the Californian sun having found the ideal specimen to blaze upon. Without a doubt, he would be firmly toned all over.

The urge to glide my fingers over those muscles intensified the incessant throb in my pussy.

I inhaled unsteadily, shifted my gaze and focused on securing my belt as he slid onto the seat opposite me. A moment later one arm extended toward me.

Annoyingly agitated with my skittish emotions, my head jerked up. He was unbuttoning his cuffs, casually folding back his sleeves, exposing thick, brawny arms overlaid with silky wisps of hair.

The innate grace flowing through the moment was almost hypnotic.

God. Enough.

The man was mouthwateringly attractive, granted. But I'd never lost my head or hormones like this, not even during the brief months I thought I was in love with Scott Wyatt, the man Chance planted in my life to manipulate me. Even before I found out his true motivations, Scott didn't set me on fire with a mere look.

After he was done with his hot little arm-porn display, Caleb rested his arms on the table. "Do you want a drink?"

"I'm good, thanks."

He nodded and glanced at his watch. "It is three in the morning, and we land in about forty-five minutes. We can use the time to discuss the case, or you can get some sleep?"

"You're giving me a choice?"

He smiled. "I'm not a complete ogre, Lily, regardless of whatever impression Maggie gave you."

It unsettled me that he'd read me so accurately. But wasn't that why I chose him? He'd risen to the top of my list almost immediately when I searched on the dark web because he was a maverick to the core. Totally unscrupulous when he went after something he truly wanted.

And the way he was staring back at me strongly suggested I was somewhere on his *want* list.

Maybe that was the reason I should've been bone-tired but felt oddly invigorated despite being awake for twenty hours straight. If I'd been coding, I'd be getting ready to crash hard by now.

My stalker's latest "gift" arriving in my mail this morning had wiped rest from my mind.

That unwelcome reminder refocused me. "I'm fine to answer your questions."

His brisk nod signified the switch back to fixer mode. "We'll get to the background stuff when you've had some sleep. For now, tell me when you first realized you'd attracted someone's attention?"

I didn't need to think hard. The memory was etched in my mind. "About seven weeks ago I received a piece of what looked like my code in an email. It was a very rough copy but it got my attention. And no, I wasn't able to find out who sent it."

"So we could be dealing with corporate sabotage."

The possibility shocked me. "You think one of SDM's competitors could be behind this?"

The underhanded tactics that went on in Silicon Valley weren't a secret, but usually they involved throwing enough money at an acquisition to secure it or throwing even more money at a problem to make it go away.

His mouth twisted. "You'd be surprised at the lengths companies would go to get an edge on the market. If your code is as revolutionary as you say it is—"

"It is," I confirmed. The possibilities of my algorithm scared me a little but I was extremely proud of what I'd achieved. The thought of someone stealing it filled me with equal parts fury and fear.

Caleb leaned back but it didn't release me from the raw force field of his personality. I was convinced he'd need to be in another state for that to happen.

"Then I suggest we make a list of the top twenty companies you think might benefit from this code."

I shook my head. "That'll be nearly impossible to investigate before the deadline."

A fierce light blazed in his eyes. "Make the list, Lily. I'll take care of it."

I got the unassailable impression that he would. The depth of that belief scared me a little. But it excited me even more. Which was ludicrous and a lot disturbing considering I detested being taken care of.

Not true. You hate that no one's cared enough without having an ulterior motive. Just like you hate that soft place inside you that wants to be taken care of.

I tightened my gut against the abrading truth. But it was no use. Lately, I hadn't been able to suppress thoughts of my stepfather as easily as I used to. Truth was, my stalker had amplified the yawning cavern of my life. He, or *they*, had exposed vulnerabilities that made me feel raw and fearful and *alone*. It was that last sensation I especially despised. I wanted that aloneness gone, and if I had to endure Caleb Steele for a while to achieve a return to normal, then so be it.

"Okay, I'll have it ready for you in the morning."

"Good. Tell me when you first noticed this wasn't just an online thing?" he whipped back, sharp eyes narrowed.

A swell of fear met quiet fury at the recollection of that first violation. "Two weeks ago I got another piece of code in the mail. It's a long way from the one I was working on, but someone out there is taunting me with knowledge of what I'm working on."

A muscle rippled in his jaw. "Did they make demands? Ask for money?"

"No."

"They're trying to scare you into changing your routine. Trip you up in some way. When was the next time?"

"He left me another code on top of my bike outside a coffee shop four blocks from my house."

His mouth thinned. "So he knows where you work and live."

I fought the shudder that rolled up my body. "Looks like it."

His hands curled into loose fists but his breathing didn't change. He carried on staring at me with a level look, then nodded for me to go on.

"The last time was yesterday morning. I received another code, but with a picture of me attached."

"A picture?" Caleb asked.

I nodded, a sheet of ice unravelling through me at the recollection. "It was taken two days ago. I was shopping."

"Fuck." Caleb's jaw rippled with tension before he leaned forward, bristling with quiet fury. "What happened to the package?"

"I have it at home."

His expression tight, he reached for his phone and had another conversation with the unflappable Maggie, issuing terse instructions about retrieving the package and having a discreet service dust it for prints. Just as briskly, he hung up and dropped the phone on the table between us.

"Tell me about your online activities, outside of the work you do for SDM."

"That's a very broad question." The plane dipped, taking a little bit of my stomach with it. "You want to know if I messed up somewhere?"

"I'm sure you didn't but something you did triggered this."

The logic was too sound to dismiss. I tried to suppress it but my unease grew. "You don't think I covered my tracks?"

A smile twitched his lips. "You're a coder. I'm sure you can clear your caches in your sleep. And I'm not talking about porn. Although I'd love to know which sites you prefer."

A flush heated my chest and spread lower to my abdomen. "Mr. Steele—"

"Lily?" he responded with a heavy dose of snark.

I took a calming breath. "I don't leave a trail of where I buy my lingerie or post minute-by-minute details of where I'm going to be at any given time of day. I know how to protect myself."

"And yet he found you," he stated with bracing finality.

After a moment, I looked at him. "What do you want to know specifically?"

"Coders make decent hackers. If you hacked your way into a job with SDM, you must be great. What's your hacker handle?"

All of a sudden the name that sent shivers down the spines of faceless dark web hackers felt pretentious. "Cipher Q."

His brows slowly rose. "You're Cipher Q?"

Another emotion swept in to mingle with the cocktail swirling inside me. This time it was most definitely not *unpleasant*. "You know about me?"

He shrugged. "Cyber crimes are a problem for a few of my clients. Maggie and a few people on my payroll keep an eye on things like that for me. A few months back she wouldn't shut up about some big-deal hacker contest going on. You won, if I remember correctly?"

The kick of pride warred with the need to set him

straight. "Yes, but it was all aboveboard. No cyber crimes involved."

"Who came second?"

"Nordic Razor."

"What do you know about him? How did he take coming second?"

"You think he's doing this?"

His shoulders rippled beneath his shirt as he shrugged again. "Not everyone likes losing to a woman."

I shook my head. "It's not him."

"I'll be the judge of that. I need the names of every-one who took part in the contest, too."

"At this rate I'll be spending all my time compiling lists for you. I won't have time to work."

He shot forward and the force of his dominant per-sonality hit me like a tidal wave. "You won't be working at all if this situation escalates. Did you forget already that I'm in control here?"

I'm in control.

Words I'd heard far too many times in my life. Words that had imprisoned me for far too long. My teeth met in a grinding clench. "I don't like being ordered around, Mr. Steele."

"Too bad. Until this bastard is in custody, you'll not only do as you're told, you'll also learn to love it."

Maybe it was something in his voice. Or the words he used with me. But my fury faded, along with that carnally needy, traitorous voice that wanted to say, *Yes, Caleb. I'll learn to love it.* That tingle between my thighs still throbbed, but it was with a different sort of need.

A burning need to, for once in my life, grab and

keep the upper hand. To put this man in his place once and for all.

Because, fuck that noise. My days of pretzeling myself to please others were nearly behind me.

I unclipped my seat belt and was out of my seat before I fully processed my actions.

Being pint-size had its advantages. It made crawling on top of the table a piece of cake.

I relished Caleb's unguarded intake of breath as I leaned forward and shoved my face in his. With a couple of inches separating us, I caught every fleck of surprise in his eyes as he watched me.

"You really think you're in control here?" I murmured softly.

A slow, assured smile widened his sexy mouth. "I know it," he rasped.

"I see." I scooted another inch closer, glided my tongue over my bottom lip. His demeanor changed. His ravenous gaze dropped to my mouth and his next breath wasn't quite so steady. "You didn't ask me how I found you to handle my problem, Mr. Steele."

His eyes grew wary. Good. "Maggie handles background stuff."

I nodded. "Hmm. She did ask me the right questions. But I'm afraid I told a little white lie. I don't personally know the client I named as my reference. I found him, and your whole client list, some other way."

A muscle ticked in his jaw. "You hacked me."

I allowed myself a little smile. "No, I *skimmed* you. But you know what I could've done if I wanted to?"

His eyes narrowed. "What?"

"Uncovered every…single…detail about you."

Silence throbbed. The muscle jumped faster. "What's

to stop me from bending you over this table right now, giving you the spanking you richly deserve before I dump you in Palo Alto and walk away?" he breathed through gritted teeth.

The erotic image of his palm turning my ass pink threatened to wipe off my smile. I ignored the balloon of heat dampening my panties and traced my fingers over his jaw, suppressing a gasp at how warm and vibrant he felt.

His sharply exhaled breath washed over my face.

"Because I took a little peek at your active cases. I wanted to make sure I'd be your number one priority. Your most exciting case finished two weeks ago. You're a man of action, and you're bored, Mr. Steele. Right now mine is the juiciest case to drop into your lap."

My thumb skated dangerously close to his lips. He bared his teeth, and another image flashed into my mind—how those perfect whites would feel grazing my clit.

"I could always take the vacation I've been promising myself for a while now," he rasped.

"You won't. Because I also saw the way you looked at me when I walked into the room tonight. The way you're looking at me right now."

My fingers drifted down his solid neck to his collarbone, then over his hard chest to rest on his belt. Without breaking eye contact, I closed the gap between us and brushed my lips, whisper-light, over his, reveling in the instant clutch of lust that darkened his eyes.

"I know you're rock-hard for me, that you've imagined a dozen different positions in which to fuck me."

I drew back and pried my gaze from his to the fists clenched with white-knuckled control on the table on either side of my body. "But you won't touch me, not until you catch my stalker. Because you don't mix business with pleasure. I know that about you, too."

My hand dropped to its final destination, gliding over the stiff, mouthwateringly impressive bulge behind his fly from root to tip. A strangled growl left his throat.

"So, you think you're in charge, Mr. Steele? Dream the fuck on."

CHAPTER FOUR

Caleb

JESUS FUCKING CHRIST.

I stared at her, torn straight down the middle between fury and pleading. Between shoving her ass out of my plane and begging her to stroke my cock again. Harder. Between admitting that yes, she and her case intrigued me, and the urge to say *to hell with it*.

Back in her seat, she stared at me, a saucy smile lifting her delicious mouth. A smile I promised to wipe clean the first opportunity I got.

Shit.

Women with mouths like hers shouldn't be allowed to swear unless there was immediate, no-holds-barred fucking involved. Because between that, the almost-kiss and tortuous stroking of my dick, I was now guaranteed to walk around with a hard-on strong enough to shatter glass.

Even my fury at her invading my privacy wasn't enough to calm the fire raging in my crotch. The knowledge burned, though, along with a need to know what else she found when she went… What did she call it? *Skimming?*

Did she know about my mother's suicide? About the desperate but ultimately fruitless measures I'd used to try to save her? About that one session with the child psychologist after my meltdown? Thankfully, the nightmares that had dogged me since her death weren't on record anywhere.

Still…she'd crossed the line.

Why?

"That was a dangerous little play you staged there, Lily. Is control really that important to you?"

The answer blazed in her eyes before she lowered them. "Isn't it to everybody?" she fired back.

Okay. Control, or giving it up, was an issue for her. I tucked away that piece of info.

But despite her spine of steel, I didn't need to look hard to spot her apprehension. Plus, she was on edge. Clients in that state tended to knee-jerk the hell out of situations.

I took a breath as the plane taxied to the hangar. "You went to a lot of trouble to hire me. Don't fuck it up by digging into my life again. Trust me, I'll know. And I won't give you a pass next time. In return, I'll loop you in as much as I can. Deal?"

She stared at me, the fire raging in her eyes for another second before she offered a curt nod. "Deal."

I rose from my seat, uncaring that my erection still throbbed stiff and eager in my pants.

She'd stoked the fire. She deserved to burn a little. And from the pink staining her cheeks as her beautiful eyes dropped to my crotch, she was burning all right. Still twisting with fury and lust, I leaned down and whispered, "As for your assessment about how many ways I want to fuck you, try a few dozen times north of your calculation. And, guess what?"

Defiant eyes met mine. "What?"

"I know you want me, too, so I guess I won't be the only one suffering, huh?"

She didn't answer, not that I was expecting one.

We both retreated into our thoughts as we exited the plane.

The ride Maggie had organized was a sturdy SUV with darkened windows, which I appreciated. Sadly, there were a million ways for stalkers to spy on their victim these days, and a million ways for victims to respond if they felt powerless.

The thought triggered a question that helped to drag my attention off Lily's small but perfect body and thoughts of what I wanted to do to her. "Do you own a gun?" I asked after stashing our bag and hopping into the driver's seat.

Her eyes widened as she shut her door. "A gun? Why would I own a gun?"

"Don't look so surprised. You'd be shocked by how many people exercise their right to carry a firearm. I don't want to be surprised down the road." I rolled my shoulder as unwelcome thoughts of Kirsten, my ex, and phantom pain from my bullet wound registered.

Lily caught the movement, questions filling her eyes as she replied, "No, I don't own a gun. And I don't intend to arm myself, regardless of this situation."

"Good."

She kept quiet, until curiosity got the better of her. "Were you—?"

"You've pried enough for one night, Lily. Let's focus

on why I'm here, okay?" The snap in my voice made her flinch, but I didn't regret it.

I stuck to a quieter, longer route from the airport to Lily's address in Menlo Park. She started to fidget when we turned into the tree-lined road that housed a row of impressive mansions.

"Will your guys still be there?"

I checked the time on the dashboard. "No. Maggie texted me when they left. They'll come back tomorrow to take care of the security inside the house."

Surprise widened her eyes. "Oh. Thanks."

I glanced over to see her worrying the inside of her lip again. "You're welcome. Wanna tell me why having them inside the house makes you so nervous?"

She averted her gaze. "I'm not comfortable with strangers invading my space," she muttered.

I sensed she wasn't being entirely truthful but let the matter drop. "Okay."

She looked relieved as I checked out our surroundings.

Half of the properties were displayed in all their sprawling glory, but the other half were hidden behind palm and fir trees. Many places for a stalker to hide.

Lily pulled out her phone and hit a button on the screen, nodding at the property coming into view. "It opens the gates."

The electronic gates were swinging open much too slowly. "They need to open faster. You don't want to be a sitting duck out here while the gate takes its sweet time to let you in. I'll get it fixed."

She nodded. "Okay."

When the gap widened, I drove through. Compared to the other houses on the street, hers was on a smaller scale but still impressive enough to blend comfortably into the neighborhood.

Built on two levels with a tapered roof, the tiered white European-style mansion took up several thousand square feet, with tall rectangular paned windows that drew an inward grimace. All her stalker needed was a decent set of binoculars and he could follow her every move when she was home. And that second floor tier was also a problem especially if my suspicion that one or all of the bedrooms came with a terrace overlooking the backyard was confirmed.

The front door looked solid enough, though. I couldn't do anything about the Roman pillars framing the front porch, but the seven-foot potted plants on either side of the door needed to be relocated.

She opened her door and jumped out. I stopped myself from growling my annoyance and got out, reaching her just as she climbed the last step onto the stone-laid porch.

I touched her upper arm. "Wait."

Apprehension flickered across her face. "Your security people were just here. Surely you—?"

"Can't be too careful. Keys?"

She dug through her satchel and handed the keys over. I unlocked the door and saw a large foyer.

"There's a light switch on your left," she said.

I flicked it on, bathing the large space in a warm golden glow. An alarm beeped from a panel next to the switch. I entered the code.

Silence settled in as I took in the layout of the first floor. Two short corridors forked from the entrance foyer on either side of a grand staircase made of wood and trellised iron. At the end of the left hallway, I saw shadowy frames of sofas and a coffee table, which meant the right hallway probably led to the kitchen.

I motioned her inside and turned the dead bolt on the door. "Stay here. I'll check out the other rooms," I murmured. The gun I'd tucked in my back before we left the airport rested reassuringly against my skin.

She sucked in a slow breath before her gaze met mine. "I prefer to come with you," she whispered firmly.

The statement wasn't made out of fear of being on her own. No, Lily was nervous.

The possible reason why hit me with a punch. "Do you live here alone?" I demanded.

"What if I do?" Her chin rose, daring me to have a problem with it.

"Hey, I'm not judging." The size of the house didn't warrant the question. "I'd rather not surprise anyone at four in the morning."

Her gaze swept away. "Oh, right. No, there's no one else here," she murmured.

"Okay, you can come. Just stay behind me, got it?"

She jerked out a nod, albeit a distracted one.

There were no surprises in the kitchen or the pantry, same for the sizeable laundry room. I double-checked the outer doors to make sure they were locked before inspecting the other rooms on my way into the living room.

I guessed the reason for her uneasiness a few minutes later.

The two living rooms connected by a long entryway with a door leading to a study weren't exactly untidy, but they weren't pristine, either.

A discarded throw on one side of the sofa, an empty glass on the table, cushions on the floor in front of a marble fireplace. Over one arm of another sofa, a tank top draped precariously with a black lace bra tucked into the sleeves. Besides the superficial untidiness, all the surfaces were clean, and the decor was tasteful enough to show someone cared enough to make the house a home.

However, when I glanced over, her cheeks were pink, adorable shades of strawberry over the cream.

"So I'm not the tidiest person in the world," she said defensively. "When I'm buried in work I forget to pick up after myself. And I gave my housekeeper time off, so..." She shrugged, then skirted the sofa, her gaze darting furtively around the room.

"You like to be comfortable in your own space. Nothing wrong with that." Except the sight of those plump cushions in front of the pale marble fireplace was restoking the fire she started on the plane.

She snatched the tank and bra off the sofa and dropped them into a cabinet drawer.

I dragged my gaze from her to properly study the room. Two sets of doors led outside. Lots of windows covered by expensive-looking drapes. All to be secured tomorrow.

As if drawn by magnets, my eyes returned to the cushions, to the hint of bright pink poking out from between two cushions. Before I could confirm what it was, Lily moved to block my view of it.

I raised an eyebrow and her color deepened.

"Shall we move on?" she blurted.

I ate the grin threatening, welcoming the chance to cool my raging libido. "By all means."

We retraced our steps to the foyer and headed downstairs to the basement.

A flick of a switch illuminated the corners of the impressive movie theater, equipped with everything a movie buff needed, including luxury loungers and an extensive 1950s-style snack and drinks bar at the far side of the room. I checked out the bar, the small pantry and the bathroom before motioning for her to enter.

She made a beeline for the front row and the object lying out in the open.

The bright pink object was the same as the one I saw upstairs, but this vibrator clearly stood out against the black sheepskin throw discarded on the middle seat facing the giant screen.

My breath locked in my lungs as an image of her spread out on the lounger with her favorite gadget between her legs sideswiped me. Before I could recover from it, another image punched through. This time I was the one positioned between her legs, seeing to her pleasure as whatever chick flick she preferred played in the background.

Only she wouldn't be able to concentrate on a single thing on the screen. Hell, no.

She would be half out of her mind, grabbing my hair and arching her back as she begged me to *please, please, please* get her off.

My pulse kicked into uncomfortable levels as I watched her grip close over the sex toy.

"Can I make a suggestion?" My tongue felt as thick as the hard-on pressing against my fly.

Her fingers clenched around the pink object. "No."

I adjusted myself before moving toward her. "If you're that embarrassed by having anyone see your naughty toys, maybe don't leave them lying around?"

"A gentleman wouldn't mention this," she snapped.

"And a lady wouldn't have crawled onto the table on my plane, teased me with her body and stroked my cock without at least buying me a drink first, but here we are."

"I didn't stroke you...it," she replied hotly. "I just..." Her blush deepened.

I laughed, enjoying her discomfort a little too much. Not so much as the memory of her hands on me because it triggered a craving for more of the same.

"Lily, I don't really care what toys you play with so there's no need to feel bad about it. I am curious about what else you have stashed around the place, though. Personally, I like cold beers in coolers handy around my place but I guess with you it's sex toys? Is it super-efficiency or do you just get crazy impatient when the mood grabs you?"

Sharp, irritated green eyes aimed lasers at me. "I'm going to bed, Mr. Steele. Please take that as a sign that I won't be answering your inappropriate questions." She shot for the door, moving quicker than I anticipated.

I intercepted her before she reached the foyer. "I haven't checked upstairs yet."

"Then I suggest you get on with it." She headed for the stairs.

"Stop." There was more grit in my tone, more pressure in my grip.

"Don't talk to me like I'm Maggie, Mr. Steele," she bit out.

My thumb slid over her skin before I could stop myself. "I would never mistake you for Maggie. You're in a class of your own, sweetheart. And call me Caleb." The gruffness in my voice was a direct testament to what touching her was doing to me.

It had some effect on her, too, if her parted lips and the small gust of breath that escaped was evidence enough. I was completely stumped by the effect of that tiny sound on my dick.

The undercurrents that had swirled around us since we first set eyes on each other strengthened by the minute.

Shit, I needed to cool off before I did something crazy, like drag her close and taste her sinful mouth properly.

"Let's get this over with. Same rule applies: you stay behind me."

After confirming everything was good, I grabbed the bags from the car, fighting the temptation to pour myself a drink. Much as I wasn't looking forward to sleeping under a strange roof, I couldn't compound my rest with alcohol. The nightmares always found a way to filter through anyway.

Teeth clenched, I headed back upstairs.

Maybe choosing the bedroom next to Lily's wasn't the brightest idea. Most nights the nightmares only triggered cold sweats. But there were times when that last image of my mother ripped...*sounds* from me.

I eyed Lily's door. She'd shut it firmly in my face after a curt good-night.

A tight smile tugged at my mouth. She wouldn't appreciate being called a spitfire but that was exactly what she was. Despite the dark clothes and alabaster skin, she blazed red-hot underneath, a fuse ready to explode.

My grip tightened on the doorknob. Was she using her little pink toy right now to take the edge off her irritation with me? To bring much-needed relief from the shadows lurking in the dark?

Fuck, I was in danger of dying from blue balls if I didn't get myself under control.

CHAPTER FIVE

Caleb

IT WAS BARELY daylight when the ashen image of my mother's lifeless face jerked me from sleep to the pinging of the alarm. I ignored my racing heart as I sprinted for the door and yanked it open, relieved that it wasn't the continual blare announcing a possible intruder. Until I remembered that I was dealing with a tech-savvy stalker.

Downstairs, I took a moment to listen. Only the muted chorus of birdsong broke the silence.

Followed a second later by the faint splash of water. The gun I grabbed from the nightstand before leaving my room bumped against my thigh as I moved toward the open living room door and stepped through it.

Thirty feet away from the back patio, the pristine lawn gave way to stone tiles and a larger-than-average pool.

And right there, swimming without a care in the world, was Lily.

Irritation and disbelief drove me past the large ivy-twined oak pergola with the center fire pit and the loungers that stood to one side of the swimming pool.

My gaze was fixed on the figure weaving through the water, completely oblivious to my presence.

I watched her swim one lap. Then another. I breathed in and out. Slow, deep to get myself under control.

No joy.

"Lily." My voice pulsed with the quiet fury running through my veins.

She didn't stop. Her strokes were flawless and efficient, her strong kicks propelling her swiftly away from me toward the far end of the pool. I trailed after her, watched her execute a neat underwater flip, turn and launch herself into another lap. The move was smooth enough for me to see the wireless swimming earbuds plugged into her ears. My pissed-off barometer ticked up another notch.

I tugged my T-shirt over my head and stepped out of my sweatpants before diving into the pool. Two hard kicks later, she was in front of me. Alarm flared in her eyes as my hands closed on her arms. She fought back, clawing and thrashing the water before she realized who she was fighting.

In that time an unhealthy number of what-if scenarios whizzed through my head, darkening my already foul mood.

"Are you out of your mind?" I made no effort to keep my temper from showing.

She sluiced water out of her eyes with one hand and attempted to push me away with the other. The hell I was budging. "Can you not yell at me, please?"

"I asked you a question."

"Well, you're not going to get an answer if you don't let go of me. Or lower your voice by a couple of thousand decibels."

Fine, so my voice was a little loud. It was barely daylight and I'd slept like shit. "I said—"

"I heard you the first time. I'm pretty sure the neighbors heard you, too." She attempted to break free. I held her tighter, propelling her from the center to the side of the pool.

The water wasn't deep but with her small stature, her feet dangled above the bottom. When she tried to move again, I trapped her with one leg.

She wriggled, braced one hand on my shoulder. The small charge that detonated inside me at her touch was perfectly echoed in her expression. A tiny hitch in her breathing, and then her hand disappeared into the water. "What are you doing?" Her voice squeaked but that fire that was never far from the surface blazed pure challenge with her glare.

I shoved away the effect of her hand on me and glared right back. "I think that's my question. What the hell were you thinking, coming out here on your own?" I demanded.

The first rays of the sun chose that moment to emerge and bathe her face in golden light, illuminating the pearls of moisture dotting her pale, beautiful skin. I couldn't take my eyes off the three fat drops clinging to her top lip. Or the pure temptation of her full lower lip.

"I couldn't sleep. Swimming relaxes me—wait, why am I explaining myself to you?" She shifted impatiently, her toes brushing my bare calf.

I clenched my teeth and tried not to let the heat stabbing my groin distract me. Now that I had her attention, it was probably wise to let her go.

Not until I made my point.

"Do I really need to spell it out to you? And these

things in your ears?" I tugged the earbuds out and tossed them onto the tiles. "How the hell do you expect to hear anything with them plugged in?"

"I always swim with my earbuds in. And no, I can do without that narrow-eyed judgment. This is my home. My life. I can do whatever I want."

"You have a thing for control. Trust me, I get it. But you don't know when this creep will step things up another level. Why the hell didn't you wake me if you wanted to swim so badly?"

She blinked. "I swim every morning, and I don't need your permission to do it."

"For fuck's sake. That's what I'm here for—"

"I'm not going to live in fear and let some random stranger pull my strings!"

The forceful words hit the tranquility of the cool morning. Echoed all around us before settling like a boulder between us. Lily froze as if her outburst had electrified her into silence. The stunned look on her face confirmed she hadn't meant to voice them.

When she went a little pale, I frowned my concern. "Lily—"

"Let me go!"

Her hands rose in the water. One braced on my stomach, the other brushed my upper thigh, then my bare hip. Her green eyes went wide. A moment later her gaze dropped down my chest, and then lower. She gasped. "Are you...*naked*?"

Despite my disgruntlement, I smiled. "I don't get my favorite sweatpants wet for just anyone, sweetheart."

Delicious heat poured into her cheeks as her hands jerked away from my body. "Oh, my God!"

"Why the outrage? Just a few hours ago you were stroking—"

"Shut up!"

I followed the blush, unable to take my eyes off the alluring sight of it. God, I wanted to taste that blush, trail it with my tongue up and down her body.

"My, what a hot little temper you have. I could—"

The words choked off as the hands that pushed me away a minute ago clutched my head and yanked me down to meet her waiting lips.

She kissed me. Then bit me. Hard. Then swallowed my stunned groan into her open mouth as she swiped her tongue over the sting. Once, twice, then with slow, dragging licks that rained fire through my body.

Jesus.

I parted my lips to better taste her. She immediately slid her tongue into my mouth, pressing her velvety lips harder against mine as she licked her way inside the way I wanted to lick her pussy—bold and relentlessly. She nipped the tip of my tongue. I groaned again at the taste of her. She was just like I imagined she would be.

Heaven and hell.

Sin and absolution.

Pleasure and—

She pushed me away as quickly as she'd pulled me close. My stunned brain was still absorbing her spectacular taste when she whirled away, planted her hands on the edge and launched herself out of the pool.

"What the fuck—?" The rush of saliva in my mouth as I watched the water glide off her body was disgraceful enough to make me grimace. Jesus, she was breathtaking.

Her glare didn't hold much power, diluted as it was

by her arousal. "That was to shut you up. Nothing more."

My eager gaze raked her incredible body, took in her erect nipples, the pulse racing at her throat. "You sure about that?"

She looked off to the side. After a minute she balled her hands. "Swimming alone is off the table for now. I'll agree to that."

"Let's make a list so there's no confusion. Five minutes in the kitchen okay with you?"

Her eyes still refused to meet mine. "Fine."

Beneath the water, my cock pumped to full, eager life as the sun rose higher, giving me an even better view of her.

The black one-piece was skimpier than most two-piece suits purely because it was held together by a crisscross of ties designed to draw attention to her impressive curves. I stared my fill while telling myself if my gawking made her uncomfortable then it would be a little payback for what she'd just put me through. But I accepted that my reasons were far baser.

She looked even smaller in her bare feet. God, handling her during sex would be infinitely delightful. She turned away and my gaze dropped to her heart-shaped ass, her shapely legs and the cutest ankles I'd ever seen.

I bit back a groan as my groin kicked hard.

Hell, at this rate, I'd need a cold shower before I could conduct a coherent conversation.

When she reached the lounger and grabbed a towel, I struck out for the far side where I'd dropped my clothes.

I hauled myself out, hoping the cool air would do what the tepid water hadn't been able to achieve, and calm my excitement.

Her sharp intake of breath reached me as I bent to pick up my pants.

Don't turn around. Don't—

I turned and surprised her gaze on my ass. On any given day, I would've tossed out a cocky remark, encouraged her to look her fill if she promised to let me do the same. But we were already in uncharted territory and it'd barely been twelve hours since we met.

Not to mention, there were cameras out here, set up by my team, recording every second of our little show. Set-jawed, I pulled on my pants. First priority after our talk would be to access the security feed and delete that stretch of footage.

She'd disappeared by the time I locked the doors and went into the kitchen. Her coffee machine looked as if it hadn't been touched since it came out of the box. After setting it up, I grabbed two mugs and waited for the machine to do its thing.

She walked in just as the first cup filled. The thin, long-sleeved sweater wasn't temperature-raising in and of itself except it was cropped, exposing a good three inches of her midriff. Paired with black leggings hugging every glorious inch of hip, thigh and legs, it was incredibly potent. I swallowed a groan and busied myself making the second cup. Which took all of ten seconds.

"How do you take your coffee?"

She looked surprised at the offer. "Umm…cream with two sugars and a splash of vanilla."

I found the ingredients, stirred them into her cup and handed it over. "If it sucks, keep it to yourself."

She accepted the coffee, took a careful sip, then blinked. "It's good. Thanks."

I got mine and joined her at the kitchen island. "Why

buy a coffee machine if you don't intend to use it?" I asked just for something to do other than stare at the mouth whose taste was now stuck in my head.

"I didn't buy it. It was here when I moved in, along with most of the furniture." Her reply was the stiff, don't-go-there kind.

I ignored the alarm bells. "How long have you lived here?"

Her face tightened. "Three years."

"And you've only worked for SDM?"

She nodded and leaned her hip against the counter. I forcefully redirected my gaze up to her damp hair, anything not to stare at the silky stretch of bare midriff skin or the luscious curve of her hip.

"So why not a condo nearer to SDM's offices in Sunnyvale?" This part of Silicon Valley was CEO territory, usually favored by those with families.

Her long, sooty lashes swept down. "Accommodation came as part of my signing package and this one was available. It was supposed to be temporary until I found my own place but…it grew on me. When the opportunity came up for me to buy it, I did." She shrugged. "Also saved me time on house-hunting."

The well-rehearsed answer heightened my suspicion that something else was going on here. I left it alone for the moment.

"Besides swimming, what else takes you outside on a day-to-day basis?"

"Nothing I can't live without for the time being."

"Great. So we're agreed that you'll give me a heads-up before you head outside?"

Rebellious green eyes met mine across the granite top. "If it'll stop you from diving naked into my pool, then yes." Impatiently, she set her half-finished coffee on the counter with a snap. "By trapping me in my own home, isn't he winning?"

"You're not trapped. You just won't be doing stuff by yourself for a while. Besides, if he thinks you've got someone else in your life he might show his hand sooner."

She frowned. "Someone in my life?"

I shrugged. "He doesn't know who I am. That'll make him nervous. Enough to show his hand, I'm hoping."

She absorbed the words for several beats. "And if it doesn't?"

I felt my face harden. "Then we'll step up the game, take the fight to him."

My days of sitting around, waiting for things to happen were long behind me. Trusting other people to do the right thing for my mother had cost her the ultimate price. She'd suffered for years until she'd taken the only option she felt available to her, leaving me to deal with the aftermath.

The bitter pill I've swallowed all these years rose to the back of my throat again. Ruthlessly I pushed it back down.

Her gaze dropped for a moment. "The other reason I hired you was because your success rate is one hundred percent. I guess you're good at what you do," she murmured as she toyed with the handle of the mug.

I silenced the cocky bastard inside that wanted to strut at the hidden meaning in her words as she tugged one corner of her lower lip between her teeth. "I have a lot riding on finishing my algorithm," she added.

The admission wasn't an easy one and I admired her a hell of a lot for voicing it. It was probably why I skirted the counter to stand in front of her. Why I tucked my finger under her chin and raised her gaze to mine. "We'll catch the bastard. I promise," I said.

Her nostrils quivered delicately as she took a breath. This close, I could see the faint shadows and fear she was fighting lurking in her eyes. She'd been brave up to this point but the edges of her composure were beginning to unravel. I opened my mouth, to promise fuck knows what, but she stepped back.

"Um, about that kiss…"

The memory of it blazed a path through me. "Yeah?"

"It was out of line. I'm sorry."

"I'm…not."

She stiffened. "What?"

I tossed out an offhand shrug, despite the wide pit of *what-the-fuck-are-you-doing* yawning before me. "Technically, I didn't break my rules. *You* got me hard as fuck on the plane. *You* kissed me in the pool."

Her eyes widened. "And that makes it okay?"

"That makes me…okay with not losing any sleep over it." In fact, the more I thought about it the more I grew okay with it.

"Is that how you usually give yourself a pass?" she asked, her face tightening.

"Since you're the only client I've allowed to…handle me like that, I'll say no."

Lily's mouth dropped open.

My answering smile felt tense as thoughts of Kirsten flared up. With her, I did all the chasing, right into the trap she set for me. Since her, my personal encounters had been kept strictly sexual, with a time limit of no more than two months. I'd discovered that was when nesting behavior began cropping up.

One or two women had called me a cold bastard. I'd
learned to live with it. I could probably live with Lily's
brand of shutting me up, too, although I was a little unnerved that I was inviting her to smudge the lines. "So
if the urge takes you, feel free to go with it."

She gasped. "Are you serious?"

I shrugged.

"Well, it won't," she said briskly. "Are we done here?"

Disappointment cut sharp but I brushed it off. "For
now. My team will be here at nine to finish setting up
inside. What are your plans for today?"

"I'm going to the office in a couple of hours. It's
quieter on the weekend. I get a lot more done there."

"We'll go together."

She nodded and walked over to the sink with her
cup. After rinsing it, she bent over to place it in the
dishwasher. I ogled her heart-shaped ass for a cock-
hardening few seconds before redirecting my gaze.

"I'll have the list ready for you in half an hour," she
said as she walked out.

I leaned against the counter after she was gone, willing my hard-on to subside even as I tossed around the
rationale I'd given her for bypassing my rules.

Would she take it? Did I really want her to?

Hell, yes!

The powerful need behind the thought propelled me
from the kitchen in search of something else to occupy
my mind.

For the next hour I explored the two acres attached
to the house, assessing possible weak points and compiling a list for the security team to tackle.

In the garage I found a gleaming black single-rider
motorcycle with chrome detailing next to a compact

Mini. Both were characteristically diverse, but some-how encompassed Lily Gracen's personality perfectly.

Smiling, I finished the check and returned to the house. I set myself up in the dining room and sent emails to Maggie and the security team. Then I logged on to the security feed, played it through until I reached the moments from the pool.

The cameras displayed shots from different angles, but the one placed in the pergola perfectly captured the moment I reached Lily. It showed the tight expression in both our faces as we talked. Her shock at finding me naked. The moment she pulled my head down for that memorable kiss. The perfect arch of her spine and ass as she rose from the water two feet from me, and my blatant hunger as I stared.

I selected the seven-minute frame and moved my finger to the delete button. Only to pause at the point when she glanced over at me after I came out of the pool. Her gaze didn't linger for more than a few seconds, but the effect of watching her watch me pull on my pants was an extreme turn-on. Like a testosterone-filled sucker, I hit Rewind. Watched the kiss. And again. Until my balls screamed under the pressure I was putting on them. Until my dick roared with the need to fuck.

Hard and fast and rough.

Damn. I wish I hadn't watched it. Lily was an extremely attractive female with a delectable exterior wrapped around a core of steel. Not to mention a healthy sex drive she wasn't shy about satisfying with sex toys.

But despite my weakness for strong, intelligent women, rules were rules. They'd kept me at the top of my game for the best part of a decade.

I shut the laptop and shoved away from the table. My

hand slipped beneath the waistband of my sweatpants and I gave myself a quick, jaw-clenching few strokes before standing up.

I wouldn't touch her while she was my client. But there was nothing stopping me from ensuring the ball was kept front and center in her court.

CHAPTER SIX

Lily

HIS SECURITY TEAM arrived right on schedule.

Three men carrying six large black cases grunted various forms of hello before they went to work.

Ninety minutes later they were done and gone. The setup was state-of-the-art and discreet enough to almost blend into the decor but their presence still felt intrusive.

"How soon do you want to head to the office?" Caleb asked after running me through the security procedures.

I paused halfway up the stairs and turned to face him. He was right behind me, so close I could smell traces of chlorine mingling with his natural body scent, which didn't help my desperate need to forget what happened at the pool.

God, he'd tasted incredible—erotic, intoxicating and potentially addictive. Everything I imagined a real man tasted like. And that was with a kiss I'd surprised him with.

Like on the plane last night, taking control had felt... wonderful. Liberating. I went to sleep craving more of it. I woke to the memory of my hand stroking his thick, hard cock. It was what drove me to the pool to cool off.

Except I'd left it craving more of Caleb.

He was waiting for an answer. And I was staring at his mouth like a horny idiot.

I turned away sharply before that left brow completed its mocking ascent. "I just need to transfer data from my laptop to my office work station. So ten minutes?" I needed to be free of his distracting presence for a few hours. The man brought new meaning to the term *larger than life*.

"Sounds good."

Five minutes later I was standing in my closet, assessing my clothes with a critical eye. The notion that I was taking extra time to dress because of *him* intensified my churning emotions. But the powerful thrill that came from knowing Caleb Steele was attracted to me was unstoppable. It was the kind of power that could go to a woman's head.

But power was corruptible. I should know. Between Chance and my stepfather, they'd used their power over me to control my every move.

It wouldn't be like that between Caleb and me, though. He'd given me the green light. Hell, he'd *urged* me to use my power.

And I'd be lying if I didn't admit I was sorely tempted.

God, you're losing it.

I tugged off my leggings and replaced them with black leather pants. I kept my sweater and usual accessories of leather wrist cuffs and choker but I hesitated before reaching for my favorite red lipstick. It drew attention to my mouth, and made me feel sexy but after this morning, did I want to encourage that around Caleb?

Yes, you do. Maybe, even a little too much...

Frowning, I impatiently reached for the peach lip balm.

The earlier I got to the office, the quicker I could disappear into my work and forget my stalker, and Caleb, existed.

He was waiting at the bottom of the stairs, eyes on his phone when I reached the landing. I hated myself for half hoping he wouldn't look up while my stomach churned in hope that he would. Both wishes were answered when halfway down the stairs his head slowly lifted. His gaze collided with mine before those unnervingly hot eyes swept down my body, all the way to the tips of my heeled boots before conducting a slower return journey.

Hell, he wasn't even hiding the fact that he wanted me anymore. Now he'd told me to come for him, he was granting me unfettered access.

By the time I reached the last step, the simmering heat that hadn't quite dissipated since our pool encounter was stoked into foot-high flames, licking their way up to my nipples and turning them into traitorous points of need that stood out against my thin sweater.

As if he could read my thoughts as easily as he could read my body, his gaze dropped to linger on my breasts, then rose to my face again as his breathing altered.

I'm not sure how long we stood staring at one another.

His phone beeped with an incoming message. His gaze dropped for a second, and then he stared back at me.

"Are you ready?" His voice was gruff.

My head bobbed a nod.

As he turned to open the door, I noticed he'd changed

into dark jeans, a black T-shirt and a dark brown leather jacket. "We'll take the SUV."

I stopped. "I usually go to work by bike but I understand that it's no longer a viable option. So we'll take my car."

"No disrespect to your car, but I prefer not to arrive with leg cramps. And before you say it, no, I won't follow while you drive your car."

"But—"

"Sorry, this is one of those nonnegotiable scenarios we talked about. The safe house is also still an option."

I stalked to the SUV and yanked open the door, worryingly aware this man had the ability to unbalance me with very little effort.

I studied his profile as he started the engine and rolled the large vehicle toward the gates. After he drove through, he flashed me a smile, intensifying the heat blazing through me.

God, had I not stood my ground last night, I would currently be ensconced in a cabin in the middle of nowhere with him.

Mr. if-the-urge-takes-you-feel-free-to-go-with-it.

Erotic thoughts and images bombarded me, enough to keep me silent as he drove toward SDM's Sunnyvale offices.

At the checkpoint, I showed my ID, confirmed that Caleb was with me and directed him to my parking spot.

A curl of pride drifted through me as I saw him read the sign attached to my name—*Junior Vice President— Programming & Coding*. Despite the yoke around my neck in the form of my debt to Chance and my stepfather, I knew I'd earned this position. That I was capable of conquering even bigger mountains. It was what

I intended to do the moment I was free of my twin oppressors.

Caleb's glance showed cool respect.

A knot loosened in my chest. Which in turn made me madder that I'd wanted to see that respect in his eyes. Wanted him to see me through another set of lenses than those of a powerless victim needing help from a fixer.

Throwing the door open, I jumped out.

"Lily, wait—"

I was half a dozen cars away when he caught up with me. "What?"

"You don't rush off and leave me behind. Understood?" he gritted out. He was annoyed, too, but trying to hide it with a fake smile. His fingers slipped around my wrist, his gaze scanning the parking lot before returning to mine. "He could be anywhere, including right here in this parking lot, waiting for an opportunity to strike."

I felt the blood leave my face. His hold tightened momentarily, a gesture of comfort despite his annoyance. "I know it's a pain in the ass but it will become much easier if you accept a few temporary changes."

"Like agreeing for you to become my shadow?"

Annoyance receded to leave a smile that looked more genuine. "I was thinking more like your second skin but I'll settle for shadow."

I tried not to recall the feel of his golden skin against mine and failed miserably. "Okay, can we go now?"

"Sure."

And just like that, he'd gotten his way again. Deciding that keeping score would only mess with my sanity, I headed for my place of work.

SDM's San Francisco offices were shaped like two

bananas facing each other, connected by glass and steel walkways on every floor. The hardware development and tech team took up one building, and the software, programming and coding team took up the other.

I entered the left building and smiled at the guard behind the security desk. "Morning, Charlie."

The stout, middle-aged man smiled back. "Morning, Miss Gracen."

"This is Mr. Steele. He's a…consultant visiting from LA for…a while. Can you sort out a security pass for him?"

Charlie's gaze swung to Caleb before he nodded. "Sure thing."

Caleb handed over his ID for verification, took the pass handed over and studied it with a frown as we headed for the elevator.

"What?"

He leveled his blue-eyed gaze at me. "You're a lousy liar."

Heat rushed into my face and I redirected my attention to the LED floor counter. "I'll take that as a compliment."

From the corner of my eye, I caught his deepening scowl.

"Something else bothering you, Mr. Steele?"

"Charlie suspected I wasn't a consultant, and yet he gave me a security pass anyway. I wasn't searched. Like those rent-a-cops in LA, he would've been useless if I truly wished you harm," he snapped.

I hit the emergency stop button on the elevator, my temper once again bubbling to the surface. "First of all, Charlie is good at his job. The normal procedure for bringing a guest into the building is way more stringent than that. He let a few things slide because *he knows me*. Second, you assume that if you'd been holding a weapon on me I would've folded like a cheap noodle. I can take care of myself. If you don't believe me, try me."

The words were hardly out of my mouth before he lunged for me. Strong hands gripped my waist, lifted me high and pinned me against the wall.

"What the hell?" My voice was a husky mess.

"Okay. Challenge accepted."

I tried to snatch the breath he'd knocked out of me with his action and proximity. All I got was a knee-weakening hit of his intoxicating scent. That and intense deep-blue eyes.

His gaze dropped to my lips. He exhaled, long and deep, still staring at my mouth for breath-stealing seconds. His grip tightened around my waist, imprinting heat from his touch directly onto my skin. A low, insistent throb started between my legs.

I dropped my satchel and brought one knee up, only to have him block me with a smooth deflection a few inches before it made contact between his legs. His low laugh made me see red. I slammed both wrists against his neck. The gleam in his eyes mocked me and I knew he could've evaded me if he'd wanted to. But with the semi-blunt spikes from my cuffs digging into his carotid, he was going nowhere.

His thumbs pressed into my hipbones, his body pinning me harder into the wall. "And here I thought those cuffs were just to drive up a man's blood pressure," he breathed against my lips.

The ends of his hair teased my fingers, sparking a need to twist them into his hair. "You can't really be talking since I've just virtually ripped your throat out," I murmured.

He gave another laugh. "True. Score one to you."

"Great. You can...let me go now." Why did the second part of that sentence stick in my throat?

He shook his head. "Not until you agree to stop calling me Mr. Steele."

"And if I don't?" I challenged.

"Technically, I'm dying. I deserve a last wish, don't you think?"

"And your last wish is for me to say your name?"

His gaze dropped to devour my mouth. "Yeah. But I wouldn't mind another taste of you, too. Or those hot little hands on my cock again. Hell, I'll take whatever you give."

"You... I..."

"Ball's in your court, baby," he encouraged thickly, then flexed his hips, offering the vivid imprint of his cock between my thighs as he gave a strained laugh. "Literally."

Dear God. He was thick. And long.

The ache between my legs intensified a thousand times, plumping my clit as my pussy clenched hungrily. I tunneled my fingers through his hair, then grabbed a handful, exerting a little force as I hooked my legs around his waist.

His chest vibrated with a smothered growl as he planted himself more firmly between my thighs. The layers of clothing between us were all but nonexistent as he pressed the solid rod of his cock against my sex.

"Fuck," he groaned. "Your hot little pussy feels so good against my cock."

I lowered my head until our lips were millimeters

apart. Then I slowly undulated my hips, deepening the friction.

"Shit," he growled, his gaze darting between my mouth and where we were pressed together below the waist.

"You like that...Mr. Steele?" I drew my hips back up, nice and slow.

His jaw clenched tight and a shudder powered through him. "You teasing little witch. You'd like nothing better than to see me come right here, wouldn't you?" he muttered.

I wanted him to lose a little control, but not with the bothersome layers of clothes between us. I wasn't going to tell him that, though. "Would you die happy, then?"

"Not even close," he hissed. "Not when I'd rather have you, hot and wet and tight around my—"

"Hello? Is everything okay in there?" A disembodied voice asked from the panel on the elevator wall.

Caleb's jaw flexed, and he swore under his breath. "We're fine," he growled without taking his eyes off me.

"You sure? We have a technician here if you need help?" the helpful voice offered.

"Let me go," I muttered against his lips.

For a charged moment he resisted. Then his grip loosened and he allowed me to slide down the wall. With every inch, the heat of his erection singed me, announced its potency in a way that made my nipples sting and my pussy wetter.

It was ten kinds of inappropriate but for the life of me, I couldn't summon an ounce of regret. All I could think about was what it would feel like to have that thickness *inside* me.

"To be continued, I hope," he murmured against my cheek as my feet met the floor.

He took a step back. Then another. Reluctantly, his hands dropped. Then, without taking his eyes off me, he stabbed the button that released the elevator.

The small rattle before the carriage continued its journey restored some sanity. But even then a large part of me was suspended in disbelief at what I'd done.

Sex with Scott—before I found out that Chance had planted him in my life to control and spy on me—had been lukewarm at best.

What happened to my body when it was within touching distance of Caleb was nothing short of stupefying.

I avoided looking at him as I led us through the open plan space that led to my corner office. Like most tech companies in Silicon Valley, the space was designed to invite easy lounging with the aim of sparking ideas through socializing.

I entered my office, set my satchel down and fired up my three monitors. From the corner of my eye, I saw Caleb checking out the area before refocusing on me.

When he started walking toward me, I reached into my satchel. "Here's the list you asked for."

His hot gaze lingered on my face and mouth for a few ferocious moments before he took the piece of paper. "Thanks."

"If you need somewhere to work, there's a spare desk and computer next door."

He reached into his jacket and I forced myself not to ogle the way his T-shirt stretched across his torso. "No, thanks. This is all I need." He waved his phone at me.

He walked across the room, dropped onto the sectional sofa next to the wall and propped one foot on the coffee table. A minute later his fingers were flying over the keyboard.

I greatly resented the fifteen teeth-grinding minutes it took for me to focus, but eventually I was back in the groove. I spent the next few hours going over the tweaks I'd made that morning.

The snags my coding had hit were frustrating, but I couldn't rush this or SDM would miss the first major beta-testing deadline.

Not gonna happen.

My burning need to be done with Chance depended on everything going smoothly.

There were times I wished I hadn't hacked him. Times I wished I'd called his bluff when he'd turned up at my house with a patrol car and threatened me with jail unless I did what he—and my opportunity-grabbing stepfather—wanted.

Thoughts of how easily Stephen Gracen had thrown his own stepdaughter under the bus slashed painfully through me.

I was stealthily breathing my way through it when Miranda, my assistant, entered.

Her gaze swung to Caleb. And stayed.

His head snapped up, but the laser-eyed scrutiny he'd given my other employees was nowhere in sight. Instead, a slow smile broke over his face as he stared at my tall, attractive assistant.

"Hi," he drawled, slowly rising to his feet.

Miranda's toothpaste-white smile lit up her face. "Hi, I'm Miranda." She strode to him, her hand outstretched. "And you are?"

He took her hand. "Caleb."

"Caleb. Hi," she repeated. Then just stood staring up at him.

I slowly disengaged my clenched jaw. Cleared my throat. They both looked at me.

I opened my mouth to explain Caleb's presence, then remembered his gibe about me being a lousy liar. When his eyebrow started to creep up, I redirected my attention to Miranda. "I wasn't expecting you in today."

She reluctantly dropped Caleb's hand, but I noticed a pronounced sway in her hips as she crossed to my desk. "It was either go off-road biking with the guys from design or finish the assignment you gave me on Wednesday."

"It could've waited till Monday," I replied. Her work had nothing to do with my secret project but she had an aptitude for programming that I utilized when necessary.

She shrugged. "Programming beats the risk of a broken arm, no matter how exhilarating the boys claim biking can be." She glided a hand over her sweater dress and glanced at Caleb. "I prefer a different type of excitement."

He slid his phone into his back pocket and crossed his arms, and I swore Miranda groaned under her breath.

"I'll let you get on with it, then." I couldn't help the irritation filtering through my voice.

She nodded, then flicked Caleb one last glance. "See you around?"

Caleb smiled. "I'm sure you will."

To his credit, or more likely because he knew he could have her if he wanted, he didn't watch her sashay to the door. Instead, he turned his blue gaze on me.

Oh, hell no. I wasn't about to answer questions about Miranda.

The tall brunette could double as a supermodel any day of the week, and was constantly hit on outside the office.

And technically, she didn't fall under Caleb's no-dating-clients rule.

I fixed my gaze on my screen and continued working.

He got the message and returned to the sofa.

An hour later his shadow fell across my desk.

The breath I sucked in didn't quite catch. Irritated by my body's continued betrayal, I raised my head. "Can I help you?"

His mouth twisted in a parody of a smile. "You seem different. Much less...tense." He snapped his fingers. "That's it. You look relaxed."

I cursed the flush that crawled up my neck. "I don't know what you're talking about."

"Sure you do. You're in your element."

"Is this conversation going anywhere? I have a ton of work—"

My breath rushed out when he leaned across the desk and drifted a finger down my cheek. "You really don't need to be so jumpy around me. You especially don't need to get defensive every time I give you a compliment."

"I wasn't—"

"You want to pretend you're offended because I said you're more at home here with your computers than in that gilded cage you call a home. But you don't have to be."

The accuracy of his words made me jerk away from his touch.

My house was luxurious on many levels. But there was more to what I'd told Caleb last night. Truth was, it was also my cage. Chance had stashed me there when I'd first arrived in San Francisco because he'd wanted me isolated. *Still* wanted me isolated. For now it was a place to eat and sleep but it would never be my home.

Caleb was watching me closely, reading my every expression.

My gaze dropped to his throat as I cleared mine. "I'm not. You're mistaken."

He sighed. "What's your favorite restaurant?"

I blinked. "What?"

"Food. Lunch. Where?"

"Why?"

"Jesus. You love making me sweat, don't you, Lily?"

My fingers curled around the edge of my desk, unable to stop myself from replaying those moments in the elevator. The feel of his cock between my legs, his strained voice as he whispered his wishes to me.

All that power and glory under my control…

He leaned closer, sunlight glinting off his dark, mahogany-tipped hair. "What's going through that mind of yours, I wonder?"

I dragged my gaze from his body and named the Japanese restaurant I liked. He tapped it into his phone and I heard a whoosh of a text.

"Why do we need to go out at all? This place has a takeout service. We could just order in."

He shook his head. "Like I said, it's time to change things up a little. Your stalker knows your routines so let's introduce a new element into the equation."

"Let me guess? You?"

"Yep. We're putting ourselves out there. Besides, I

have questions about the people on the list you gave me. I prefer we do it somewhere we won't be interrupted." He jerked his head to where a couple of analysts conversed outside my office. One of them looked up and started to wave.

Caleb's glower froze it dead. They quickly dispersed.

"Wow, you must be very proud of yourself," I said.

He turned back. "Last night you told me what you're working on is top secret."

"It is."

He indicated the clear glass windows. "I would've thought you'd be locked away in a basement somewhere in one of those Faraday Cages."

I opened my mouth, closed it again and tapped a command to shut down my laptop.

"Come on. I'll show you how it works. Then maybe you'll stop glaring at everyone who comes into my office."

He smirked. "I can't make that promise. And I didn't glare at *everyone*."

No. Miranda got the full effect of his megawatt smile. I didn't want to examine why that bothered me so much.

In the elevator, I made sure to keep a distance between us although I didn't escape the sizzling heat of his gaze as he lounged against the opposite wall.

Damn, I'd probably never ride an elevator again without thinking about Caleb Steele.

The code I inputted dropped us down to Basement Level 3. The guard outside the elevator took Caleb's electronic gadgets. We walked down a corridor to a silver metallic door.

"To answer your question, both buildings are equipped with specialist reflective glass that makes it hard to spy on monitors from outside. And then there's this." I led him into a warehouse-size room completely empty except for the large meshed structure in its center with a desk and one chair.

"The Faraday Cage," Caleb muttered.

I nodded.

"What's that?" He nodded to the pedestal set up against the left wall with a small laptop built into it.

"Every keystroke I make on my laptop or work station upstairs is immediately saved into that laptop. Every twenty-four hours, I transfer data from the laptop to the supercomputer in the cage. Hacking it isn't impossible, but it'll be very difficult. And I didn't come down here to work because as you can see there's only room for one down here." I didn't want him prowling outside the cage, like a predator wolf, disturbing me with his presence.

Caleb walked around the cage, examined every inch of the space before returning to where I stood.

"You designed all this?"

I licked my top lip. "Yes."

His gaze heated up, his eyes telling me he wanted to touch me and do other intensely filthy things to me. Things forbidden by his rule. "All that beauty and brains in this killer little package."

That darned swell of pride rose again, mingling with the sizzling fires his eyes evoked in me. "Is that your way of saying you're impressed?"

"It's my way of saying I'm *very* impressed."

Before I could stop myself, I was smiling, shamelessly basking in his praise.

His eyes dropped to linger on my mouth, and his nostrils pinched a little as he inhaled. "You have a beautiful smile, Lily. You should use it more often."

I knew Caleb was attracted to me, but the look in his eyes as he called me *beautiful* shook loose something mildly disquieting inside me.

Just shut up and enjoy the moment.

Except I was enjoying too much of it altogether.

I was paying him to be here. Once his job was done, this would be a distant memory.

Unless you make it infinitely memorable?

I turned away sharply, the potency of that temptation taking me by surprise. Under the guise of taking the laptop to the Faraday Cage to transfer my latest work, I couldn't stop thinking about the possibilities.

Caleb and me.

Doing the dirty.

Last night he'd given me the green light. This morning in the elevator, he'd all but begged me to third-base him.

What was stopping me?

The discovery that Scott was just a pawn strategically placed in my life and not just a guy I'd met at a party and subsequently dated had left a huge deficit in my trust bank, not to mention a gaping vacancy in my sex life. This might be my chance to balance the sex part without the messiness of wondering about authentic emotions.

Plus, if our three brief encounters were an indication, the sex would be off the charts.

"Lily."

God, that voice. Would he sound like that when he was deep inside me, pounding my brains out?

"Lily?"

I snatched in a breath, schooled my expression and turned. "Yes?"

"You done?" he asked with a raised eyebrow.

"Uh-huh."

"Good. Time for lunch."

As we entered the elevator, I remembered other fragments of our conversation upstairs. "You said you had questions."

He was watching me with hooded eyes as if he knew the thoughts running through my head. "Yeah," he replied absently.

"What kinds of questions?" I asked.

He slid his hands into his back pockets. "Different kinds. Personal and professional. Wanna start with the personal?"

My breath caught. "I—"

"Great. When was the last time you had sex?"

CHAPTER SEVEN

Caleb

"You're going to have to answer me sometime."

After a sharp intake of breath and a furious blush, which took all my severely tested control not to trace with my fingers, she'd clammed up.

To be fair, having a couple of SDM employees join us in the elevator had put the brakes on that conversation.

But she'd maintained silence in the SUV and all the way to the restaurant.

I parked in front of the Japanese restaurant, ignoring the valet waiting for us to exit the vehicle.

"I'm happy to repeat the question if you want? Sex, Lily. When—?"

"I heard you the first time," she snapped, puffing out an annoyed breath as she reached for the door.

I stepped out, a little annoyed with myself, too. Truth be told, I didn't intend to ask her that. Not immediately.

But as suspected, with every revelation of her brilliance, I grew more attracted to Lily Gracen. I'd come within a whisker of calling bullshit on my own rules and kissing her in the Faraday Cage room. After that little cock-teasing incident in the elevator, who the hell would've blamed me? Shit, I was getting hard just thinking about the way she'd worked me between her legs.

And yes, I was a little peeved that she managed to get herself under control before I did. All the same, this was a subject that needed addressing, so why the hell not?

I made eye contact with the two-man security team I had Maggie send ahead, and escorted Lily into the restaurant. The waiter showed us to the private booth I requested.

"Lily." Maggie called this my rumbling volcano voice. "This will go a lot faster if you didn't stop to dissect every question or take offense at it."

She barely blinked at my don't-fuck-with-me tone, studied the menu for a minute before she closed it with a snap. "What has sex got to do with anything?" she hissed.

I shrugged. "Maybe nothing. Maybe everything. I thought you were in a hurry for this to be over?"

"I am, but—"

"How old are you?" It was another pertinent question I hadn't yet asked. She was over the age of consent but the flashes of innocence I spotted every now and then demanded investigation.

"Twenty-four," she answered with a frown. "How old are *you*?" she tossed back.

If she didn't know then she'd told the truth about skimming my past. That put a plus tick in her favor.

"I'm asking the questions here, but if it'll make you cooperate, I'm twenty-nine. I'm six-foot-four. I have all my own hair and teeth. Oh, and I'm single."

A hungry little expression flitted across her face but she hid it well. "How long have you been a fixer?" she returned.

"You must have missed what I just said about questions."

"I'm supposed to trust you with my safety. I deserve to know a little bit about you, don't you think?"

Fair point. In her shoes, I would have a few hundred questions, too. She wasn't a blind follower. Another turn-on. Still… "You get three questions. *After* you answer all of mine."

That earned me a sarcastically raised eyebrow that somehow managed to connect straight to my cock. Fuck.

"What's your deal with SDM? You said you had history," I said.

Her face immediately shuttered. "They put me through college and hired me straight after."

Interesting. "And college was?"

"MIT."

"You're from the East originally?"

The waiter arrived at our table. Lily ordered a soda and six bite-size platters of assorted dishes without consulting the menu.

"I'll have what she's having but with a beer," I said.

The waiter nodded and hurried away.

"Why does it matter whether I'm from the East or not?" she asked warily.

"Is that one of your questions for me?"

"It's a query generated by the fact that I think you're wasting time on pointless questions."

She was unsettled by my line of questioning. Which triggered a need to know more. "You're being stalked, Lily. You don't think details of your background will inform me as to who is after you?"

Her shoulders slumped a little but in direct contrast,

her chin angled up. "Fine, I grew up in Maine, but we moved to Boston when I was ten."

"We?"

"My stepdad and I. And before you ask, neither of my biological parents are in the picture. They haven't been for a very long time."

I crunched on that piece of information for a minute. I wanted details but sensed it wasn't an easy subject, so I dropped it. I had ways to find that out on my own anyway.

"You have a boyfriend?" Living alone didn't mean she wasn't seeing anyone.

Her mouth—her very fuckable mouth—compressed but I spotted the flicker of anguished fury in her eyes. The kind that came from a nasty betrayal. "No. I don't have a boyfriend. If I did, I wouldn't—" She stopped short.

"What? Have sex toys?" I shrugged. "That could indicate a voracious appetite, not the absence of a sex life. Although I'm guessing you're not the kind of girl to wrap your legs around a man's waist and rub your pussy so beautifully against his cock if you belonged to another?"

"God, you're unbelievable," she said under her breath.

"I'm plain-speaking. There's a difference, sweetheart." Mixed signals led to complications. After Kirsten, I wasn't prepared to take that risk.

"When was your last relationship, casual or otherwise?" I pressed. It was obvious I would need to pry every piece of info from her.

Her gaze dropped, and she toyed with the tableware. "Eight months ago."

"How long were you together?" *Where did you meet? I hope he was a lousy kisser and even worse in bed.*

Jesus, Caleb. Get a fucking grip.

"Six months."

Not long by any stretch, but long enough for me to be mildly jealous at the thought of some guy having a claim on her.

The waiter's arrival gave me a moment to examine that jealousy, grimace with disgust at myself for sticking steadfastly to my second and third rules.

I watched her pick up a roll of sushi with her chopsticks and dip it in teriyaki sauce. I did the same and we ate in silence for a while.

"Who ended the relationship?"

She froze. I couldn't stop myself from staring at her glistening mouth, wondering how it would feel when I slid my cock between her lips.

I looked up. She was staring at me. Her cheeks heated up as she accurately read my thoughts.

"Answer the question, Lily."

She dropped her chopsticks, her face tightening again. "I did. And you're wasting your time with this. Scott isn't the one doing this."

"I'll be the judge of that—"

"No! I know what I'm talking about so please drop it," she hissed.

"Not until you tell me why any guy whose veins aren't filled with ice water would quietly walk away from you?"

Her lashes swept down for a moment, then rose again, a challenging fire in her eyes. "Not every guy I come into contact with is a potential stalker."

"Scott wasn't just any guy, though, was he? What aren't you telling me, Lily?"

She remained silent for a long stretch. And I waited her out, biting down my impatience.

"Because Scott wasn't just a guy I met at a party. Chance paid him to seek me out."

Shock bolted up my spine. "What? Why?"

She swallowed and her hands balled into small fists. When she lifted her gaze her beautiful green eyes were far too haunted. "Because he wanted...*wants* to control me."

Jesus. "Again, why?"

"What does it matter?" she snapped. "All you need to know is SDM and Chance need this algorithm. It'd be absurd for him to jeopardize it by having someone stalk me, so just...just take my word for it that it's not Scott, okay?"

I didn't voice the world's worst cliché right then because I didn't want to piss her off even more, or sound like a hormone-addled teenager but, fuck me, she was so incredibly gorgeous when she was mad I lost the ability to think clearly for a minute.

I let her take the deep breaths she needed to calm down.

"You slip into Bostonian when you're agitated, you know that? It's cute."

She looked adorably nonplussed before she shook her head. "Nothing about any of this is *cute*, Mr. Steele."

"I disagree. I wonder, do you sound like that during sex, too?"

Green eyes snapped fire at me. "You'll *never* find out."

I couldn't help myself. I had to touch her again. I reached out and traced the curve of her lower lip with my finger. Soft. Firm. Satin-smooth. "Are you sure about that, Lily?"

She inhaled sharply and her eyes turned a shade darker. "Can we not turn everything into a sexual tennis match? It's really exhausting."

Reluctantly, I retreated. "Has there been anyone else since Scott?"

She picked up her chopsticks again. "Someone briefly. Nothing serious."

"Who, and for how long?"

She sighed. "Mark Callen. For two months. He bought me a coffee at where I get my breakfast. I… I wanted to make sure Chance wasn't still interfering in my life."

My jaw gritted. "Was he?"

She shook her head.

I relaxed a little. "Did you sleep with him?"

Her glare burned me but I didn't let up.

"No," she answered eventually.

I was swimming in relief when she took a sip of her soda. I watched her throat move, wondering why the hell I found that so sexy.

Hell, was anything about her not sexy?

Yeah, the way she kept snippets of information from me. That didn't turn me on even a little.

That Chance thing really pissed me off, though. I made a note to have the asshole checked out.

As for Lily, I wanted to know everything about her. Lily Gracen fascinated me the way no other woman had.

"So you went out with him for two months but didn't sleep with him. What the hell did you do? Hold hands and read each other poetry by candlelight?" I asked.

"So what if we did?" she lobbed straight back.

"Then I'd say it's great you dumped the dickless wonder. You deserve way better than that."

"God, you really are a Neanderthal, aren't you?" she snapped before pushing her plate away. Apparently, we were done eating.

"No, I'm a man with basic but fundamental needs. If I have to endure the R word, then I sure as hell expect some regular fucking as part of the bargain. Otherwise, what's the point?"

"So sex has to be a guarantee in a *relationship* or you're out?"

I took in her white-blond hair and the choker around her neck that howled at me like a damn siren call. The semi-erection that flared to life if she so much as breathed in my direction thickened behind my fly. "I like sex. It's the single decent thing the good Lord granted humanity. I feel zero guilt for loving it. So yes, sex is a hell of a priority for me."

Fresh heat flared in her cheeks, but she still delivered the most dick-torturing smile I'd ever seen. "Except when it comes to your clients, though, right, Mr. Steele?"

Dammit. She was too fucking much. I breached the gap between us, spiked my fingers into her hair and tightened my fist.

She glared at me but didn't struggle to get away. "I'm beginning to think you enjoy taunting me by refusing to use my name," I breathed.

"I don't have a problem with saying your name."

I tugged her even closer. "Then do it."

She looked me straight in the eyes, her tongue darting out to moisten her lips. "Caleb."

I tilted her head until she had no choice but to raise

that gorgeous face, offer up those luscious lips to me.
"Again."

She glared fiercer at my instruction, then parted her
lips. "Caleb."

The soft, whispered delivery was deliberately pro-
vocative. I knew it. But it still chopped me off at the
knees. "Fuck." With a groan, I lowered my head, but
stopped a breath from her lips. "Kiss me, Lily."

"Why?" she breathed defiantly even as her eyes devoured my mouth.

"Because you're *dying* to. Take it, baby. Take what
you want."

Her ragged moan was music to my ears but hell for
my cock. All the same, I let go of her, put the power
in her hands and nearly roared with triumph as she
leaped on me.

And goddamn it all to hell if she didn't taste twice
as heady, twice as decadent, as before.

It started with one hot little sound under her breath
as my teeth grazed her bottom lip. A cross between a
whimper and a sigh, it snaked down my groin, curled itself around my cock and stroked me into rigid life. And
that was before I'd even tasted her properly. I nipped
her again, resisting the urge to take a deeper, more satisfying bite.

The promise of more lay within, but I was more than
content, for now, to just sample her plush lips. Over and
over. To hear the tiny sounds turn into moans, to feel
her strain toward me as her own hunger clawed at her.

Her hands delved beneath my jacket, clawed at my
T-shirt before she slipped them underneath.

In that moment I stopped caring that we were in a
public place.

A breath I didn't remember holding expelled from me as her small nails dug into my skin. I suppressed a growl and fought the need to ravage, reminding myself that besides every shitty thing happening in her life, she hadn't had sex in a while. Exhibiting even a fraction of the wild craving whipping through me might send her into retreat mode, and fuck if I was going to allow that to happen.

But God, she was exquisite. The way her lips clung to mine was driving me insane.

"Jesus, you taste amazing." I couldn't help the words from spilling out when we broke apart to get a hit of oxygen.

She tensed. I sucked her bottom lip into my mouth and trailed my tongue over her velvety skin. A sigh and a moan rewarded my effort.

I'll stop in a minute.

We hadn't finished our talk. Plus, we needed to put on the brakes before we were thrown out for public indecency.

Besides, I couldn't sustain this much longer. Not without throwing my rules out the window, flattening her to the booth seat and delivering on every single promise and filthy fantasy I'd harbored since she walked into my life.

But I *could* drag her a touch closer. I *could* slide one hand down her back and mould it around her pert little ass, reconfirm that her flesh was as tight and supple as I imagined.

I would stop. Right after she gave me another of those exceptionally indecent moans.

CHAPTER EIGHT

Lily

HOLY. SHIT.

What the hell was happening to me? Why did Caleb only need to crook his finger before I threw common sense out the window and jumped him?

And these sounds I was making? Yeah, I *really* needed to stop moaning like a whore in church. But up until a minute ago, he'd let me take the lead in our little make-out session.

Then something flipped.

Now, the way he was using his mouth, his tongue, heck, his teeth? In the few times I let him kiss me, Mark's teeth always managed to collide with mine, generating an unpleasant nails-on-a-chalkboard sensation.

Caleb knew how to use his. Little nips at the corner of my mouth that shot fire straight between my legs, even bites on the very tip of my tongue where I had no clue I was so sensitive.

Our previous encounters, I'd felt like I'd plugged into a steady current. *This* was probably what it felt like to bungee jump off a helicopter over a live volcano after being injected with pure adrenaline.

Three numbskulls from the research department confessed to doing that once for the intense rush. I still believed they were completely insane, but if what they experienced was remotely close to what I was feeling now, then…yeah…I got why they would chase such a thrill.

Caleb's tongue swiped between my lips, instantly igniting a yearning to feel it swiping between my legs on its way to concentrate on my clit, now throbbing insistently.

And God, his hand was kneading my ass in that superhot way again.

His hand slipped lower to the curve of my butt and nudged me closer until somehow, I was in his lap. Was that the slow grind of the thick erection against my thigh? Holy…God. He felt even bigger than this morning in the elevator.

The thought of all that power and girth inside me freaked me out a little. Okay, a *lot*.

Until I reminded myself that I had the power. I could stop anytime I wanted. By simply pulling back. Letting go.

Let go!

I dragged my hand down from where it'd ended up on his ripped chest. Down to his waist, to the solid square of his belt buckle. Any lower and I would touch his cock again. I moaned at the intense urge to do just that.

Then I heard the faint clink of cutlery.

We were in a restaurant. In a private booth, yes, but still a public place. And for the third time since I woke up, I was sucking face with the man I'd hired to find my stalker.

Oh, God.

Maybe that adrenaline kick I imagined had really been a hormone shot? Because the sensations racing through my body all craved one thing—Caleb's cock inside me.

I scurried backward from the hot body and the erection digging into my thigh. One hand was still buried in my hair, imprisoning me as he stared down at me with fiery eyes that promised as much filthy fucking as his lips had pledged.

"Lily." His voice was thick. He cleared his throat and swallowed.

Those few precious seconds helped me put more daylight between us. I grabbed his wrists and tugged his hands from my body. He dropped them but not his searing gaze.

I busied myself by picking up my glass of soda and taking a sip I prayed wouldn't choke me. Thankfully, it went down smoothly, cool enough to restore a tiny bit of sanity. "So, you think this little display helped?"

His eyes narrowed. "What?" He shifted away and dropped one hand into his lap. I forced myself not to watch him adjust the bulge behind his fly.

"My stalker. If he's watching. You think it helped or was it all a waste of time?" I forced out as I smoothed my hands over my hair. My scalp still tingled deliciously from when he'd grabbed and pulled my hair. Did he do that during sex, too? I slammed my thighs together before the image of him doing that added to the fire scorching my pussy.

He exhaled sharply. "That wasn't why you kissed me and you know it."

"Do I?" I challenged because, *dammit*, I was out of sorts in more ways than one, and this seesawing from being in total control to losing it around him was driving me nuts.

His eyes gentled. "You don't need to panic, Lily. I'm not going to use this against you. That's what you're afraid of, isn't it?"

My breath shuddered out as panic flared. "Stop talking as if you know me. You don't!"

"I know that control is important to you. Is it because of what your asshole boss did? I'd be wary, too—"

"Tell me why you're so hung up on *your* rules. Is it because of what a *client* did to you?" I lashed out, terrified of how effortlessly he was probing beneath my skin.

A muscle rippled in his jaw. "We're not talking about me."

I forced a laugh. "That tells me everything. Who was she?" I pressed.

His whole face grew taut. "Nobody you need to concern yourself with," he bit out.

The confirmation that someone somewhere had affected him enough to drive his guard up hit me with unnerving disquiet. Nearly as much as his accurate divining of my panic.

"Fine. Can we leave now?" I cringed at the stress in my voice.

He inhaled slow and deep, and then pulled out his wallet.

"I have an account here. They'll put it on my tab," I said.

He scowled as he placed a couple of hundred dollar bills on the table. "I brought you to lunch. I'm paying."

Outside, the brilliant sunlight reminded me it was still daytime. That I had many more hours of work ahead of me.

About to get in the SUV, I caught Caleb scanning the street, his gaze alert. I knew he had men out there but the fact that he was in fixer/protector mode despite the turbulence between us shook loose something I hadn't felt in a long time.

Warmth.

The memory of it was ephemeral—the contented seven-year-old tucked in her mother's arms with no clue that a mother's love could be temporary like everything else.

You're truly losing it.

I slammed the door and shook my head.

Like the outbound journey, neither of us spoke as we drove back to SDM but I knew I had to say something as he pulled up into my parking space.

I undid my seat belt, faced him and opened my mouth. He grabbed me and pulled me across the center console.

"I know it's insane, and we'll both probably regret it, but fuck, I need to kiss you again," he breathed roughly against my mouth.

Before I could take a breath, his tongue slid into my mouth. Wet and insistent and carnal. It was the dirtiest promise of sex I'd ever known. Over and above every inappropriate sexual thing he'd said to me since we met, it was that decadent slide of his tongue against mine that did me in. My hands returned to dig into his waist, my torso straining across the small space to slide against his.

He banded one hand around my waist and lifted me over to his side. And just like that the heat of his cock was a living thing against my ass, announcing its insistent virility. I moaned, half-ashamed at how easily

I'd fallen into the kiss, half-fearful of his sensual power over me.

Slowly, that fear built, insidiously reminding me that this was no longer my default setting. I was so close to true freedom for the first time in my life. I couldn't become a slave to my hormones or my emotions.

I pushed at Caleb's chest before the hand sneaking up my waist could cup my breast. "Stop!"

He froze immediately.

I took a breath. "Let me go."

He stared at me for a full minute, his chest rising and falling in harsh pants. Then his hands dropped from my body.

I hopped over into my seat, struggling with my own breathing.

"Jesus," he swore under his breath, slammed his head against the headrest and closed his eyes. After tense seconds he opened them. "I'm…" He stopped and gritted his teeth. "Hell, I suppose you want an apology?" Before I could answer, he continued, "You're not going to get one because I'm not sorry. You, with that tight, gorgeous body and that bruised, ripe mouth, are fucking irresistible," he growled.

My lungs deflated in a giddy rush. Heat spiked through my blood, and my panties grew shamelessly damper. Every atom in my body strained to jump into his lap and continue where we'd left off. I curled my nails into my palms until tiny bites of pain brought a little clarity.

"I'm afraid you'll have to resist."

To my surprise, he nodded. "Understood."

My jaw threatened to drop. I caught myself, then

shifted my gaze from his face. Now I'd successfully drawn the line, I didn't know what to do next.

He answered by stepping out and escorting me inside.

In my office, he calmly returned to the sofa. While I spent the next hour rewriting the same code.

I called it a night at six. He drove us home after stopping to pick up the takeout I'd ordered.

Over dinner, he asked me a bunch of work-related questions, probing my routines and those of my team. Any trace of the fever that overtook us in the restaurant and the parking lot was wiped from his features as he listened and made notes on his laptop.

Just before nine, he sat back in his chair, his eyes on his screen. "That's enough for today. I'll see what I can dig up with this info." His tone was impersonal as he stood and picked up the plates and empty cartons. He helped clean up and stack the dishwasher, maintaining a chilly distance that made my stomach muscles tighten.

You wanted this. Professional distance is good.

When we were done, I turned to leave.

"Remember, you need to let me know if you're going outside," he said.

My face felt stiff so I didn't even attempt a smile. "I haven't forgotten."

He stared at me for a beat then nodded.

In my den I made a stab at work for a solid hour before giving up and giving in to a burst of resentment. I swiveled in the seat and stared out the window.

Caleb probably thought he was only doing his job, but his interrogation had peeled back a thin layer of memories I wanted to keep buried.

Boston. My mother.

Frustration threatened to build as I paced from window to wall and back again. My restlessness eventually drove me to the cinema room and I halfheartedly settled for a new rom-com I wasn't really in the mood for.

I startled awake to a blank screen and a sore neck. When my disorientation cleared, I noticed a blanket that had been draped over me and there were cushions I'd dislodged in my sleep, which weren't there before.

My heart lurched as that warmth encroached again, teasing me with its comfort. I pushed it away, got up and stumbled upstairs to bed.

Caleb Steele, like everyone in my life, was a transient, *paid* presence.

Nothing else.

Sunday was a repeat of Saturday, minus the mind-melting making-out sessions, the probing questions into my sex life and the sexually loaded banter.

That set the course for the next three days.

On Thursday we returned to the Japanese restaurant and picked our way through an uncomfortable meal.

As he wove through light traffic on the way back to SDM, I glanced at him, that little morsel he'd let drop on Saturday returning like a nagging toothache.

Who was the client who'd triggered his rule? Was he or, as I suspected, *she*, still in his life?

At a stoplight he speared me with dark blue eyes. "Something on your mind?" His tone was cool. That plus the absence of his mocking eyebrow lift rattled me more than I cared for. It was like he had become a different person after the episode in the parking lot.

I reminded myself that I'd only known him for a handful of days.

That first night and day had been…out of the norm. Intense. We were both fighting for control. We'd reached an understanding and now he was focused on what he came here to do.

This was the real Caleb Steele. End of story.

So this unsettled sensation that had carved a small hollow in my stomach was misplaced. Right?

I looked away from his piercing eyes. "Nope. Nothing at all."

He drove on, dismissing me as coolly as he'd done for the past few days.

Unfortunately, the sensation knotted inside me wasn't as easy to dismiss. Admitting I wanted the dirty-tongued, brooding-eyed Caleb back was…hard.

I glanced out the window, frowning at my reflection when I caught myself biting my lip. I had more important things to dwell on than which version of my fixer I preferred. Besides, what the hell could I do? Crawl into his lap, drag my fingers through his hair and kiss him the way I'd wanted to do on Saturday before sanity returned?

The dragging sensation in my belly gave me the answer.

I avoided his gaze for the remainder of the journey.

The fretful but excited buzz in the air when we reached my floor was a great excuse not to hunt for an answer right then.

"What's going on?" Caleb asked as we entered my office.

"We're presenting a midseason upgrade on two SDM products to the board tomorrow. The day before is always a little frantic."

His gaze narrowed slightly as he watched me. "That doesn't include what you're working on, does it?"

"No. That's still confidential. But I'll be giving a presentation of my own to three of the board members tomorrow, too."

"Which members?"

"Chance and two of his colleagues." I couldn't keep the stiffness out of my voice.

He noticed. "He's coming here?" he rasped.

I swallowed at the volatile vibes oozing from him. "Yes."

His gaze narrowed on me for several heartbeats. "Okay, I'll need the names of the colleagues."

I gave him the names, unable to stop the chill spreading over my nape. "Why?"

His stare was direct. "Everyone who has access to you is a suspect until I catch this asshole. Don't underestimate anyone, Lily. And if you can help it, don't trust anyone, either. That way you'll avoid any nasty surprises."

He turned away but not before I caught a flash of pain in his eyes.

Add the confounding emotions coiling through me, it rooted me to the spot for several heartbeats until a knock on my door snapped me free. By the time I finished dealing with my team member's query, Caleb was on his phone.

We worked late into the night, then headed down to the seventh floor where the in-house catering staff had laid out a buffet-style meal in the dining room.

Although Caleb stayed close by, he didn't engage in conversation. I tried not to glance his way, but it proved almost impossible. Especially when Miranda slid into the seat next to him, and he gave her one of those smiles that had been absent for almost a week now.

I turned away, finished the chicken parmesan I didn't really want, while doing my best to reassure the two tech newbies on either side of me that they wouldn't tank their presentation tomorrow.

I wasn't sure what made me glance over at Caleb halfway through my conversation. His eyes were fixed on me, a ripple of muscle ticking in his jaw as he clenched his teeth.

Abruptly, he stood and walked around to where I sat. "Are you done eating?" He glanced pointedly at my plate.

"Yes."

"You ready to head out?" he asked, flicking a cold glance at one newbie, who cowered away from the arctic mountain glowering at him.

I considered calling Caleb out on his rudeness, but it had been a long, draining day. I really wanted to get out of here. And it had absolutely nothing to do with wanting to get him away from Miranda, who was eyeing Caleb with barely disguised hunger.

I swallowed a knot of irritation. "Don't stay too long, Miranda. I need you back here by seven."

Her gaze swung to me, and I swore I caught a flash of something nasty in her eyes. A moment later it was gone. "Sure thing, boss. I'll make sure you're all set to go."

Caleb's impatient hand gripped the back of my chair, and I rose.

Maybe it was the don't-mess-with-me vibes he gave off as we left the building, but nobody approached to talk to me. I continued with last minute prepping on my tablet right until we drove through the gates of my house. And then I couldn't hold back the grain of irritation that had grown since dinner.

I cleared my throat. "I need a favor," I said briskly.

He paused with a hand on the door. His eyebrow twitched but didn't exactly lift. "Normally, a request like that is couched in a more…friendly tone."

I fixed my gaze somewhere around his chest to avoid New Caleb's cool, disinterested expression. "Tomorrow is an important day for me. So I need you not to…" I paused, a little annoyed with myself for needing to utter the words.

"It would help if you actually complete the sentence?"

The mild mockery lacing the words made me forget not to look into his face. His eyes weren't disinterested. They were neutral. Enough to make that odd little band around my chest tighten.

To hell with this. "Stop flirting with my assistant," I snapped.

He sat back in his seat, his eyes narrowing. "Why?"

"Excuse me?"

"What do you care who I flirt with?" he drawled.

"You're supposed to be a professional. Do I really need to point this out to you?"

He gave a careless shrug.

"Fine. Your…attention hasn't impacted her work. *Yet*. But—"

"You're worried she's becoming preoccupied with getting into my pants and you have a problem with that?" The words were delivered with a little more of that zing I was used to.

Hot little fires began licking through my veins, sparking electricity that engulfed my breasts, stung between my legs. "I only have a problem with how it pertains to my work. She needs to be on her A-game for tomorrow. So, yes, I'd be grateful if you'd dial down the low-voiced charm, and all that *smiling*."

The smile I'd just denigrated lit up his face. It was slow and deadly. It was also so drop-dead magnificent that I couldn't look away. Couldn't breathe. Couldn't do anything other than absorb it. Bask in it and God help me, grow intensely, claws-out possessive over Caleb smiling at another woman like that. And right in that moment of admitting that I was mindlessly attracted to him, I wanted to die.

Especially when that smile turned stupidly smug.

"Why, Lily, if I didn't know any better, I would think you were jealous."

CHAPTER NINE

Caleb

I WATCHED HER stalk to the front door, her body stiff with outrage.

My smile dimmed as my gaze swept feverishly over her, greedily taking one of the few long glances I'd been reduced to stealing all week. A part of me remained pissed off that she'd put the brakes on what had seemed like a slam-dunk acceptance of the green light I gave her.

Hell, three insanely hot make-out sessions in twenty-four hours was a record, even for me, although that first time in the restaurant had been a simple exercise in taking her down a peg or two, but had quickly escalated into something mildly earthshaking.

Okay, nothing about what happened between us could be classified under *mild*. I would've fucked her in broad daylight in the front seat of my SUV if one of us hadn't come to our senses.

Still. The part I was having a hard time dealing with was how hard it'd been to stick to my own rules this week. I'd spent more than a few sleepless nights reliving

Lily's taste, enduring a raging—pun intended—storm in my cock I was yet to get under full control.

As I watched her stab the code to turn off the alarm, though, I couldn't help my gratification at this latest revelation.

"I'm not jealous," she denied hotly as if she'd read my thoughts.

I shut the front door and slid home the dead bolt. "Really? You're sure acting like it."

Her grip tightened on the satchel she never left home without. "Of course you would think that."

I strolled over to her. "I did wonder why you felt the need to instruct Miranda to come in on time tomorrow when she's never been late."

"And how would you know that?" she challenged huffily.

I cracked a little smile, watched her eyes drop to my mouth before she averted her gaze. The slow, torturous burn in my loins intensified. The wall I'd deliberately erected between us to help honor her wishes crumbled a little. I was tempted to give it a healthy kick, but deep down I knew she was right to want to keep things professional between us.

Besides, I wasn't sure I wanted to test my control just yet. Lily was as sensational as I imagined she would be. And that was with barely a taste.

"I know how to get the information I need," I answered her question.

Her eyes narrowed. "Was that what you were doing tonight? Gathering information?"

I shrugged. "Sometimes it's best to use honey, not vinegar."

She nodded and turned toward the stairs.

"Are you going to bed?"

Her eyes met mine for a second before she looked away, the pulse at her throat picking up speed. She let go of the satchel to drag her fingers through her hair. At some point this week, she'd repainted her short nails a dark purple shade that looked almost black. Something about the way it contrasted against her shock-white blond hair raised my temperature.

"No. I was thinking of going for a swim. I need the exercise to…de-stress a little."

Fuck, I had a dozen positions in mind to help her de-stress. And that was for starters. I forced the lid back on my runaway libido. "You nervous about tomorrow?" I asked.

She knew I was asking about Chance and tensed for a moment, and then she deliberately avoided the subject. "I shouldn't be. The code is working perfectly. But…" She shrugged.

I'd been looking into Chance Donovan and had a few thoughts on the bastard CEO. But I didn't want to add to her stress.

So, even though Lily in a sexy swimsuit and within touching distance was so not a good idea, I jerked my head toward the stairs anyway. "Go get changed. I'll meet you in the living room."

"Thanks," she said, looking relieved that I'd let the matter drop.

I stayed at the bottom of the stairs, unable to take my eyes off her perfect ass as she sprinted upstairs. Yeah, I was a glutton for punishment.

That punishment increased a hundredfold the moment she entered the living room. My hand froze on the French doors, and I swallowed hard.

She was wearing a see-through black mesh T-shirt over a burnt-orange bikini. Two things struck me hard just then. First, that while her signature black suited her alabaster complexion, the dark orange was even more flattering, drawing attention to her pint-size perfection.

Second, that the wall I'd built to contain my insane attraction and strict rules didn't stand a chance of staying up.

"Everything okay?" she asked, her eyes a little wide as she took in the joggers and T-shirt I'd changed into.

Fuck, no. "Sure." I held the door open for her.

She walked past me, trailing light, sensual perfume that made me want to bury my face in her neck. Her back view was just as spectacular as her front, the tight globes of her ass barely contained in the bikini bottom.

A dangerously high percentage of blood rushed south, emptying my head of every thought except the one that fixated on what I wanted to do to her body. "How long do you need?" I croaked, dropping onto the lounger and hitching up one leg before she turned and saw the steel rod tenting my pants.

She paused at the edge of the pool and glanced over her shoulder. The setting sun's rays worshipped her cheek, her arms, her stomach and thighs. "I normally swim a hundred laps. So…forty-five minutes?" she murmured.

"Yeah. Fine." *Wow, you'll be drooling like a brain-dead idiot next.*

She grabbed the bottom of her T-shirt and pulled it over her head. A groan rumbled up my throat as she dove cleanly into the water with the smoothness of a practiced athlete.

It took twenty laps for me to get myself back under

acceptable control. Of course she chose that moment to pause at the far end of the pool to smooth back her wet hair and slowly swivel her head until her gaze rested on me. Her lips parted as she sucked in air to regain her breath.

She didn't utter a word. Neither did I. And yet, a thousand conversations passed between us.

Later, I would appreciate that this was the moment we both accepted that we were far from done with each other. That the rules and barriers and words we'd thrown up in an attempt to stop this sexual juggernaut stood no chance.

She clung to the edge of the pool for a full minute, her sexy green eyes never wavering from mine. Then with a lithe twist of her body, she dove underwater.

Every cell in my body wanted to join her. If for nothing else, to cool down before the top of my head blew clean off. But I stayed put, counted down her laps until she reached ninety-eight.

I jumped up, grabbed a towel from the stack next to the lounger and was waiting when she climbed the shallow steps.

Just like last time, delicious droplets clung to her skin. I wanted to lick each and every one off, then concentrate on licking her between her legs.

Instead, I held out the towel. Her eyes met and clung to mine as she accepted it and wrapped it around her body. "Thanks."

My eyes drifted to the wet curl clinging to her cheek. Unable to resist, I smoothed it behind her ear, then went to retrieve her T-shirt.

"Let's get you inside." I didn't give one tiny shit that my voice was a gruff mess. Or that my cock still stood at attention. I saw her eyes drop to it before, reddening, she glanced away.

She followed me inside and lingered in the living room as I locked the doors. "Drink?" I needed one badly before I did something foolish.

She passed the towel through her hair before lowering it. "Umm... I shouldn't."

I handed back her T-shirt. "That doesn't sound like a definite no," I said, then held up my hands. "But I'm not trying to corrupt you or anything so if you want to head up to bed, don't let me stop you." The breath trapped in my lungs told a different story to the words falling from my mouth. I wanted her to stay. Badly.

She dropped the towel on the coffee table and shook her head. "No. I'll just lie in bed worrying about stuff. Or I'll be tempted to tinker with the code some more. Bad idea," she said with a laugh.

It was the first time I'd heard her laugh. The soft, tinkling sound hooked into me, feeding a need to hear more of it. "Okay, so what do you do to distract yourself?"

She looked away, fidgeted, then dragged the T-shirt over her head. "I normally read. Or watch a movie downstairs..."

It was an easy decision. "I vote for downstairs." She had a bar down there, after all. "I'll have a drink. You can join me. Or not." I cocked an eyebrow.

The barest hint of a smile curved her mouth as her gaze touched on my brow. "I get to pick the movie."

I shrugged. "Your theater, your choice. I'm just coming for the booze."

Her smile widened a little more.

We went down together, her bare feet slapping lightly on the polished wood. I crossed to the bar shelves stacked with expensive alcohol. She went to the sweets stand and returned with a large cone cup filled with assorted candy.

She popped a pink marshmallow into her mouth, then held out the cup to me. I chose a jellybean and pointed it at her. "These things will rot your teeth."

"Luckily I have an excellent dental plan." Her sexy grin exhibited perfect teeth.

I refocused on pouring my bourbon. "You sure you don't want anything?"

She inspected the row of drink bottles behind me. "Okay, I'll have a lemondrop martini, please."

I laughed. "You folded much easier than I thought you would."

She plucked another marshmallow from her supply before placing the cup on the counter. "I rarely fix it myself because it never comes out right. You look... comfortable behind the bar, like you know what you're doing."

Our eyes met. Locked. "So this is a test?"

Her lips slowly parted. "Maybe."

"And if I pass?"

Her gaze swept down for a moment before stunning green eyes met mine again. "I'll let you help me pick the movie."

I slowly set down the bourbon, biting my tongue against spilling what I really wanted for my prize. Hell, she knew it already. Knowledge flamed in her eyes. Whether she would choose tonight to do something about it was another matter.

I gathered the ingredients and watched her watch me fix her drink. I slid it across the counter to her, lifted my glass of bourbon and waited.

She picked up her glass, took a delicate sip. Her tongue slid across her bottom lip. My cock jumped. "It's good."

"Just good?"

Again, her eyes flicked to my raised eyebrow, and her mouth twitched. "Okay. It's perfect."

"You're welcome." I reached into the freezer, plucked out two ice cubes and dropped them into my drink. Anything to lower the inferno raging in my groin.

Grabbing her candy and drink, she hopped off the bar and headed for the red leather lounger with drink holders on either side.

Perfect for two.

On Saturday night, when another damned nightmare had ripped me from sleep, I'd wandered downstairs, heard the movie running and came to check on her. I'd toyed with waking her but with tensions running high, I thought it best to leave her alone. As I'd made her comfortable, she'd made a small, forlorn sound that ripped through me.

As I joined her now, questions crowded my mind. Asking more personal ones would mostly likely hurl us back onto the battleground. So I stuck to a less volatile one.

"I've ruled out most people on the list." Including her ex. A discreet probe into Scott Wyatt's activities showed he'd been mostly out of town in the weeks before the stalking started, and was currently engaged in a long-distance relationship with a new woman in Seattle. He was lucky he was out of my reach.

A trace of unease flitted over Lily's face. "Okay. So who's left?"

I paused. My answer could risk her acting differently

around the people left on the list. "I haven't been able to rule out Nordic Razor yet. Could he have seen what you were working on when you were online?"

She tucked her legs underneath her, rested sideways on the lounger, and took another sip of her drink. "No. I use a separate computer for social activities."

I set my glass in the holder. "Why Q?"

"What?"

"Cipher Q. What does the Q stand for?"

She toyed with a damp strand of hair. "What do you think it stands for?"

"I thought it was Quantum. But I'm going with Queen," I replied.

Her head dipped, that hint of shyness and innocence adding to her appeal. "It's silly, I know. And vain. But…"

"But you wanted to feel empowered at a time when things felt out of control?"

Her mouth dropped open a few seconds before she shut it. "I don't like it when you do that," she murmured.

"Do what?" I asked gently.

"See…too much."

"I won't hurt you, Lily. Not with any information you give me. I can promise you that."

After a moment, she nodded.

Grasping that tiny leeway, I probed softly, "How old were you when you started hacking?"

She looked a little trapped by my question, but she answered, "Thirteen."

"I'm guessing it was your stepfather who made you feel…less?"

A shadow crossed her face and she remained silent for a long time before she nodded. "He was saddled with me after my mom left. Every now and then he would let me feel his displeasure."

My fist tightened. "Did he hurt you?"

"Physically? No. In other ways…yes."

I took a sip of bourbon just for something to do so I didn't drive my fist through the wall behind me. "Tell me what he did."

Her nostrils quivered as she sucked in a breath. "I don't have all night."

"Then tell me exactly how you got involved with Chance."

"When I was fourteen, I hacked him. I was good back then, but I wasn't great. He hired another hacker to find me, and turned up at my house with the cops. He gave me a choice, work for him or go to jail."

"Your stepfather didn't tell him to get lost, I take it."

She gave a bitter laugh. "Not when Chance started throwing money his way, he didn't."

She flinched at my tight curse. I reached across the counter and placed my hand on hers. She stared at it with a sad smile before she inhaled long and deep.

"Anyway, between them they hammered out a deal that he'd pay my stepfather a monthly fee for my maintenance, then my college tuition fees on condition that when I left MIT I'd devote all my time to developing something big for him."

"The algorithm?" I asked, my chest and throat tight with the effort it took to keep my fury inside.

She nodded. "I had the beginnings of the idea back then."

"Why didn't you walk away when you turned eighteen or even twenty-one?"

Her lips tightened and she shrugged. "I gave him my word I wouldn't."

A simple answer, but such a powerful statement as to the true depths of Lily Gracen. I would've thought it impossible, but I grew even more attracted to her in that moment.

"And the Scott thing? How did you find out?"

She smiled unapologetically. "I hacked his phone records and confronted him."

"How did Chance take it?" I realized I was searching for another reason to punch the guy's lights out when I met him tomorrow.

"He claimed he was looking out for me. I called bullshit and threatened to walk then. He promised it would never happen again." The information was coming out in charged little bites.

"Lily—"

She shook her head. "No more. You're ruining the mood."

I cupped her cheek, my thumb caressing her lower lip until she had herself back under control. "Don't feel bad about letting me in. I know a little about how that feels like."

Wide green eyes locked on mine. "Really?"

I heard the throb of pain in my voice and inwardly grimaced. I could've answered differently, thrown her off with a shrug or said nothing at all. Instead, the last word I expected to say surged from my throat. "Yes."

She waited. Then a breath huffed out. "That's all you're going to give me?"

Curiosity swirled in her eyes, making my chest pound for a different reason. "Yes. I don't want to ruin the mood, either."

Her breath grew shaky. As did her hand when she raised her glass to take a healthy gulp. She stared at me for several heartbeats. Then, visibly shaking it off, she grabbed the remote and aimed it at the screen.

"Lowlights." Her command activated the lights, dimming the overhead lights and leaving only a set of lowlights running along the floor.

Onscreen, the system had grouped her entertainment into genres and then favorites. She clicked *favorites*. A long list rolled down the screen.

"These are all your favorites?" I asked skeptically.

"Uh-huh."

The title she clicked on caught my eye, and another raw memory spiked through me. *"The English Patient?"*

She glared at me. "It's a classic."

"If you want to weep into your martini glass the whole time then fall into a coma from boredom, sure."

"You've seen it?"

My teeth clenched as I toyed with evading. "Yeah, I've seen it. It was my mother's favorite, too."

Naked, hesitant curiosity lit her eyes. *"Was?"*

I threw back the remaining bourbon. What the hell... "She died. Fifteen years ago." Because she fell through the cracks. Over and over again until she hit rock bottom and never rose. I swallowed my bitterness as Lily leaned closer.

"When you were fourteen?"

I jerked out a nod. Silence throbbed between us, then I indicated the screen. "Are we gonna watch this movie or what?"

Her head swiveled to the screen, then back at me. She held out the remote. "The deal was you could help me pick. You've vetoed my first choice. Show me what you got."

I accepted it, allowing my fingers to graze hers. She exhaled sharply.

God, I wanted to feel that puff of breath on my face. Reluctantly, I turned to the screen. Surprisingly, only half of the movies were chick flicks. Top-notch detective movies and psychological thrillers had made the cut.

I frowned as the list kept going. "There are over a hundred here. How can they all be your favorite?"

She stared at me. "Is it too difficult? I can help you out if you want?" I caught a hint of teasing challenge.

I snorted and selected one.

She grimaced. "Uh, no. I love Bruce Lee but not tonight. The sound effects alone will give me a headache."

I scrolled some more until she laid her hand over mine. "This one," she breathed.

"Revenge?" It was the original movie with Anthony Quinn, Kevin Costner and Madeleine Stowe. I couldn't remember the plot line but I'd probably seen it. Movies had been a huge escape for Mom the few times depression released her from its merciless talons. To be honest, they'd been an escape for me, too, because for a blessed stretch of two or three hours, I could stop worrying about her. She'd even summoned a laugh when we watched a comedy.

"Yes. It doesn't have a high rating but I love it. Unless you want to find something else?"

I tore myself from the past. "This will do." I hit Play and pointed to her empty glass. "Do you want another?"

She stared wistfully at the martini glass. "No, I better not. I'll take a soda, though."

I grabbed a soda for her and bottled water for myself. She broke the tab, curled her lip over the top and drank half the contents, while I forced myself not to stare at her throat.

The movie's plot became clear within twenty minutes. Sex. Corruption. Forbidden lust. Betrayal.

I settled in and tried to give it my full attention. Lily set the cup of candy between us and stretched out her legs. She ate another marshmallow, then held out a jelly bean to me. I took it, chewed, and steeled myself not to stare at her exposed thighs. Or her flat belly beneath the mesh top. Or the slight mound of her pussy.

Jesus.

A few minutes later she shifted again, turning onto her side to face me as she slid one leg up against the other.

She rested her head on one arm, and started toying with the ends of her short hair.

Hell, something about the way she played with those white-blond tips turned me on beyond comprehension. A moment later her other hand dipped into the candy cup. She didn't pick one, just rummaged through it, her gaze still fixed on me.

"Are you going to settle down or are you planning on fidgeting through the movie?"

Dark-tipped fingers traced the edge of the cup.

"I still feel...wired," Lily stated, her voice hardly above a husky whisper.

Alcohol, sugar, unscripted revelations and lust didn't sit well together. Add the flimsy top and bikini she wore, and it was an explosion waiting to happen.

I grabbed the candy cup and moved it to the other

side of my seat. "Maybe you should stop stuffing your-self with sugar, then."

Her lower lip protruded in a sexy pout, drawing my eyes to the luscious curve.

Lily made a small, muffled sound under her breath. "Caleb."

God, *now* she chose to say my name voluntarily. In that damn dirty, cock-stroking voice.

Her free hand dropped onto the space between us, then drew tiny circles on the leather.

"Maybe it's time to call it a night." I didn't mean it. At all.

She dragged her lower lip between her teeth. "No. I…can't. I'm wound too tight," she whispered.

"Tell me what you need." *Hell of a time to be the better man, Steele.*

She blinked slowly, sultrily, and her hand bunched into a fist. A moment later her gaze swept over my chest, then dropped lower to caress my rigid cock. She took a deep breath. "I've decided to accept that pass."

I stopped breathing. "What?"

Beautifully lusty, gorgeously defiant eyes met mine. "You heard me. You gave me a loophole in your rule. I'm taking it."

Filthy little fires leaped through my body. "What exactly are we talking about?"

A wickedly saucy smile curved her lips. "You'll see. Wanna get my Bob?"

Shit. My cock was very ready and extremely capable. I gritted my teeth for a second. "Your little pink toy. You sure?" I rasped.

"I need release and the way I see it, I have two

choices. I can let you fuck me or help me some other way. I'm not ready for the first one yet."

What the hell did she have in mind? "Lily—"

"Are you in, Caleb?"

As if I could answer any other way. "Where is it?"

Hectic color stained her cheeks as she nodded to the small bathroom next to the bar. "Under the first blanket in the closet," she whispered.

I sucked in a sustaining breath and rose from the lounger.

Fuck, I pushed her into testing my self-control. Now my cock was hard enough to hammer nails, and my balls were on fire.

Way to go, champ!

I entered the bathroom and tossed the first blanket. The bright pink sex toy gleamed at me. I wanted to leave it there, tell her I didn't find it.

I could easily give her what she craved with my mouth. My fingers. My tongue. But I knew I wouldn't be able to stop there.

I grabbed the gadget and returned to find her half sitting up, her breathing elevated. That mesh top was driving me nuts. As for her bare, supple thighs and the shadowed space between them—

"We need some ground rules," she blurted. "We keep our clothes on, no matter what. Deal?"

Her eyes were wide and shiny, and goddamn it, she was the most beautiful I'd ever seen her. And I wanted to see her come so badly, my back teeth hurt from the need. "Deal," I croaked.

I crawled back onto the lounger and laid the vibrator between us.

She looked down at it, and fresh flames lit up her alabaster cheeks. "Caleb—"

"I'm yours to command, baby. Just tell me what you need."

"Kiss me," she instructed.

God, yes.

Spiking my fingers through her hair, I yanked her down and fused my mouth to hers, heard her sexy little whimper, right before she melted into me. I didn't need to cajole my way in. She opened her beautiful mouth and I licked my way inside, unable to stop from groaning as I got another taste of Lily.

She eased back against the seat. I followed until my chest was pressed against hers, her firm, plump breasts rubbing against me as she breathed.

I deepened the kiss, sliding my tongue against hers, biting the tip of it when I recalled how much she liked it last time. She rewarded me with a moan, the hands exploring my back quickening their caress. Her fingers traced the waistline of my joggers, then tentatively dropped to my ass. I bit gently on her top lip. Her nails dug into my ass, even as her legs parted to accommodate me.

The flames licking through my veins intensified as I broke away and glanced down between us. Less than six inches separated us. I only needed to drop down a fraction for my cock to brush her bikini-covered mound. And if I angled downward I would easily slide between her legs, rub the underside of my cock against her clit. Get her off that way.

My breath shuddered out as I glanced into her glazed eyes. At her bruised lips.

Fuck me.

She was in charge, and as much as it unsettled me, it was also the headiest thing I'd ever experienced.

Slamming on the brakes was hard. But I planted my hands on either side of her head, increased the gap between us and drew up my knees to bracket her thighs. From my position, I had an intoxicating view of her from head to toe.

"What now?" I rasped.

One hand scrambled blindly for the vibrator. Then hesitated.

"Go for it, sweetheart. Before my good intentions take a flying leap." Her breath kept hitching as if she couldn't catch it. When her gaze dropped to my mouth, I dropped my head and delivered a quick, hard kiss. "Now, Lily," I commanded hoarsely.

She brought it up between us, and flicked it on with her thumb. Noticing the low setting, I raised my eyebrow.

"I've never used number three before," she blurted.

I put my thumb over hers and flicked it up two more. "Then I'm glad I'm here for your first time." My grin felt as tight as the pressure in my groin as I returned to my original position. And waited.

Slowly, she lowered her hand, and then paused with the sex toy above her belly. Then she raised her gorgeous eyes to me. "You do it."

Fuck. I drew in a strangled breath. "You sure?"

She caught her lip between her teeth and nodded jerkily. She handed me the vibrator, then lowered her hand and drew aside the crotch of her bikini.

At the first sight of her pretty pink pussy, I nearly lost my mind.

Fighting the irrational jealousy rising within me, I

slid the vibrator against her wet clit. A sharp gasp broke from her lips as her back arched off the lounger.

My arms shook with the effort it took to stay upright. "Fuck."

"Oh…God." She shuddered as I pressed the vibrator harder against her clit. "Ahh…"

The scent of her wetness rose between us, triggering fresh agony in my balls. "God, your pussy smells incredible, Lily."

Another set of shudders unraveled through her, ending in her undulating her hips against the pink toy. Beneath the mesh and bikini top, her nipples were hard little points that begged to be tasted.

Saliva filled my mouth as I fought with the rampant urge to rip her clothes off and do just that. Instead, I contented myself with planting openmouthed kisses down her satin-smooth neck, licking the frantic pulse racing at her throat. Biting her earlobe.

"Caleb. Oh." The groan was dragged from her as her face pinched and her eyes rolled shut.

"Are you close, baby?"

She shuddered, her hips moving faster. "Yes… Yes!"

"Open your eyes. Look at me. I want to see your gorgeous eyes when you come," I instructed, barely recognizing my own voice.

Her lust-glazed eyes met mine. "Caleb… I'm coming," she said in a hushed whisper. "Oh!" Her hips exploded and she screamed.

My fists bunched hard, tension screaming up my spine as I locked my knees to stay put.

Dear God, she was glorious.

I lost the fight halfway through her release, and slanted my mouth over hers. Her lips clung to mine as

I devoured her every panted breath, desperate not to miss a moment of her glorious climax.

After an eternity, her convulsion died down. That was when I realized her arms and legs were locked around me. When the smell of her hit me, I knew I was in deeper trouble.

Clamping an arm around her waist, I lifted her off the lounger and staggered for the door.

"Caleb?" Her voice was still slurred.

"I'm taking you to bed," I said through clenched teeth.

Her breath hitched. "No."

"Don't worry. I'm not going to pressure you. You're going to bed alone. And we're definitely going to fuck," I promised, "but not until this shit is taken care of."

Her legs clamped tighter around me. Which delivered the fresh hell of having my eager cock sweetly cradled by her very wet pussy.

I stumbled on the stairs as she buried her face in my neck and gave a low moan. "But…what about you?" she whispered, performing a slow, torturous grind against me.

"I'll take care of it…later." My mouth drifted from the corner of hers to the delicate shell of her ear. "Or I'll save it for you."

She whimpered. A glorious sound. I tunneled my fingers in her hair and pulled her head back.

"Would you like that?"

Her blush deepened, but she met my gaze. "Yes."

I groaned, tightened my hold on her and vaulted up the stairs.

In her room, I pulled back the covers and set her down in the middle of the bed. Her legs stayed locked in place for a beat before she released me. I kissed her soft lips and reluctantly stepped back. "Get some sleep. I'll see you bright and early."

Resolutely, I headed for the door.

"Caleb?"

My hand tightened around the door handle, and I squeezed my eyes shut for a bracing second before I looked over my shoulder. "Yeah?"

She twisted a corner of the duvet between her fingers, making no move to cover herself. "Thank you. For...tonight."

My fevered gaze scoured her body to the shadows between her legs, unashamed of the savage hunger most likely blazing on my face. "Don't thank me just yet. I intend to fuck your lights out the second this shit is handled. And it won't be a nice, gentlemanly fucking. Good night, Lily."

CHAPTER TEN

Lily

MY INNER ALARM nudged me awake just shy of 5:00 a.m., after the soundest sleep I'd enjoyed since my stalker problem started. I stretched, rolled over and froze as memories of last night flooded in.

Heat surged through my body, pooling in my pelvis, before rushing up to engulf my face.

OMG!

I lay there, breath held, bracing myself for extreme vulnerability slash acute mortification. I'd bared parts of my past I'd never told another soul to Caleb. And then I'd let him use my vibrator on me!

Weirdly, neither sensation arrived. Emotionally, I felt unburdened, like a heavy cloak had been lifted off my shoulders. And neither by word nor deed had Caleb judged me.

Sexually, I felt…sensational. Like I'd won a grand prize in a contest I didn't even know I was competing in.

Great sex had always felt like a gift granted to other people, a sleight of hand everyone else had mastered but me. I wasn't ashamed to confess that was the reason why I invested in the very best sex toys. But…last night…

I came harder than I ever had…and we didn't even have sex. I was one hundred percent sure it had nothing to do with the higher setting on my vibrator. The only other time I'd tried the highest setting, all I could think about was the noise and what possible damage the overload of electricity was doing to my clit. It ruined the experience.

But last night I unlocked a previously unknown inhibiting door and been rewarded with an amazing experience.

The memory of him crouched over me, big, hot, wild, with barely restrained hunger stamped on his face, his hand between my legs, and dirty, beautiful words pouring out of his mouth…

Yeah, that certainly guaranteed the unforgettable encounter my instinct had been nudging me toward from the start.

I felt empowered, like I could do it all over again, no problem.

I gulped down the moan rising in my throat.

Despite laying down the caveat, there'd been a moment, right before that incredible climax hit me, when I'd wanted to beg Caleb to pull out his thick cock jutting boldly against his pants. Beg him to *fuck my lights out*.

His gruff, sexy promise echoed in my head, ripping free a ravenous moan. I wanted that. Badly.

Except it wouldn't happen until my stalker was caught.

My stalker.

My code.

The SDM presentation.

Reality drenched me like an icy waterfall, catapulting me out of bed and into the shower. Someone was still out there, watching, waiting for me to slip up. I clenched my teeth against the skin-crawling sensation that threatened to ruin my day and tried to regain my buzz.

I never quite got it back. My mood plummeted further when an email from Chance buzzed on my phone just as I was heading downstairs.

I entered the kitchen to find Caleb at the coffee machine. In the few seconds before he turned around, I hungrily ogled his V-shaped torso draped in a fitted navy blue shirt, tucked into tailored pants that framed his mouthwatering ass.

The ass I'd gripped all too briefly last night before he'd called a halt to my exploration.

He turned, two mugs of coffee in his hands. We both froze as his eyes met mine.

The memory of last night pulsed between us, hot and heavy. His heated gaze swept down and up my body, its intensity heightening with each pass. I was glad I'd taken extra care with my attire.

My black dress was a combination of a corset top and flared skirt, which I teamed with three-inch-heeled ankle boots. My makeup was flawless, too, with an added confidence-boosting layer of eyeliner and mascara, topped off with my favorite scarlet lipstick.

"Good morning," I murmured, eager for something to dissipate the charge rippling between us before I did something embarrassing, like stare at his crotch and wonder if he'd given in and jacked off last night or whether he'd kept to his promise to save it for me.

"Morning," he responded, striding forward to hand me the coffee.

We drifted to the center island, both lifting our mugs to take an idle sip while his eyes made another pass over my body. Then he reached out to touch the silver star dangling from the middle of my lace choker. "You look…incredibly beautiful," he said throatily.

My whole body reacted to his words, going from zero to furnace-hot in seconds. "Thank you."

His eyes slowly narrowed. "Something's wrong."

I waved my phone. "Email from Chance. He's bringing someone else to the meeting today."

He tensed. "Who?"

"He didn't say."

"Has he done that before?"

"Not at the last minute, no." I took another sip of coffee, swallowing it down with my anxiety.

"And you're worried," he observed.

I shrugged. "I can do without the extra pressure."

He set his mug down and cupped my cheeks. "I've watched you all week, batting away problems from your team without so much as pausing to look up from your keyboard. You'll kick ass today. I've no doubt."

Like last night, his gentle touch, together with the encouraging words, sent fierce prickles to my eyes. I blinked rapidly, dead certain I didn't want to cry in front of Caleb. "Thanks."

One thumb drifted along my jaw. "You're welcome," he murmured.

His gaze dropped to my mouth, and a different emotion swirled around us.

He stepped away first, picked up his cup and finished his coffee. "You ready to go?"

My nod was as shaky as the emotions zipping through me.

In the hallway, he picked up the waist-length jacket I dropped next to my satchel and held it out for me. I stood in front of him, put my arms through the sleeves, secretly breathing in the heady scent of aftershave and pure man. When I went to do up the single button, he brushed my hands away, pulled the lapels close and secured it.

Then he gripped my waist tight and pulled me back into his body. "I don't know how well you slept last night," he breathed in my ear, "but mine was pretty damned fucked because all I could think about was how magnificent you looked when you came. Just thought you should know."

I was struggling to breathe as he shrugged into his leather jacket and we left home without exchanging another word.

What could I say? That knowing he hadn't slept made my panties wet? To hell with waiting for my stalker to be caught. I wanted him to pull over and bang me on the backseat.

Conversation became redundant as his phone blared to life. He reached for it, his brows creasing when he looked down at the screen.

"Ross," he answered with a cool voice. "Yes, Maggie told me you've been trying to reach me. I've been a little busy." His eyes flicked to me before returning to the road. "What can I do for you?"

Traffic was light, and with the radio in the SUV set to low, I heard the other voice on the line. "The band won't take me back."

Caleb suppressed a sigh. "Have you been showing up for rehearsals like we agreed?"

"Every day. I even blew off my weekend plans to put in some extra work. They said it was too little, too late."

"It's only been a week. Maybe they're testing you to see whether you'll disappoint them again. Where are you right now?" Caleb asked.

There was a moment's hesitation before Ross-who-ever-he-was answered, "At the Beverly Hilton."

A muscle rippled in Caleb's jaw. "Didn't we agree you wouldn't go back there again?"

"Yeah, but if the guys won't take me back then what's—?"

"You better not be thinking of pulling that stunt again or I'll hang up right now and block your number permanently," Caleb interrupted harshly.

"I won't… But it's hard, man," the other man whined.

"That's what happens when you let people down, Ross. They stop trusting you." His voice gentled. "If you really want this, you just have to keep trying. They'll come around eventually."

"And if they don't?"

"Then you have to find answers elsewhere. You're talented. You just need to take a little more responsibility for your life. Ultimately, it's down to you whether you want to succeed or fail."

"I…want this. The band," Ross said.

"Then you know what you have to do."

A sigh echoed down the line. "Yeah. Umm…thanks, man."

"You can thank me by checking out of that hotel and getting your ass back home." He hung up and slid his phone back into his pocket.

Silence throbbed through the vehicle for a few blocks.

"You're good at this… Being a fixer."

The corners of his mouth lifted, but the smile didn't quite reach his eyes. "Thanks. That's high praise coming from you."

"I mean it. It can't be easy dealing with people who aren't always receptive."

He eyed me. "Are you including yourself in that?"

I hid a grimace. "Maybe. But what you said to him, just now…is that why you're a fixer? Because people let you down?"

His face tightened. "That's too heavy a conversation for this time of the morning, sweetheart."

"You're avoiding."

"And you're searching for something to take your mind off your meeting. This subject isn't it, Lily." There was a touch of warning in his voice.

"Why not? I've told you my secrets. You owe me something. *Quid pro quo.* Isn't that what it's called?"

His lips flattened. But he blew out a breath a moment later. "Yeah, a bunch of people let me down. But more than that, they let my *mother* down when she needed them the most. It's not a good feeling, being that helpless, so fixing became my thing."

"When did you start?"

"Officially? When I was twenty. Unofficially, shortly after my mother died. There was a lot of fixing to be done in Trenton Gardens." There was a hard, bitter note in his voice that drew shivers down my arms.

"I don't know where that is."

"Consider that a good thing, baby."

I looked at his rigid profile, and burning with a need I couldn't suppress, I tapped the name into my phone.

And grew colder. "Trenton Gardens, home of the most notorious gangs in South Central LA. Five people are killed there *every week*!" I read out loud with growing horror.

A flash of anger lit his eyes as he glanced at the phone, but then he gave a grim shrug. "Not exactly fairy-tale reading, is it?"

I put my phone away, my chest tightening with sympathy for this man with the hard exterior and flashes of tenderness. I wanted to know more, uncover his layers.

"I hear you sometimes," I murmured.

His body tensed. "Excuse me?"

"In the night. You don't sleep very well, do you?" I probed gently.

"What makes you think I'm not checking on things? Keeping you safe?"

"Are you?"

His fingers tightened around the steering wheel. "Leave it alone, Lily."

"My mother left just before I turned eight. I didn't sleep through the night for a year," I blurted. "My stepdad and I woke up one morning and she was…gone. Left a note to say she was never coming back and we shouldn't try to find her. Even after we received papers the next week from her lawyer granting my stepfather full custody of me I still thought she would come back. Stephen was sterile and couldn't have children of his own. That's the only reason he kept me."

Caleb cursed under his breath. "That's his loss, Lily, not yours."

I attempted to shrug his sympathy away, but my shoulders didn't comply. "I wasn't entirely blameless. It…hurt, knowing my mother could leave without a second thought, and my stepfather would've walked away if he had children of his own. I acted out. Sometimes."

"That's still not an excuse for what he did."

"I know, but…" I shrugged.

"Deep down you wish things had turned out differently," he said.

I sniffed away the unexpected tears. "Stupid, right?"

"No. Not stupid at all," he murmured, reaching out to glide a finger down my cheek.

Damn, there he went, being all gentle again. A fat drop rolled down my cheek.

He cursed again as he turned off the ignition. A distracted look outside showed we were in SDM's parking lot. It was still early enough that there were only a handful of cars around, the nearest one six bays away.

When his thumb brushed my chin, I tried to pull away, more than a little terrified of the softening happening inside me. He clamped his fingers in my hair, forcing me to look at him.

One brow was cocked, but his eyes were gentle. "I told you this was too heavy for this time of the morning. You should listen to me more often."

Another tear slipped free. I tried to laugh it away. "I have no idea why I'm crying. I'm over all of that. Counting the days until I put him and Chance in my rearview."

His fingers tightened on my nape. His other hand patted his lap. "Come here," he commanded.

My breath caught. "Why?"

"So I can make you feel better," he answered, his voice lower, deeper, curling around my turbulent emotions.

I shouldn't.

I really, *really*, shouldn't.

My hands slowly went to my seat belt, freeing it despite the voice screeching warning at the back of my head. Caleb's seat, already extended fully to accommodate his long legs, afforded me plenty of space as I crawled into his lap.

The hand on my nape speared into my hair and the other clamped one hip.

"Open your jacket," he instructed.

Hands shaking, I complied.

The sun wasn't fully up yet and the tinted windows shielded us as I braced my knees on either side of him. The moment my hands landed on his shoulders, he pulled me down and fused his lips to mine.

Caleb ravaged my mouth like I was his last meal, and I was more than happy to be devoured.

Between my legs, his erection thickened, pressing insistently against me. Shamelessly turned on, I ground against him, earning his tortured groan. We kissed until the need for more oxygen forced us apart. He kneaded my ass, encouraging me to grind against him. The feeling was intensely exquisite.

God, I could come from just rubbing my clit on his cock.

The thought drew a hungry moan but when I tried to dive back into the kiss, he stopped me.

"I didn't see a zipper on your dress when I helped you with your jacket earlier. Where is it?" he demanded hoarsely.

I motioned dazedly to my left rib cage.

"Take it down for me, baby," he said, his eyes still consuming me.

My racing heart tripled its tempo but I couldn't have stopped myself if a freight train was bearing down on me. I lowered the zipper until the corset gaped to reveal my breasts.

Caleb stared at me for another tense second before his gaze dropped. He exhaled sharply. "Fuck." His hand dropped to brush the back of his knuckles over one tight nipple, making me jerk against him. "I wondered whether these would be pale or dark." His gaze flicked to my face, absorbing my reaction as he repeated the gesture over the twin peak. "I have no clue which I would've preferred because seeing them now...they're fucking perfect." The words ended in a groan as he yanked me forward and clamped his mouth around one tight bud.

"Oh, God!"

He suckled me, hot and urgent, then flicked his tongue mercilessly over the sensitive bud, all the while dragging my damp center back and forth over his erection.

He transferred his attention to the other nipple, catching the freed, wet bud between his thumb and finger.

Stars exploded across my vision. "Yes!"

My fingers dug into his hair, desperate to keep him right where he was. I threw my head back as my hips took on a life of their own, fixated on riding him to the bliss that hovered on the horizon.

"Holy fuck, you're beautiful," he groaned against me, staring up at me with an intensity I couldn't fathom.

"Caleb..."

"You have no idea how gorgeous you are, do you?"

I couldn't breathe. This man was unraveling me, piece by piece. Body and soul. And I couldn't think of a single reason to stop him.

My body was a knot of seething sensation, waiting for some unknown directive to explode. Caleb wrapped one hand around my throat, restricting but not hurting. The other slipped beneath my dress and nudged my panties aside.

My fingers dug into his shoulders.

"I wasn't going to. But I need to feel you, Lily."

"Yes." Agreement was as easy as breathing, my need unstoppable.

His eyes hooked into mine, Caleb dragged his tongue across my nipple as he sank one thick finger inside me.

A tight scream erupted from my throat. He added a second finger and pleasure rained on me, quickening the movements of my hips as I chased ecstasy.

"Damn, you're so fucking tight," he exclaimed harshly, his breathing a ragged mess. "I can't wait to bury my cock inside you."

"Caleb…" I couldn't form any other words other than his name as he drove me insane with his fingers.

Sweet vortex swirled closer, sucking me down.

The hand around my throat bore me down onto piston-fast fingers. His thumb circled my clit and pleasure like I've never known before completely unraveled me. I came hard.

Somewhere in the midst of blinding ecstasy, Caleb covered my mouth with his, riding the waves with me until my convulsions ebbed away.

I collapsed in a boneless heap on top of him, panting like a bitch straight out of heat. He rained kisses on my neck and jaw, his hand caressing my ass.

"You okay?" he asked gruffly in my ear.

I hummed, mindlessly floating on a sea of bliss. The fingers inside me crooked, making me gasp one last time before he pulled out.

He gently nudged me upright, made me watch as he put his fingers in his mouth and licked off my essence. A fierce blush lit up my skin as he pressed his mouth against mine. "You taste even more sublime than I thought you would. The list of what I'm going to do to you is growing by the hour, baby. I've just added eating your pussy for hours to it."

I groaned, my senses firing up all over again. Before my orgasm-addled brain could return to reality, I scooted sideways and reached for his belt.

He tensed. "Lily?"

Maybe it was the orgasms that made me bold. Maybe it was his words of praise that tapped into a reserve of strength inside me. Either way, I slowly brushed my fingers over his mouth before replacing them with my own. "Shh," I whispered. "You're not the only one who gets to bestow awesome gifts this morning. I'm feeling generous, too."

His eyes widened a touch, right before his gaze dropped to my mouth. And locked, with blazing hunger flaring in his eyes. "Lily…" Hoarse anticipation thickened his voice.

"Will you let me, Caleb?" I lowered his zipper and slipped my hand beneath the waistband of his boxers. "Make us both feel good?"

He slammed his head against the headrest and groaned, long and hard and pained. "Do you really expect me to refuse an offer like that?"

I pulled him out, gasped and just…stared. *God.* He was huge. Thick and hard and insanely hot. Caleb's cock was everything I'd dreamed it would be and more. "You're beautiful." Tentatively, I stroked his hard length.

A rough sound erupted from his throat. "Dammit, Lily…"

Trepidation threatened to overcome me as the difference between watching a few porn clips and giving my first blowjob hit home.

I stroked him harder, loving the velvet-steel feel of him, loving the way his teeth gritted and his cheekbones flushed with color.

Lost in my ministrations, I startled when he cursed, "Fuck, stop licking your lips like that and put your gorgeous mouth on me before I come."

Heart racing, I slowly lowered my head and kissed his crown. A hiss flew from his lips as his hand slid up my back. I trailed kisses over his length, and then dragged my tongue up the underside of his cock, earning myself another deep groan.

Still sliding my hand up and down his glorious shaft, I flicked my tongue in rapid succession over his slit. His hips jerked against my mouth and frantic fingers dug into my hair. "Fuck!"

I sucked and pumped him with long, even strokes, establishing a rhythm that drew harsh pants from him.

"Yes! Fuck, yes, just like that," he croaked, his other hand fumbling for my breast.

Sensation curled through me as he fondled me almost frantically, his movements growing jerkier as I kept up a relentless pace on his cock.

A glance up showed his eyes squeezed shut, his chest heaving as he sucked in desperate breaths.

I reached between his legs, stroked his balls, and his fingers tightened painfully in my hair.

"God, Lily, don't stop. Don't fucking stop."

Impossibly, he thickened in my mouth. I drew him deep, right to the back of my throat and held still, glorying in his utter lack of control when he ground himself mercilessly against me.

"Take it. Fuck, take it all," he panted, right before a pure, animalist growl rumbled from his chest, then erupted in a hoarse shout as he came furiously in my mouth.

I swallowed him down, the salty muskiness of him weirdly addictive. When his body sagged against the seat, I licked him clean, then allowed him to pull me upright.

"Jesus, Lily. That was sensational," he breathed against my mouth.

The smile that curved my lips was pure feminine power. My first blow and I hadn't sucked at it. A wicked little laugh broke loose before I could stop it.

"Enjoying your power, are you?" he croaked.

"Maybe," I replied breathlessly.

He pulled me in for a deep, long kiss. When we parted, we stared at each other for several heartbeats, both adjusting to the shifting landscape beneath our feet.

His gaze scoured my face; then his thumb brushed my lower lip.

After he zipped himself up, he reached into the center console and handed me packet of tissues. I took one and reached between my legs.

He caught my wrist. "No. Not there. I want you to walk around the office today with a reminder of how good this moment felt. Each time you get anxious, re-

member this moment. Remember that you're phenomenal. Okay?"

The huge lump that rose in my throat prevented me
from speaking. After I nodded, he took the tissue from
me, and gently wiped my smeared lipstick. Then he
wiped his own mouth before reaching for my satchel
and the small makeup bag I kept in there.

He watched as I repaired my makeup, his intense
gaze fixed on my face. Only then did he zip me back
up, button my jacket and let me slide back into my seat.

"You ready?"

I took a deep breath and let my gratitude show in
my smile. "Yes."

His return smile was gentle if a little dazed around
the edges. "Let's go."

The morning presentation went without a hitch,
with an eager audience comprising the tech media
and bloggers, applauding when the two-hour event
was done.

Over the years, Chance and I had perfected the art
of being in the same room but speaking only the barest
minimum to one another.

Afterward, I returned to my office with Chance.
Caleb had grudgingly agreed to keep out of sight while
I dealt with Chance but I knew he was nearby, and that
gave me a layer of comfort I didn't know I needed till
it was time for the second presentation.

The beta test started off well, my tweaks making the
algorithm as fast as I promised it would be.

Right up until the moment the compression sequence
slowed to a crawl. My heart jumped into my throat.

Seventeen excruciating seconds ticked by before it sped up again.

But the blip was the only thing that mattered when the screen turned black and the lights went back up in the conference room.

CHAPTER ELEVEN

Lily

"I CAN FIX IT," I blurted. "It's just a small area of the code."

Chance looked furious. "We thought these wrinkles would've been ironed out by now."

"I still have three weeks of beta testing before the final deadline."

Walter Green, the man Chance had brought with him, frowned. "You said it would be ready, Donovan."

"I was assured it would be," Chance responded.

I ignored the men and fired up my laptop. Scrolling through the code, I zeroed in on where the problem was. Heart pumping, I forced myself to analyze it line by line. After forty lines, I stopped. "It's fixable," I repeated. "But I'll need time."

"How much time?" Chance snapped.

I bit my lip. "A week. Ten days, tops."

Silence greeted me.

Walter Green rose and left the room without saying a word. The other SDM executives also left.

Chance Donovan's gray eyes lanced me. The rest of him looked as harmless as a middle-aged CEO with a wife and three kids could look. But from the moment we met, I'd glimpsed a layer of menace in his eyes that pushed all my self-preservation buttons. "This is disappointing, Lily," he rasped.

I forced myself not to waver. "Who's Walter Green?"

"He's the guy who decides whether SDM sinks or swims. Delivering this algorithm, correctly and on time, and earning the freedom you claim to so badly crave, feeds directly into that. Is that clear enough?" he said.

"Yes," I murmured.

"Good. Now, what's this I hear about a new consultant?" he asked.

I struggled not to tense up as I trotted out the line Caleb and I practiced. "He's from LA. He's helping me with preliminary info on a possible gaming app my team is working on."

Suspicion flickered through his eyes. "Why don't I know about this? And why is he staying at your house?"

Why wasn't I surprised he knew Caleb was staying with me? "Because this is still *preliminary*. And because I don't need your permission to have a houseguest."

His eyes narrowed and he didn't speak for a long time. "Remember what's riding on this project, Lily," he warned, then left without further comment.

I buried my face in my hands.

A minute later Caleb arrived, swiveling my chair to face him before tugging my hands down. He'd been listening on my laptop so I didn't need to repeat what had happened. His solid presence took away some of my apprehension.

"Apart from my regret that I wasn't here to punch

that asshole in the face, the problem is only a minor bump in the road, right?"

"Maybe. Maybe not."

He frowned, crouching down in front of me. "Meaning?"

"The mistake looks…sophisticated. I triple-checked everything yesterday. I could've missed it—"

"You think you were hacked?" he asked.

The icy hand on my nape wouldn't let go. "I don't think so but it's possible…" I stopped as another thought occurred to me.

"What?"

"I added a last-minute tweaked version this morning from the team."

"Which team?"

"Sanjeet's team. But—"

His fingers brushed my lips, halting my words. "You want to think the best of everyone. I don't want to take that away from you, but you have to accept sooner or later than not everyone is decent."

My heart lurched. "I know, but I trust them."

"Give them the benefit of the doubt if you want. Let me worry about who's at fault here. Okay?"

Chest tight, my gaze settled on my laptop. "What's their end goal, Caleb?"

"The stalking is most likely to keep you off balance while they try to get their hands on what you're working on."

The thought drew a horrified shudder. "That can't happen."

"It won't," he ground out. With a decisive click, he shut the lid. "It's almost eight. You've been up since five this morning. I'm taking you home."

I shook my head. "I can't. The team always goes out to celebrate after a presentation. They'll expect me to be there."

"Where's it happening?"

"Q Base in Cupertino."

He pulled out his phone to relay the instruction to his security team. Then he cupped my shoulders. "You're officially clocked off for the day. Understood?"

Feeling numb, I nodded.

I was grateful when Maggie called and kept Caleb on the phone for most of the time it took to drive to Q Base.

Thumping music when we entered the club further prevented me from making meaningful conversation with Caleb or my team.

I exchanged high fives with anyone who stopped at the VIP lounge reserved for SDM, but the first chance I got, I headed to the main bar.

"You want a lemondrop?" Caleb leaned down to ask in my ear.

Memories of last night flooded in, knocking aside a bit of my melancholy. "Not unless you're making it," I said before I fully grasped how revealing my answer was. His lips curved in a smug smile. "They don't make it that well here. I'll have a noche azul," I added in a rush.

He ordered my drink and bourbon for himself.

Since it was early by clubbing standards, we had most of the dance floor to ourselves. But an hour later the place was packed.

I excused myself to go to the ladies' room, and returned to find Miranda seated next to Caleb. Frozen, I watched her lean in close and whisper in his ear.

A smile crept up his face but he shook his head. She leaned in closer, her bare leg sliding against his.

Hot, green bile curdled in my gut, merrily aided by the two cocktails I'd consumed. I wanted to stalk over, uproot her by the hair and lay my claim on him.

But other than the two orgasms he'd given me, a few shared confidences and a promise to screw each other's brains out sometime in the future, what hold did we have on one another? For all I knew, Caleb could be gone from my life this time next week.

The thought slashed through me, sharp and unexpectedly agonizing.

I made a U-turn, heading for the bar. Someone stepped in front of me. He looked familiar.

Mark, the ex who'd turned out to be harmless.

"I thought that was you," he said.

"Hi." I summoned a bright smile.

"Long time, no see."

"Yeah…"

He cocked his head at the dance floor. "Wanna dance?"

I looked over my shoulder. Caleb's eyes were fixed on me, narrowing as it flicked between Mark and me. Even from across the wide space, I witnessed tension climbing into his body.

I turned back around. "Sure, why not?"

Mark grinned. We headed to the dance floor and, with a sense of wild abandon, I threw myself into the dance. Seconds later Caleb materialized beside me.

"You. Beat it," Caleb snarled at Mark.

Like a true analyst, Mark assessed the situation, saw he was on a losing streak and beat a hasty retreat.

Furious blue eyes glared at me. "What the fuck are you doing?"

I lifted an eyebrow. "I should ask you the same thing. You just deprived me of my dance partner."

"You said you were going to the bathroom," he accused.

"I did. Only when I returned, you seemed…busy."

His jaw clenched. "So you decided to let some punk drool all over you?" he bit out.

I shrugged and his gaze dropped to my cleavage. I discarded my jacket a while ago, and without it my attire had transformed from quirky but acceptably professional to risqué.

"Not just some guy. I let my ex *dance* with me. Now that you've driven him away, are you going to take his place or just growl at me? You're certainly putting on a great show for our audience."

He didn't so much as flick a glance at said audience. He stepped closer, towering over me. I tilted my head, met his furious gaze full-on. Then I placed my hands on his waist. He tensed. Still watching him, I began to move, swaying my hips to the slower tempo of the song now playing. Then I added subtle shoulder shimmies.

His gaze dropped again to my cleavage and a light shiver rolled through him. I dragged my nails across his abs as I swayed deeper. His hand landed on my back and yanked me closer.

"Are you trying to make me lose my shit, Lily?" he rasped in my ear.

I pouted. "I'm just trying to *dance*."

He stared down at me for tense seconds. "Fine. Let's dance."

Over the next five songs, Caleb effortlessly proved

how incredible he was on the dance floor. Smooth moves drew increasing attention until every pair of female eyes was fixed on him.

His wicked smile flashed with increasing frequency, until I was turned on beyond belief.

Enough to make me forget my disgruntlement. Enough to make me grip his hand tight as he led me off the dance floor.

"Want another drink?" he asked as we found a quiet spot near the bar.

"No, thanks."

"Okay." He smoothed a lock of hair behind my ear, then caressed my jaw.

I looked into his gorgeous face and smoldering eyes.

Heart hammering, I bit the inside of my cheek. It was now or never. "Caleb?"

"Yeah?" His voice was gruff, as if the feelings swirling inside me gripped him, too.

"I don't want to wait."

He pulled back, blue eyes piercing as they searched mine. "If this is because of what happened at your presentation—"

"No, it's not." I swirled my tongue over my lip, nerves consuming me. "Please, Caleb. You said you wouldn't hurt me with anything that happens while on this case. I'm saying the same to you. I want you…"

Then he leaned in, one hand braced on the wall above my head. "Just so we're clear, you want me to what, exactly?" he demanded.

I slid my hand up his chest, over his shoulder to his nape and drew him down to me. "I want you to break your rule and take me home," I whispered in his ear. "I want you to take my panties off. I want you to undress me. Or I... I can keep my dress on if you want. And I want you to fuck my lights out. Like you promised."

A deep shudder rolled through him. He continued to stare at me for several heartbeats. "Jesus." He buried his face in my neck, breathed out harshly, then plucked my hand from around his neck. "I knew I wouldn't be able to hold out for much longer. Are you sure?"

"Yes."

His jaw clenched as he tried to fight it for one more minute. Then: "Let's go."

Each mile from Cupertino back home felt like an eternity.

I was hot, getting hotter and wetter every time I glanced at Caleb's tense profile. At the thick rod of his cock pressing against his fly. He changed lanes suddenly, his thighs flexing as he stepped on the gas.

"I like the way you drive."

He flicked me a heated glance. "I like the way you're looking at me."

On impulse, I reclined my seat by thirty degrees and propped up my legs on the dashboard. The skirt of my dress slid down to midthigh.

Heat turned to flames. "Christ, Lily, you're going to get me arrested. I swear to God, if I get pulled over before I've fucked your phenomenal pussy, I'll spank your sweet ass until you can't sit down for a week."

Why did the thought of that sound insanely heavenly? "I have bail money. I'll help you out," I said, sliding my skirt higher.

He swerved into the faster lane, splitting his fevered attention between the road and my thighs. Then he groaned. "Stop. Please, baby, let me get us home in one piece. Then you can show me this insanely sexy, naughty side of you."

My fists bunched. "I don't know if I can wait."

"Well, I'm not fucking you on the side of the road our first time, that's for damn sure," he growled. He reached over and gripped my thigh, pressing my flesh a little roughly before snatching his hand away. "Behave." His terse plea almost made me smile.

"Okay." I released my skirt and draped my arms around the headrest, exposing a generous amount of breasts.

"For fuck's sake! You think that's better?" he rasped hoarsely.

"Hmm. Maybe I'll take a nap. Wake me up when we get home?"

He cursed again as I closed my eyes. A few sharp turns threatened to dislodge my feet from the dashboard. My saucy smile melted away as the minutes ticked by. By the time we arrived home, I was as breathless and as on edge as Caleb.

He turned off the ignition without glancing my way. Stepping out, he stalked over to my side and yanked the door open. His chest rose and fell rapidly as he scoured my reclined body.

Slowly, his eyes locked on mine, he reached over and unsnapped my seat belt. When I attempted to rise, he pressed a hand against my midriff. With his other hand, he trailed his fingers down my inner thigh. Torturously, he slipped beneath my skirt, just as he did this morning. When he reached his destination, his fingers fingers boldly against my mound, cupping me through my panties.

"Jesus, Lily, you're fucking soaked," he muttered with a groan.

He circled his fingers, applying pressure over my engorged clit. I whimpered before I could stop myself.

The sound triggered him into action. He scooped me up, kicked the door shut and strode to the front door. Opening it, he set me down and deactivated the alarm. "Stay put."

The security check took less than five minutes. Anticipation had me breathless by the time he trotted back downstairs. On the second to last step he stopped, hands clasped behind his back.

"Come here." The order was gravel-rough.

On shaky legs, I teetered over to him. With his elevated position, my eyes were level with his fly. And excruciatingly aware of what lay behind it.

He stared at me. Then he nodded at his crotch. "See what you've done to me?"

My head bobbed up and down.

"What are you going to do about it?" he demanded thickly.

I swallowed as a dozen erotic images flashed through my mind, all starting and ending with my hands on his body. My hands found his chest, felt the hard muscles shift beneath my touch, then trailed over his abs to his waist.

Then, breath held, I slowly slid his belt free. Twisted open his button and lowered his zipper.

His broad chest expanded in a deep intake of breath, his eyes dark pools of hunger tracking my every move. Whether it was those incisive eyes or my own insecurities that suddenly pummeled me, I wasn't sure. I froze, my mouth drying as I struggled to breathe.

* * *

With a snatched breath, I slipped my hand beneath his waistband and closed my fingers around him.

His breath hissed out between gritted teeth. He swallowed hard but didn't move an inch. I tugged his pants and briefs lower, exposing the cock that had fueled more lurid fantasies all day.

I stroked him once. Twice. He grew thicker, his dick pulsing in my hold. Emboldened, I tightened my grip, pumped him a few more times.

A tortured groan rumbled from his throat as his fingers sank into my hair. "Fuck, Lily, that feels so good."

I stepped closer, breathed in his earthy scent. But it wasn't enough. I wanted more. I wanted to devour him. I yanked down his pants, cupped his heavy balls. He groaned again, a drop of precum glistening at his broad head.

I flicked my tongue against his slit and he jerked against me. I went to taste him again, but his fingers clenched in my hair, pulling me away.

"No." The denial was torn reluctantly from his throat.

My fingers tightened around him, making his abs clench hard. "Caleb, I... I want you in my mouth." This morning hadn't been enough. I wanted more.

He shuddered, but still shook his head. "I'd love for you to blow me again, sweetheart, but right now, I'm dying to be inside you."

Before I could protest, he scooped me up again like I weighed nothing, pivoted and hauled ass up the stairs. The hallway passed in a blur, the door to my bedroom slamming shut to his kick.

He set me down on the side of the bed. Eyes pinned to mine, he made short work of his buttons and shrugged off his shirt. He was ripped and tanned all over, hairless except for the thin strip of silky hair that arrowed from his belly button to frame his groin.

"You're so hot," I gushed, unable to stop myself.

Dark color flared across his cheekbones, and his nostrils flared as he toed off his shoes and socks. "Keep talking like that and you won't get to walk straight for a week," he growled.

The very idea made me weak. I sagged onto the bed with a pathetic whimper.

With a smug smile, Caleb bent over me, pressed his forehead against mine as he nudged me backward onto my elbows. He grabbed my knees and made room for himself between my thighs, then fused his lips with mine.

The kiss was ravenous to the point of decimation. Strong fingers kneaded my calves, then drifted down to tug off my shoes. He continued kissing me as his hands reversed direction, trailed up my thighs to slip beneath my dress. He started to pull down my panties, then halfway through he muttered under his breath and ripped it free.

At my gasp, he smiled against my lips. "Sorry."

"You're not really, are you?" I challenged between kisses.

"No," he confirmed, then sucked my tongue into his mouth in a move that melted my brain.

God, the man could kiss. I'd lost the ability to think straight when he pulled away. From his back pocket he took out a pack of condoms and tossed it on the bed.

I was staring at the box, wondering if I would be lucky enough to get through the pack by morning, when he grabbed my thighs and dropped onto his knees. Utterly captivated, I watched Caleb trail his tongue slowly up one inner thigh, then the other, but maddeningly staying away from my needy center.

"Get the lights up in here. I want to see your beautiful pussy properly," he said as he bit lightly on my flesh.

Pleasure shivering through me, it took a moment to realize the only light in the room was the one on my dresser, set to come on automatically at nightfall.

My breath puffed out as my lungs remembered how to work. "Lights," I croaked. Nothing happened. I cleared my throat. "Lights."

The lamps on my nightstand flared softly, chasing away the shadows. Baring me to Caleb's avid gaze. His mouth dropped open, a hot breath escaping as he stared.

And stared.

I squirmed. "Caleb…"

"Shh. Give me a moment," he rasped.

A moment to what? I squirmed harder.

He lifted his gaze and his eyes were on fire. "You're fucking exquisite, Lily." Hunger and worship throbbed in his voice.

In that moment I knew it was entirely possible to orgasm from dirty talk alone. Except it wasn't just dirty talk. Because my heart was flip-flopping in my chest in a weird, terrifying way.

This was just sex. My heart shouldn't…couldn't get involved. No way—

Fear melted into pleasure as his tongue licked me in one long sweep.

Sweet. Heaven.

My eyes rolled as I collapsed onto the bed. He repeated the caress several times, then spread me wider and went to town.

Caleb was a connoisseur, using every part of his mouth on every part of my pussy until I was one delirious mess.

"Please, Caleb," I begged when he drove me to the edge for the umpteenth time, only to withdraw. My fingers speared into his hair, tightening when he started to pull away. "Make me come. *Please, please, please.*"

"Fuck," he groaned against me right before he sucked my clit into his mouth.

I shot off like a rocket, my legs fighting to close as fireworks exploded behind my closed lids. He kept me wide open, working me into a frenzied orgasm that felt like it would last forever.

Convulsions were still rippling through me when I felt him tug on my zipper and remove my dress.

"Caleb," I sighed.

"I'm right here, baby. Hold on." His voice was tight. Edgy.

The sound of ripped foil preceded a hiss from him as he rolled it on; then he crawled over my body. One arm circled my waist, and he tossed me higher up the bed.

"I've been craving this since the moment I saw you," he said, his tongue sliding over one nipple.

My nails dug into his shoulders as fresh waves of pleasure washed over me. "Me, too."

His mouth curved in a smug smile. "How hot were you for me?" The question was rasped against my throat as he grazed my skin with his teeth. He was marking me. I didn't care one little bit.

"Umm…"

He paused and tracked the blush creeping up my neck. "You wanted my cock pounding your pretty little pussy even as you were snapping at me, didn't you?"

I wriggled, half-shamed, half-impatient. "Yes!"

"Don't fret, baby. You're going to get it exactly as you wanted it."

He matched words to action.

With one hand planted next to my head, he trailed the other over my breast, my quivering belly to my pussy. He slid two fingers inside me, his eyes absorbing my reaction. His face tautened at my gasp.

"Please, Caleb, I'm ready. Don't wait."

His teeth gritted, but he continued to fuck me with his fingers, stretching me for another minute before he drew my leg higher, and nudged my entrance with his cock.

Slowly, excruciatingly, he pushed inside me, filling me, stretching me to the point of pain. "God, you're so tight."

He withdrew. Pushed back in. I bit my lip to keep from crying out.

He tensed. "Lily?"

I shook my head. "I'm good."

"You're not good. You're so fucking small," he bit out tersely.

I dug my nails into his back. "Don't stop! Please don't stop." I clamped my legs around him, raised my hips to meet his next thrust. Pain and pleasure collided and I screamed.

"Shit!"

"More," I begged.

A wave of uncertainty flashed across his face. Then it morphed into something else. Something hot and dangerous and guaranteed to send me to another stratosphere. Incredibly, it made me wetter. He felt it on his next thrust when his cock seated deeper inside me.

A mini-roar erupted from his throat. "Jesus, you're incredible."

I hauled myself up on one elbow, fused my mouth to his for a hot moment before dropping back down. "More, please, Caleb."

He didn't need any more begging. He fucked me until my vision blurred and my heart pounded against my rib cage. Until sweat dripped from his body to mine, and my screams mingled with his thick groans.

Until one last series of pounding ripped me from reality and I blacked out from pleasure. I wasn't sure how long I blissed out. But when I resurfaced, he was still a hard, unspent presence inside me.

Tension still gripped him and sweat dotted his upper lip. "Did I tell you how much I love watching you come?" he rasped.

I shook my head, stunned by his control.

"Well, I do. I could watch you all day." He started to move inside me again.

"Oh, God… I can't."

He kissed me, hard and quick. "Wrap your legs around me and give me one more, baby. Just one more."

He caught the heels of my last climax minutes later, unraveling me as he roared his own release. I was fairly sure I passed out again.

When I came to, I was stretched on top of him, his arms clamped around me with his chin resting on top of my head.

My hand trembled as I caressed his chest. "Caleb?"

"Hmm?"

"I… I don't think I can move."

A low, deep laugh rumbled from him. "That's okay. I can't move, either."

A happy little note strummed in my heart, the first warning that I had let in a seemingly harmless virus that could potentially compromise my very existence.

Because as I drifted off to sleep it struck me that I would be totally okay if he didn't move from my bed.

Not tonight.

Not tomorrow.

Not ever.

CHAPTER TWELVE

Caleb

IT WAS SEVEN o'clock and I'd been up for an hour. I should get up. Draw clear lines by returning to my room.

I didn't engage in cozy heart-to-hearts. I never fell asleep in a woman's bed. Or, worse, woke up and... *lingered.*

Yet I couldn't move.

Because I had no clue where the line was anymore. I'd given Lily the green light to blur it, and I'd completely obliterated it by sleeping with her.

And hell, I'd barely scratched the surface of my need for her. I couldn't get enough of Lily. Her silky softness. Her smell. The way her eyelids fluttered as she dreamed.

I breathed out slowly, reluctant to wake her even though my eager dick was raring to go again.

One taste and I was addicted. Enough to remain in her bed, enjoying her slight weight draped over me as I waited for her to wake up so I could indulge all over again.

Despite being more than a little rattled that I'd also experienced the soundest, nightmare-free sleep in years.

The jagged, heart-pounding images that usually taunted me with how I failed to save my mother were so inherent I'd accepted their presence.

Last night they didn't materialize. It was disturbing to even consider that Lily had anything to do with it. That something as simple as sharing bits of our past with each other had achieved this result.

It was absurd, right?

Unbidden, other moments filtered through—her pain during our first lunch in the restaurant. Her tears when she told me about her stepfather. Exposing her vulnerability at the possibility of one of her team sabotaging her work.

After the sort of childhood Lily had experienced, many people would've cut their families out of their lives and closed themselves off.

I was surprised she hadn't.

Stephen Gracen parked himself on his favorite bar stool in his favorite Irish pub most days before noon and stayed till closing, his tab settled courtesy of the money he'd made off his stepdaughter's talent. The guy I sent to Boston to check him out had reported that while Gracen hadn't exactly talked trash about Lily, he hadn't been complimentary, either.

Gracen was either too bitter or too stupid to realize the gem he had in his stepdaughter.

I'd met several Silicon Valley types who thought they were hot shit because they could string code together that baffled the common man.

In the past few days I'd discovered that Lily, despite being a highly intelligent woman who was mostly likely being paid millions for her professional skills, wasn't in any way a pampered princess.

She was caring and considerate.

And she'd shared her deepest pain with me.

Scattered across several events, they'd seemed minor but put together they were huge. Put-your-trust-in-another-person huge.

When was I remotely okay with being that guy?

I eyed the bedroom door, wondering again why I wasn't hightailing out of it.

Because you want the same from her.

The sharp ache in my chest answered the inner voice.

I shifted again, uncomfortable at the fresh turmoil churning inside me.

This was why I didn't do feelings. So far, every encounter between us had come packed with them, even the moments she'd accepted my help to ease her stress sexually. They were all emotional land mines that usually had pushed my eject button.

I gritted my teeth. I liked her. A hell of a lot. But feelings and fucking didn't mix well. Period.

She stirred against me. I looked down and saw her watching me with contemplative eyes. It was that same look she'd given me before prying secrets from me yesterday in the car.

"You look seriously...*serious*." Wary questions lurked in her eyes, traces of unease and all those pitfalls I suspected came with the morning after a night of earth-shattering sex.

"For a genius, I expected more eloquence than *seriously serious*." I kept my voice light.

Her hand drifted up my waist to my chest even though her eyes remained dark, searching. "Okay, how about this." Her thigh brushed my hard-on. "Is that one of my sex toys in your lap or are you just extremely happy to see me?"

Sex. This I could handle.

Talking about my mother and how I would have her back in a heartbeat, if only for a chance to do things differently, push harder, shout louder until my voice was heard, until she got the help she needed, I most definitely couldn't.

I smiled past my disquiet, willing my emotions to detach again as I rolled her over and slid two fingers beneath the choker we never got round to taking off last night. "In case I need to spell it out, your battery-operated boyfriends have had their privileges revoked for the foreseeable future. I'm taking care of your every need from now on."

The words echoed with an unnerving sense of permanence, sending another spike of unease up my spine.

Something flitted through her eyes before her lids swept down, cutting me off from her expression. When she looked back up, her eyes contained nothing but hot sexual promise. "If it's going to be anywhere near as good as last night…"

I brushed my lips over hers, teasing even though I wanted to plunge in and devour. "That better not be a challenge, baby. Or I'll be forced to give you a demonstration."

Her breathing picked up, her pulse racing against my fingers. "Yes, please."

Before the words were out of her mouth, I was sliding my tongue between her lips, giving her a vivid taste of what was coming.

A moan rolled from her throat as her fingers dug into my back. My dick jerked, homing in on that place between her open thighs. When her eager wetness greeted it, my vision blurred.

For the first time in my life, I wondered what it would be like to take a woman bare, to glide skin on skin. To come at the gateway to where a new life could be created—

Christ, what the hell is wrong with you?

I dragged my mouth from hers, scrambling for sanity before I did something unthinkable, like ask if she was on the pill. If another man had ever been with her the way I suddenly craved to be.

Irrational jealousy bubbled up, joining the deranged carnival going on inside me. The hand fondling one gorgeous breast tightened.

She inhaled sharply. "Caleb?" Bewilderment laced her lust-soaked voice.

Get yourself together!

I dropped a contrite kiss on her mouth. "Shower or pool?" In the hour before she woke, before perplexing thoughts ruined my mood, I listed all the places I wanted to fuck her.

She blinked, then murmured, "Shower."

Thank fuck. I didn't think I'd make it to the pool.

I scooped her out of bed, grabbed a condom before walking us into the bathroom. Like mine, there was a huge copper roll-top bathtub and a separate shower stall.

I held her against me as I turned on the shower and adjusted the temperature. When my hands slid from her ass to her waist to set her down, the arms around my neck clung, forcing me to look into her face.

"Caleb, are you okay?" she asked, still a little hesitant.

Hell, no, I wasn't. But I wasn't going to attempt to

explain something that puzzled the shit out of me. "You took your time to wake up. I've been rock-hard for you for over an hour," I deflected, cupping her breasts and mercilessly teasing her nipples.

The tactic worked. Her head dropped back and she whimpered. I continued to fondle her as I nudged her against the wall, watched the spray hit her chest and cascade down her body. I'd never seen anything more beautiful.

She made another innocent, dirty sound and I couldn't help but press my mouth against her, gliding my tongue against hers to devour the sound.

My hand slid down her belly, through the trimmed thatch of hair to her sweet, soaked pussy, before inserting two fingers inside her.

Her hand fisted my hair as she gasped.

"Good?" I demanded against her mouth.

"So, so good," she moaned.

I finger-fucked her slow and steady, until her eyes rolled and her thighs shook. Until her cries echoed through the steam.

Only then did I slide on the condom and flip her around. "Brace your hands on the wall and arch your back for me, my dirty little angel."

A smile laced her arousal. "I see you've started with the pet names again."

"I never promised I would stop. Besides, you could lead a man straight to his doom."

She sent me a sultry glance over one shoulder. "Just a man?"

Something bit hard inside me. "Fine. You could lead *me* straight to the gates of hell. Is that what you want to hear?"

Her eyes searched mine. "Maybe."

I hooked one finger into the choker, using the leverage to bring her head back to align her face with mine. "That back still isn't arched. Do I need to spank obedience out of you?" I growled against her throat.

Her whole body shook. Then, with a slow sensual stretch that wouldn't have been amiss on a mermaid, she curved her spine, until her gorgeous twin globes perfectly framed my cock.

I looked down and nearly lost my mind. "God…Lily. You know exactly how to drive me insane, don't you?"

Her answer was to rise on her tiptoes. "Fuck me, Caleb."

With a less than gentle touch, I grabbed her hip and yanked her back onto my waiting cock.

She screamed. My insanity tripled. I forgot to breathe, forgot to think. Forgot everything but the need to bury my cock inside her over and over again.

"Yes. Yes! More," she panted, delirious in her pleasure.

"You're a greedy little thing, aren't you? Always demanding more."

Her fingers clawed the tiles. "Don't stop. Please don't stop."

She continued to beg. I gave her everything until we were seconds from imploding. Then she reached up, covered the hand I had on her choker, locked her eyes on mine and croaked, "Tighter."

A little shocked and a hell of a lot more turned on than I'd ever been in my life, I hooked another finger beneath the tight lace.

She started to come. Endlessly. Gripping me with muscles that demanded my complete surrender. I clung to sanity just so I could watch her for one more soul-shaking second. And holy hell, Lily Gracen, lost in ecstasy, was beyond magnificent.

In that moment before the bottom fell out of my world, I wished I could freeze time. Wished this transcendental moment would never end.

Transcendental. Soul-shaking. *Feelings*.

The next shudder that gripped me had nothing to do with my phenomenal orgasm and everything to do with *emotions* attempting to shift the center of my gravity.

Enough.

The stern warning didn't stop me from kissing her crown and sliding my hand down her back before I pulled out. We both groaned and subsided into silence, words seeming superfluous in this aftermath. I disposed of the condom, turned her around, then directed the flow of water over both of us.

Her eyes were still glazed, but as I reached for the simple lock that secured her choker, her gaze darted to mine.

I froze, waiting for her to speak.

Her nostrils quivered as she sucked in a breath. "I… want you to know…I've never done that before," she muttered. "I was just…"

I brushed my fingers over her lips, absorbing the electric delight that lit through me. "You don't need to explain, sweetheart. If it helps, the effect on you was fantastic for me, too."

A deep blush swept over her cheeks as she caught my hand in hers and kissed my knuckles.

The move was unexpectedly sweet. For a split second, I wanted to succumb.

I returned to my task and undid the choker. Red

marks ringed her neck, a perfect imprint of the lace pattern. I trailed my lips over the mark, still caught in the cycle I couldn't break free from, feeling a little perverse that the sight of it aroused me.

The gel I picked up smelled like Lily. I washed her from head to toe, lingering in places that made her gasp.

Then she held out her hand for the bottle. I handed it over and braced my palms over the wall above her head. I was hard again before she was halfway down my chest.

I didn't reach for her. I needed a moment to regroup, to make sure I could emerge from whatever was happening between us with my faculties intact. When she sank onto her knees, I squeezed my eyes shut and locked my jaw as her small, wicked fingers washed my cock, my balls, then finally moved lower.

I was so focused on not grabbing her for another mind-blowing fuck, I didn't realize she'd ducked under my arm to wash my back until she gasped.

Shit. The scar.

Gentle fingers touched my left shoulder blade where the bullet grazed me. "What happened?"

Her soft sympathy reached inside me, further weakening rigid foundations. My shrug didn't hit the offhand mark as I turned. "Trigger-happy client. Let's get out of here and I'll tell you the full story over breakfast."

She looked disappointed but she didn't say anything as I rinsed off and grabbed a towel. In the bedroom I gathered my clothes, aware that her gaze grew more guarded with each passing second.

I tightened my gut against the urge to reassure her. It was better this way. I wasn't about to break open a box of hearts and flowers. Even if I once possessed such a box it had been smashed beneath the reality of repeated promises made and broken with callous indifference. Every single promise made to help my mother had been broken.

Then Kirsten came along and drove the knife in deeper.

I wasn't about to speak words I didn't mean or give reassurance that I couldn't back up. "I'll see you downstairs in ten?"

She blinked, then jerked out a nod.

I walked out, suspecting that the word *bastard* was lit up in Lily's mind right now. I slammed the door in my room, then stood frozen in place. Could I have handled it better?

No. Maybe. Minutes ticked by, then I heard her walk past my door.

Fuck it. I threw on fresh clothes with an urgency I didn't understand, and rushed downstairs to find Lily hovering by the front door wearing a tight black T-shirt that ended where a pair of leather shorts started. Those shorts ended at the top of her thighs, leaving an indecent amount of leg showing. She wore minimal makeup, but her eyes were darkly outlined, and her lips gleamed a faint pink. The wrist cuffs were back in place, as was a new, broader choker.

God, if she was trying to torture me, it was working. She looked phenomenal.

I swallowed my tongue, spotted the keys in her hand and realized she was dressed for *outside*.

"Where are you going?"

Her chin lifted. "For breakfast. Where else?"

"Lily—"

"Oh, and I'm driving this time." She twirled the keys. "You can come with me or you can follow me."

My jeans and T-shirt were okay to go out but I would've followed regardless. She stepped outside and hurried to the garage.

"Lily, let's talk about this—"

"Let's not," she snapped. "And if you even *think* about physically restraining me, I'll rip your balls off."

I believed her. But I still shook my head as I followed her to the garage. "No can do, baby. I catch the smallest sign of danger and I'm getting *very* physical. Count on it."

I let her glare at me for a full five seconds before opening the Mini's door for her. She slid behind the wheel. Going around I said a prayer and contorted myself into the passenger seat.

She drove fast without breaking limits and considerately without being a pushover. Me, she completely ignored. We passed several respectable cafés before she stopped at an upmarket bistro. She surprised me by bypassing the parking lot and heading for the drive-through lane. It wasn't your average drive-through. Shiny food trucks displayed glorious baked goods, bacon, cheeses and everything in between.

Two guys and a woman manned the trucks. The woman smiled when she spotted Lily. "Hey, girl." She handed over two big paper bags with the bistro's logo on it.

"Thanks," Lily replied.

I deposited the bags on the backseat and reached for my wallet, but she was already driving away.

In between ensuring I wasn't blocking the blood flow to my legs and trying not to drool over her legs, I decided to maintain silence. Ten minutes later she pulled up to an abandoned lot with a tall wall erected on the south edge. She drove to the center, stopped next to a bench and turned off the engine.

I stepped out with our food and looked around. "What's this place?" I asked.

"It used to be a drive-in theater." She reached into the bag and started setting out the food. Bacon. Bagels. Cream cheese. Coffee.

I had zero appetite but I accepted the coffee. She laced hers with cream and sugar, took a sip and set it back down.

"Who owns this place?"

"For now, the original owner. Next month, maybe me."

I nodded at the food. "Why the drive-through? Why here?"

She stared into her coffee. Then shrugged. "Your guys didn't have a chance to check out the bistro first. And I knew I could be alone here."

I. Not *we.*

I waited a beat. "You're pissed."

Her mouth firmed. "Give the man a prize."

My jaw clenched. "Enough. You've made your point with your little tantrum."

Anger flashed across her face. I watched her rein it in. "Fine. Talk to me, then, Caleb. Convince me I didn't just sleep with an asshole who couldn't even be bothered with conversation after he fucked me."

"Jesus…"

"Leave him out of it. This is between you and me."

Absurdly, I wanted to smile. But her beautiful face was a picture of hurt she was trying to hide. I dragged a hand down my stubbled face. "Full confession. What we did kinda…blew my mind."

Shock replaced hurt, and then her expression slowly softened. After a minute she nodded. "Me, too," she whispered, blushing fiercely.

"Okay. Now that we've got that squared away, how can I make you feel...less pissed?"

She grabbed a sliced bagel, tore a piece, but didn't eat it. "I want to know you, Caleb. Tell me something."

I took a deep breath. "You know I grew up on the rough streets of LA."

Her hand trembled as she stared wide-eyed at me. "Yes. Was it after you lost your mom?"

Christ. I weighed the option of evasion against the return of her hurt, and grimaced inwardly. "It was before. And after. She was a manic-depressive. The moments of light in her darkness were very few but for the first nine years of my life she had medical insurance and a decent doctor to prescribe her the right medication."

"Caleb—"

My fingers brushed her lips, silencing her. "I don't like telling this story. Let me tell it once and be done. Okay?"

A small nod.

My chest tightened as memories flooded in. "She lost her job and the domino effect of no insurance, losing our house, ending up at a halfway house, then a shelter, sent her into a deeper hole. I was eleven before we were assigned a place in Trenton Gardens."

Lily winced but I couldn't let her sympathy affect me.

"But it was too late. She'd lost the will to..." I took a breath. "I was the only thing she fought for. Every time social services tried to take me away, she would fight to keep me. I've no idea how she did it, but she won. But then she would spiral back into darkness. I couldn't help her. I called every helpline I could find, wrote a dozen letters every week to anyone I thought could help. The doctors we managed to see were hopeless. Twice, she tried to end her life. Every time they sent her home from the hospital with a damn leaflet. I even pawned her jewelry to pay for an appointment with a private doctor. The pills he prescribed helped. When she ran out I called my social worker and asked her to help me get her more. She just…laughed at me." Anger and despair I hadn't felt in a long time swelled inside me. I withdrew my hand from Lily's, clenched it in my lap and took another breath. "Anyway, she succeeded on her third attempt."

"Oh, God…"

Tears spilled down her cheeks. I opened my mouth to tell her not to cry for me. Then stopped. I *wanted* her soft sympathy. It was a salve to a wound that had never healed. Shedding tears for my mother was one of the many things I hadn't been able to do for her. Maybe Lily's tears would be enough to let her know how sorry I was for failing.

Lily got up, walked round and slid into my lap. "I'm so sorry." Her arms circled my neck. I hugged her close, breathed in her goodness. And just like in the bathroom, I never wanted this moment to end.

I never wanted to let her go.

Which was crazy. We'd only known each other for a week. And…dammit, I didn't do feelings!

I looked around and grimaced. "Can we continue this at home?" I said, raising my eyebrow.

For some reason my cocked eyebrow made her smile. "Too wide-open-spaces for you?"

"Something like that," I said, looking down at the table. "Breakfast is ruined, though."

She shrugged. "I wasn't that hungry anyway."

I scowled. "A woeful waste of good bacon."

Her smile widened as she stood up. "We have bacon at home," she suggested.

Unable to keep my hands off her, I grabbed her and trailed my hands up her thighs. "Is there an offer in there?"

Her fingers tunneled through my hair, gently massaging my scalp. "If you want. But I don't break out my culinary skills for just anyone."

I caught a trace of pain through the flippant words. "Why not?"

Green eyes darted away, then came back. "Stepdaddy issues. In return for him…tolerating me, I had to cook for him. It made me hate cooking."

I caressed her damp cheek. "He doesn't deserve your love. Or your pain."

Her eyes misted. "It's not easy to brush it off."

True. I'd lived with guilt and anger for so long it was fused into my DNA. "I get it."

"Caleb?"

"Yeah."

"I was thinking…maybe your presence has achieved the opposite of what we hoped. Maybe instead of bringing my stalker out into the open, he's given up?"

"Sorry to disappoint you, but assholes like that don't go away easily. I'm close to catching him. Trust me. Okay?"

Small, soft hands framed my face. "Okay."

My hands coasted higher, brushed the underside of her breasts. Her breathing altered. "Let's go home."

She nodded.

We threw the uneaten breakfast in the trash. I winced as I folded myself back into the car. "This is the second thing I'm punishing you for when we get back."

Her eyes widened. "What's the first thing?"

"Driving me insane with those fucking shorts," I griped, reaching down to adjust my hard-on. "That was the intention, wasn't it?"

Pink flared in her cheeks. "Maybe."

"Well, you are *definitely* getting your ass spanked for it."

Hot anticipation washed away the last of the sadness and pain in her eyes.

When she pulled up at a stop sign, I dragged my gaze from her slim thighs to her face, then her hair. "Has your hair always been this color?"

She shook her head. "It used to be dark blond." She grabbed a lock at her right temple. "This part started turning whiter when I was twelve. It was cool at first. Then I got tired of it. So I went white all over."

"I like it. A lot."

Her gaze latched on to mine. We stared at one another, pure electricity zinging between us. The driver behind us honked impatiently. She jumped, then laughed. Her laughter triggered mine, easing the tension of the past hour. The lightness stayed as we drove through the gates. As I threw her over my shoulder and rushed through the front door into the living room.

Maybe this…unburdening thing wasn't catastrophic after all.

Maybe breaking my rule for her wasn't the end of the world.

Maybe—

We froze as the TV flicked to life of its own accord. Except that was impossible. Not without electronic intervention.

That intervention arrived in the form of neon green bits of code raining down the screen, then a masked face framed by a black hoodie. I pushed Lily behind me as if it would protect her from the loud, distorted voice that filled the room.

"Hello, Lily Gracen. First of all, congratulations. You're very close to achieving perfection with your code. Don't be frightened. I represent interested parties wishing to form a partnership. Apologies if I've made you a little…uncomfortable lately. But I urge you not to give the code to SDM or I'll have no choice but to stay in your life a while longer. Think about it. I'll be in touch. Oh, and tell that fixer to go home to LA. He won't be of much use to you."

The strangled sound Lily made cut to the heart of me. I took a step toward the TV just as it went blank.

A loud pop shot through the house, then an eerie silence echoed in its wake.

CHAPTER THIRTEEN

Caleb

"WHAT ARE YOU DOING?"

"We're getting the hell out of here." I spotted an overnight bag and handed it to her. "Pack what you need but do it fast."

She reached for my hand. "Caleb—"

I turned away, fist clenched, the need to punch something running wild through me. "Lily, the asshole hacked your Wi-Fi, sent the transmission, then hit the house with an electromagnetic wave that killed the electricity on the whole street. You're not staying here. Not until I have my hands around his fucking throat."

To her credit, she didn't dawdle. She stuffed clothes into the bag, added essentials, then grabbed her satchel and purse.

Ten minutes later we were driving away from the house.

"Your guys searched the area. Did they find anything?"

My security team's presence had provided some reassurance, but not enough to close the horrified black chasm in my stomach at the thought that from the moment we returned to the house, we were sitting ducks. It snatched my breath. Reminded me of the consequences of dropping my guard.

"Caleb?"

I gathered my scattered thoughts. "They found motorcycle tracks behind the house."

She flinched at my cold tone, but said nothing for a couple of miles. "Where are we going?"

"To the airport."

"And then?"

"We're swinging by my place in Malibu. Then I'm taking you to the safe house in Lake Tahoe." I should've done that in the first place. Regardless of the fact that bringing her home had produced the desired effect of drawing the stalker out, the flip side was much worse. The EMP blast could've been knockout gas. Or—

"So you still don't know who it is?"

My fingers tightened on the wheel. "No."

She didn't speak much after that. Neither did I. I was too busy playing worst-case-scenario.

Anything could've happened to Lily.

My jet was ready when we arrived at the airport. We took off immediately. Leaving Lily in the club chair upfront, I retreated to the back of the plane and dialed Maggie.

She answered on the first ring. "Boss, how can I help?"

"I've left three guys in Palo Alto to track down this bastard. I need another team at the Reno safe house."

"I'll get right on it."

I hung up, then went through my contacts. Every favor owed to me, I shamelessly called on. By the time we landed in LA I was in a better frame of mind.

My house in Malibu was set on a bluff that overlooked a private beach. The helipad that came with the property had been used only a handful of times. Today it came in handy as a way of avoiding LA's horrendous traffic.

I walked in and my steps slowed. The last time I was here I was in complete control of my world, my only focus on being bigger, better, *badder*.

In the space of seven days, the ground had shifted beneath me, attempted to change my orbit. All because of the stunning woman who stopped beside me, her eyes lighting on the space I'd claimed, possessions that proclaimed my success. That fierce yearning to hang on to her clobbered me again. I smashed it to pieces.

No more breaking rules.

"Hang tight. I'll be right back." I sprinted upstairs to my bedroom to retrieve the weapons I kept in the safe.

I came down to find her at the window, staring at the ocean with her arms wrapped around her middle. She turned at my approach. "Can't we just stay here?"

The urge to say yes pounded me. "No. This place is secure enough but it's in my name. Any fucker with a computer can find it. I need you off the grid."

Resigned, she nodded.

We headed outside and reboarded the chopper.

"Chance will need to know I'm going off-grid."

My teeth gritted. "No, he doesn't. You still have time before your deadline. And frankly, I don't want him anywhere near you right now."

Again, she didn't react as expected. She was either in shock or afraid. Neither of the two sat well with me.

"Lily..."

Her fingers curled in her lap. "What if it's someone close to me? What would that say about my judgment?"

"You're not blaming yourself for this." That ball was squarely in my court.

"Since you don't know *who* it is, that's easier said than done," she murmured.

I had no answer to that so I remained silent as we reboarded the plane and took off.

There was very little in the way of conversation during the flight.

Many times I opened my mouth to say something, then decided against it.

Action, not platitudes.

Maggie had lined up another SUV for us, and I high-tailed it out of the airport with one eye on the police scanner on the dashboard. I wanted to get us to the cabin on the Nevada side of the lake as quickly as possible without attracting attention from the cops for speeding.

Twenty minutes later I breathed a sigh of relief when I spotted the turnoff for the dirt track leading to the cabin. I'd kept it overgrown on purpose. There were no signposts or no trespassing warnings to attract inquisitive neighbors.

The Jeffrey pines lining the track and surrounding the property were ideal for mounting security cameras and other intruder-warning triggers.

I pulled up in front of the cabin in Knots Peak, killed the engine and glanced over at Lily. She was staring at the log building that would be her home until I came through with my assurance to catch her stalker.

My gaze slid past her to the three-leveled property. The one-bedroom dilapidated structure I bought five years ago had been expanded into a no-cost-spared piece of real estate worth ten times its original price.

It was one of three safe houses I owned around the country. The other four were overseas but this was my favorite. On the rare occasion I took downtime from fixing other people's problems, the cabin was my first choice.

There would be no downtime, though. I'd dropped my guard, messed around with a client and the bastard had gotten close.

Fury and guilt bubbled inside as I threw open the door. "Let's get you inside."

I grabbed her bag and walked her to the front door. A palm print and alphanumeric code released the lock.

Rugs spread out in the wide hallway and over polished wooden floors throughout the cabin muffled our footsteps. Exposed oak beams propped up high ceilings in the living room, and light filtered in from a wide window facing the lake.

I stashed her bag in the bedroom before returning to the living room. Still clutching her satchel, she stood at the window, lost in the view.

"The window is one-way glass so no one can see inside. Even at night you'll be able to see the lake. That should help a little." Shit, I sounded like a damn realtor.

She turned, wary eyes catching mine. "Help with what?"

I shrugged. "Not everyone likes being stuck in the middle of nowhere. The lake will give you something to look at."

"I'm okay with it," she replied, although her sleek white throat moved in a nervous swallow. I dragged my gaze away from the smooth landscape of her skin. Giv-

ing in to those insane yearnings was what had landed
us here.

"Good. Security-wise, the outer doors are made of
solid oak. It would take a very large ax or a sizeable
explosive device to breach it. The woods for half a mile
radius are part of the property. There are a few booby
traps to prevent intruders."

She frowned. "What kinds of traps?"

"Very effective ones," I gritted out, partly to reassure
her, partly to reassure myself.

She flinched; then her lips pursed.

I dragged my hands down my face and walked over
to her. Every cell in my body was dying to touch her.
But I'd already let too much *personal* get in the way.

It was time to revert to Caleb Steele, Stone-Cold
Fixer.

Jaw set, I moved toward the French doors. "I need
to go through the cabin's security with you. Familiar-
ize yourself with the property."

"Why are you being so cold?"

Her soft, bewildered words were like a punch to the
gut. I steeled myself against it before turning to face her.

"You wanted to know what happened to my shoulder? I got involved with a client. Kirsten was an actress,
one of my first clients. She'd made a couple of wrong
choices in the past. The studio she was working with
was threatening to fire her over some revealing pictures. She begged me to help. She was beautiful and I
was young, foolish and…into her." Lily's gaze dropped
and a look I couldn't fathom crossed her face. "When
she needed a car, I gave her mine. When she needed a
place to stay, I asked her to move in with me." My bitter laughter seared my throat. "Hell, I believed we were

in a *relationship*. Right up until I found her banging the director. Even then I thought she was the victim. I punched his lights out and caused general mayhem that ensured my fledgling career tanked before it'd taken off properly. And Kirsten's response? She went off her head because I'd just ruined her chances for another movie and decided she didn't want me in her life after all so she tried to fucking shoot me."

Lily blanched. "Oh, my God!"

I shrugged despite the fury of bitterness and anger dueling inside me. "Luckily, she was a very lousy shot. Anyway, if it hadn't been for Ross's father, I'd still be fixing problems for gangsters back in Trenton Gardens. He gave me a piece of advice, one I'd already figured out the hard way—never get involved with a client."

A horrified little sound escaped her throat, scraping on my nerve endings. "S-so you think this is my fault?" she whispered.

I opened my mouth to say *hell, no*, but then stopped. She was partly to blame. She'd gotten under my skin with her soft sympathy and her flashes of innocence and her incredible inner strength in the face of adversity and her gloriously tight body. Even now, she continued to drive me insane with her jaw-dropping beauty.

"I think my point has been proven conclusively that shit happens when you break the rules," I said. "Besides, you were on a mission of your own, weren't you?"

She gasped and her eyes darkened in pain. I turned away. My point was made. And I still had a stalker to catch.

"Security tour. Now." I crossed to the French doors on the other side of the living room and stepped out onto the porch, not looking back to see if she was following.

The sky was a clear blue, and the cool air was drifting in from the lake. It was all so fucking idyllic.

When I heard her behind me, I went down wooden stairs leading to a sloping garden. A staggered limestone feature tumbled water into the rock pond one level lower and stopped next to a covered hot tub. I bypassed it, trying not to think of Lily immersed in the swirling bubbles, completely naked, with the setting sun gleaming on her glorious skin.

A few hours ago I would've said, *forget the fucking tour, let's go to bed.* But my sex-addled brain had put her in danger.

We skirted the garden and the high stone walls to stop at the side gate. "This leads down to the lake. And a boat for a quick getaway if you need to. The code is 40998061."

Fear sparked through the shadowed swirls in her eyes. I forced myself not to react to it.

After a few beats she placed her thumb against the panel, and the gate sprang open. The scent of pine and earth grew as we stepped onto the uneven path and walked in silence to the jetty. "Have you driven a boat before?"

"No."

"The keys are hidden beneath the sixth slab…right here." I tried to ignore the feel of her silky skin as I caught her arm and pointed to the wooden plank. "It's screwed in but loose enough to pry apart in a hurry if you need to."

The boat was a few years old but was kept in good condition and fully fueled at all times.

She hopped down before I could help her, and then took a step away from me. I gritted my teeth against the grating discomfort in my chest and pointed to the ignition. "Twist to the left and hold. Engine should kick in. Then push the lever. Ignore everything else."

"It looks pretty straightforward."

"It might not be if you're panicking," I bit out.

Her cheeks lost color, but she nodded. "Understood."

We returned to the house and I took her round the lower level to another door. "Same code as the gate but backward."

"16089904," she repeated instantly.

Hell, even scrambling to maintain distance, I couldn't help but admire her incredible brain.

The large room that doubled up as a games room and gym took up most of the square footage of the cabin. It was also self-contained enough to use as a sleeping place for the odd bodyguard or two when needed.

I bypassed the doors connecting the short hallway to the stairs leading up and headed to the far wall. When she joined me, I pushed on the fourth wooden panel. A five-foot partition sprang open to reveal a small spiral staircase. "This takes you straight up into the kitchen. After you."

She sprinted up lithely on the balls of her feet. I took the stairs much slower, unable to take my eyes off the ass that'd cradled my cock in the shower this morning.

Her steps slowed as she neared the top.

"Is there a problem?" The question emerged with a tight croak.

I stopped two steps below her, keeping us at eye level. Close enough for me to lean forward and taste the sinfully gorgeous mouth currently pinched with tension. I locked my knees hard and reminded myself that my wayward cock had brought us to this.

"You didn't bring in your bag from the car. And you've just given me a very detailed tour. Why?"

Chains shackled my chest. "Because I'm returning to Palo Alto."

"You're leaving." The statement was final and chilled.

Unaccustomed dread slowly filled my chest.

I'd pushed her into accepting that what happened with us was a mistake, and yet seeing that acceptance in her eyes had lodged a cold, hard ball in my gut.

I braced a hand against the banister as another truth bit me hard. I'd told her to *trust me*. And had done zero to back it up.

My failures, rehashed just a few short hours ago, slashed me in half.

Bitter laughter seared my throat as patterns were laid bare.

My success rate with jobs that didn't require emotional expenditure was near perfect. Those I allowed myself to care about were doomed to failure. My mother. Then Kirsten. Now Lily.

And yes…I cared about Lily. Hell, I was damned sure *caring* was too mild a word for it.

I gathered every last scrap of emotion, knotted it into a cold ball, and buried it deep. Then I forced a nod, despite my veins beginning to fill with icy water. "I can't find your stalker stuck here with you. I need to get back, rattle a few cages."

Her eyes, no longer that gorgeous shade of green I loved, shadowed even further. Then she gathered that admirable strength and nodded. "I see. You better get to it then."

Something that tasted uncannily like anguish billowed up from my feet to lodge in my throat. No amount of bracing myself could prevent it saturating every corner of my being as I watched her walk to the sofa and snatch up her satchel.

"Lily." I said her name for the simple, selfish reason that I couldn't bear the distance between us.

She glanced impatiently at me. "What?"

I pointed to the fridge. "You didn't have any breakfast. You need to eat something."

Her gaze swung blankly to the fridge. Then she frowned. "I'm not hungry."

"Well, eat anyway. You'll need—"

"I'm not a child. I'm capable of feeding myself when I need to, thanks."

I opened my mouth. My phone beeped. I read the message and my heart sank.

Me, the man of action who abhorred drawn-out goodbyes, was reeling that his time was up with Lily Gracen. "Your security team is here."

She nodded stiffly as I introduced her to her three minders. Two disappeared to take up positions around the perimeter. The one tasked to stay inside with her at all times retreated to a respectful distance.

"Was there anything else?" she asked coldly.

There were a thousand things. But everything started and ended with the fact that I'd failed her. So not a single word emerged.

Slowly her eyes grew colder, her face a mask of disappointment as she strutted to the door and pointedly threw it open.

"Goodbye, Caleb." The echoing finality behind her words stayed with me long after my plane soared into the sky, racing me away from her.

CHAPTER FOURTEEN

Lily

HE WAS GONE.

Forty-eight hours later I still couldn't believe how quickly everything had turned to ash. When Maggie called last night to ask if I needed anything, I had to bite my tongue hard to stop myself from asking about Caleb.

What good would it have done? He blamed me for pushing him into territory he'd never wanted to revisit. And he was right. I'd taken advantage of our insane chemistry just so I could prove I was in control. And I was the one bleeding with no end of the ravaging pain in sight.

The truth wasn't hard to accept. The pain that came with it was.

I'd allowed myself to hope. To care.

If only I hadn't let the moments of gentleness and protectiveness weave into my heart. If only he hadn't opened up at the drive-in…

If only the phenomenal sex hadn't left me raw and reeling and craving the impossible.

From the start he'd made it clear sex was off the

table as long as I was his client. And I'd seen that as a challenge.

Misery clawed through me. My heart shuddered and I blinked to stop the fierce prickling that preceded tears.

God, was it even possible to fall in love in seven short days?

My inability to catch my breath, the endless turmoil in my mind and the anguish coursing through my body, screamed *yes*. Butting heads with him at the start had been my mating dance. Giving him my body had gone hand in hand with giving him my heart. A heart left battered even before it'd had a chance to soar.

If I had to pinpoint when it was well and truly doomed, it was the moment he confirmed why he became a fixer.

I couldn't even hate him for that. He'd never hidden himself from me.

Maybe it was better this way. Having happiness snatched from me before I truly tasted it would be a blessing somewhere down the road.

I stared at the horizon, watching the fingers of dawn trail the inky blue sky. Down by the water I spotted Kurt, the minder who'd pulled lake duty. I didn't sleep a wink last night. Surprise. But I managed to snatch moments of lucidity, long enough to confirm that it was Sanjeet's code that sabotaged the beta test.

Further anguish weighted my heart, but I was thankful I didn't have to deal with him just yet. I would repair the code on my own and test it vigorously before the next meeting.

Because now more than ever, I needed total control of my life. I had a feeling I'd need it because this ravaging pain wasn't done with me by a long stretch.

Caleb

I jerked awake from a sleep filled with alternating images of losing my mother, then Lily. As I watched, screaming, their images blended, then drifted farther and farther out of reach.

I dragged myself upright to a sweat-soaked T-shirt and guilt-laden relief that immediately morphed into pain.

It'd been like this for the last four interminable days.

In the cold light of day, I could distract myself with something else, although success in that area was dwindling. But in my dreams I was helpless against the savage craving; helpless to fight the powerful emotions that poured out of my soul, wrenched me from sleep only to mock me with the emptiness of my reality.

I stared out the window of the cabin's guest room, the peace I usually found here shattered.

Why the hell did I put her in my bedroom?

So you can torture yourself with visions of her when she's gone, why else?

Perversely, the thought that I'd have *something* to hang on to soothed me a little.

Jesus.

I rose, changed my T-shirt, added sweatpants and grabbed my phone. As I approached the door, my heart began to race.

I told myself the smell of coffee didn't mean a thing. Lack of sleep and the couple of drinks I had on the plane equaled a foggy brain. I could've set the coffee machine myself when I rolled in at…whatever o'clock.

I entered the living room, saw her, and thoughts of time dissolved.

She sat cross-legged on the sofa nearest the window, beneath the worshipful rays of the morning sun.

The leather and lace comprising her usual work attire had been swapped for a less dramatic getup of black T-shirt and jersey shorts. But a choker still circled her neck, cuffs binding her wrists.

She hadn't seen me yet. I needed an uninterrupted minute to imprint her on my memory. Some of the things I said couldn't be taken back.

Hell, my behavior had been beyond shitty. So yeah, the chances of her being gone by nightfall were extremely high.

But God, I needed another minute, because I'd missed her beautiful face...her body...so damn much.

She was spectacular, if elusive, in my dreams but the reality was infinitely better. I approached, the contrasting black-and-white vision of her a magnet I couldn't resist.

She was completely absorbed in her work, her fingers dancing in a hypnotic blur over the keyboard. Earbuds firmly in place cut her off from me.

But then, greedily, I wanted those beautiful green eyes that had invaded my dreams every night since I left on me.

As if she heard my thoughts, her fingers froze.

Her head snapped up, her eyes widened, then dimmed. Her resting expression was a punch in the gut. I tried to absorb it as I strolled closer.

"Hey." She eyed me warily as she plucked her earbuds out. "I didn't...when did you get back?"

"Very late. Or very early."

Her eyes grew more guarded. "Is...everything all right?"

I hesitated.

The moment I answered, it was over. There would be nothing keeping her here. A shamefully large part of me wanted to stall, like I'd wanted to freeze time in the shower, and at the drive-in. Hell, every moment with Lily deserved to be preserved in amber.

But the universe selfishly ticked forward. Gritting my teeth, I indicated the sofa. "May I sit?"

She stared blankly at me, then down at the space before shrugging. "It's your house, Caleb." Her voice was a chilled rasp.

I ignored the ache sucking oxygen out of my lungs and sat down. When she tensed and tucked her legs firmer beneath her, I bunched my fist on my thigh.

Wow, you blew it good this time, Steele.

"Caleb?" Her fingers were curled tensely around the lid of her laptop.

I cleared my throat and fired up the video app on my phone. In a dark gray room, across a desk and two chairs, two men faced each other.

I pointed to the younger man. "Do you know him?"

She set her laptop aside. "No. Should I?"

"His name is Eric Vasiliev. He works for Baitlin Tech."

She blinked. "Baitlin was on the list I gave you."

I nodded. "He's also Sanjeet's roommate."

Alarm widened her eyes. "Okay. Who's the other guy?"

"A friend of mine. He's in law enforcement. He did me a solid."

"How?"

"He interviewed the remaining people on the list, helped me fill out a few blanks."

Her breath caught, hope filling her eyes. "Are you saying... Have you caught my stalker?"

I smiled. "Yes. You don't need to worry. They're in custody. And your algorithm is safe."

Relief drenched her face. She covered her open mouth with one hand. "Oh, my God," she whispered.

I wanted to touch her so badly my hand burned with the need.

She took a few more breaths, and then her gaze returned to the screen. "Did Sanjeet have anything to do with it?"

"Not directly. But he unwittingly started the whole thing. Eric saw what he was working on during a Face-Time call and asked a few questions, enough to get an idea of what you were working on."

"But Sanjeet was just a third of the team, and the others didn't know about each other."

I hit the second video in the folder. "They didn't, but she did."

Lily stared at the video, hurt and anger flashing across her face. "Miranda?"

"Yeah. She had access to you. All she had to do was listen and watch and tell Eric when to strike."

"But...why?"

The throb of anguish in her voice cut through me. I wanted to absorb her pain. "Money. She was dating Eric. They hatched the plan together. All they had to do was destabilize the team, stalk you in the hopes of you making a mistake. If that didn't work they were going to move to outright blackmail to get the code. They had a bidding war going with six countries."

"She told your friend all of this?"

I nodded. "We got it all on tape."

"Oh, my God." Her eyes filled with tears.

Unable to hold back my need, I reached for her. She flinched away, jumped to her feet and paced to the window.

I threw my phone on the coffee table, swallowing the boulder of pain in my throat.

After a minute she swiped her eyes. When she faced me, her face was a controlled mask. "So it's over. I can leave?"

Every ounce of power concentrated in keeping my jaw clenched just so I didn't have to answer. But the part of me that yearned to give her what she wanted forced my head to nod. "The police will need a statement from you at some point, but with the confession they have it should all be straightforward."

Then, unable to sit still, I surged to my feet. "Lily—"

"I want to leave. Now. Please."

No. *Hell, no.*

One look at her face showed my firecracker was back, ready to rain fire and brimstone on me if I didn't grant her wish.

"Lily, we need to talk."

She shook her head. "I need to pack." She darted down the hallway so fast she was a blur.

I followed because, fuck it, I was tired of feeling like shit.

I knocked. At her silence, I entered. She was holding a top, staring blindly into her suitcase. I took another moment to memorize her face.

Her head snapped up, and her face tightened. "What do you want, Caleb? We said everything that needed saying last time."

"No we didn't. I have more to say."

She looked mutinous for a moment, and then her cute chin lifted. "Fine, let's hear it."

My fists tightened, the magnitude of my need an overwhelming weight pressing me down. But I pushed ahead. "I don't want you to leave. We're not done. Hell, we barely even started. I want you back."

A look flashed through her eyes but it was gone too quickly to read. "Wanting me back suggests you had me in the first place. Did you?" she queried almost carelessly.

"What?"

She threw the top into the suitcase. "Let's forget that for a minute. You want me…back…for how long?"

I frowned. "Lily—"

"A week? A month? Two months?"

I shrugged. "It's something we can figure out together."

She laughed, an acid-tipped sound that whipped blades through me. "How? What criteria would you use? When the sex isn't so hot anymore? When your next exciting case came up?"

"If you want a time frame I'm not going to give you one," I snapped with more heat than I'd intended.

She paled. I reached out. She flinched. This wasn't how I'd intended it to go. At all.

"Lily, I—"

"Why did you become a fixer, Caleb?" The question walloped me from left field. Her voice was wooden but her sharp eyes were prying beneath my veneer.

I didn't want to be analyzed. Not while this rawness lived inside me. "Why the hell not?" I snapped again.

"That's not an answer. Shall I tell you what I think? You enjoy the control it gives you. But more than that you enjoy the transient nature of your work. You don't have to invest in the long-term. You go in, all guns blazing, you fix whatever's wrong. And then you *leave*. Don't you?"

I stared at her, trying to summon fury and detachment. All I achieved was a widening of the chasm between us. Fuck it. "Yes," I threw out.

It was the truth, after all.

She whirled to face the window, then almost immediately turned back again. "Well, there's your answer. You can't guarantee anything beyond your next *fix*. That's what you live for. That's all you'll ever care about. But you know what else you can't guarantee? That your neat record will hold out. Sooner or later you'll have to accept that some things can't be fixed."

The raw ache intensified. "What the fuck are you talking about?"

She sighed. "It doesn't matter. I just know that I don't want to be your next fix, Caleb."

Somewhere beneath the roaring in my ears, I heard the sound of her suitcase zipper and the echo of her footsteps down the hallway.

Moments later an engine started, revved, then slowly faded away.

CHAPTER FIFTEEN

Caleb
One month later

"WHY ISN'T THE Landon file on my desk? I asked for it twenty minutes ago. What's going on?" I snarled as Maggie hurriedly slammed her laptop shut.

"Nothing!"

I eyed her, the irritation that had been living beneath my skin for weeks threatening to erupt. "If you want to watch porn, do it in your own time, not on company property. And seriously, I thought you were a much better liar than that?"

"Okay, first of all, ewww. Second of all, double ewww!"

"You have five seconds to fess up before I fire you for inappropriate use of office property."

With a long-suffering sigh, she opened her laptop, and hit Play.

The sweet, sexy voice that lived in my dreams flowed through the speaker. Heart lodged in my throat, I rounded Maggie's desk.

And there she was.

Lily. Giving another interview.

I'd taken pains to avoid all forms of tech news since she left me in Lake Tahoe.

I tried to summon the anger I'd carried with me since she walked out. All I managed was the ashen aftertaste of a poorly handled situation.

I don't want to be your next fix...

I snorted under my breath. Lily Gracen had proven that she was one long fix, one I couldn't get away from whether I was awake or asleep.

She'd burrowed herself firmly beneath my skin, made it so I couldn't take three steps before she crossed my mind. I wasn't sure whether to be pissed with her or feel sorry for myself for allowing her close.

Some things can't be fixed...

Ironically, in letting her smudge the lines, she'd forced me to redraw my rigid boundaries, forced me to examine the hard chains I'd wrapped around myself since my mother died. A few had been rusty, surprisingly easy to break, letting me breathe easier than I had in a very long time.

Some others not so much.

All in all, she'd forced me to examine far too much. Which was why I was still leaning heavily in the pissed column.

And there she was, without a fucking care in the world.

Stunning in customary black. With...a pair of stylish, boxy glasses perched on her nose.

Holy fuck.

That last day in Silicon Valley, sitting in the passenger seat of her cramped-as-hell little car, watching her laugh while wearing those saucy shorts, I thought she couldn't get any more sensational.

I just discovered she could.

"Umm…boss?"

I scowled. "What?"

"Just checking that you're breathing, is all."

I wrenched my gaze from the screen. "I'm not paying you to sit around watching online videos all day, Maggie."

She nodded sagely. "Then I guess you won't want the thing I just sent to your phone."

My scowl deepened. "What thing?" I pulled my phone from my pocket.

It was an invitation to a black tie event. Hosted by SDM. Five thousand dollars a plate. Starting at 8 pm. Tonight.

A tremble rolled up my arm and down my body. "Why the hell did you send me this?"

"Because I'm terrified one of these days you'll develop actual fangs and claws and all my parents will find when they come looking for me is a dried up husk."

"Trust me. If I turned feral you wouldn't be my first choice of a meal."

I knew someone who tasted sweeter. Glorious, in fact. Someone whose every breath I would die for, given half a chance.

"Fine, but just FYI, this is her last gig for SDM. Who knows where she'll disappear to afterward?"

The words struck pure dread into my heart, pissing me off even more. I stomped back into my office. "Can't go. I'm busy."

"Actually, you're not. But okay."

I threw myself into my chair, vowing not to look at the invitation. I lasted five minutes. "Maggie!"

"Yeah, boss, I have your tux right here."

Great. This was my chance to rectify a few things with Lily Gracen.

Once and for all.

Lily

The terrace of the Griffith Observatory was great for many things, including its stunning views of nighttime LA. But decked out in spotlights and caviar towers and champagne fountains, it was magnificent. That was before the celebrities and Fortune 500 CEOs who'd flown in from around the globe added their dazzle to the occasion.

After two weeks of hard publicity, tonight was the official launch party stroke fund-raiser for SDM's compression algorithm. And my final appearance as the ambassador for the most talked about development in the tech world. After tonight I was free. I'd never need to set eyes on Chance Donovan, or my stepfather again.

Even though the latter thought brought a pang of pain, I was okay with it. For the first time in my life, I could truly move forward with no baggage.

I closed on the sale of the abandoned drive-in movie theater today, and immediately applied for permission to convert it into offices. I was starting my own tech company and even though I was scared spitless, I was also excited.

If nothing else, starting a company from the ground up would take my mind off thinking about Caleb.

Whoever said time healed all wounds was a dotard. With every passing day, the hole in my chest grew wider, deeper. There were times when I feared the thing could just expire from the brutal trauma it endured daily, simply because it craved one night of perfection that would never be repeated.

But did you make absolutely sure it couldn't be repeated? Or did you shut the door because you were hurt and never looked back?

Those lingering questions were the reason I hadn't erased his last message from two weeks ago from my phone. Or maybe I was just a glutton for punishment.

Had he moved on? Was he currently buried neck deep in a new exciting case?

"I have no idea what it does, but I hear it's revolutionary. What did they call it again?"

"They called it the Angel Algorithm," a deep, magnificent voice said.

Dear God. His voice...

"Why *Angel*?"

"Because it's the creator's middle name," Caleb replied.

"Oh, how special," the female guest gushed.

"I couldn't agree more. She's one of a kind."

Heart in my throat, I turned around. He stood six feet away. Resplendent in a black tux and snowy white shirt. His face looked a little thinner but the designer stubble and slightly windswept hair worked for him so splendidly, I couldn't have pried my eyes off him if an earthquake cratered the ground beneath my feet.

The crowd seemed to part between us, and he loomed, magnificent, over me. "That was right, wasn't it?"

Breath totally depleted, I nodded. "Short for Angela. Chance let me name it." After witnessing the code that would make him and his company billions, he'd been so ecstatic he'd allowed me to name it. Regardless of how our relationship had begun, it was ending on my terms, with an achievement I was proud of. I'd chosen to let go of all grudges.

"It's a beautiful name." Caleb's voice was a little gruff, his eyes a fierce blue that blazed over me from my crown to my feet and back again. "Hello, Lily."

"Hi," I whispered.

"You look…incredible."

"Thank you." In honor of tonight, I'd gone a different way with my clothes. Dressed top to toe in white, the only splash of color were the red soles of my white platform heels. Diamond-and-pearl pins secured my slicked back hair, and even the choker around my neck was white leather.

Caleb's eyes lingered there the longest, setting my body aflame. "Lily, can we talk?"

Say no. Save yourself more heartache. "Yes."

Relief drenched his face. He started to reach for me. Someone bumped into me, sending me one stumble forward.

"Okay, enough of this shit," Caleb growled. He relieved me of my half-finished champagne glass, meshed his fingers with mine and tugged me through the crowd.

"Where are you taking me?"

"You'll see."

"But…I can't leave the party."

"You've given Donovan the algorithm. You've done his speeches. You don't owe him a thing. Besides, we need to revisit our last conversation in Lake Tahoe. There are a few things I never got around to saying." He gripped me tighter as I navigated the steps to the lower level, then increased his pace again.

"God, I haven't missed this bossy side of you at all."

I tried to project irritation but the wild hum in my veins wasn't anger. It was...*joy.*

"Sure you have. Or you wouldn't be hurrying to keep up with me."

He was right. I would go anywhere with this man, but at what price?

"I still want to know where we're going."

"We're here," he replied in a hushed voice, then pushed the door open.

I entered, and gasped. "We can't be in here," I whispered halfheartedly. But my excitement tripled as I gazed up at the stunning constellation splashed across the planetarium roof.

His fingers trailed up my wrists, my arms, to cup my shoulders. I redirected my gaze to his, saw the raw emotion stamped on his face.

"I'm fucking pissed at you."

I gasped. "What?"

"You heard me. But God, I've also missed you. So much," he confessed raggedly.

I stopped myself from blurting out that I'd missed him, too. "Have you? You were shitty to me."

His face clouded with pain. "Believe me, I know. I'd do anything to take it all back."

My throat clogged. Excitement faded and harrowing pain rushed at me. "Would you? Why?"

"Because you didn't deserve it. Not a single one of the things I threw at you."

"Are you sure? Because there's no shame in admitting you don't have room in your life...for me." It hurt me to say it, but it needed to be said.

He shook his head vehemently. "That's not—"

"I saw how devastated you were when you told

me about your mom. You blame yourself for her. You moved heaven and earth for her and she still died, and after that you were never going to become so wrapped up in anyone else. Am I right?"

He stared down at me for the longest time. Then he exhaled harshly. "Yes. I'd love to say I fought hard to shut people out, but…after she died, it was easy to close the door, to bottle the pain and become the lone wolf no one depended on. Until Kirsten."

My heart twisted with pain for him. For me. "And she let you down, too."

His mouth tightened. "I don't want to talk about her. She's not important. Not anymore. She was just another crutch I used to distance myself. The option to walk away on my own terms before things got heavy with anyone was mine alone. I was okay with it. Until I met you. You forced me to take a long, hard look at myself."

My lungs flattened. "Caleb…"

"Walking away from you was the hardest thing I've ever done, Lily," he confessed forcefully.

Remembering brought more pain. "Then why did you?"

"I let my guard down with you. My instincts warned me about Miranda but I saw how close you were to your team. To her. I knew you would be hurt if it was her and I didn't want you to experience that pain. I hesitated when I could've acted sooner. Then the breach happened and all I could think about was that I could've lost you. In the end I did anyway by pushing you away, when I should've pulled you close."

"I thought you were into her. Miranda."

Caleb's fingers brushed my throat and I realized I was clinging to his wrists. "I'm into one particular pint-size blonde, with a heart of gold, the courage of a lion and a body designed to stop traffic."

"She's into you, too, but she was terrified all you'd ever want was to be a fixer. That she wouldn't be able to compete with your calling. You chose to do what you do to help people but also to stay connected to your mother. I... I didn't know if I could compete with that."

"The moment you walked into my life, the competition was over. I would've come after you whether you were a client or not. My heart and my soul craved you even before I knew what was happening. That second time in Lake Tahoe was my piss-poor way of telling you I couldn't live without you."

"Oh, Caleb."

"I've been wretched without you. The thought of waking up every morning for the rest of my life without you..." He stopped and shook his head, urgent hands cupping my cheeks to tilt my gaze to his. "If there's any part of you that feels a fraction of that, please give me a chance to make us both happy."

Bright, shining hope billowed through me. "Do you mean that?"

"With every bone in my body," he breathed.

"Oh, my God."

Fevered eyes pierced me. "Is that... Are you considering it, Lily?"

"I don't need to. I was thinking of what it would be like to wake up each day with you."

His fingers trembled against my cheek. "And?"

"I would love that, Caleb. So very much."

A blinding smile erupted. "God, Lily... I love you."

Hope turned to joy, filling my battered spaces with

new, vibrant life, and my eyes with tears. "I love you, too," I wailed.

Caleb stared at me for a stupefied moment; then my big, magnificent man snatched me in his arms, but not before I caught a suspicious sheen in his eyes.

He fused his lips to mine, and my heart sighed with happiness. Still bound in his arms, I felt him moving. Felt him sink into a seat before he placed me before him.

His hands worshipped my face, my neck, my fingers. Adoring eyes pinned me as he slid his hands under my dress.

"I saw you on TV." His fingers drifted up my thighs.

"Yes, I've been doing a lot of that lately," I whispered.

He nodded. "You looked…incredible."

"Yes, you said that already," I teased.

He hummed as he skimmed the edge of my panties. "I had this fantasy as I watched you give that *Tech-Crunch* interview."

"Yeah?" I was beginning to pant and I didn't even care.

He hooked two fingers into the lace and dragged it down my legs. "Hmm. You were rattling off all these big tech words and numbers. And I promised myself if I ever got you back, I would have you recite the Fibonnaci Sequence while I fucked you long and slow."

My gasp echoed around the large room. "Oh, my God."

He tapped my legs. I stepped out of my panties, and he stuffed them into his jacket pocket. "That's not all. You would be wearing nothing but a choker, those boxy glasses and black heels you wore for the *Wired* cover shoot when you announced you were starting your own company. I'm incredibly proud of you for that, by the way."

My heart threatened to burst with happiness. "Did you watch *all* my interviews?"

"Every single one. Twice. I bought all the magazines, too. I've had a very busy afternoon." He plucked a condom from his wallet, handed it to me, then reached beneath his cummerbund and lowered his zipper.

"Wow. If I didn't know better, I'd say you were obsessed with me, Mr. Steele."

His eyes clung to mine. "It's more than an obsession. You're my reason for breathing."

My fingers shook as I tore open the condom. Then the shaking suffused my whole body as he took out his big, beautiful cock.

I leaned over him, kissed his gorgeous lips before bending lower to kiss the crown of his penis. His strangled curse was music to my ears.

The moment I glided the condom on, he pulled me close, tugged my legs on either side of his lap, and he stared up at me with eyes shining with unfettered love. I braced my hands on his shoulders and sank down, slowly, excruciatingly impaling myself on him. His groan mingled with mine.

When he was fully seated inside me, he held me still.

"There are over a billion stars above our heads right now. But I bet we could touch every one of them if we tried really, really hard."

I cupped his jaw in my hands. "I'd love nothing better than to reach for the stars with you. Oh, Caleb. I love you."

"I love you, too. I'm going to spend the rest of my life making you incredibly, sublimely happy," he vowed.

I sealed my lips to his and silently promised that, for as long as the sun rose each morning, I would love and worship him, too.

* * * * *

PLEASURE PAYBACK

CHAPTER ONE

Neve

A SINGLE WOMAN walks into a bar...

I felt a little bit like a cliché as I entered the VIP-only bar on the twentieth floor of Hotel M and perched on the stool at the far end of the long smoked-glass counter. At nine p.m. on a Thursday night in late May it was surprisingly quiet, with only a few people seated at the tables, the stunning views of Boston at night their backdrop.

The junior suite I'd splashed out eight hundred bucks for had a fully stocked minibar, more than adequate for my needs. If that failed I could order anything from Room Service.

But...

A single woman walks into a bar. At ease and in control. Because she owns several like it across the East Coast.

Much better.

It'd taken risks to get to this point. Bold risks that had fuelled several sleepless nights. Financially, by gambling every last penny I had on this once-in-a-lifetime deal. Emotionally, by attempting to keep my grandparents' legacy alive while also fighting to keep the lines of communication with my mother open despite the bitterness and resentment spewed my way every time I braced myself and called.

That particular thread was frayed to the point where I secretly feared my next phone call would be the one that severed our ties for ever. It was why I hadn't called her in five weeks. Why that dull ache in my chest sharpened every time I thought of reaching out to my one remaining relative even though more often than not she hadn't been there for me.

To stop myself from dwelling on it, I'd channelled all my energy into making sure the ambitious expansion I was pursuing went off without a hitch, while smothering the whispers of doubt at the back of my mind instigated by those very same phone calls.

'Are you sure you know what you're doing, Neve?'

'Shouldn't you leave this to more experienced people?'

'You'll lose everything, then where would you be?'

Cautionary, maternal words that would've touched me had they not echoed the same lack of belief in my abilities from the moment I could walk.

I'd smothered the voice, confident in my business plan and the numbers I'd crunched so hard I could taste them in my sleep.

And it'd paid off. That instinct that this would work had earned me an invite to the big leagues.

My goal was within my grasp—a hard-won affiliation deal between Cahill Hotels and Cephei Hotels, my six small but thriving boutique hotels.

So where was the harm in staying out of my comfort zone for one more night? Besides, this was one of

Boston's most prestigious hotels. The hundred-year-old iconic building, recently bought and expertly renovated by the renowned Mortimer Group, sat on prime real estate on Beacon Hill with majestic views of the Charles River. I'd planned on staying at a cheaper hotel, but had fallen in love with the blend of old-world and contemporary decor. It struck that sweet spot of appealing to young artsy types while catering to a mature demographic. Exactly what I was aiming for with my own hotels.

It also didn't hurt that it happened to be the venue for my meeting.

Excitement fizzed higher.

By this time tomorrow I would've signed the biggest deal of my life and set myself on the road to a wider expansion of the hotel and spa group my grandparents had started sixty years ago as a tiny four-bedroom B & B.

Not bad for an almost twenty-nine-year-old.

The thought widened my smile. Enough for the bartender to pause in the act of lining up shot glasses to look my way, interest sparking in his eyes.

I dimmed my smile a touch as he sauntered towards me.

'What can I get you?'

'Whiskey sour, please,' I said, sliding more firmly onto my seat.

He nodded. 'Coming right up.'

I sighed with relief when he moved away after a brief perusal.

Male attention didn't bother me. Hell, I enjoyed a bit of flirtation when the mood took me. But I preferred to be in control of the situation, always. What my mother called a flaw I saw as the cornerstone that would ensure I didn't end up like her, dependent on the wrong men, depressed and resentful when they inevitably let her down. Because of her I'd learned early in life that total independence was my key to maintaining control.

It was why I'd sworn to build on my grandparents' hard work, why I intended to control my own fate, no matter what. Why I was here tonight, on the cusp of achieving my biggest win yet.

My whiskey sour arrived at the same time as the tall stranger claimed my periphery. A deep compulsion pulled my gaze in his direction; he pulled back the bar stool farthest from me, and hitched one taut, muscled thigh onto it. Bemused, I watched the bartender fall over himself in a hurry to serve him as I wrapped my fingers around the ice-cold glass even as my temperature spiked to furnace-high at the sight of him.

Dry-mouthed, I stared, a hungry tingling sparking inside my belly before nose-diving low and deep.

Dear God, he was hot.

Incandescent.

The kind of *hot* you initially dismissed as impossible without elective surgery. Or as a trick of light. Or an expert make-up artist's brush on a vain model.

As I was busy checking him out, a chilled bottle was placed in front of him. He examined it for several seconds before twisting the cap off his sparkling water. Under the elegant half-moon lampshades hanging over the bar, his hair appeared black until closer examination showed the dark mahogany highlights. A slash of dark eyebrows were gathered in a thunderous frown but they didn't stop me from noticing that he had the most insanely long eyelashes I'd ever seen on a man.

He looked remote. Forbidding.

As he poured the water into a glass, I shamelessly stole the seconds to further examine him. A superbly cut suit draped his body. Dark navy with thin pin-stripes and, underneath it, a matching waistcoat and white shirt, finished off with a stylish tie, currently tugged loose, around a masculine neck that framed a square, rugged jaw sporting designer stubble, and a face so impossibly breathtaking, it was a struggle not to gape like a drooling fool.

I sipped my cocktail, hoping the pleasant burn would calm the butterflies flailing in my belly. All it did was awaken impulses that had gone dormant in the hunt of fulfilling dreams.

The bartender murmured something to him. The stranger shook his head and waved him away with a flick of an elegant hand.

My gaze dropped to that hand. To delicious possi-bilities. To stepping further out of my comfort zone.

I cleared my throat, even then unsure whether I sought to attract his attention or steady my own nerves.

He tensed slightly, his movement slowing. It was the only indication that he'd noticed me. After a moment, he lifted his glass and gulped down half his water.

The bartender sauntered over to me. 'You want an-other?' He nodded to my glass.

I looked down, a little startled to see my almost empty glass. 'Yes, thanks.' He was back moments later with a fresh drink. On the wildest whim, I said, 'A shot of your best whiskey for him too on my tab.' I cocked my head at the stranger. He looked like a single-malt-savoured-slowly kind of guy.

The bartender hesitated. 'You sure about that?' he asked in a low, concerned voice.

I wavered for the tiniest fraction. 'Of course, I'm sure.'

Trepidation and…yes, anticipation scrambled through me as the bartender reached for the bottle from the top shelf, poured a shot and set it in front of the stranger.

He stared at the expensive amber-coloured drink as if it were poison. As if it were his worst enemy and he were moments away from pummelling it into oblivion with his bare fist. After an eternity, long after the bartender had gestured at me and taken a step back, that sexy head swung my way and I was caught in the headlights of his mesmerising stare.

Sharp hazel eyes widened as if, despite sensing me a moment ago, he was surprised by my presence. For one indecent moment, something hot and filthy and carnal twisted in that gaze, firing up the blaze in my belly, conjuring a fleeting burst of feminine satisfaction.

Far from the look he'd given the glass, he stared at me as if he wanted to devour me, stark hunger I'd never glimpsed before stealing over his face for several blistering seconds.

Right before his jaw clenched tight. 'Thanks but no, thanks. I don't pick up women in bars,' he said.

Momentarily dumbfounded, I couldn't speak. Not when I was confronted by further potent scrutiny from his unique, piercing hazel eyes and the cut-glass English accent that sent a pulse of heat straight to my clit.

I relocated my tongue. Assembled enough composure to swivel to face him. 'Great. Neither do I.'

My comeback triggered a twisted smile. Only to disappear seconds later beneath the quiet carnage of whatever was eating him up. I should've left him alone then. Should've listened to instincts I'd trusted above all else thus far. Ones that warned that tangling with this man would be extremely thrilling, but also deadly.

But he was rising from his seat, nudging the glass of whiskey along the counter as he sauntered towards me. Two stools away, he stopped. Stared with a blatant heated interest I felt to the tips of my toes.

'I also don't accept drinks from strangers.' His second delivery wasn't drenched in ice but it was still cool enough to draw a shiver.

For the first time in a long time, I ploughed ahead despite the warnings to retreat. Despite wondering how on earth my mother went back for more of this kind of treatment when the tops of my ears were already burning from one rejection. 'Now I think you're just trying to hurt my feelings.'

One lean shoulder rose and fell. 'You'll get over it, I'm sure,' he said.

His gaze lingered, dropped to my crossed legs, then back up, pausing for longer than was polite on my cleavage, then up to rest on my lips.

The pulse between my legs throbbed harder, my breath fracturing the longer he stared.

Maybe it was his inability to look away, *despite his words*, that bolstered my confidence. Or maybe I was making excuses.

But for whatever reason I wanted to draw him out of the funk eating him up. I was in a celebratory mood and wanted someone to celebrate with. And he intrigued me. A lot. Enough for me to slide off my stool and venture closer, accepting that my motives weren't wholly altruistic.

Long before my last boyfriend, Gray, had tossed his bags into the back of his Chevy and made a false promise to call when he reached his new job in Chicago eight months ago, I knew the relationship was as dead as the lacklustre sex we'd been having. When he'd failed to call, my primary emotion had been relief.

I hadn't been fucked to anywhere near my satisfaction for longer than I could remember.

This stranger, with the harsh, handsome face, brooding eyes and wickedly sexy hands, could cure me of the ache between my legs. Barring that, he could make it so my evening wasn't wracked with the last-minute doubts plaguing me. Doubts that had fuelled my decision to come down to the bar instead of celebrating solo in my room.

He watched me with a dark gleam in his eyes, his nostrils flaring as I paused with one stool between us. Slowly, he blinked, a slightly bewildered look whispering over his features, as if he couldn't make up his mind whether I was friend or foe.

Walk away. Return to the safety of your suite.

My feet had other ideas though. They stayed put, compelled by that look in his eyes.

Time slowly ticked by, the atmosphere thickening as we stared at one another, acknowledged the dirty desire eddying around us.

'You shouldn't let it go to waste.' He tapped a fingernail against the whiskey glass without taking his eyes off me.

'It won't if you drink it.'

His mouth firmed. 'Do you make a habit of buying

four-hundred-dollar shots for strangers?' he asked, one eyebrow quirked.

This time eighteen months ago, that price tag would've made my eyes water. Not any more. Pride swelled inside me for all I'd achieved and I shrugged. 'I can afford it. And you look like you need it.'

He stared at me for a beat, shifted closer and leaned down until his lips brushed my ear. 'You don't have the faintest clue what I need,' he breathed, sending a wild shiver down my spine.

I swallowed as his scent—rich and earthy and mouth-watering—engulfed me. 'Don't I?' I challenged faintly.

Hazel eyes ringed with darkness clashed with mine. 'You're looking for someone to tangle with. Nothing wrong with that. But I'm not your man.' Despite his words, I heard the throb of betraying lust in his voice.

He wanted me, and that dark, torrid longing stopped me from calling quits to this strange but exhilarating exchange. I'd never done this before. But I'd never pulled a multimillion-dollar deal together before either.

His dark intensity was a little scary but that only amped up my buzz.

'You take yourself far too seriously.'

His sensual lips twisted as he straightened. 'You have no idea.'

'Go on, enlighten me,' I invited, aware that he hadn't moved away. If anything, he'd leaned closer.

He stared at me for an age, myriad expressions flitting across his face. A few too fast to catch. Others lingered. Interest. Lust. Bleakness. Hard-edged determination.

'It's private,' he finally said in a tone that reeked of deep, dark secrets.

'If you want privacy, you shouldn't have come to a bar.'

From close by, I heard the bartender's swift intake of breath. I ignored it, keeping my attention on Tall, Dark and Acerbic.

'Tell you what. Let me return the favour and we can call it even, hmm?' He lifted a hand and beckoned the bartender.

I flicked my hand too, belaying the order. 'No need. I'm all set. Two drinks is my limit anyway.'

He flicked a glance at my glass with something approaching approval. 'That's probably wise.'

I raised my glass, wrapped my lips around the thin straw and sucked. The cold tartness went nowhere near cooling the fires his darkened gaze stoked as it landed on my mouth. Beneath the soft layer of my black wrap cocktail dress, my nipples tightened, my skin tingling under his scrutiny.

Whoever this man was, his words were saying one thing but his body was betraying him mercilessly, broadcasting his interest.

Shamelessly feeding off it, I slowly swirled my tongue over my bottom lip.

Hunger, raw and potent, blazed in his eyes then slammed mercilessly into me.

'Did you need something else, Mr Mortimer?' the bartender interrupted.

He blinked, then frowned at the intrusion.

Mr Mortimer? Of The Mortimer Group? Inside, the butterflies in my stomach somersaulted. Surely that wasn't a coincidence.

Did I really just try to buy the owner of this amazing hotel a drink?

The bold and reckless demon inside me grinned wide even as the less effervescent Neve cringed.

But why the hell not? He was wildly attractive, with the kind of sexual charisma that set women's panties alight with alarming frequency. What was wrong with wanting a piece of that?

The grim set to his jaw put paid to that wild fantasy.

I was already at my two-drink limit, a hard cap I'd set myself after witnessing countless times what alcohol did to my mother. The dark depths of despair interspersed with endless bitter rants about the world at large and me in particular whenever she'd had more than a few. Much as I'd told myself that it was the alcohol talking, the barbs she'd thrown my way had found their mark.

Thoughts of my mother dampened my mood. Tucking my purse under my arm, I turned to the bartender. 'Put the drinks on my room, please. Suite 6799.'

I felt Mortimer move, his shadow looming closer. My insides tightened, my pussy throbbing at the thought of further tussling with him.

But as much as I wanted that thrill, my screaming instincts had other ideas. Curbing the need for one last thirst-quenching look, I turned on my heel and walked out of the bar.

Twenty minutes later, fresh from a hot shower, I shrugged into the complimentary satin robe, tying the belt loosely around my waist. Drawn to the spectacular view, I was halfway across the carpeted suite when the hard triple-rap on the door froze my steps.

For some absurd reason my pulse jumped. It could

be many things. The concierge delivering my final bill before I checked out tomorrow. The complimentary turn-down service listed among the numerous guest perks.

Still, my blood thrummed with excitement as I pulled the door open.

He stood with hands rammed deep into his pockets, his hair a little dishevelled and his tie still loose, exposing the beginnings of a mouth-watering, hair-dusted chest.

For a pulse-racing stretch of time, we stared at each other, neither of us making a move.

'You shouldn't blurt out your room number in front of strangers,' he rasped, his gaze climbing from my legs to clash with mine.

'Even the stranger whose hotel I'm staying in?'

Only the fleeting gleam in his eyes said I'd correctly guessed his identity. 'Especially him.'

'Thanks for the tip. And thanks for installing the peephole and latch to ensure I have the choice of only opening the door to people I feel I can trust.'

A muscle ticced in his jaw, a telltale sign that he was fighting urges or demons. 'You think you can trust me, Neve Nolan?'

It shouldn't have made me hot and wet, the fact that a powerful man like him had taken the time to find out my name. But, boy, did it.

I shrugged, and when the robe slipped off one shoulder to reveal my upper arm and the slope of one breast, I didn't adjust it. I stood stock-still and let his gaze caress skin I'd exposed.

He stared long and hard. Then cursed tightly.

'Bloody hell, I shouldn't be here,' he muttered, his fingers clawing through his hair.

He started to turn away.

Something sharp and urgent pierced me. 'And yet here you are.'

He froze. Lust and something harsh swirled through his eyes as our gazes reconnected. 'Tell me to leave you alone, Neve.'

I shrugged again, projecting calm I didn't feel. I didn't want him to walk away but I wasn't going to beg. 'You're a big boy. If you don't want to be here, you know where the elevator is. If not...' I left the sentence hanging, released the door handle and turned my back on him for the second time in under an hour.

I wasn't one for calling bluffs. Yet something urged me to challenge this towering force of a man caught between desire and demons. I put the distance of the suite between us and made it to the window and the view beyond. But not even the spectacular vista of night-time Boston could divert my senses from his solid, overwhelming presence.

The door closed with a sharp snick and my pulse leapt. Through the window's reflection, I watched him prowl towards me. He arrived behind me and stopped, saying nothing, his sandalwood and earthy scent swathing me.

Between one breath and the next, he spun me around, long, lean fingers meshing into my loose hair, gripping it tight enough to send delicious tingles to my pussy. Slowly he tipped my head back, stared deep into my eyes. 'You're an exceptionally beautiful woman, Neve.'

'Thank you,' I murmured, lava-thick lust oozing inside me.

He nodded, a brittle little gesture incongruent with the liquid heat in his eyes. 'But you should be debating the wisdom of letting me entangle you in my life. I'm having a very bad day, you see,' he grated, then gave a hard laugh. 'Scratch that. I'm having a very bad fucking *year.*'

'I can tell. On the flip side, I'm having a pretty good one, with the expectation of a great one tomorrow. The way I see it, we can balance each other out brilliantly. I don't want to celebrate alone and you don't want to sink into that hell I see swirling in your eyes. Correct?'

He drew closer, wedged one thickly muscled thigh between my legs. My burning centre rubbed against his leg and at the moan I let loose, his cock thickened against my hip. 'Beautiful, irresistible *and* intuitive. Where did you come from, Neve Nolan?'

I blinked up at him and smiled when his cock jerked against my leg. 'Connecticut. I'm here in your lovely city for one night only.'

He laughed under his breath. 'This isn't my city. I'm visiting too.'

'Then let's make the most of it,' I replied.

He pondered that for a few seconds, and a little of the chaos in his eyes abated. 'Ships passing in the night, and all that?'

'Hmm. But it would also help if you told me your first name.'

One eyebrow spiked. 'Help with what, exactly?'

'With whose name I scream when you're balls-deep inside me. Or would you like me to scream some random name?'

His fingers tightened a fraction, enough to shower me with fresh waves of decadent tingles. 'No, darling, I most certainly would not. The name you'll want when you hit that special place is Damian.'

I reached for my belt and tugged the ends free. The robe parted enough for him to see I was completely naked underneath.

Enough to draw a rough sound from his throat.

'Nice to meet you, Damian. Now take off your clothes.'

He didn't comply. Not immediately. His gaze dropped to my mouth for the longest time, his eyelids half masts of sinful need he couldn't hide as he released my hair and stepped back. Impatient fingers tugged his tie free and made short work of his shirt. Belt, shoes and socks followed. In less than a minute, Damian Mortimer was down to his boxers.

He was exceptionally built. Ripped in all the right places with a happy trail that drew my gaze down to the thick erection pressed against soft cotton.

Need flooded my system. Hard and fast and merciless. Enough to make me groan and slide my fingers over my belly to the furnace raging between my legs. He gave a thick curse as his gaze latched onto the brazen movement of my fingers.

I was wet. Soaking. And I was more than enjoying the rabid look in his eyes as he watched me caress myself.

He groaned, almost as if against his will.

'You like that?'

One large hand curled around his cock and stroked. 'Fuck, yes.'

With my free hand, I shucked off my robe. My

shoulders met the cool glass and I gasped as my nipples peaked to painful points. 'Come here, Damian.'

Lust propelled him forward, even as a hard look lanced through his eyes. It was that same look I'd seen at the bar after I bought him the drink. But I didn't care. Not enough to stop and examine it. We were both adults and this was a one-night-only thing.

Hands braced on either side of my shoulders, his breathing harsh and frantic, he stared down at the busy fingers between my legs. I raised my chin, aligned my face to his in silent command.

With a grunt, he fused his lips to mine, kissed me with brutal urgency, his tongue tangling with mine as if he couldn't help himself, and, God, it was just what I needed after long fallow months where work dominated my life. To be kissed, *desired*, as if I were the harvest after a terrible famine. My hungry lips clung to his, my moans filling the room as my reawakened body blazed.

Damian plastered his glorious body against mine. When his hands left the glass wall to curl around my nape, I slid my free hand beneath his waistband and grasped his hot, velvety length. He jerked within my closed fist, a tortured grunt leaving his throat at my eager caress.

'Jesus, that feels good.'

The guttural confession made my pussy clench tight, need making my fingers work faster. God, I was close and he hadn't even touched my erogenous zones yet. The wet sounds of our lips and my fingers grew louder and he wrenched away.

'Need a taste.'

Still brazen, I shook my head. 'Not yet. I get to go first.'

His eyes darkened until they were almost black save for the tiny gold flecks within the burning depths. 'You want to wrap that gorgeous mouth around my cock?' he croaked.

'I want nothing to occupy your mind except how good your cock feels sliding down my throat,' I replied, gliding sinuously down the glass until my knees hit the soft carpet.

A wild tremor shook his frame as he stared slack-jawed down at me. At my parted lips. Past my hard-tipped breasts to the fingers working my pussy.

'Tell me you don't need that.'

A spasm of bleakness darted over his face and he shut his eyes for a split second. 'I need it. More than you could possibly know.'

I offered him another smile. One that slowly disappeared as he pushed his boxers down his muscular thighs and kicked them away.

Sweet heaven.

He was thick and long enough to elicit a momentary pang of alarm. But need eroded alarm, leaving behind savage hunger.

The back of his hand traced my cheek in a jerky caress before he recaptured my nape. With one hand braced on the wall, he slid his length between my lips.

Eagerly I welcomed him, wrapping my lips around his bell-shaped head before gliding my tongue over his slit. His salty, heady essence exploded on my tongue, dragged a whimper from deep inside. One taste and I wanted more. When his hips drew back I chased after him, greedily meeting his thrust.

We both groaned when he hit the back of my throat.

I glanced up his spectacular body, our gazes clashing as I sucked him deep. His nostrils flared wide, then, unable to resist giving me what I wanted, Damian began to fuck my face. With every penetration I took him deeper, wanting as much as he was willing to give.

'God. You're bloody spectacular,' he growled.

The sexy, guttural voice made me wetter. I sank my middle finger deep, feverishly imagining him filling me up until I was stretched tight, until there was nothing but him.

His fingers tightened on my nape and with a harsh groan, Damian exploded in my mouth. The force of his climax spiked my lust and I rode the wild, frenzied wave.

Lost in mindless pleasure, I barely noticed him move away, grasp my arms and lower me to the carpet. But I felt the heat of his body when he covered mine with his, when he brushed his fingers over my mouth and caught my gaze.

'Christ, did you just come sucking me off?' he demanded hoarsely.

'Hmm,' I murmured, my hips still riding the tail end of my climax.

He leaned closer, brushed his lips over mine before trailing kisses over my jaw and neck. 'Holy shit, I don't think I've seen anything sexier,' he rasped in my ear. My shiver drew a laugh from him. 'I hope you're not overly sensitive. Because I don't think I can wait to fuck you.'

He reached for his trousers, pulled out a condom and tugged it on. 'On your knees,' he growled.

I rolled over and surged up onto my hands and

knees, dragged my hair over one shoulder so I could watch him position himself behind me. 'Hurry.'

A smile twisted his mouth as his eyes met mine. 'Is that gorgeous pussy hot for me?'

'Yes. I need you.'

The smile dropped from his mouth, followed by his gaze a second later. The inkling that I'd just committed a faux pas rushed out of my head the instant Damian surged hard and deep inside me.

I screamed, my fingers digging into the carpet as searing pleasure shot up my spine. Firm, almost cruel hands dug into my waist and held me still as he withdrew and plunged deep inside again. As anticipated, Damian was thick enough to fill me almost to the point of pain despite my slickness. That added bite dragged another scream from me as he slammed in from behind, setting a pace that made my back arch in bliss.

'God, yes! Just like that,' I moaned.

One hand moulded my butt, trailed up my spine to rest between my shoulders. He pushed my torso down to the carpet, and I screamed all over again as the angle seated his cock deeper inside me. Pure instinct had me dragging my legs wider apart, and with one last thrust, I started to unravel.

Clever fingers tormented my clit as the first wave hit me, prolonging my release until my body was trapped in relentless convulsions. Just when I thought I'd crawl out of my own skin with the savagery of my climax, Damian roared with his own release, then stilled inside me.

We collapsed onto the carpet, for the longest time saying nothing as we caught our breaths.

Then a smile I couldn't stop creased my face.

'I knew I liked your hotel.'

He chuckled, a deep but rough sound. As if he hadn't laughed for a while. From our curious exchange tonight, I guessed he probably hadn't. 'Just *like*?'

'Fine, I *really* like it.'

His eyes gleamed. 'Which part do you like the most?'

'I have to choose?'

He wrapped a hand around my waist. 'Let's start with this room.'

'Everything. The lamps. The view. The bed.'

'Hmm. We haven't made it to the bed yet. What especially do you like about it?'

'It's sturdy. It could pass for an antique even though I know it's not. It gives the guest a feeling like they're sleeping in a bed fit for a king or queen. Or a naughty courtesan sneaking in for a tryst.'

He stiffened slightly. 'Is that what turns you on, Neve? Illicit assignations with strangers you meet in bars?'

My breath caught on a dart of hurt. 'If you're trying to be offensive, don't waste your time. I've never done anything like this before but I don't regret it.'

I read his scepticism loud and clear. Told myself I didn't care.

I knew my truth but couldn't help adding, 'There's nothing wrong with that if all parties are free and consenting adults.'

He inhaled slowly, his gaze turning turbulent. I sensed his withdrawal even though his arm tightened around me. 'And what would you have me do in this tryst of yours?'

I draped my arms around his neck. 'I'd like to move to the bed, test my theory for real.'

'As you wish.' His concession held a definite bite.

Perhaps I should've called a halt to things then. But Damian Mortimer was kissing me as he carried me across the floor. Potent kisses I wanted to enjoy just for a few more hours. We were consenting adults after all.

So why fight it?

Damian

I tried.

Fought to resist her.

When I couldn't, I wanted to punish her for reminding me of everything I wanted to forget. For tempting me enough to break the rigid rules I'd ring-fenced my life with for twelve long months. Most of all, I wanted to punish her for unwittingly re-enacting that sordid little scene downstairs.

The one that reminded me of the worst moment of my life.

That reminded me of why I was here on the wrong side of the pond when I yearned to be back in London, in the place I thrived and loved the most.

The part of me that knew it was irrational to take things out on this woman whose brazenness shouldn't have been a turn-on—and yet had touched parts of me I'd thought were withered and dead—winced. But hell, I was drowning beneath the bitterness and vitriol festering inside me.

And she…

I tossed her on the bed, watched the most beautiful woman I'd seen in a long time beckon me with a come-hither smile.

She was irresistible. Just enough for my needs. Because after that phone call, after hearing the anger and bitterness and disappointment, I'd wanted to dive into a bottle of whiskey. I'd wanted to forget that I'd betrayed the one person closest to me.

Gideon Mortimer.

My flesh and blood. But more than that, my best friend.

But even that avenue was now closed to me.

A casual drink at a bar was what had started my descent into hell.

But Neve Nolan wasn't off limits. She was wide open and willing, a tangible port in a black sea of despondency and frustration.

I intended to take with no regrets.

Just for tonight, I would break my own rules. And if regret came in the morning, I'd toss that too into the seething abyss that was my life.

CHAPTER TWO

Neve. Two years later...

DESPISE. LOATHE. ABHOR.

Nope, none of them quite fit.

I hate Damian Mortimer.

There. That was better. I've hated him with every single breath I've taken for the last two years. Since he took my offer of relief and turned it completely against me. Since he crippled my business and trashed eighteen months of back-breaking work and sacrifice with nothing more than a few gruffly muttered words to Malcolm Cahill.

This TV show was my one attempt to exact some payback.

Every day since that fateful morning after, when Malcolm Cahill shattered my dreams, I've vowed to teach Damian Mortimer an unforgettable lesson.

That he hadn't even bothered to hide his part in the demise of my affiliation deal with Cahill Hotels was just the first in a despicable series of low blows that had started with his disappearance from my bed the morning after our night together. Hard on its heels had come Cahill's phone call.

'I'm sorry but I've had second thoughts, Miss Nolan. My partner, Damian Mortimer, believes this deal isn't as viable as I previously thought. I'll no longer be going forward...'

Bruised but undaunted, I'd risen like a phoenix from the ashes of near catastrophe, rebranded myself from Cephei Hotels to Nevirna Resort and Spa Hotels and seen steady growth, with the best quarter so far under my belt. Something I hoped my grandparents would be proud of, even if my mother believed I'd made a mistake.

My gut clenched against the dart of pain as my thoughts lit on my mother. Another area of my life Damian Mortimer's betrayal hadn't helped. Another area I needed to heal, despite the sinking feeling that the promise I'd made to my grandparents might never be fulfilled. They'd gone to their graves never having repaired their rift with their daughter. They'd made me promise to keep trying with my mother.

Lately, that battle seemed unwinnable.

Fresh from the loss I'd suffered at Damian's and Cahill's hands, I'd called my mother in a moment of weakness, for a shoulder to cry on.

Her advice had been the same—sell the resort she believed was hers by birthright and give her her due share. My refusal had estranged us for six months.

But I'd become adept at problem solving and putting out fires through sheer hard work.

The incredible success I'd achieved in those two years had drawn the attention of the producers of *Raider's Den*—a TV show I wouldn't usually lower myself to. But the discovery that this was a Damian Mortimer project was too tempting to resist. What better way to beat the devil than on his home turf?

If the rumours were true and he planned to return to England, this was my last chance to teach one particularly arrogant, insanely sexy Brit a lesson.

With a deep breath, I settled into my seat and read through the pre-show paperwork one last time. The show had been separated into four segments according to specialised industries. My segment contained sixteen young contestants, each hoping for start-up funding and partnership for their business in the hospitality industry.

I was scanning the list of contestants when the double doors to the conference room opened.

Sunlight pouring through wide rectangular windows on the fortieth floor of Mortimer Plaza, the five-star hotel and retail tower in Manhattan, lovingly illuminated the stunning physique of the man who entered.

He wore a suit. Bespoke. Naturally.

For several betraying heartbeats, anger took a step back to accommodate the hot spike of lust that lanced my belly before detonating in my pussy. Even as I clawed back control and fought the urge to squirm in my seat, the traitorous dampening between my thighs mocked me.

It brutally reminded me that the only thing better than Damian Mortimer in a three-piece suit was Damian Mortimer naked. Gloriously ripped. Utterly divine.

His soul as dark as a tar pit.

Remember *that*.

But even the stern admonition didn't stop my recollection of spectacular, mind-melting sex.

I'd believed I knew what good sex was before I met Damian. Oh, how pathetically wrong I was.

If I despised one thing more than the man himself, it was that since our night together my body hadn't come even close to craving what he gave to me with anyone else. I only had to think about him for every cell in my body to come alive, for my needy pussy to remind me of its continued famine and for those X-rated thoughts about that arrogant bastard to hit the play button.

The dating app my assistant had defiantly signed me up to had resulted in two mind-numbingly boring dates, after which I'd deleted it.

Even my vibrator had taken a much-needed holiday, leaving me pent up and aggravatingly in need of a good seeing to.

Which made me hate him even more.

So was it any surprise that by the time his towering six-foot-plus frame reached me I was already seeing red?

His gaze skittered past the other mentors already seated as if they were part of the furniture, sauntering as if he weren't twenty minutes late. 'Gentlemen,' he drawled on his way to his seat at the top of the table.

Then his eyes lit on me. His stride didn't break but a hard light flickered in his gaze and muscles twitched in his jaw. Then followed the slow elevation of one eyebrow.

'Neve, I didn't know you were a part of this meeting.'

'It's Miss Nolan, and I'm shocked, *Mr Mortimer.* I was under the impression you knew everything.'

He didn't so much as flinch at my sarcastic tone but his eyes reflected wariness and mild shock.

He probably wasn't used to women talking back to him and preferred everyone to ask how high when he said jump. He'd kept the producers hanging on for weeks before finally committing to the latest *Raider's Den* production last week.

He probably hadn't even read the brief that announced that three of the members of the panel wouldn't be returning for the new season and would be replaced by three new mentors, including me.

I took a calming breath. 'I hate to throw out clichés so early in the morning but time *is* money for me, Mr Mortimer. So if you're certain you're absolutely present, can we get started?'

That drew varying looks from my fellow Raiders, ranging from bemusement to wariness. One sniggered.

A scathing look from Damian wiped the look off the man's face.

'I had my assistant send my apologies twenty minutes ago to say I was running late. If that won't suffice, I'll be sure to draw you a pint of blood once the meeting ends if that's what you need to appease you?'

I'd silenced my phone for the meeting so any incoming emails wouldn't have registered. I hit the home button on my phone and there it was, a message from Damian Mortimer.

Shit.

Stupid heat crawled up my neck but it didn't stop me from boldly meeting his sardonic gaze. 'Keep your blood. I wouldn't have the first idea what to do with it.'

'You sure?' he enquired mockingly, one hand reaching for the leather binder in front of him.

'These days I'm just a little more selective with my tastes. Shall we proceed?'

He paused, eyes narrowed, his jaw tightening at the insult. 'Since I'm chairing the meeting, you'll have to curb your enthusiasm for another minute while I get up to speed. Can you do that, Miss Nolan?'

I forced a smile, tried to quell the effect of the deep-voiced, cut-glass English accent that reminded me far too much of a certain young royal prince and shrugged. 'Of course, although I would've thought you'd be all caught up by now.' Another shameless dig, but I couldn't help myself.

His eyes gleamed with that flint-hard expression I'd spotted the first time we met. Some things hadn't changed, then? Whatever demons he'd harboured two years ago still snapped at his heels.

Satisfaction I'd expected to feel about that never arrived, leaving me faintly bewildered. I forced the sensation away and watched his gaze drop to the document before him. For the sixty seconds he took to speed-read, my stupidly compulsive gaze dragged over his face, noted the harsher lines etched into his features.

There were other changes too. Lips that had delivered magnificent orgasms were no less sensual now than they'd been two years ago but they appeared sterner, as if he spent too long pursing them. The skin around his eyes looked strained and his hair was longer. And yet, not a single thing detracted from the jaw-dropping package.

His head reared up suddenly, and I couldn't avoid the piercing gaze that crashed into mine or the eyebrow elevated in silent query.

'Let's get started. First of all, welcome to the team, Miss Nolan.'

Okay, not what I was expecting. 'Thank you,' I responded briskly.

He stared a moment longer. The scrutiny was fleeting, but my skin reacted feverishly to the heat of his gaze on my face and chest before he swung his gaze around the room.

'Gary, Preston, welcome,' he addressed the other mentors. 'The rest of you know the brief. This may be a TV show but it's a profit-making venture, catering to the discerning. Our viewers are in the upper-middle-class demographic. They're engaged by savvy, intelligent investments, not by us playing up to the cameras. I don't need to tell you that if you make a crap investment, it's not just your money on the line but your reputation. And more than that, it's *my* reputation. So don't fuck it up.' His gaze travelled the room, met mine, lingered.

Gary Withers leaned forward. The newspaper mogul had branched into venture capitalism a decade ago, and was known for his aggression. He was definitely one to watch. 'Heads up, when I see something I like, I go after it, no holds barred. I didn't come here to pussyfoot around.'

Damian's gaze left mine after lingering one more second. A second that felt like a whole hour and left me annoyingly breathless.

'The show isn't live. It can be stopped at any time. If you need reminding that you're being an ass, Gary, it'll happen.'

Damian's evenly delivered words drew chuckles around the room, but the steely undertone registered.

It was clear who was running the show.

The need to take him on, and win, burned brighter. 'We're sticking to the two offers, two mentors maximum per pitch, correct?' I asked.

He nodded. 'Correct. It's been a tacit rule since the show started.'

'But not everyone's averse to bending the rules, or screwing a fellow mentor over, are they?'

The atmosphere grew strained, thick with the unspoken words I wanted to flaunt at him. Those laser eyes narrowed again. 'If you're seeking an ironclad promise, Miss Nolan, you're not going to get one.'

I smiled, letting my cynicism drape my lips. 'Of course I'm not. Where's the fun in that, right?'

His gaze dropped to my mouth, blatant mockery in his stare. 'Exactly. Don't forget that this is business. But no reason why it can't be pleasurable, as well.'

The note in his voice caught me deep and heavy, snagged at the taut strings of lust I'd thought were long since slackened from disuse. Beneath the conference table, I squeezed my thighs together as his gaze lingered, the green in his eyes standing out the longer we traded stares.

A throat cleared. 'Since we're talking…possible leeway, how about we lift the rule on pursuing prospects outside the show?' Preston Roper, owner of Roper Casinos, asked.

'Once the six-month non-compete deal with your fellow Raiders passes, sure,' Damian replied.

Preston groaned. 'Seriously? Six months? You know how quickly the market can change in six months.'

'Not my problem,' Damian replied. 'Anything else?'

Other queries arose and were batted away by Damian. The man knew his stuff. I couldn't deny it. But the devil was an expert in his line of work too.

'Just so we're clear, can you confirm that you haven't seen the pitch list? That you haven't cherry-picked projects for yourself?'

He stiffened and a chilly breeze wafted through the room. 'Are you calling my integrity into question, Miss Nolan?'

Yes! 'I'm the newbie. I'm making sure we're all on the same page.'

Long masculine fingers drummed on the table for a moment before he replied, 'As it's been since the be-ginning, only the senior producer knows what the can-didates will pitch. They're picked based on a module that matches our business needs with the candidates. Otherwise we'd all be wasting our time. If I wanted to attach my name to a fixed, mindless reality TV show, I wouldn't be on this project.'

I raised my eyebrow. 'So that's a definite no, then?' I goaded.

A tight smile flickered over his lips before he an-gled his chair away from me. 'If there are no more questions, I'll let the producers know we're good to go.'

Satisfied I'd made my point, I closed my folder and stood.

'A word please, Miss Nolan?'

Although framed like a question, one look at his taut face said it wasn't. He couldn't have stopped me from leaving, of course, but I was intrigued by what he had to say. More than I suspected was wise.

The others trickled out, and immediately the atmo-sphere thickened. Or it could've just been my inability to take a full breath around this man. Irritation ramped up. 'I have somewhere else to be, Mr Mortimer.'

He nodded briskly. 'I won't keep you long. Please sit. And it's Damian, as you well know.'

I raised a surprised brow as I retook my seat. 'Two *pleases* in one minute. That must be a record for you.'

Several seconds ticked by as he eyed me. 'Are we going to have a problem, Neve?'

A hot little fizzle lit up my midriff when he said my name—soft, sexy, dangerous, much like the way he had that night. I actively ignored it.

'You tell me. There's nothing in the contract that stipulates one member of the panel isn't allowed to fuck another. And despite all the professional vibes you've been attempting to throw out, I can tell you're a little...*affected*. So maybe you should be asking yourself that question?'

He cursed under his breath. 'You go straight for the jugular, don't you?'

'I'm just stating facts.'

Firm lips pursed as a muscle ticced in his temple. 'Did you read the email my assistant sent?'

The question threw me for a second. I rallied quickly. 'What does it matter?'

'If you had, you'd have seen that I was late because I was dealing with a personal matter. One that went on longer than I anticipated. I detest being late but it couldn't be helped. You have my word it won't happen again.'

The unfettered admission threatened to dissolve my anger, much as I'd let the bleakness in his expression sway me two years ago. But the simple truth was Damian Mortimer believed himself above the rules that governed mere humans. So what if he admitted to a single flaw? He had more damning ones lodged in his soul. Ones he probably didn't think he needed to answer for. 'If that's supposed to be an apology for your tardiness, I accept.'

'Doesn't answer my question though. This is my last appearance on this show. I want things to go smoothly. So again, are we going to have a problem?'

'With my participation in this show? Not a one,' I replied.

'Why do I sense you're playing semantics with me?'

'You have a terrible imagination?' Or a much-needed prickle of a guilty conscience?

His eyes narrowed. 'You seem…different. Were you this distrusting of everyone two years ago or have I done something in particular to earn yours?' he enquired tersely.

Hell, no, he wasn't going to do this. 'Are you serious?'

'When it comes to business I'm nothing but. But if I recall our one and only encounter was less business, more…something else?'

Something else. Something that didn't even warrant its proper definition in his book?

Sex. Filthy, sheet-clawing, scream-yourself-hoarse fucking.

I searched his face for acknowledgement of what had been a highly memorable encounter for me in more ways than one. All I got was the apathetic stare of a bored business mogul.

Had I been *that* forgettable?

It stung. And in that burn my resolve to make him pay solidified.

Perhaps it was feminine pride getting the better of me. Perhaps it was that indomitable aversion to failure sparked to painful life one unforgettable night spent in a child protection service's halfway house when the threat of losing everything had loomed large and scarily real. Unwilling truth be told, twenty years later, that threat of being alone, of never seeing the mother who'd wilfully admitted to caring very little about me, still lingered at the back of my throat and chose times like these to manifest itself, much to my dismay.

Whichever it was, as I watched him, my goal settled heavy and unmoving inside me.

Damian would succumb to me sexually.

Before we were through with this project, I'd make it impossible for him to forget me. This time *he* would be the one stumbling away in bewilderment.

Purpose sizzled, then blazed. Through my veins and all the way to my fingertips. Until I could see nothing, *taste* nothing but the need for retribution.

Maybe I'd known this was coming. Perhaps it was why I'd chosen my clothes with extra care today, why I'd drifted past a closet full of pencil skirts and matching jackets to settle on the low-cleavage pinstriped dress with the short pleated skirt and matching bolero jacket, complemented by my highest work heels. It was definitely why I'd made an appointment with my hair stylist yesterday, shaved my legs and dabbed on my favourite perfume.

It meant that when I leaned back and casually freed the single button holding the jacket fastened, Damian managed to hold out for all of three seconds before his not so jaded gaze dropped to my breasts. And when I rose from the table and casually walked to the nearest window, I didn't need to look back to know his eyes were fixated on my gym-honed ass.

Time ticked by as I leaned on the narrow sill, pretending interest in the frenzied bustle of Lower Manhattan until the force of his stare branded my skin. Until the heat pulsing between my legs, frantically rousing my lethargic libido, compelled me to turn around.

I perched against the window, subtly angling my body towards the sunlight. 'Trust is earned. As for distrust...' I shrugged. 'Let's just say I've learned to start with a negative balance and let those who are worth it win their way into my graces.'

Damian shifted in his seat. Eyes two shades darker than they'd been minutes ago rose from my hips, paused on the small but tasteful diamond pendant stroking my cleavage, to my face. 'That's a jaded way to approach life, isn't it?'

'Didn't you refuse a drink I bought you back in Boston on those same grounds?'

His eyes narrowed. 'Those were different circumstances.'

'And the rumour that you've resigned from six projects in the last month. Is that boredom or because you've stretched yourself too thin?'

A watchful gleam entered his eyes. 'It's neither. Every partner I've dealt with has walked away more than content, not that I owe you an explanation for the way I operate.'

But you owe me an explanation for why you stabbed me in the back for no reason!

I reined in anger and hurt. 'By the same token, I

don't owe you an explanation on how I approach my relationships.'

We stared each other down for a long silent stretch. Then his mouth twitched. 'If nothing else, our friction will make for good entertainment.'

I forced a smile. 'And that's all that matters in the long run, isn't it? Good *entertainment*?'

Another frown attacked his forehead. 'With all parties walking away with a handful of sound business deals, of course.'

'Of course,' I echoed, unable to keep bitterness from staining my voice.

Damian rose and approached. A couple of feet from me, he stopped. This close, with the sun highlighting every feature, it was difficult to look away from his physical perfection. 'I was under the impression that you were a strong, level-headed woman who wouldn't let one encounter cloud her business judgment. Are you going to prove me wrong?' he taunted baldly.

God, I hate, hate, hate *Damian Mortimer.*

By the skin of my teeth, I managed to pin my smile in place. 'Are you referring to the same encounter where you played hard to get when I bought you a drink but couldn't resist showing up at my hotel room afterwards with a hard cock and a couple of tired one-liners?'

Annoyance flared his nostrils. 'You think telling you you're beautiful was a glib one-liner?'

I cursed the heat staining my cheeks. 'I've heard more original lines.'

'It was true then. It's true now. One thing you should know about me, I believe in the truth at all times, Neve. Even when it's brutal to hear,' he said in a deep matter-of-fact voice that still transmitted straight between my legs.

God, how could he be so detached, so insufferable and yet virtually stroke my clit with a few choice words?

My flush deepened. 'But you believe I'm the type of woman to let flattery or sex get in the way of business? Or do you imagine I'm secretly holding out hope for something else?'

His gaze blazed bright before it dropped to my lips. My stupidly tingling lips. 'You didn't exactly hate what happened between us,' he murmured. 'You were just as enthusiastic as I was once you let me in.'

I didn't. And I was. It was what happened the next morning I had a huge problem with. 'Like you said, *Mr Mortimer*, whatever friction we create will play well for the cameras. So what are you worried about?'

He visibly reined himself in, a stark look shadowing his eyes before he shook it off. 'I don't like surprises. If you're hiding something up your sleeve...'

I couldn't help myself. I chuckled.

Irritation sparked his eyes. 'Did I say something amusing?'

'Amusing? No. Ironic, yes. You want assurances? Well, I can assure you that it's going to be one hell of a ride.'

CHAPTER THREE

Damian

*STUNNING. EXQUISITE. BREATHTAKING.*

Three inadequate words that sprung to mind when I first saw Neve Nolan in my hotel bar two years ago.

Three words that still didn't do justice to the woman staring me down with fire in her eyes and determination etched into her captivating face.

My unfettered reaction to her then had propelled me to do the unthinkable. I'd dropped my guard. Put myself in a situation I'd known I'd regret the next morning without taking into account how much. Or the mess it would create in the wake of slowly uncovering the truth of what had happened the night I'd supposedly betrayed Gideon.

The growing possibility that I might have been drugged by someone I'd trusted had fucked me up worse than I'd imagined.

Long before that night in Boston, trust had been a shitty mirage I'd given up on. Once upon a time I'd had an innocent child's trust that my parents would stick around, deliver a modicum of care and attention in a family seething in dysfunction and strife. They hadn't.

My only truth was hard work and the bone-deep knowledge that everyone in my life had an agenda and a price.

Unsurprising, therefore, that I'd been in a worse than dire mood when Neve had crossed my path.

I'd been reeling from the possibility that there might not be a way of repairing the bridges I'd burned, and my encounter with Neve couldn't have come at a worse time. Compounding my mistakes by repeating them, by succumbing to that filthy temptation when I should've hit the button for my penthouse suite instead of the one that led to Suite 6799... Well, that had been yet another demon I'd been prepared to live with.

But regardless of my personal foibles, I wasn't a Mortimer in name only. Regardless of my mood, I'd achieved what I'd gone to Boston to do—assess the viability of merging one of Mortimer Group's smaller but hugely successful companies with Cahill Hotels, and a lesser known outfit. I'd advised Cahill to reject the bid from Cephei in favour of another hotel chain who were a better fit. The Cahill deal was one of many successes that had fattened the family coffers while I'd continued to search for truth and answers.

Now, three long years later, my investigators had exhausted every avenue to find the evidence of Penny's treachery.

Now Gideon would be forced to listen.

Acid bitterness bit deep, as it did every time I remembered the consequences of letting down my guard.

That particular mushroom cloud still hung above my head, contaminating my every interaction. My family hadn't exactly shunned me, but it was probably because they didn't know the full truth.

I sucked in a breath, pulled myself together and re-focused on Neve.

She'd signed on the dotted line to participate in *Raider's Den* before I had been made aware of her involvement. By then it had been too late to…what? Get her thrown off the show? Further complicate my life with a possible lawsuit?

She wasn't thrilled to see me. Perhaps I could use that to keep her at arm's length despite the havoc her close proximity was already wreaking on my libido. Because it was becoming clear that my chaos-loving demons might have severely compromised my judgment when we'd first met, but my body's unfettered reaction to her when I'd walked into this room today was brazen evidence that the chemistry that'd compelled me to her suite that night still raged strong.

Hell, she was even more spectacular now than she'd been two years ago. My dick had surged to life at the first sight of her, and the damn thing hadn't subsided since.

Well, too bloody bad.

I was done empire-building on this side of the Atlantic.

My mouth twisted at the thought of what Great-Grandfather Mortimer would've made of my particular situation. Probably slapped me on the back with pride that I could still make millions for the family trust even with betrayal staining my bones, my personal life in shreds and my soul in tatters.

I stared into the slate-blue eyes assessing me. She was up to something. The fire burned too bright in her eyes, for starters.

Unfortunately that fire only reminded me of the

blaze we'd created, the thrilling noises she'd made when I'd fucked her. As crashing and burning went, the all-night-long fucking in her suite had singed deep, left an indelible mark on my cracked soul.

To make matters worse, the downside of my stringent no-booze-thanks-to-Penny ban meant every sizzling second of our encounter was seared into my memory. Every slide of Neve's silken skin, every hot gasp as I'd rammed into her unbelievably tight pussy had echoed in my head for a very long time after I'd walked away from her. For weeks, I'd sported a hard-on that had abated only after a teeth-clenching jerking off.

In another time and place, she would've been a prize worth pursuing.

Not today.

Not with a very personal, way-past-due goal of righting wrongs in front of me.

Neve Nolan, with her magnificent body draped in clothes that displayed her very fuckable assets, would be resisted on every front.

Her lips moved, drawing my attention to her plump, lightly glossed mouth. The memory of sliding my cock between those lips, the enthusiastic way she'd sucked me off, almost drew a groan from my throat.

I frowned. 'Beg your pardon?'

'I said your phone's buzzing. You should get that. No doubt your highly exclusive presence is urgently required elsewhere,' she said dryly.

Yeah, she was seriously pissed about something. Absently, I reached for my phone. One glimpse of the London number and every ounce of my focus shifted.

Chest tightening, I started to press the answer button. Then hesitated.

Neve was watching me, had most likely caught whatever was reflected on my face. I schooled my features. 'I need to take this. I'll see you tomorrow morning for the first day of filming.'

Her brisk nod belied the curiosity in her eyes. I watched her walk away, unable to stop my gaze from roaming her backside and jaw-dropping legs as she left the room.

The insistent buzz dragged my attention to the phone.

Aunt Flo. As close to a mother as I could get despite my own mother being alive and well.

I stabbed the answer button. 'Did you get my message?'

'You have better manners than that, dear boy,' she snapped.

I breathed out slowly. 'It's been a testy morning.' My patience was running thin on all fronts.

'It's been a testy few *years* for us all.'

My fingers tightened around the phone. 'Regardless, the stonewalling ends now. It's time.' The oppressive guilt wasn't getting lighter. It suffocated me even more these days, the passage of time an amplified klaxon I could no longer ignore.

No matter what had happened that night three years ago, it was time to face it.

'Some would say it's too little too late. Or too much too soon, depending on which side of the fence you're standing.'

'Too bad if my timing isn't convenient for everyone,' I snapped, frustrated anger licking through me.

She sighed. 'It's never going to be good for one of you. For what it's worth, I'm proud of you for taking the bull by the horns.'

The pit in my stomach yawed. 'In case you've forgotten, I've been trying to wrestle this damned bull for three years.'

'I'm aware. But you may have to give it a little more time. The company is in the middle of a delicate negotiation—'

'The Russian stadium deal,' I said. As a top executive, I received regular memos on all high-level deals.

'Yes. And I have my hands full dealing with some of your more pig-headed relatives on the board, not to mention attempting to manage Gideon.'

Hearing his name tightened the band around my chest. 'Why does he need managing?' I asked with more than a little snap. The Gideon I knew could manage the family company I'd been meant to co-head with him in his sleep.

Aunt Flo hesitated, making me grit my teeth. 'What's going on, Flo?'

'Your cousin is suffering a bit of a...regression.'

'In what way?'

'In all the bad ways. When he's not working himself into the ground, he's partying too much at that private club of his. He's been spiralling for months. It's only a matter of time before he completely unravels. The family's meeting this week to decide—'

'You better not be thinking of ousting him,' I butted in icily. 'Not after everything he's done for the company.'

'He won't be if I have anything to do with it. He'll hate me for telling you this but I know you're just as iron-willed as he and liable to do something rash, so this is just to give you context.'

Bitter laughter barked out of me. 'Rash? I listened when you said relocating to the States was what was best for all. But enough is enough. It's been three years.'

'I know it's been hard for you, son.'

She didn't know the half of it and I wasn't sure I was ready to tell her the true extent of what Penny had done. Hell, *I* was still trying to wrap my head around the fact that she'd *drugged* me. That deep suspicion now dictated I checked and rechecked every drink I took in public like some paranoid fucker. 'Good, then you should know I'm wrapping things up here and I'm coming home in the next few weeks with or without this thing being resolved. I'd prefer the former but it won't stop me either way.'

'What did I do to deserve the number of grey hairs you two are dishing out to me?'

A reluctant smile broke through my frustration. 'I have it on good authority that you have an excellent colourist in Sloane Square.'

'He's earned his money in the last few months, that's for sure,' she quipped, then sighed again. 'Gideon is preoccupied with this Russian deal. You occupy yourself with wrapping up your life in America. Leave everything else to me.'

'For now, Aunt Flo. Understand that I won't let this be for ever.' I ended the call nowhere near satisfied by the outcome.

Waves of frustration, anger and guilt rolled over me, followed closely by the yawning pit of despair and shame that inevitably arrived with it. The black hole of unanswered questions didn't erode the reality that I'd let myself down in the most spectacular way.

Two drinks that had turned into three, then four. Then…total blackout.

Somewhere along the line that night, I'd let my guard down and trusted Penny Winston-Jones, Gideon's ex-fiancée.

Only she hadn't been his ex…

And in so doing had betrayed the one person who meant the most to me.

I gripped my phone tighter, the urge to go against Aunt Flo's advice pummelling me. Only the reminder that she'd been there for me when my own parents abandoned me stopped me.

She would probably forgive me eventually if I went against her advice but could I afford to add another black mark against me?

I slid my phone back into my pocket just as Rachel, my executive assistant, knocked and entered.

'Your next appointment is here, sir,' she announced.

As the primary representative for The Mortimer Group, I'd freed myself from the everyday constraints of a single role to explore deals that would suit the family company. It was meant to be a temporary deviation from my usual role as President of Global Expansion so Jasper, my younger brother, could learn the ropes. The grand plan had been to eventually co-CEO the entire Mortimer Group with Gideon.

In the aftermath of Penny's treachery, that idea had crashed and burned along with our relationship, resulting in this self-imposed, godforsaken exile. One I intended to end *ASAP* now my investigators had presented me with the near certain facts of what had happened to me that night.

Briefly, I toyed with cancelling the meeting, calling fuck it to the whole day and burning rubber out of Manhattan. I could head to the Hamptons, grab my surfboard and pound the waves until I was too tired to think. Or I could jump on my plane, head to Colorado, pick a mountain and climb it.

I rejected both ideas. Years of trying had shown the futility of attempting to outrun my demons. Staying right here, pursuing The Mortimer Group's best interest, would at least bring a modicum of satisfaction.

So I nodded to Rachel. 'Show him in.'

I'd be done here in another two or three weeks. A month, tops.

Then I intended to throw the gates of hell wide open and confront the devil.

Neve

The warehouse in the Meatpacking District in Manhattan where the latest series of *Raider's Den* was being filmed had been decorated to resemble a pirate ship. Treasure chests with costume jewellery spilt out over red embroidered silk strategically placed around a wide rectangular platform on which were set six throne-like antique leather armchairs.

On the far side of the wall hung two banners with a matte black imprint of a skull and crossbones denoting the show's name. The rest of the space was draped in blood-red curtains, cherry-oak tables and black, red and white spotlights.

The whole marauder vibe added dramatic tension to

the show and even though I wanted to roll my eyes as my heels clicked on the hardwood plank from the audition area towards my designated seat, I had to grudgingly admit that the set designer had done a fabulous job. The scene was perfect. Enough to make me tingle.

Applicants who braved the plank to present their ideas had to bring their A games. The formidable panel wouldn't be a walk in the park.

I'd arrived an hour early not just to stop the butterflies in my stomach from turning into crows, but also so as not to be wrong-footed in any aspect of this project.

But Damian was already there, seated in prime position in the centre, once again impeccably dressed in a bespoke three-piece suit, one ankle resting casually on his knee.

It would've been cheap and snarky to mock his need to project his presence but the chair could easily have been a minor accessory. It in no way detracted from his imposing presence.

He didn't even need the spotlight poised above his head that would be activated when filming started. From producers to make-up artists to film crew, eyes flickered to him with the frequency of homing beacons.

He remained oblivious to all of it, his gaze on the document he perused.

My heels echoed louder the closer I got to him and he raised his head when I was a few feet away.

Intelligent, piercing hazel eyes flicked to me, dropped in a quick skim over my body before rising. 'Neve. Glad you made it.'

I delivered a neutral smile. 'And with a whole hour to spare.'

Long, capable fingers tapped his ankle as his eyes conducted another sweep over me. 'The commute from out of town wasn't horrendous, I hope?'

I wasn't going to be impressed that he'd remembered my flagship resort was based in Westport, Connecticut. It hadn't mattered an iota when he'd advised Malcolm Cahill to kill the affiliation deal without giving me a chance to argue my case for my business and home. 'I'm staying in town this week. To avoid any unforeseen timing issues.'

One sleek eyebrow lifted at my chilled tone. 'Am I still not forgiven for arriving at the meeting late?'

I shrugged. 'Forgiveness, like trust, is earned.'

He paused for a long stretch. 'The cameras aren't rolling, Neve. No need to show your claws just yet. We're all friends here.'

My stupid breath caught at how easily he said the words. How unnervingly sincere he sounded. How could I not have spotted this two years ago? Oh, yes. Lust completely blinded me. 'This is all a game to you, isn't it?'

He tensed. 'Beg your pardon?'

I waved a hand around the room. 'All this is one giant playground for you to roll around in, isn't it? What do you do, get up in the morning and roll a dice and decide who you're going to meddle with?'

Hazel eyes narrowed. 'I'm sure I haven't the foggiest idea what you're talking about.'

My hackles rose. 'Of course you don't. Must be hard to keep track of your games when you've been at it for as long as you have.' My voice dripped with bitter acid.

His face grew tauter, his lips twisting with that unique mixture of amusement and cynicism. 'I'm attempting to get back into your good graces but I see I'm wasting my time here.'

The utter nerve. 'It'll take more than a half-smile and a courteous enquiry about my commute to achieve that, Mr Mortimer.'

He grimaced. 'Can we drop this bloody *Mr Mortimer* crap? It's getting a little tedious, don't you think, *Neve*?' he asked pointedly, and raised a hand when I opened my mouth. 'We're supposed to be business competitors but only up to a point. You throwing out that rigid formality I hear in your voice won't make for good television.'

'On the contrary, I think the high prospect of me clawing your eyes out for a deal is exactly what will keep viewers' interest.'

His gaze dropped to the fingers wrapped around my coffee cup. 'I think you should save the clawing for something more…beneficial.'

I thoroughly despised myself for the hot throb that started between my thighs. I counteracted it by moving to the seat farthest from him. 'Don't worry, Mr Mortimer. I'm great at multitasking.'

He muttered something under his breath. Something that made my temperature kick up for no reason. 'What did you say?'

His mocking smile said he wasn't going to repeat it. 'You're in the wrong seat.'

'I didn't realise the seats were assigned.'

'They aren't. But as Executive Producer, I have a little discretion. And I prefer you next to me. Besides, Nate has already bagged that seat.'

I gave a challenging little laugh. 'Are you sure you want me next to you?'

The rapier-sharp retort I expected didn't materialise. Instead a cloud drifted over his face, his expression mirroring the one I saw yesterday when his phone rang. Now, like then, I wanted to ask if everything was okay. If *he* was okay. I staunched the absurd urge. If I wanted to play in the big leagues, I couldn't be blinded by emotion. Not unless I wanted to be chewed up and spat out again.

'It makes for good optics, according to those who're fussed about such things,' he replied in his crisp accent. Except his voice was colourless. Flat. As were his eyes. 'Totally up to you whether you want to take it up with the producers, of course.'

Oh, how very neat of him to lob the ball back in my court. Make it impossible for me to do anything but take the seat he preferred. Because how much of a diva would I be if, as one of the newest members of the group, I started throwing my toys out of the crib over seating arrangements?

I swallowed my reservations, urged my runaway pulse to calm the hell down and took the seat to his right.

A hint of a smile twitched his mouth. 'Thank you.'

'Don't thank me just yet. You might live to regret it.' A part of me already regretted it after one whiff of his aftershave immediately threw me back to when I'd experienced that scent up close and very personal.

'Maybe. Maybe not,' he answered cryptically.

The other mentors' arrivals put paid to our conversation. Final instructions were given, we were miked up and official shooting began.

The first contestant's pitch was mediocre and unanimously dispatched. Nate snapped up the second participant's golf-ball-retrieving invention suited to his golf-based hotels.

Brian and Gary battled over the next two contestants and decided to partner up in the end.

I swallowed my disappointment as the last contestant of the day pitched a sex-centric app that held zero interest for me.

It set the tone for the next few days.

By Friday afternoon my nerves were fried from being subjected to Damian for several hours a day. It was no use telling myself I shouldn't have let him goad me into taking the seat next to him. I was committed for the duration of the series.

That didn't mean I wasn't going to deny with every ounce of my being the hyperawareness generated by being this close to him. It really wasn't fair that he was so jumpable. And the guy didn't just look good. His aftershave made my mouth water with every breath I took and the smug bastard knew it, if his lingering glances when the camera swung away from us were any indication.

I gritted my teeth and attempted to focus on the producer's notes. Three more presentations before filming ended for the next five days. Another couple of hours and I'd be on my way home. I loved hotels, especially boutique hotels with their own charming identity, but I'd grown tired of New York.

I preferred the tranquillity and fresh air that surrounded my Westport resort, had done ever since my first visit to my grandparents' B & B when I was eight. The unforgettable summer when the planets had aligned and my mother and her estranged parents had attempted to patch up their differences.

The trip had been an unmitigated disaster, and by the time Mom had bundled me into her beat-up Corolla, their relationship had strained beyond repair. Somehow the blame for that had landed at my feet, just as every misfortune that occurred to Priscilla Nolan somehow found its root cause at my existence.

Of course, that hadn't stopped my mother from dumping me on my grandparents every school holiday after that summer.

But as much as it'd hurt to know I was a burden she couldn't wait to be rid of whenever the opportunity arose, I'd treasured the visits to Connecticut, had grown to love the quaint Quaker two-storey characterful B & B painted a buttercup-yellow.

Almost as much as I'd treasured the relationship with my grandparents. In their eyes, I'd seen the dashed hopes and dreams they'd harboured for their own relationship with my mother and had striven to make up for that emptiness, selfishly absorbing the affection lacking in my own relationship with my parent.

Finding out they'd left their beloved property to me in their will had seemed like a sign, a way to hang onto their legacy and to keep their memory alive; a way to hold onto a precious connection filled with love and compassion, not disappointment and bitterness.

The moment I'd scraped a decent business plan together, I'd poured my heart and soul into making my dream come true. I might have five other resorts on the East Coast, but the Westport branch of Nevirna remained my favourite place in the world.

I couldn't return just yet though. Not until I'd

achieved my end goal and knocked Damian Mortimer to his knees.

'Something wrong with the notes?' the man asked, igniting a deeper awareness that made my body hum as he approached where I stood in one corner of the converted warehouse.

'What?' This little light-headedness whenever his raw masculinity hit me was becoming a problem.

'You've been staring at that paper for the last five minutes and you're wearing an adorable little frown. Did the producers miss something?'

I opened my mouth to chastise him for ruining my concentration but the words that tumbled from my lips were the last I expected. 'Did you just call me *adorable*?'

His lips twitched. 'What if I did?'

'I'd remind you that we're in the workplace. I could sue your ass for saying things like that.'

One eyebrow lifted. 'You're in a tetchy mood. Anything I can help with?'

Yes. Stop looking so damn mouth-watering. Stop wearing those ties that match your eyes and make them look so incredible that I want to keep looking into them. I need clarity of purpose.

'Unless you have a time machine handy, no.'

Speculation flickered through his eyes. 'You're in a rush to get somewhere?'

Reluctant to tell him I missed my cottage by the lake, I shrugged. 'I'm a hands-on boss with a demanding business to run.'

'And business is your only reason?'

I frowned, irritated that I'd given myself away somehow even before I'd been able to formulate a clear plan of how I'd get Damian in my bed. 'What other reason would there be? And why would it concern you?'

The flicker in his eyes intensified. 'You've sat next to me all week. I know you're intense when a pitch interests you but otherwise you're frustratingly... buttoned-up. Maybe I'm interested in what else makes you tick.'

This was my chance to test the waters. 'It's a little late, isn't it? Didn't we already put the cart before the horse, so to speak?'

Shadows crossed his face but he still shrugged. 'Maybe you're not the only one who craves time machines.'

My breath knotted in my throat. 'You sound like you have regrets.'

'A bloody boatload of them.' His gaze met mine, and a wave of heat slammed into me. 'But in other ways, I wouldn't change a thing.'

Right. The sex had served its purpose, insulated him from whatever demons had hounded him that night for a little while. Even if he'd regretted it after, he'd still indulged himself.

His asshole ways, however, were ones he wouldn't change. Not if it allowed him to walk away with the deal that should've included me.

'Well, I'm not interested in your little getting-to-know-you expedition, so save us both the time-wasting, hmm?'

His gaze swept down for a moment, his mouth twisting ruefully. 'It might make for good television but, as sexy as they are, I'm growing weary of you glaring at me all the time. You have a spectacular smile. I'd love to see it again.' His low, deep voice shot flames straight to parts of my body that made me want to clench my thighs.

'The whole point of a one-night stand is that it's uncool to keep bringing it up.'

He stepped closer and leaned against the wall next to me. The stance threw his body into a sexy position that made my heart beat faster.

'Do you regret it?' he demanded abruptly, a throb of something indefinable in his voice.

I bit the inside of my cheek, resisted the urge to lie and tell him that I regretted every moment of it. 'I'm an adult. I made a consensual decision to sleep with you, and the experience wasn't awful.' I should've left it at that, but again my tongue got the better of me. 'Do you?'

Aquiline nostrils flared ever so slightly, and his gaze dropped hungrily to my mouth before rising again. 'I regret certain aspects of it.'

I was weak enough to step through the door he'd left open. 'Which aspects?'

His silence lasted a few seconds too long. 'There was a…recklessness I could've done without. I'm not the type of man who follows women to their hotel rooms.'

'Because you're too busy fending them off when they throw themselves at you? Got it.'

He sighed, and pinched the bridge of his nose. He seemed…weary. Worn down by a heavy weight. I steeled myself, yet again, from asking what that burden was. 'What's it going to take for you to change your mind about me?' he rasped.

'Admitting you fucked up would be a great start,' I returned sharply.

'I didn't fuck up. I fucked *you* and I don't mean that even remotely metaphorically. I fucked you as thoroughly and enjoyably as you fucked me,' he breathed in that low, lethal voice, his simmering stare starting fires in all the right places. 'That's what pisses you off, isn't it? You wish you could dismiss it as the worst fuck you'd ever had but you can't because we were that good together. Admit it.'

'You're wrong. I never disparage good sex. Treacherous assholes, however…'

His face clenched tighter than I'd ever seen it. 'Excuse me?'

From behind his shoulder I spotted the producer heading our way. 'Don't worry. I hear what goes around, *comes* around. And this time, I'm going to come out on top.'

The satisfaction I should've felt walking away was marred by the distinct notion that I was playing with lethal fire.

CHAPTER FOUR

Neve

JUST FOR THE fun of it, I went toe to toe with him on the next pitch before making a tactical withdrawal.

He knew what I was up to, of course, and his gaze grew increasingly assessing as the next contestants entered the den.

I redirected my gaze to where Chinese screens with colourful frames were being erected. There were six in total and, having learned on the first day to take my cue from the crew's excitement, I paid closer attention. I'd researched the past shows, knew there was a solitary gem that stood head and shoulders above mundane pitches.

My instincts screamed this could be it.

Surreptitiously, I noted Damian's interest and plastered on my poker face as the crew finished setting up, noting the mastery in the hand-stitched embroidery etched in the red silk cloth that covered the frames.

The cameras started rolling.

A man and woman of similar height and colouring entered, their smiles open and friendly.

'Hi, Raiders, I'm Sam Weston and this is my brother

Tyler,' the woman said. 'I earned the right to speak to you first today because I'm three minutes older than him.'

'What she means is, she didn't really give me a choice,' Tyler replied.

Chuckles echoed through the room, lightening the mood.

I angled my body subtly towards Damian, crossed one leg over the other, and immediately sensed tension rise in his body.

'We're here to ask for a seven-hundred-and-fifty-thousand-dollar investment in return for a twenty-five per cent stake in our business,' Sam stated. 'It's a huge sum, we know, but what we have to offer in return will blow your socks off.' She shared a smile with her brother. 'Please allow us to let your fantasies come true.'

They approached the Chinese screens, drew them to one side and, in sync, tugged away the silk cloth to reveal a set of large photographs.

One picture was a replica of a scene from *Alice in Wonderland*, the other a Victorian-era agency parlour. They unveiled the next frame to reveal a French boudoir, and the one after that a late-nineteenth-century Wild West drinking saloon.

The last two were equally eye-catching, every vivid detail in the picture depicting scenes familiar to book and movie lovers.

'Our business is called Fantasy Rooms. In short, we give you the room of your fantasy in any hotel room of your choice. You can be a Regency duke or an explorer for the duration of your stay and, with just three days' notice before you check in, we can transform any room to suit your ideal fantasy and provide the costumes and the props required to make your stay one hundred per cent authentic.'

A wild dart of excitement arrowed through me. When I was a child, my one guaranteed escape from the unpleasant roller coaster of watching my mother and the revolving door of unsuitable men she entertained had been through the magic of books.

My library card had been my most treasured possession almost from the day my father had walked out when I was eight. And as soon as I could afford it, I'd filled my reading tablet with more romantic fantasy books than any other.

The idea of bringing those two worlds together, incorporating them into my business, wrapped itself around my heart and held on tight. I needed to use my business head for this but I took a moment to indulge in the possibilities of what this could mean for me. For Nevirna.

I snapped into focus.

'Three quarters of a million is a hell of a lot of money. Why such a big budget?' Nate asked.

Tyler stepped forward. 'We've only worked with a few small hotels on the East Coast. We're looking to expand to the West Coast and eventually go international. The budget will go towards investing in manpower for a year. Ideally we're looking at six teams, four in each team, to be available to transform the rooms with the three-day notice we aspire to. We're also looking at hiring costume designers to produce bespoke equipment that isn't readily available on the market.'

'Bespoke,' Damian echoed. 'That's expensive.'

'But ultimately worth it,' Sam replied.

'You said you've been working with smaller hotels. Who are they?' I asked.

Tyler named a chain of hotels based in Florida. They were good but not worthy competition.

'I want an exclusive partnership.' I boldly staked my claim.

Damian glanced my way but I kept my gaze trained on the Westons. They exchanged smiling looks before glancing my way again.

'Nevirna Resorts is on our dream list, and, yes, we would consider an initial exclusive arrangement.'

My stomach dropped. 'Explain *initial*,' I pressed.

Sam smiled. 'We really admire you, Miss Nolan. You cater to the type of clients we're after. We've done tons of research and know you're working on expanding your resort into Europe and the Caribbean. Our dream is to be bigger eventually and we'd welcome the chance to grow with you but we don't want to be locked in if…things don't work out. We need to start somewhere and we think that your resort would be a good fit for us for a couple of years. Ideally we would both grow together.'

Disappointment welled up. Their concept could be huge with the right partnership. But I wasn't done fighting for the right to be their long-term partner even if all they were offering right now was two years. 'I'll offer half a million for the twenty-five per cent stake for a five-year exclusive contract with Nevirna,' I stated boldly.

'This hasn't been tested on a large scale, has it? It could be a success story or it could be a huge money pit. Convince me it's not the latter,' Damian challenged.

'It's new and largely untested, yes, but we believe in the concept and in our ability to make it worthwhile to your clients. We've also had strong interest from the Stardust group of hotels. But we think a partnership with the Raiders will better fit us.'

With a compulsion I couldn't stem, I turned my head. Surely enough, Damian was staring at me, a hard, shrewd smile twitching his lips.

He knew I wanted this deal. Knew it and relished taking me on.

Tyler cleared his throat. 'If we may be so bold, our ideal objective would be to secure a semi-exclusive partnership with Nevirna and The Mortimer Group.'

Hell, no. 'That doesn't work for me at all.'

Damian's gaze veered from mine to lock with Sam's. My heart dropped to my toes. He was about to chop me off at the knees.

But I wasn't down and out yet. 'I'll offer you six hundred thousand for a thirty per cent stake and a three-year exclusivity agreement,' I countered. 'But more than that I'll offer you a true partnership, not one where you're just another gimmick that'll easily get overlooked in a big conglomerate's fanfare. The Mortimer Group is impressive, sure, but do you want to get lost in all their noise before you have a chance to make your mark?' I challenged.

Damian stiffened and his wisp of a smile evaporated.

'Can you give us a moment, please?' Tyler requested, his voice buzzing with suppressed excitement.

They retreated to confer with muted voices. The camera followed them, leaving us alone for a minute.

'It makes good business sense to partner up,' Damian murmured from beside me.

I turned the full force of my glower on him. 'Not to me, it doesn't.'

'Why not? Your obvious animosity aside, are you seriously suggesting you don't think that this could work out for both of us?'

I shrugged. 'It probably would if I trusted you as far as I could throw you. But I don't.'

His expression bordered on furious. 'I guess I was wrong about your ability not to let past encounters get in the way of a sound deal. I'm…disappointed.'

To my infernal annoyance, my heart dipped. As if his opinion mattered. As if the echoes of my mother's voice in his words were real.

I wanted to slap the look off his face. But despite myself I was fascinated by Damian's effect on me when no one else so far, besides my mother, had ever made me doubt myself. Wasn't that why I'd acted so out of character that night in Boston?

Despite having reached into my burgeoning business and yanked the heart out of it, he still both terrified and thrilled me.

Every time he looked at me, whenever I smelled that intoxicating aftershave, I got that stupid urge to trace my fingers over his square jaw, intimately acquaint my skin with his stubble.

It was insane.

I really needed to get it together.

'Even if I trusted you, which I don't, five years is a long time in business. I don't want to be stuck with an absentee partner. You evaded my query earlier so here's your chance to quash the rumours that you're relocating back to England shortly.' His reputation as a genius with the Midas touch was unquestionable, but still…

His shrug was laid-back but the tension vibrating from him told a different story. 'I'm part of a family that runs a multibillion-pound conglomerate. Even if I were permanently based here in New York, I'd still have varied business interests that demand my attention. But regardless of that, we have an opportunity here that's guaranteed to be wildly successful with me as part of it.' His voice brimmed with arrogant confidence.

'You're very sure of yourself, aren't you?'

'I don't need to crow about my successes, Neve. They speak for themselves.'

'Spoken like a true egomaniac.'

Far from being irritated by my waspish response, he gave an insanely sexy smile. 'Keep giving me compliments like that and I might just fall for your charms.'

'Sorry. My one compliment started and ended there.'

His smile slowly dimmed. 'Shame.'

Before I could ask what he meant, the Weston twins returned to the stage.

Sam smiled and I cautioned myself not to get excited. 'We love everything you stand for, Miss Nolan. My best friend and her fiancé stayed at your hotel the week before they got married and they adored it. We really want to go with you…' my heart dropped as she paused and meshed her fingers together '…but on the basis of a two-year deal with The Mortimer Group attached as a possible future partner and Mr Mortimer as a consultant. For that we'll offer Mr Mortimer a ten per cent share of our company.'

Damian shrugged. 'It's not the perfect deal but it's interesting enough. I'm in.' He glanced at me. His gaze wasn't challenging. It was almost...hopeful.

Silence thrummed through the charged space.

Aware of the cameras trained on me, I cleared my throat. I was a strong, intelligent businesswoman. I couldn't afford to crow at the win I sensed within reach or exhibit my fierce reluctance to have Damian attached to my business.

Besides...wasn't this the perfect opportunity? His professional involvement would be abstract but he'd be within reach of the sexual plans I had in mind long enough for me to deliver that final coup de grâce my soul, and my pride, needed.

I plastered on a smile, aware that the fifteen-second suspenseful silence we'd agreed with the production team to add extra drama to the show was slowly ticking by.

Again, I met Damian's gaze. Hope had given way to blatant, challenging hunger. One that dared me to come out and play. My skin grew hotter, that insane urge to tangle with him and *win* this time rushing through me again.

A two-year deal with the twins and Fantasy Rooms was the best thing that I could deliver to my hotel right now. It was the perfect platform from which to launch myself internationally, to show my mother that I could make an even better success of her parents' business despite her doubts.

And by the end of that term I'd prove to the twins

that they were better off with me in the long run than with Damian.

'Have mercy, Neve. The suspense is killing us all,' Damian mocked with a half-smile. 'I know this is a TV show but do you want your potential new partners to have heart attacks before they sign on the dotted line?'

A little embarrassed, I glanced over at the twins, who were staring at me with identical expressions of apprehensive hope.

Tyler's imploring brown gaze met mine and a part of me grew excited for them because their dream was coming true.

Perhaps it was a little foolish to lay my heart on the line for them but I intended to protect their business just as fiercely as I would mine so they'd never know the kind of betrayal I'd felt at the hands of Damian Mortimer.

Fortified by that belief, I nodded. 'I'm in.'

Sam gave a shocked, ecstatic gasp. Tyler's smile stretched wide as he fist-pumped. My own smile widening, I stood and approached them.

'Thank you,' Sam gushed.

'I'm excited…we're both excited you're on board,' Tyler said as he held onto my hand, still grinning wildly.

The camera zoomed in, and I sensed Damian approach. My stomach dipped as I felt heat from his body caress mine.

'Congratulations,' he offered, shaking Sam's hand.

His gaze slid to where mine was still held in Tyler's and narrowed imperceptibly.

The observation sent a pulse of electricity through

me but I ignored it. The other Raiders joined us, offered congratulations of their own.

Damian thrust his hand at Tyler. They shook hands abruptly as the director shouted cut.

'We're so glad you're on board, Miss Nolan. You're our inspiration, the reason we decided to come on the show,' Sam said with a wide smile.

'I'm beginning to feel like a spare part,' Damian drawled, brittle amusement tilting his lips.

'No,' Tyler piped up. 'We hoped you'd be on board too but Nevirna was always our target. No offence.'

'None taken. For your sake, I hope your gamble pays off,' Damian said in a cool tone.

'So what happens now?' Sam asked me.

'Now I get my lawyers to put together a contract package. I expect Mr Mortimer will also do the same. But before that I'd love to see a real-life sample of your work.' I already had my ideal fantasy room in mind.

'Of course,' Tyler responded immediately. 'We'd love to show you a full scale of our work. We put a few of our outfitters on notice on the off-chance we might need them. We're at your disposal to start immediately if you wish.'

Impressed by their forward thinking, I reached into my jacket and handed over my business card. 'You'll have my email with specifications within the hour and I'll tell my hotel manager to expect your call. She'll have a room ready for you to start on tomorrow. But that means you'll have to travel to Westport tonight.'

'No problem,' Sam said.

'And when you're done with Neve's place, you will do one of mine,' Damian added. 'I'd also like a demonstration before I fully commit.' He addressed the twins but his gaze was fixed squarely on me.

Immediately lewd images invaded my brain, supplying reel after reel of every hot, dirty fantasy I wanted to indulge in with him.

'Will it be at Mortimer Plaza?' Sam's excitement broke into my lurid thoughts.

Damian's gaze darkened, as if he'd read my filthy fantasies. 'I'll decide on a location later. But we'll both inspect the finished work to make sure we are on board. Which means I'm coming to Westport too. Any objections?' He directed the question to me.

I forced an easy shrug, despite the wild blaze invading my pelvis. 'Not at all.'

Damian shot a few pertinent questions at them. I parried with a few of my own. Then we parted company.

The moment our mics were taken off, Damian stepped closer. Against my will my breath caught, every sense vividly aware of the way his broad shoulders blocked out the rest of the room. Hell, even his five o'clock shadow made my fingers itch for its rough bristle against my skin.

'You think you can let go now, express how you really feel?' he rasped.

'Excuse me?'

'The buttoned-up poker face thing is great when you don't want to give yourself away but surely you can crack a smile now you've won?'

'I'll consider it a true win when you're not affiliated with any of this.'

Dammit.

I pressed my lips shut but it was too late.

Laser eyes narrowed. 'Why does my presence bother you so much?'

'It doesn't,' I snapped with excessive heat and instantly knew I'd left myself wide open to the dark speculation growing in his eyes.

'Then you won't object to a sit-down tonight to discuss the best way forward with this deal,' he parried smoothly. So smoothly, I didn't feel the shackles closing in until I was trapped.

He knew I'd planned to return home to Westport tonight, having heard me say as much to the director when we'd discussed the final segment of shooting.

But he wouldn't throw me that easily.

I made the exaggerated show of looking at my watch. 'I can delay my car service for an hour…' I raised an eyebrow when he shook his head.

'For a deal worth over half a million dollars, surely you'll want to devote more time than a measly hour to this?' he drawled in that laconic way that was at odds with the dangerous fire gleaming in his eyes.

I sucked in a slow steadying breath, aware that his gaze was moving over me again, lingering at my throat, on my breasts. Making me hot and hungry when I needed a cool head.

The goal here was sexual domination. My domination. *My win*. 'Fine. I'll give you two hours.'

He nodded. 'Perfect for dinner. I'll book us a table at Mortimer Plaza—'

'No. I'm staying at the Wilton Grand. It has an excellent restaurant. I'll make reservations.' No way was I meeting him on his turf. To hell if that suggested I was a little scared of being seduced by the elegance and grandeur of his hotel all over again the way I was last time. I'd learned the hard way how to pick the weapons for my battles.

'My driver's outside. He'll take us to your hotel,' he said.

'I have a few things to take care of first. We can meet at the restaurant at seven-thirty.'

He nodded after a brief hesitation. 'Very well. I'll even endeavour not to be late,' he said with a touch of sexy mockery that irritated and made my breath catch at the same time.

This is where you walk away, Neve.

My feet refused to obey, because the way he was staring at my mouth made my pussy throb and clench with a furious need that excited me way too much. He prowled another step closer and somehow my back was against one of the Chinese frames and we were hidden from view of the crew.

'Neve.'

God. His voice. Low. Sexy. Deep.

The craving he sparked terrified me. 'Are we done here? I need to get going.'

He made an irritated little sound under his breath. 'I'm looking forward to dinner. It might even give us the chance to put all this…*hostility* to bed.'

The mention of bed immediately conjured up more explicit images that made my thighs clench and my nipples hard. To redress the sensation of being so…off balance in his presence, I subtly leaned towards him, gratified when his gaze dropped to my mouth for the umpteenth time this evening.

Slowly, I slicked my tongue over my lower lip and smiled when his breath caught. 'You know what? I'm actually looking forward to seeing you try.'

My mental fist-pump as hunger spiked in his eyes stayed with me all the way back to my hotel and through my quick shower. Right up until my phone beeped with an unwanted reminder as I was slipping on my dress.

Call Mom.

My finger hovered over the delete button only to be knocked away by surging guilt and the reminder of the promise I'd made to try, no matter what. The weight of my grandparents' own pain for the bond they'd never managed to forge with their own daughter burrowed deeper into my heart. Stomach clenched with nerves I should've been used to by now, I hit the call button, a quiet obstinacy not to fail at this too urging me on.

She answered on the fourth ring.

'Hey, Mom.'

A pulse of silence. 'Neve. I was beginning to think you'd permanently lost my number.'

Relief darted through me at her sharp tone. She hadn't hit the bottle. Yet. 'Sorry. I've been a little busy.'

'Of course you have. Chasing another overambitious venture, I expect? I don't suppose you listened to my advice and dropped that silly TV show gimmick?'

Relief was replaced with a spiky ache that tunnelled deep. 'No. I went ahead with it. The exposure will be good for business.' I wasn't going to mention Fantasy Rooms. Not until it was a done deal.

She made a derisive sound under her breath. 'I guess we'll see, won't we?'

My fingers tightened around the phone, suspecting what was coming. 'Mom—'

'Did you stop to think how your grandparents would feel about you turning their place into a spectacle?'

Tears prickled my eyes. I blinked them back. 'They knew how much I loved the place so I hope they'd be proud. I hope they'd be pleased that I managed to hang onto it instead of selling when times got hard.'

Like you wanted me to.

'You mean when you were forced to change the name of the hotel my father chose so your mistake didn't follow you around?'

'It made good business sense to rebrand. Start fresh,' I argued.

'You think you know better than me, don't you?'

I sighed. 'No. I just… I just wish—'

She laughed, a bitter sound that scraped my nerves. 'Wishes are for fools, Neve. All the wishing in the world didn't stop your father from leaving us. From erasing us from his life like we were nothing and high-tailing it back to England.'

The pain in my gut intensified. 'You could have gone back with him like he wanted. *We* could've still been a family—'

'Are you saying that was my fault?' she asked sharply, and just like that we were back inside the vicious little circus of resentment and recrimination that had peppered our lives from the moment my father had walked out the door.

I fought to keep my voice even. 'No, Mom. I'm not saying that.' But the part of me that had always judged her a little for her decisions wouldn't be soothed. From the letters I'd discovered as a teenager, Richard Nolan had loved his wife. Enough to uproot his life to follow her to the States. Enough to forgive her first infidelity and the many that had followed. It was only after I was born that my father had put his foot down. He'd thrown down the gauntlet of his desertion in the hope that she would come to her senses. She hadn't. He'd walked away.

Seven years later he was dead and I was left with a parent who'd spent the best years of her life looking for love and validation in all the wrong places.

I swallowed my knotted heartache and lowered the phone long enough to check the time. 'I have to go, Mom.'

She didn't respond for a long moment. 'New Jersey isn't the other side of the world, Neve.'

It felt like it most days. 'I know. I'll visit when I can.'

I ended the call with shaking fingers and lacerated emotions. I straightened my spine and attempted to pull myself together. My problems with my mother weren't going to go away any time soon. But I was going to be late to dinner if I didn't move my ass.

I was shown to our table mere minutes before Damian walked through the restaurant. His laser-sharp gaze fixed on me as he strode through the room, again oblivious to the heads he turned with the sheer jaw-dropping magnificence of his presence.

Even with the width of the table between us, his sexual dynamism hit me like a wild tropical wave. Right up until he froze, his eyes narrowing. 'Is everything okay?'

I bit the inside of my lip, cursing the shaky composure that hadn't quite righted itself since the call with my mother. 'I'm fine.'

He sat down, no...he *lounged* as if he owned the

place, drawing attention to the dark olive-green shirt that clung to his streamlined torso, the open collar revealing a swathe of hair-dusted skin that made me itch with that infernal need. The casual jacket and matching trousers were also dark, the overall effect nothing short of spectacular.

When he flicked open the single button to his jacket, I shifted in my seat, desperately wishing I were immune to his obscenely handsome face. A little perturbed, I busied myself powering off my phone, while attempting to tamp down my body's involuntary reaction, deny the effect of that unnerving stare as it continued to sizzle deep inside me.

As there had been two years ago, there was a mildly puzzled texture to his stare that thrilled me with the possibility that *he* couldn't help his visceral reaction to me.

Was that why he'd behaved so appallingly after our night together?

Why are you finding reasons to excuse his behaviour?

And what did it matter now, when I could use it to my advantage? 'There are a hundred other deals out there that you could put your name to. Why are you intent on attaching yourself to Fantasy Rooms?'

His mouth twisted slightly and the heat lessened in his eyes. 'So much for thinking this would be a cordial dinner.'

'I don't have time to beat around the bush.'

The waiter approached. Damian ordered a bottle of water, then raised his eyebrow at me.

'A glass of Chablis, thanks.'

The waiter nodded and left.

Damian eyed me. 'It's a great business opportunity. The Mortimer Group owns thousands of hotel rooms across the world. A concept like this, with innovative marketing targeted at an exclusive clientele, could eventually add considerable revenue to the business. And once you get over your dislike of me you'll realise this could be hugely beneficial to you too, regardless of my involvement. Or perhaps even because of it,' he tagged on after a few seconds.

'Deals struck on the show are binding, but there's a cooling-off period, isn't there?'

His eyes narrowed. 'Are you attempting to insult me again?'

I shrugged. 'I'm merely triple-checking facts.'

'Triple-checking or trying to piss me off?'

I sent him a saccharine smile. 'Which one suits you best?'

'Careful, Neve, or you might get a reaction you're not entirely ready for.' His gaze didn't stray from my face but I felt as if he'd stripped me bare, branded my skin with his words. And more.

'I'm a big girl. I can handle myself. And while we're discussing the subject of handling, let's talk about your so-called role.'

One corner of his mouth tilted. 'So-called? You make it sound imaginary.'

'You know exactly what I'm talking about.'

'You're still hung up on rumours?'

I raised my eyebrow and waited.

'Tell my why you looked troubled when I arrived and I'll tell you.'

My stomach dropped in alarm. 'We're not here to get personal. We're here to—'

'Discuss business. I know. But my reasons *are* personal. And you've been probing all week. So those are my terms.'

'I could get up and walk out of here. You know that, don't you?'

'And leave all those questions buzzing in your head unanswered? I don't think so.'

I needed ammunition; to probe his weaknesses to achieve my own goals. If I had to give a little to gain a lot… 'Phone call with my mother a little while ago. We have a…fraught relationship.'

His gaze remained steady on me. Penetrating. Almost…encouraging.

I dropped mine to the table, a little puzzled as to why I felt compelled to elaborate. 'She's my only remaining relative. The one I've had the longest relationship with even though it's been difficult at best.'

'And you hate failing. So you persevere,' he stated simply.

Icy chills chased over my skin at those simple, insightful words. 'I'm human. I don't actively *like* failing.'

He continued to watch me, his gaze far too knowing. Slowly his expression altered, becoming… understanding. And not at all to what I wanted. 'We both know it's more than that. We're all marked in some way by dynamics we can't control until it's too late. It's nothing to be ashamed of.'

My instincts blared dire warnings. Much as they had two years ago. But I remained seated, arranging my own features into a question. One he was required to answer now I'd exposed a precious layer of my skin.

His lips compressed. 'It's true. I'm wrapping things

up in the States. I'm returning to London in a matter of weeks.'

'Because you're bored?'

'Because it's long bloody overdue,' he returned in a gruff whisper, as if the words were torn from his soul.

The waiter arrived, setting down our drinks with barely a murmur, as if afraid of disturbing the atmosphere. We ordered our food after a cursory look at the menu and I barely registered his retreat.

'You sound as if it's been a prison sentence.' The mild scorn I attempted failed. In its place was a quietly churning urgency. A fierce need to understand this man. To understand *why*.

I wrapped my fingers around the bulb of my wine glass and waited.

His jaw rippled with tension. A shamefully heated part of me wanted to run my lips over the spot. To taste the chaos. 'A prison sentence is finite, even if one's release is via death. Mine is…fluid.'

'And you think running from it will solve your problem?'

That bleak darkness I'd glimpsed two years ago blazed through his eyes. 'You misunderstand. I'm done running from it. I'm *returning* to it.'

Facts gleaned from research clattered among the industry rumours I'd absorbed over time and informed my response. 'You're supposed to be co-CEO of The Mortimer Group and yet your title doesn't state that.'

'To be co-CEO I have to be an active member of the board. I'm currently not.'

'Because of your fluid sentence?'

He cracked open his bottle of water, pouring it with an intense focus that made me think he wasn't going to respond. Then he shrugged. 'Like you, I don't like failure. But I understand the wisdom of a tactical retreat. I didn't expect mine to last three years.'

'Who?' I asked boldly.

Again, time stretched, a tensile cord that vibrated with every mercurial sensation that'd connected us since the moment we'd set eyes on each other.

It seemed a little obscene to be thinking of sex in this moment but the second his gaze clashed with mine, I was back on my knees in that hotel room, staring up at him with parted lips, inviting him to lose himself in me.

Intuitively, I knew he was in that moment too. His fingers curled a little too forcefully around his glass, his eyes gleaming with fiercer fire.

Through it all, my question clawed at the air between us. Demanding a response.

'Gideon. My cousin. We had a disagreement. In hindsight, retreat was a mistake.'

His answers were bullet-sharp, wrapped in bitterness, a deeper, more potent strain of what I'd witnessed two years ago. Funny thing was it seemed aimed at himself.

This time I knew better than to entertain sympathy, to get carried away with even the remotest delusion of saving him. Hell, I couldn't even save my own broken relationship with my mother.

'What makes you think you can fix anything now? What makes you think you can reverse time and fix something you turned to ashes?' I demanded with all the bitterness lodged in my heart.

CHAPTER FIVE

Damian

WE'D TAKEN A wrong turn somewhere. And I didn't need a compass to know that the fault was mine. My motives tonight hadn't been wholly altruistic, true. But I hadn't anticipated this…*deep dive* into matters I never discussed with anyone.

My plan when I'd challenged Neve into spending more time with me had been to delve into a conundrum of my own. To uncover why she still remained irresistible despite her bristling hostility. Why she made my cock hard by simply walking into a room when she was far from easy or accommodating.

The problem was that I wanted her. So bloody much it'd taken on a life of its own this past week. I wasn't so far gone as to label it an obsession but…

My cock hardened, throbbing with a terrible ache that made me shift in my seat.

Bloody hell. Was I so fucked up now that this sort of thing turned me on? She was responsible for the broken curse on my libido, sure. Since our night in Boston I'd fucked three other women. Carefully vetted, willing women. None of them had come close to plumbing the depths of the peculiar hunger that had tunnelled itself into unreachable places inside me.

That hunger accelerated out of control with each moment I spent in Neve's presence. But alongside that craving for the kind of filthy, sublime sex that'd taken me out of my head for a blessed few hours was another unspeakable yearning.

To simply...*know* her. I shifted again but this time my unease had nothing to do with the ache in my dick and everything to do with the need to answer the censure in her eyes.

'The past is the past. It can't be changed. But I can control how the future pans out.'

'So he should simply accept that you've done your time? That you'll impose your will on him whether he wants it or not?' she demanded sharply.

'I intend to lay out the evidence and let three years of time and distance provide their own clarity.' And yes, if necessary, force Gideon to confront what we've both been hiding from—that the betrayal wasn't as cut and dried as we initially believed. That, according to what the investigators had uncovered, he'd had a lucky escape.

Neve's response was curtailed by the waiter's arrival. He set our plates before us in a silent flourish before making himself scarce again.

She made no move to pick up her cutlery. I wasn't in the mood to eat either.

'What?' I asked when she stared at me with mild disbelief.

'I'm trying to decide if you're that much of a hypocrite or just plain egotistical.'

I ignored the sharp pang in my chest. 'I've been

called many things in my time. Thankfully I have a thick skin. And I also think it's time we refocus on why we're here.'

The quicker we did that, the sooner I could address the pressing problem of the need to fuck this woman into oblivion at the earliest opportunity.

I watched her fight whatever was eating at her. Seconds ticked by before she blinked her gorgeous blue eyes and picked up her fork.

Something like relief spiked up my spine. 'I asked my team to find a location for my Fantasy Room. As of half an hour ago it was a toss-up between Mortimer Plaza London and a château I own in the Bordeaux region of France.' I locked my gaze on hers. 'I'm leaning towards the latter.'

'Why are you telling me this?'

'We wrap up *Raider's Den* filming next Wednesday. We can be in France by Thursday to inspect the second set-up.'

She froze. 'You want me to go to France with you?'

'Why not? I'm coming to Westport tomorrow. As majority partner in this deal, I thought you'd welcome the opportunity to see more than one. I've already spoken to Sam and Tyler. They're on board with the schedule.'

'You made plans with my partners without me?' Hell, even her prickly tone was sexy. I suspected very little detracted from Neve's allure.

'We had a conversation. As a consultant, I believe I'm allowed to do that. If you object to any part of it, feel free to speak up when we meet tomorrow.'

'I have a business to run. I can't just fly off to France.'

'You're looking to expand into Europe. This could be the perfect opportunity to do some on-the-ground scouting.'

Her lips compressed, drawing my attention to them. Reminding me how it felt to slide my length between them, how enthusiastically she'd sucked me off. My balls hardened to stone.

Fucking hell.

'I don't need to. I know exactly where my expansion vision will take me.'

Her bristling demeanour told me she didn't intend to share it with me.

I sighed. 'Look, I know you don't want me anywhere near this deal but I have no intention of walking away so it'll benefit us both if we're on the same page when it comes to dealing with Sam and Tyler.'

'What *will* it take to get you to walk away?'

For one dirty little second I was tempted to give in to my basest instinct. Tell her another night in her bed. Another mind-blowing night fucking her every which way she allowed me, just so I could be cured of this insatiable craving.

But that knotted need in my gut stopped me. That need that had nothing to do with sex and everything to do with…something else.

Jesus.

'Right now, in this moment? Nothing, darling. But feel free to ask again in a month's time.'

Her eyes darkened with quiet fury. 'Don't call me *darling.*'

'Why? Does it remind you of Boston?' I dared because one of us had to acknowledge this *entity* threatening to consume me alive. And as much as she'd pretended otherwise, I'd seen her checking me out all week when she thought I wasn't looking. 'Does it remind you of when you begged me to make you come, *darling*? Make that tight, wet pussy even wetter with my tongue before I pounded you into a screaming orgasm?'

A deep blush stained her cheeks and her fork clattered to the table. With adorably uncoordinated movements, she called over the waiter, snapped open her purse and handed over her credit card. 'I think I've lost my appetite.'

'All your *appetites*? Or just for food?'

She surged to her feet and I got a control-shredding view of the way her dress clung to every mouth-watering curve. Curves I wanted to plunder in every decadent way available.

'This meeting was clearly a waste of time.'

I dragged my gaze to her stunning face. 'I disagree. I'd say we've both learned a few things about each other.'

Her chin lifted. 'Like what?'

'Like the fact that this insane chemistry between us isn't going away. The fact that I want to pin you up against the nearest wall and taste every delicious inch of you, starting with your pussy, which I'm willing to bet is wet right now. If you stop bristling long enough to take a breath, you'll admit you want that too.'

The charged step she took towards my chair granted me an even better view of her spectacular legs. And the hard bullets of her nipples outlined clearly against her dress.

Fuck.

My breath knotted in my lungs as she bent forward, placed her hand on my chest and brought her lips to my ear. 'Here's the thing, *darling*. You're right. I won't deny that something about you makes my pussy ache. Something about you makes me want to rip your clothes off and ride you until one of us stops breathing. But tell me, Damian, why would I lower myself into fucking an asshole who will only turn around and stab me in the back again come morning?'

It was a testament of my shoddy state of mind that she was halfway out of the restaurant before her words registered.

But not even the cold drench of those words could put out the flames in my groin as I staggered to my feet and went after her.

Neve had a few things to answer.

Right before I fucked us both into next week.

Neve

I'd barely kicked off my shoes and tossed my clutch onto the sofa before he knocked. Hard and insistent.

Just like last time, I didn't bother checking the peephole before I opened the door. 'This feels like déjà vu. Of the unpleasant kind.'

His shrug was easy. Self-assured and sexy as hell. 'Last time I invited you to tell me to leave. This time I'm not going until we clear up a few things.'

'This isn't your hotel. I can have Security up here in minutes.'

'But you won't. I'm not a physical threat to you and we both know it.'

I hated how he could read me. How he could tunnel past all the bullshit to the heart of my unwelcome needs. Like right now. He was looking at me as if he knew not only the anger in my heart but how much I was still turned on from our little exchange downstairs. He wasn't exactly smirking about it but the knowledge was a solid, writhing thing between us.

'What do you want, Damian?' I snapped, hanging on tight to the door handle despite the frantic need to seize my chance, throw it wide open, let him in. Let him *inside* me.

'First of all, you forgot this.' He held up his hand to show my credit card tucked between his fingers.

Dammit. So much for my smooth exit. Frowning, I took it, tossed it onto a nearby table and reached for the in-room phone. 'I didn't sign for dinner. I should—'

'I took care of it. If that offends your sensibilities, you can pick up next time.'

'There won't be a next time.'

'Again, I disagree.' A whisper of a smile teased his lips as he propped a shoulder against the door frame. But his hazel gaze maintained that single-minded ferocity that punched fresh heat into my belly. I struggled not to fidget as his gaze rushed over my body. 'I didn't get the chance to say before, that dress looks incredible on you.'

The cocktail dress I chose to wear tonight was my favourite. The black off-the-shoulder number made of soft merino wool clung to my curves and ended a few inches above my knee. Wearing it added a boost of confidence and made me feel sexy in a way I'd needed.

'Invite me in, Neve. The quicker you do, the sooner we can be done.'

His tone didn't suggest he wanted to be done. Far from it.

Here was my opportunity to unleash everything I'd bottled up inside thus far. But the burning between my thighs mocked me with *something else*. I ignored it and stepped back.

Damian entered another hotel suite of mine, this time with his demons very much under control. They weren't gone, far from it. I'd caught a glimpse of them as he'd talked about his cousin. Gideon. The reason for the darkness that lurked in his eyes. But he had a tighter leash on them.

Or he was focused on other things. Like…me.

The thought made my insides clench in a way that both shamed and excited me.

I preceded him into the living room, cleared my throat and turned to find him shrugging out of his jacket.

'What are you doing?' I detested the hint of a shriek in my voice.

'Getting comfortable,' he responded, draping his jacket over a chair before he unbuttoned his cuffs and rolled back his sleeves. Damian in full relaxation mode was doing unspeakably erotic things to my sex. 'I have an inkling this will take a while.'

A little stupefied, I stared as his brawny forearms were slowly exposed, my panties growing damper with every passing second.

When he was done, his eyes slowly lifted to mine and held tight. Damn the man. He knew what he was doing.

Just as he'd done when he'd used sex to addle my brain two years ago, just before he'd turned around and chopped me off at the knees.

Two could play at that game.

I reached up and freed my hair from its loose knot and spiked my fingers through it.

His gaze dropped to my breasts and his Adam's apple bobbed before he refocused on my face. 'Neve—'

With a jerk, I stepped away from him and from temptation, denying every lustful urge that rammed at me, and headed for the bar.

'I'm getting myself a drink. Want one, Mr Mortimer?' I threw over my shoulder.

He shook his head. 'No. I don't want a drink.'

'Then what *do* you want?'

'For starters, I really want you to cut the *Mr Mortimer* shit,' he said.

Memories of groaning his given name as he rammed his cock deep inside me, of screaming it as the best orgasm I'd ever had rippled through me, charged through my brain. I wasn't ashamed to admit it was part of the reason I was reticent about calling him by his first name.

I surfaced from that lustful reverie to find his gaze drifting to my legs.

'*For starters?* Sounds like you have a list.'

He shook his head as he strolled towards me. 'Not a list. Just one more item up for discussion.'

'What is it?'

'What did you mean when you said I stabbed you in the back?'

Shock and fury propelled me around, my drink forgotten, everything inside me stilled into immobility by his sheer audacity. 'Are you serious?'

His brow pleated. 'It's a damning accusation. Of course I'm serious.'

I forced myself to relax. *Control.* I had to maintain

control. 'Which part of what happened two years ago do you need reminding of? It's obviously not the sex because you seem to have perfect recall on that score. So it must be the fact that after screwing me in my hotel room, you had no qualms about leaving my bed to screw me over.'

His intense hazel eyes had the audacity to widen before he frowned. 'I was in Boston for one night. The only person I met up with besides you was Malcolm Cahill.'

'Ah, so you do remember. Give the man a prize.'

Shadows darkened his features. 'Neve—'

The slow burn of anger ramped up. 'Don't you dare say my name that way. Don't you dare make out as if what you did was excusable or that I'm blowing it out of proportion.'

He stepped towards me, stopped and shoved his hands in his pockets. 'To do that I'd have to know what you're talking about. I'm not sure exactly why you think I screwed you over. The Mortimer Group was in partnership with Cahill's hotel group. I met up with Cahill to discuss an affiliation deal with a small outfit called Cephei Hotels.'

'Yes,' I said fiercely. 'An outfit owned by me. As you damn well know.'

He tensed. 'What?'

'God, please don't pretend you didn't know that. That's beneath you. How long did you even consider my proposal before you dismissed it out of hand and almost bankrupted me in the process?' I asked, years of bitterness making my voice hoarse.

He was still staring at me as if I were an apparition. 'Cephei Hotels was *you*?'

'Cut the shit, Damian. I heard your side of the phone call when Malcolm called me to break the news, less than an hour after you left my bed, I might add. What was it you said to him? Something along the lines of small fry like me having no business playing with the big boys?'

His tension increased. 'Those were Cahill's words, not mine.'

'But you had quite a bit to add, didn't you, as you and your buddy pulled the rug from under me?'

A muscle ticced in his jaw. 'He's not my buddy. Cahill is a shark but he was a necessary alliance for what I was trying to achieve in Boston.'

'What about my alliance? He was all set to sign with me. Then you got involved and he went with Crown Resorts. I'm bigger than they are.'

'*Now* you are. Two years ago, you weren't.'

My fingers curled into fists. 'Because you saw to it that I wouldn't be given the chance. We had a verbal agreement. My trip to Boston was to get the contract signed. Only the morning after we spent the night together, the deal was suddenly off the table.' Two years' worth of acrimony and fury bubbled, threatened to erupt. 'Was the sex *that* bad?'

He speared me a hard look. 'Self-deprecation doesn't suit you.'

'Then what was it?' I pressed. 'Were you bored? Was messing with me and my business some way to add a little spice to your life?'

He raked his fingers through his hair. 'Believe it or not, it wasn't personal.'

'Really? It felt *extremely* personal. You came to Boston to finalise your portion of the deal. You knew the name of my hotel. You must've known who I was when you met with Cahill.'

His lips flattened. 'Names didn't interest me. I was interested in facts and figures. Yours didn't add up.'

'And you deduced that after, what, an hour? Do you know how long I spent getting that deal together? How hard I worked and how many chips I cashed to make it work?'

'That was your problem,' he fired back. 'You were betting your every last cent on a partnership that would've crushed you within a year. I could smell your desperation in the figures.'

'You bastard.'

The jibe hit its mark and his eyes narrowed. He exhaled harshly as he absorbed it. 'If you think I'm that despicable, why did you sign up for the show?'

I wasn't going to expose my true motives. Not until I had him on his knees. 'Maybe I wanted to look you in the eye and tell you to your face what I think of you. Looks like not enough people have done that in your life.'

A touch of apprehension whispered over his features. 'And now you've done that? Now you've satisfied yourself that I'm a complete bastard, are you going to draw a line under it?'

I laughed. 'You'd love that, wouldn't you?'

His face tightened. 'Remember what I said, Neve. I don't like surprises. And I especially don't like the wool being pulled over my eyes.'

'You should've considered that before you dismissed me out of hand two years ago.'

'How long will it take you to get this out of your system?'

I laughed again. 'I wasn't aware I was on a deadline. There is one on how much time I want to spend in your company though, so if you don't mind I'd like you to leave now.'

He didn't budge. 'Whatever you have up your sleeve, bear in mind what adverse impact it could have on our new partnership.'

'Absolutely none. I want this project with Sam and Tyler to work. My feelings towards you won't impact that.'

Something gleamed in his eyes. 'I'm glad to hear it. But you're wrong on one score. I'm equally invested in this. Perhaps more than you know. So I'm going to be keeping an eye on you.'

Absurdly, I grew hot despite being raw inside from his admission that he'd unapologetically screwed me over. I had a feeling that wound would take time to stop stinging.

Thanks to him, almost overnight my business had dried up, word of mouth already a serious threat to my business. Within weeks the bank had been threatening to pull its funding.

It'd taken the best part of a year of back-breaking hard work, total rebranding and an aggressive marketing plan to ensure that I didn't go under.

I'd emerged from that ordeal better and stronger but the lesson had been hard and a part of me remained battered and bruised by the experience. And *no* part of me was ready to let Damian off the hook.

I'm equally invested in this. Perhaps more than you know.

His words ricocheted in my head. I eyed him. 'Why? This is just a small cog in your family business. Besides, you don't strike me as someone who's into fantasies. Nightmares maybe?'

The corner of his mouth kicked up, and that small action fired heat straight to my clit. 'This is as good a swan song as any. As for my fantasies, they're many and varied. Maybe when that homicidal look is no longer in your eyes, I might be inclined to show you one of them.'

My ache in my midriff felt at odds with the heaviness in my breasts and the softening in my pelvis. How could I despise him and want to fuck him blind at the same time? 'That's assuming you're still sane by the time I'm done with you.'

His gaze fired up, dropping to my mouth. 'You do realise the more you hint at your nebulous plans for me, the more I'm inclined to let you go through with whatever it is you have up your sleeve?'

My smile came easier this time and I realised, with a little shock, that I was enjoying tussling with him. Perhaps a little too much.

'You do realise that was my intention?' I murmured, keeping my voice low and husky. His gaze flicked to mine, stayed and held.

'It's the first time a business partner has threatened to keep me in line. Normally it's the other way round.'

'Maybe more of us should do that.' Still keeping my voice low, I took a single step towards him.

His eyes dropped to my breasts. His lips moved in the tiniest pout, as if savouring my taste, before his scrutiny moved lower to caress my hips and legs before slowly trailing back up again.

By the time our gazes reconnected, I was left in no doubt that he wanted me. Badly.

'It's never happened before because my partnerships start with a baseline of trust. Perhaps we should aim for that between us?'

'I don't trust easily, Mr Mortimer.'

His nostrils flared as his fingers trailed down my arm. Tingles shot from the point of contact to my needy pussy.

'What's it going to take for you to call me Damian?'

You and your rock-hard cock, driving deep into my pussy.

For a moment I thought I'd said the words out loud. I gasped softly as his fingers closed on my elbow.

'Damian. There, does that work for you?'

The blaze in his eyes grew dangerous and potent. 'I'd love to say *once more, with feeling*, preferably as a prelude to sealing our deal the way I'm sorely tempted to, but for now I'll take it.'

I didn't need to ask how he would seal the deal. His eyes spelled it out explicitly. And, worse, I wanted to let him. *Badly.*

I remained still as the sexual cyclone churned and heated up the air around us, making my fingers itch to reacquaint themselves with his hard body, experience that glorious mouth and the magic of his hands.

Unable to help myself, I let my gaze fly up to land on his mouth. Would he taste just as spectacular as he had two years ago?

Two years ago…when he'd stabbed me in the back after sleeping with me.

My insides froze.

Damian made a frustrated sound under his breath. 'There's that look again. Tell me how to fix it and I promise to give it my best shot.' The demand was low and deep. Almost as if he meant it. Almost as if my distrust aggravated him.

I attempted to step away, but he kept hold of me. His thumb slowly caressed my pulse, spiking arousal higher, hardening my nipples into needy points.

'Give me a starting point, Neve. We can work our way towards whatever goal you want.'

'Really? Whatever I want?'

He gave a solemn nod. 'Within reason, of course… but I'd prefer we don't have bad blood between us.'

Again his words were grave, containing a wealth of unspoken meaning.

But there was no way I was going anywhere near his questionable olive branch. There was one burning question I still needed an answer to, though. One he hadn't yet answered to my satisfaction.

'Would knowing who I was, knowing who you were screwing over, have made a blind bit of difference?'

He held my gaze for an uncomfortably long time. My breath froze in my lungs; I was suddenly unsure whether I wanted the truth or evasion of some sort. *The truth*, my brain and heart demanded. No matter how much it hurt to hear it, I wanted the truth from Damian. Always.

'No,' he said after nerve-stretching silence. 'It wouldn't have. You weren't ready for a deal that big.'

I flinched. That stung just as badly now as it had two years ago. As had his addendum to Malcolm Cahill.

'Was that why you told him not to speak to me? I asked for a face-to-face meeting to plead my case. You advised him to tell me no. Why?'

He shrugged. 'I didn't want things to drag on un-necessarily. I wanted to be done with it. With Boston.'

My breath caught. 'So it *was* personal.'

He turned abruptly, stalked to the window and looked out onto a glittering, electrified Manhattan. After an age, he faced me.

'You're a stunning, sexy woman.' His lips firmed as if he didn't want to admit the words. 'But I didn't intend to fuck anyone that night. Hell, I almost didn't come to Boston at all. I could've phoned in everything I wanted to say to Cahill. But I needed to get out of New York. I needed to focus on something else besides the fact that I'd hit another bloody wall with Gideon.'

It didn't appease me to know why there had been raging demons in his eyes that night. 'So you redirected your shit my way?' I probed.

Again he stared at me as if he was making up his mind about something. 'Only a handful of people know the full details about why I left England. Without boring you with the nitty-gritty of it, I'll tell you that your little…performance at the bar hit the wrong notes…right after you hit all the right ones.'

I frowned. 'I'm confused.'

He exhaled harshly. 'I saw you when you arrived at the hotel. Even before I knew your name I was fuck-ing hooked. Call me crass if you will, but I watched you crossing the lobby and wondered what you'd taste like. Wondered how loud you'd scream when I made you come. I was dying to be inside you long before I sat down at the bar. Which was an inconvenient nov-elty considering I hadn't fucked anyone for a while and wasn't planning to.' That last part was delivered with a heavy dose of bitter bewilderment that doused my arousal.

'Why not?'

'Because the last woman I met at a bar before you left an unpalatable taste in my mouth.'

Curiosity bit at me. Hard. But the stiff lines on his face told me he wouldn't elaborate. Even the little he'd told me seemed to torture him. 'So I made you hard crossing the lobby and you decided to punish me for buying you a drink?'

His hand scraped over his jaw to grip his nape. 'When you put it like that I sound like a bloody asshole.'

'Your words, not mine.'

Harsh lines etched deeper between his brows and bracketed his mouth. 'I didn't take kindly to you being that irresistible. To knocking my damn socks off with that defiance and sexiness. I don't think I take kindly to it now, to be fucking honest,' he admitted raggedly. 'I should stay away from you, focus on…straightening a few dented parts of my life. But instead here I am, being driven bloody insane by this…*need*,' he continued, his gaze raking feverishly over me once more. 'But the bottom line is if we were in the situation now like we were two years ago, I'd take the same stance with you and with Cahill. So my question to you is, what are we going to do about it?'

Pain and hurt warred with sharp questions.

Who? Why? When?

But Damian wanting me, perhaps even despite himself, surged power through me, heady and triumphant, temporarily shoving away the ache of his admission that he'd screw me over again. All he'd done really was show me that I couldn't trust him with what was precious to me—my business. My legacy. The reminder that this was just sex settled, *thankfully*, deeper inside me.

I closed the gap between us. Head tilted, I looked into his face. Past the shadows cast by demons to the sizzling-hot arousal and undeniable need.

His *and* mine.

What his actions had cost me burned just as bright, perhaps even more considering there wasn't any remorse on his part.

But he'd just handed me the two things I craved more than anything else in this world. The two things I needed to see my way clear of this cloud of lust and bitterness to my end goal.

Power and control.

And fuck if I wasn't going to grasp them with both hands.

CHAPTER SIX

Neve

I SLICKED MY tongue over my lower lip, revelled in his thick, muted groan. 'What would you like me to do about it, Damian?'

His gaze devoured my mouth with naked hunger. It was more than animalistic need. It was consuming in a way that mildly terrified me. 'You don't need me to draw you a bloody map, Neve,' he said gruffly before closing the space between us to drag me against his body. The heavy column of his cock branded my belly. 'You know what I want.'

My pussy clenched, reminding me how desperate it was to be filled. I placed a hand on his chest, registered solid muscle and a strong heartbeat beneath his shirt.

'Do I? Our wires crossed badly somewhere along the line two years ago.'

'In the aftermath, maybe. But not with this.' He lowered his head until our lips brushed. It was like being caught in an inferno. 'Never with this.'

My resistance was swept beneath the fiery lust that blazed through me. 'You want to kiss me.'

He pinned me closer until my pelvis was flushed with his. Until the outline of his thick, hard cock was imprinted between my legs. 'Fuck yes. I want to kiss you and more besides. You know how long it took to get a good night's sleep without jerking off to the memory of you sucking me off?'

My breath rushed out, along with a cheeky, unfettered little moan as he rocked his hips against me. The friction released liquid heat, slicking my pussy.

I'd never thought I'd enjoy giving a blowjob until I met Damian. Taking him in my mouth, hearing his hiss and grunts of pleasure had triggered mine in a way I'd never imagined. I wanted the experience again.

But on *my* terms.

'How long?' I stoked the fires of his memory, shamelessly eager for the validation that our night together had impacted on him too.

'Too damn long. And it wasn't just the memory of you giving me head either. It was those insane sounds you made when I spread you wide and rammed inside your pussy that drove me nuts for weeks. It was learning how every inch of your body responds to being fucked. How you felt when you came on my cock.'

I shuddered through the explicit memories.

He'd taken his sweet time, driving into me over and over until I hadn't been able to think or see straight. Until I hadn't been sure whether to beg him to stop or plead for more.

Another groan vibrated inside me, but I forcibly snapped it off when I realised what he was doing. He was wrestling control from me. With each roll of his hips, each heated word that made me dig my fingers into his shoulders, I was seconds away from begging him to actively and enthusiastically refresh my memory.

With superhuman effort, I smothered my need, placed my hands over the fingers digging in my hip bones, melting me from the inside out. 'You've told me what you want. Now let me tell you what I want.'

His gaze hazed for the moment, going blurry as if he'd retreated inward, and then he gave an abrupt nod.

'You turn me on. But I won't be as easy this time around.'

Abruptly, he released me and placed a few feet between us. I struggled to keep the bereft hollow in my stomach from showing on my face.

'I didn't think you were easy the first time around,' he said in clipped tones. 'The torment of being under your spell is still seared in my brain.'

I almost laughed but I throttled it back because I realised that laughter was directed at myself. At my unstoppable craving for a man I should've left alone. At thinking I was in control when I'd been his sexual slave. 'I might take you to places you don't like.'

Again the corner of his mouth kicked up but the action was a lot less mirthful this time. His fingers traced my collarbone slowly, leaving a trail of fire that nearly made me moan again. 'I'm a big boy. If words fail me I'll find another way to communicate. I guarantee you.'

His response triggered a need to test his boundaries. Test *my* boundaries. So much it terrified me.

I whirled away and headed for the bar. I didn't really want to drink but I craved respite from the rampant arousal surging through me.

His gaze followed me, heavy and wanting, as I plucked a fresh glass off the tray.

'I'm getting that drink now. Do you want one?'

A hard mask descended over his face as he strolled towards me. 'I get my own drinks, thanks.' The words were sharp and chilled with an underlying note I couldn't decode.

It reminded me of that night we'd met. His refusal of my drink and the water I'd seen him stick to since. It was either a peculiar ritual exclusive to him or...

My brain threw up blanks. I searched his face but his expression remained closed. He watched closely as I fixed myself a dirty martini and added the three olives I preferred.

He didn't move from his spot on the carpet. His fists were curled tight and a quiet fury vibrated from him.

Instinctively, I knew his reaction wasn't aimed at me. 'Is everything okay?'

He took a visibly relaxing breath although his harsh expression remained. 'I'm fine,' he said abruptly.

'Hmm.'

He watched me for a handful of seconds before perching on the opposite stool. Even with the counter between us, the force of his charisma and sheer gorgeousness hit me square in the chest.

It grew worse when his elbows landed on the hard wooden surface, his bare forearms drawing my gaze to the wispy hairs that covered his golden skin.

It was hard to swallow, just thinking about his hard, packed body. Only the sound of his voice drew my attention back to his insanely gorgeous face.

I grimaced inwardly. This was going to be much harder than I'd thought. Relief spiked through me when my phone buzzed. I pounced on my clutch, fished out my phone and read the message.

'It's Tyler. They've arrived in Westport and are already setting up.' I sent a quick reply and placed my phone on the counter.

His lips twisted. 'Now that we've established where we both stand from two years ago, are you going to clue me in on whatever you have planned?'

I didn't even bother to deny the allegation. 'No.'

'Getting back to business for a minute, I'm prepared, if the trial period is successful, to throw the PR and marketing skills of The Mortimer Group behind this project. For free.'

My hackles rose. 'I don't need your charity, especially if you think it'll grant you special privileges of the sexual kind.'

'I prefer to see it as goodwill. You seem to think this is just a whim for me. I'm giving you my word that I'm committed to this project and will stick to the agreements we make.'

'I have a solid marketing department of my own, thanks.'

He eyed me. 'You don't have to give up control to get what you need, Neve. Not unless you expressly wish to.'

My heart lurched, then kept on falling as I spotted the astute intelligence in his eyes. Somehow he'd latched onto my governing essence. The one that warned against giving in to the reckless lust prowling inside me. Not until I could handle any fallout.

We sized each other up for a long stretch. And even after my gaze dropped I knew he was still staring at me because my whole body tingled wildly. I set my glass down between his outstretched forearms and re-sisted the temptation to trail my fingers over his skin.

'I have an early start. I'm going to call it a night.'

'You haven't finished your drink.'

I shrugged as my phone buzzed again. Tyler, with gushing remarks about the Westport resort that made me smile. Soothed me in ways I hadn't known I needed.

'Tyler again?' Damian asked curtly when I set the phone down.

'Hmm. He likes the resort.'

Damian snorted.

'Problem?'

His smile was cocky. 'None that I foresee.'

His arrogance grated.

'You sure?' I goaded.

'You want me, Neve. You might be a little con-flicted right now about how much but we'll work through it.'

The grounded assurance in his voice made some-thing fragile lurch inside me. 'Why should I go through the trouble? Why not pick someone else en-tirely to scratch my itch who isn't you?'

Thunder rumbled over his face, devouring his cock-iness. 'If you're trying to pick another fight with me, forget it. You want me just as badly as I want you. You're not going to fuck anyone else just to spite me.'

Again his conceit grated. Badly. I forced a smile as I rounded the bar. 'I guess if you say so then it must be true,' I mocked.

He caught hold of me before I could walk past him. 'Tell me this is another game,' he breathed, irritation stamped all over his face that made me want to smile and smile and smile.

'Why, Damian? Would it bother you?'

His lips flattened as if he didn't want to answer. Then, 'Yes, it'll fucking bother me. I don't know what the hell you think you're playing at but—'

'I haven't been fucked properly in a very long time, Damian. I was busy, you see, trying to get back on my feet after what you did. But now my business is thriving again and I'm on the brink of striking an exciting new deal. Why the hell not see to my needs with an orgasm or six with someone I have a connection with?'

I was goading him. It was turning me on. I needed to stop.

The fingers gripping my waist dug in. Not enough to hurt but enough to confirm I had his sizzling, unwavering attention. The weight of it dripped right through to my bones. 'You have a connection with *me*,' he replied cuttingly, right before his mouth crashed on mine.

A part of me had seen this coming the moment I'd started taunting him. That part joined the rest of my body to sing with lustful joy as sparks turned into flames and engulfed me.

For two long years I'd relived the electrifying thrill of kissing Damian.

Reality was, oh, so much better.

There was no tentative exploration. Our tongues boldly stroked and duelled, dragging taste and texture from each other as my arms wound around his neck.

He pulled me roughly into his body, his feverish hands relearning my every curve. In turn, I ground those curves into him, imprinted myself against his hardness as hunger became a living, twisting entity I couldn't control.

He rolled his hips sinuously, refreshing my memory of how expertly he could move. My fingers tunnelled into his hair, my nails scraping his scalp in a frenzied need to keep him where he was, delivering pleasure I'd been seriously starved of.

With a thick groan, his fingers dug into my ass, tugged me up tighter into his groin and pivoted me against the bar.

Heat exploded between my legs, my clit swelling with enough crazed enthusiasm to draw a whimper from me.

Damian pulled away for a scant second and eyes ablaze with carnal intent met mine. 'You taste even better than I remember.' One hand roved my body, caressed my ribcage, my lower back, and then palmed one breast. 'And you're just as lush,' he muttered thickly before squeezing my nipple between his thumb and forefinger.

I cried out, jerking against his hold. 'Ah…'

My reaction triggered a rabid response. His breathing grew harsher and his mouth returned to devour mine. Sounds continued to trip unaided from my throat and I was convinced I'd orgasm just from kissing Damian.

Abruptly he gripped my waist, lifted me up and strode purposefully towards the sofa.

The moment my back hit the cushions, he crawled over me and dragged me into another erotically charged kiss.

Urgent hands returned to my breasts.

Double the torture, double the pleasure, he moulded

them, then toyed mercilessly with the stiff peaks, driving me even further insane. When desperation for oxygen drove us apart, he raised his head, staring down at me. The sight of lips bruised from our kiss and hair falling tangled by my hands, was almost too arousing to bear.

Lust and a touch of bewilderment crowded his face. 'I didn't think it was possible.'

'What?' I cringed at the husky slur to my speech.

'That I could be this turned on by you. Just kissing you for a minute is already screwing with my head.' He lowered his head and took my mouth in another sizzling kiss before he abruptly broke off. 'How long?'

'What?' How was he forming words when my brain was under threat of turning into mush?

'You said you hadn't been fucked in a while.'

'You think now's the time to remind me why I'm in this state?' I parried.

The stinging resentment I should've felt didn't surface. It was buried beneath the colossal weight of my arousal.

His fingers didn't stop torturing my nipples, nor did his expression show an ounce of regret. 'Tell me,' he demanded in a low, sexy voice.

Did he really think I was going to inflate his ego by divulging that I hadn't slept with anyone since him? My hands trailed down his back to dig into his ass. Simultaneously, I undulated my hips, bringing his cock into singeing contact with my pussy. 'Do you want to do this or do you want to ask questions I won't answer?'

He stared at me with eyes almost black with desire. 'Do what exactly?'

Fuck me hard. Make me scream with ecstasy the way you did in Boston.

But not until he begged for it.

I removed my hands from his ass, dropped them to my side, long enough for a wave of uncertainty to shimmer in his eyes. I wanted him to taste the possibility that I might walk away from him, leave us both high and dry.

When his face began to tighten, I nudged him away until he braced onto his elbows and knees, then reached down and slowly dragged up the hem of my cocktail dress. Feverish eyes dropped to follow the movement, his breathing growing erratic as my French lace knickers were exposed.

The hand cupping my breasts clenched for one unguarded second. 'Fuck.'

Involuntarily, he squeezed my nipples again. My back arched and another bolt of heat shot to my pussy. God, I was going to climax long before Damian got anywhere near the centre of my need. Striving for control, I drew out the moment, dragged my panties down my legs and kicked them off.

He watched me with hooded eyes that burned with the promise of insane pleasure.

I took hold of one hand and slowly pried it off my breast. Drawing it down, I kissed his knuckle, then slowly drew his middle digits into my mouth. Eyes locked with his, I flicked my tongue over his fingers, smiling when his breath hissed out.

For a minute, I toyed with him, then sucked him deep into my mouth.

'Jesus,' he groaned.

When he was near panting, I let his fingers pop free.

Then inch by inch I drew his hand down my body until it rested against my bare pussy.

'You want to know how long it's been? Feel for yourself.'

Damian boldly cupped my heat. 'Fuck, Neve, you're soaking wet,' he rasped in a ragged voice.

One thick knuckle grazed my clit and I cried out as electricity forked through my body. He repeated the action, over and over until my hips fell into a desperate, eager rhythm.

God, I was going to disgrace myself by climaxing just from Damian rubbing my pussy. How utterly humiliating would that be? I forced my body to stop twitching in an effort to make this last.

As if sensing the challenge, Damian grazed me one last time, then flipped his hand and parted my folds in a brazen V.

Fingers wet from my mouth and my own slickness pinched my clit. My hands flew to his shoulders and dug in as waves of pleasure rolled over me.

'Oh, God!'

He swooped down, tasting my pleasure with a hot and hard kiss while he intermittently tweaked my nipple. A whimper surged from my throat.

'You like that?' he growled against my mouth.

'Yes,' I replied breathlessly.

With a harshly drawn breath, he caught the corner of my lip between his teeth, bit down lightly as he plunged his fingers inside me.

My cry of pleasure was unfettered, the clench of my pussy urgent and shameless.

'Bloody hell, Neve. You're so fucking tight,' he groaned. 'So damn glorious.'

He withdrew, then fed his fingers back into me, biting me again, then licked the sting before moving back to watch the delicious havoc he was creating between my legs. Against my thigh, his cock grew thicker.

'Just watching you fuck my fingers is going to blow my load. You know that?' he slurred.

Blind need overtook me. 'More. I want one more. Stretch me, Damian. Fill me up.'

I couldn't stop the words tumbling from my lips any more than I could stop myself from racing towards the peak that promised pure bliss.

A wave of red washed over Damian's cheekbones as he inserted another finger inside me. Pressure increased. Intensified. My fingers clawed at him, desperate for more connection. 'Kiss me,' I panted.

He fell on me like a starving predator, his tongue mimicking what his fingers were doing to me.

Sensation grew too much. My fingers dug into his skin and he groaned.

'Yes, darling,' he muttered hotly against my mouth. 'Come for me. Let me feel you drench my fingers. I want to taste it so badly.' Tense hunger filled his voice, echoing mine.

No, I wasn't going to go there. This was for me and me alone.

'Harder,' I moaned. 'Faster.'

His laugh was low, sexy and *pained*. 'Yes, beautiful. Whatever you need.'

That simple concession from my nemesis flipped the switch to bliss.

With a cry ripped from deep within me, I succumbed to rapture. It flowed through me in an endless wave, singeing every cell in my body, reawakening every pleasure point.

'God, you feel amazing, but I'm dying to taste you again,' he rasped.

With a savage grunt, he reared away, gripped my thigh to open me wider before his head swooped between my legs.

He drew my clit hard between his lips, sucked and sucked and unbelievably triggered another orgasm.

'Oh, God, I'm coming again!'

'Yes,' he groaned against my pussy. 'Give it to me, Neve. I want all of it.'

Fingers digging into his hair, I surrendered all until every ounce of oxygen was wrung from my lungs. I melted into the cushions, his firm grip my only anchor to reality.

Slowly, he withdrew his fingers from me, kissed his way up my body until his lips hovered above mine.

Unwilling to let the sensation end, I dragged him down. Our lips met and I tasted myself on him. Another minute of furious kissing passed before he raised his head.

'You taste even better than I remember.' His voice was guttural. Barely coherent. And just as he'd drowned me in pleasure I wanted to see him lost in ecstasy too. Which sort of defeated the object of this exercise.

Despite my head swimming with the force of my extended orgasm, I needed to take control of the situation. I managed to curve my lips in a sultry smile. 'Well, I'm very happy for you, then.'

The stare we traded was weighted with tense, unwanted questions.

But when his head swooped low again I knew it was time to end this.

Hands that weren't as firm as I needed them to be pushed at his chest as I swung my legs to the floor.

I ignored Damian's probing gaze as I hunted for the heels that had fallen off at some point. My panties were nowhere in sight. Unwilling to suffer the indignity of hunting for them, I stood, praying my legs would support me. Relieved when they did, I adjusted my clothes, straightened my hair, went to the door and threw it open with a pointed look.

'You're tossing me out?' Disbelief rang through the cut-glass English accent.

I drew in a shaky breath. 'Were you expecting something else? Something more?'

He greeted my clear challenge with narrowed, blazing eyes before dragging unsteady fingers through his hair.

After a full minute, he stood, whatever he'd wanted to say imprisoned between his clenched teeth as his gaze flamed over my body. The sight of the erection tenting his fly nearly undid me. I might have experienced a ground-shaking orgasm but clearly my body craved more.

I held my breath as he prowled towards me, all heat and need and brooding watchfulness, his eyes probing for weaknesses.

My hand tightened on the door, fighting the desperation clawing at me. 'My car service is on speed dial, if you need it?'

His gorgeous hazel eyes lingered on my face and the flush still burning my cheeks before dropping to my chest. 'No. My driver's downstairs.'

'In that case…goodnight, Damian.'

He stopped in the doorway, filling it with his wide, magnificent body. 'You won't always have things your way, Neve.'

I clung tighter to the door so I didn't do something crazy, like lunge for him. 'You don't think so? Well, I look forward to our next skirmish.'

I shut the door in his face, but the memory of a sexily dishevelled Damian with his cock hard and his expression holding that curious mixture of bewilderment, arousal and disbelief didn't fade away as quickly as I wanted it to.

I'd triumphed over need and weakness. It should've pleased me. Instead I wondered if I wasn't digging a grave for both of us.

Damian

What the hell had just happened?

Back in my penthouse suite, high above the feverish pulse of Manhattan, I paced my living room in a semi-daze. Stopping before the wall of glass I wished were another wall in another hotel, I reached into my pocket and pulled out the scrap of contraband from my pocket.

Neve's panties.

Yes, I'd turned into *that* creep.

The feel of the delicate lace between my fingers arrested my restless prowl. My cock throbbed even harder, its anguish at being denied echoing agonisingly through my body. A quick jacking off would ease the discomfort. Hell, in my desperate state I'd probably only need half a dozen strokes to do the job. But I made no move to unzip my fly. Instead I caressed the silk for a moment, and brought it to my nose.

Her heady scent filled my nostrils and I groaned. I was compounding my problem, but between the lingering taste on my tongue, the scent of her perfume and the smell of her pussy, I had a sneaking suspicion it was physically impossible to be any more turned on than I was right now.

Hell, I didn't know whether to be pissed off or turned on by the stunt she'd pulled. Or kick my own arse for leaving her slick and wet pussy without more of a fight.

I chose the pissed route because the alternative was admitting I was seriously addicted to the insane chemistry binding us.

It was that uncontrollable reaction that had compelled me to hunt her down in her hotel room in Boston. That same visceral, unstoppable need that had bypassed all my rigid safeguards and propelled me to the woman with sparkling blue eyes that radiated determination and intelligence, and a mouth designed to bring a man to his knees.

Over the years, my contribution to the elevation of The Mortimer Group from certain bankruptcy to staggering prosperity had garnered the right accolades. With that had come attention of the female kind.

Work hard.

Party harder.

For years, I'd seen absolutely nothing wrong in revelling in that ethos. There was nothing more blissfully satisfying than losing oneself between the thighs of a willing woman after scoring a mega successful deal, especially if it involved besting an opponent.

With Gideon by my side, the ride had been doubly gratifying.

Until Penny and her lies and treachery had ruined it all.

I crushed the scrap of lace and silk a second before my balled fist shot out. I reined it in a scant inch before it connected with the glass. Breathed in. Out. Pressed my knuckles against the cool glass and attempted to rein myself in.

Anguish knotted in my chest.

Regardless of the aftermath, I was still at fault for heeding Penny's call in the first place. Misguided or not, I'd dropped my guard and trusted the words of a pathological, conscienceless liar. More than that, I'd forgotten the single most important lesson I'd learned since I was old enough to reason for myself.

Everyone has an agenda.

And nine times out of ten, it was a self-serving one. My own parents were a prime example. They'd stuck around long enough to do their duty by the family name. Then they'd walked away without a backward glance, their children someone else's burden.

Resentment tapped from a different vein threatened to rise but my issue with Hugh and Margaret Mortimer, the people I had the dubious privilege of calling my parents, *would* stay in the background of my mind, where it belonged.

After all, they'd put me completely out of theirs for most of my life.

Gideon, however...

That wound was aggravating. But more than that, now I finally knew the truth, it was a problem I could put behind me.

So I could move on?

To what?

The irony wasn't lost on me that while I was spouting off about establishing a baseline trust to Neve I had none left in my personal reserves. And surprisingly, I'd adapted to living without it.

Business-wise I kept my promises. Perhaps I shouldn't fight this need to overcome her resistance. Perhaps Neve having her own agenda was the reminder I needed to keep her at arm's length?

I grimaced at the fierce denial that tunnelled through me.

This had gone beyond business.

I wanted her. Badly. Enough to attempt to breach that wall she'd built around herself despite knowing she was right in her accusation about my actions two years ago.

I hadn't held back my verdict to Cahill because I'd believed she wasn't ready. I stood by that belief.

And hell, the morning after the night in her bed, I'd been in no mood to prolong any association with Malcolm Cahill beyond the necessary. I'd woken up burning in the reality that there'd be no definitive resolution to the hours Penny had stolen from me by drugging me that night. That there would always be a hole in my life from her actions.

I slammed my closed fist against the glass. Neve's scent invaded my senses again. And just like that I was hard as fuck again.

Forehead propped against the cool glass, I brought the fragile scrap to my nose and inhaled long and deep. The inevitable accepted, I tugged my zip down and freed my engorged cock. Tension and anticipation ramped through me as I wrapped Neve's panties around my cock and began to stroke myself.

The hard piston-fast tugs were nowhere near as glorious as I knew her tight, wet pussy would've been. My dick didn't care. Within seconds my balls drew up tight and urgent. A thick curse ripped from my throat, my vision blanked and hot spurts spilled onto my lace-covered hand.

When I caught my breath, I staggered a few steps and dropped onto the sofa and accepted my reality. Neve Nolan was a fever in my blood. One I was certain wouldn't easily be dispersed.

Acceptance brought a little questionable relief.

And two dozen churning questions.

How did I break down Neve's walls? Why the hell did I want to when my own were built on questionable foundations?

And beyond that, could I go ahead without coming clean about my past?

But fuck…how the hell did you tell the woman you were insanely attracted to that all signs pointed to the fact that three years ago you'd been *roofied* and ended up in bed with your cousin's fiancée?

A chill burrowed deep into my bones, tightening every muscle in my body in anger and frustrated bitterness.

There was no way to relate that story without inducing disgust and mistrust. Hell, I was shocked and disgusted at myself for falling for the trap of going for a drink with Penny in the first place.

As for trust, how could I begin to trust anyone when I didn't even trust myself?

The answer was shockingly clear.

I couldn't.

I was better off heeding my instinct to keep things strictly business.

CHAPTER SEVEN

Damian

INSTINCT.

That bloody useless and fickle thing changed its mind the moment I stepped off the helicopter early afternoon the next day, and saw Neve waiting on the edge of the helipad.

Last night, her cocktail dress might have looked spectacular, but the jade-green sundress gracing her body today was equally breathtaking.

The halterneck number displayed her flawless, lightly tanned shoulders and arms, and curved over her neat waist and hips to end a couple of inches above the knee, leaving her endless legs bare and immediately triggering images of them wrapped around my waist.

My situation wasn't helped by the fact that I'd spent yet another restless night fighting the temptation to return to her hotel and talk her into finishing what she'd started.

I approached, my resistance crumbled to dust as the churned air from the rotor blades whipped Neve's dark blonde hair across her face. She lifted a hand to slide strands off her cheek. A small gesture but my seriously sex-deprived state meant the motion of watching her tuck her long hair behind her ear was hell on my groin. Or perhaps it was that bold confidence in her eyes that threatened to undo me.

Undeniably, something about a strong, confident woman pushed all my buttons.

Or *had* once upon a time before another woman's actions had shattered my trust.

That I could be in the throes of resurgence…that Neve was the instrument of that reversal…unnerved me, enough to slow my approach.

She didn't seem anywhere near as afflicted. She eyed me, her smile so annoyingly neutral I yearned to pin her against the nearest wall until she begged for my cock.

'Welcome to Nevirna Resort and Spa, Westport.'

'Thanks,' I replied, unable to resist checking her out one more time before glancing around. 'This place looks great.' Much better than the pictures in the report my people had put together.

'Thank you.'

We locked gazes as a member of staff offloaded my weekend bag. For several exquisite seconds, everything we did last night flashed between us. The fire banked by that unsatisfactory jacking off roared back to life.

It was pointless to hide it so I let my lust blaze in my gaze.

Her nostrils flared for a nanosecond, my only hint that she'd registered my intention before she regained control.

'Did you have a good flight, Mr Mortimer?' Sam asked as she and Tyler joined us.

'It was uneventful.' I'd buried myself in work to stop me from thinking about Neve or Gideon.

Each problem would have my attention soon enough. One sooner than the other.

Neve waved us towards a deluxe golf buggy. 'Would you like a quick tour before you're delivered to your room?'

'Sure, why not?'

We headed for the four-man buggy and I slid beside her as she took the wheel. Unlike last night's evocative scent, her perfume today was light, wispy, like the first burst of spring. Hints of apple and lemongrass teased me, sparking an intense need to bury my nose in that sweet curve of her neck and inhale her skin. Or take a juicy bite out of her.

I contented myself with placing my arm along the top of the bench seat, letting strands of her unfettered hair fall over and caress my arm as we set off. Aware that I risked another hard-on if I stared too long at the legs exposed by her hitched-up dress, I redirected my attention to my surroundings.

Tastefully manicured gardens, artistic stone fountains, infinity pools, intimate outside dining areas perfect for al fresco or candlelit dinners—the resort was charming and very well put-together. And much bigger than I'd originally thought.

'Do you get much business from the golf club next door?' I'd spotted the golf course as we'd come in to land.

'About twenty per cent.'

I nodded. It was a balanced ratio that meant she wouldn't be at the mercy of the club if it went bust. Unlike last time when she'd had very few contingencies.

She pulled up in front of a sprawling two-storey building that looked like the main hub of the resort, stepped out and nodded to a hovering valet.

'I've arranged lunch for us. My chef cooks a mean lobster. I hope you're hungry.' Her smile was aimed at the twins but the look in her eyes was reserved for me. Echoes of lustful moans, lashes of pleasure, grunts of hunger bounced between us. My gaze dropped to her chest and her nipples were hard points beneath the thin layer of her dress.

Saliva rushed into my mouth, the need to taste the rosy buds I'd been denied last night pounding through my veins. 'I'm ravenous. Lead the way.'

The faintest blush stained her cheeks as she turned and headed inside.

The main reception area was just as impressive as the outside. A glass-and-stone muted waterfall feature formed an eye-catching centrepiece with the reception desk and seating area framed around it. Wide hallways shot off at intermittent angles and it was down one of them that she led us into the bright sunlit restaurant.

She took charge, confidently making recommendations on food and wine. I nodded without really paying attention and ate whatever was placed in front of me.

I was too busy wondering when I could get Neve alone, how best to batter down the hostility bristling from her, when I noticed the silence.

I looked up to find three pairs of eyes fixed on me with varying expressions of irritation and discomfort.

'Beg your pardon, can you repeat that?'

Sam smiled. 'We were talking about our families. Did you know that when Neve inherited this place from her grandparents it was nothing but a four-bedroom B & B?'

I switched my attention to Neve, saw the wariness in her watchful gaze. Shit, I really did a number on her if divulging news of what had to be an amazing accomplishment made her tetchy.

'I didn't know that. Consider me impressed.'

'Yeah, so were we.' Tyler smiled as he rose. 'Thank you for a lovely lunch, but, if you'll excuse us, we need to get back to work.'

I switched my gaze to Neve as the twins departed. Her expression remained sceptical but marginally less guarded.

'The other question Sam asked was about *your* family,' she said. 'Are your parents back in England too?'

I tensed, then forced myself to relax.

So she was interested in me beyond sex. While the thought was gratifying, the subject matter was far from welcome. My parents belonged to a box I rarely liked to visit. A box that represented secret childish yearnings that would never be fulfilled. A box I'd buried a very long time ago when I'd learned to thrive without emotional crutches.

I wanted to refuse but the look in her eyes compelled an answer.

'No. They live in Greece.'

She leaned forward. 'Oh? Where? I visited Athens very briefly a long time ago. Loved it. The people are so warm and friendly.'

My smile felt as tight as the bitterness twisting inside me. 'My parents didn't go to Greece for the warmth or friendliness, I'm sure. Their reasons were far less ecologically inclined.'

She flinched, and silence dropped like an anvil, smashing a briefly pleasant atmosphere. I felt a little bad. Not enough to dilute the brutal truth though.

The uncomfortable silence was broken by the waiter's arrival to clear away our plates. Neve chatted with him for a minute but through it all, my gaze resting on her face as she talked, I saw the fiery *what the fuck?* looks she sent me.

The temptation to tell her to down her sword, tell her she'd won in the business stakes this time rose.

I stopped myself just in time. I wasn't going to let sex get in the way of this deal.

Business was what I was best at. And staying close, keeping an eye on how Fantasy Rooms progressed, was prudent.

The waiter finally left, leaving me blessedly alone with Neve. Her expression didn't bode well; nevertheless my dark mood receded, replaced by deep carnal anticipation.

'Suggestion. Maybe you should make more of an effort in the presence of my new business partners, huh?'

I smiled. 'Don't you mean *our* business partners?'

Her plump lips flattened in an irritated line.

'If they wanted to keep my interest they should've stuck to talking business. But that's not what this is about, is it, Neve? I'm a Mortimer. If you didn't want to hear about my unsightly baggage or hear unsavoury truths, you shouldn't have asked.'

She glared harder. 'It's called *getting to know each other.*'

'Go on, then, it's your turn.'

'If you wanted to know, then you should've paid attention.'

Shit. What did I miss? 'I'm paying attention now.'

'You lost your chance. Now I'm more interested in what you meant about your parents.'

Tension spiked again but I throttled it down. 'Why?'

She shrugged, the action highlighting the smooth curve of her shoulder. Sunlight glinted off her creamy skin, wetting my mouth with the need to trail my tongue over it.

'I'd like to know if you inherited your rude and abrasive characteristics from them.'

The pulse beating at her throat made me harder. I itched to stroke it. Stroke her all over, right before I devoured her. I wanted to feast on her in so many ways I doubted we'd make it out alive by the time I was done. She caught the direction of my thoughts. Her colour heightened and she pressed her lips together in that way I was beginning to realise signalled, and attempted to deny, her arousal.

'You think you can handle me, Neve?'

'I've *proved* I can handle you,' she fired back. 'But of course, if you're scared of a little...revelation, you can go right back to brooding like some wannabe rock star.'

I laughed. The sound startled me, emerging from a place I thought was locked and weighted down with concrete. With a start I realised it'd been a while...hell, a long while since I'd laughed so heartily.

And I was laughing because of Neve.

The sound slowly died as I watched her expression alter.

Soften.

That heavy stone I'd carried for longer than I could remember, the one that didn't permit me to give any quarter when it came to useless emotion…shifted. Attempted to crack open. I tightened my gut against the sensation, whipping up anger that felt a little out of place.

Foolish and overdramatic.

Bloody hell, what was going on with me? This was about sex. Ultimately. So why did it feel even more precarious to know I wasn't the only one caught in this damn vortex of risky emotion and perpetual horniness?

One beautifully sculpted eyebrow rose, silently prompting an answer.

Right.

My parents.

Predictably, thoughts of them dampened my arousal, diluted the thick shroud of desire whipping around us.

'I meant exactly what I said. They didn't emigrate to Greece to be surrounded by its warm and fuzzy locals. They decided they'd had enough of their own family and wanted to live in seclusion, so they bought an island and did exactly that.'

Her eyes widened. 'You grew up on a Greek island?'

I shook my head, staring at her mouth in the hopes of allaying the deep, bruising ache that went hand in hand with this subject. But while thoughts of biting and licking that plump lower lip helped, they weren't enough. Nothing was ever enough. '*They* mean my mother and father. Alone. Exclusively. They bought their island and rarely step foot off it.'

She inhaled sharply. 'They went without you?'

I stared harder at her mouth, unwilling to confirm

whether the sympathy in her voice was reflected in her eyes. 'Yes.'

'How old were you?'

'I was nine.'

Her fingers toyed with her wine glass. I wished I had something stronger than mineral water. But my paranoia about drinking in public wasn't easy to dismiss.

Not after Penny.

Not when a six-hour black hole yawed in my memory. Fucking hell. Another subject I didn't want to dwell on for even a second—

'But…why…?' Neve asked.

For a blind moment I thought I'd spilled my darkest secret. But no. We were talking about my parents.

I exhaled sharply. 'They were satisfied they'd done their duty, I expect. Made their contribution to the great Mortimer gene pool. They left and never looked back.'

More questions flared in her eyes. I raised my hand before she could voice them.

'What's your agenda here, Neve?' I asked with a grating laugh. 'If I learned anything from my…unique childhood growing up in the Mortimer clan, it's that everyone has one.' My parents had proved that conclusively. Penny had proved that when she'd sidled up to me under the pretext of needing help and shattered the one relationship that meant a damn. 'So what's yours?'

Neve's eyes widened into pools of affront. 'Excuse me?'

'I get the business angle. You feel you were wronged and are out to right it…somehow. But this sudden interest in me? What's that all about? You want more ammunition for your little arsenal?'

A dart of hurt dimmed her eyes before the blue depths flashed with anger. 'Don't judge me by your standards.'

The laughter that rumbled from me felt less pleasant this time. 'No. You play dirtier. Remind me again who left whom high and dry last night?'

She flushed and damn if I didn't want to trace that sweet rush of heat with my tongue. 'You know what to do if this gets too much for you.'

I smiled. 'You won't run me off that easily, darling.'

'We'll see about that. And while we're at it, know that I won't be letting you steal any more of my panties.'

'Because you don't plan to take them off at all the next time I fuck you or because you won't be wearing any in the first place?'

Outrage rose swift and hot but died just as rapidly in her eyes, leaving the expression I craved. Unabashed desire. She tried to hide it by making a production of pushing back her chair and standing but her agitated breathing and the hard nubs of her nipples poking against her summer dress gave her away.

'I have work to do. You're in Suite 611. Your activation key has been sent to your phone. If you need directions or anything else be sure to let the concierge know.' She paused with her hand gripping the back of her chair, exuding a haughtiness that made every cell in my body burn. 'I trust you can amuse yourself until Sam and Tyler are ready for us to view the room?'

'Of course.'

'Great,' she said briskly. With a sexy twirl, she

walked away without a backward glance. I watched her until she disappeared from view, still puzzled as to why she hit all my spots with such ferocity. Why she got under my skin when no other had been able to penetrate the shell I'd been forced to construct to withstand unrelenting barbs from a family such as mine.

The churning in my gut intensified as I admitted that it had nothing to do with Neve playing hard to get. Although, for the first time in my life, I found *that* too a huge turn-on. Hell, everything was a bloody turn-on with her.

With an irritated snort, I stood and left the table, ignoring the tumultuous emotions dogging my steps.

My suite was impressive. Understated luxury coupled with elegant comfort was the running theme of Nevirna. The bed and lounges were sumptuous, the suite and adjoining balcony like each one I'd seen on our tour, facing a serene lake with honest-to-goodness swans gliding across its glass-smooth surface. At this time of year, with the promise of summer on the horizon, the air was fresh and clean.

Even the most demanding customer would be hard-pressed to find anything lacking in the resort. It was the sort of standard The Mortimer Group hotels strove for.

Somehow, regardless of the setback two years ago, Neve had turned her business around and made a success of it.

Under normal circumstances, she would be a great candidate for an alliance with The Mortimer Group's boutique hotels. The irony of our real circumstances produced a twisted smile.

For one thing, that curious…*itch* I'd experienced

when she showed me the door last night, and again when she walked away from me in the dining room, was growing irritatingly unbearable.

As if I needed her…somehow.

And when had I *needed* anyone?

I wanted to fuck Neve Nolan. I didn't need to…*be* with her. The whole situation was screwed up. I had no room in my life to battle this compulsion.

Not when I had Gideon to deal with and the shattered remains of a life to be salvaged in London.

But before leaving Manhattan I'd sent the board members my request to return to the board and they'd responded. The formal vote would be at the monthly board meeting. One Gideon would attend.

The three-year anguish that'd lived in my chest since that fateful night Penny had shattered Gideon's and my life wrenched at me again.

But the simple truth was that I was ready to get on with my life.

Four hours later, I stood and stretched. Beyond the balcony and landscaped gardens, the setting sun was casting an impressive glow over the lake. The scene was truly breathtaking, perfect for romantic strolls and stolen quickies between hedgerows…if you were into that sort of thing.

Was Neve into that sort of thing?

I rescued my phone, grimacing at the eagerness with which my mind raced back to her. To that sizzling half-hour on her sofa last night. To her slick, tight heat and the incredible taste of her. My hard-on was still raging when I stepped into the shower fifteen minutes later. I knew jacking off would only bring ridiculously temporary and empty relief so I didn't bother.

Which meant my mood wasn't much improved when I entered the dining room in the evening to be informed I would be dining alone. Neve was otherwise engaged and would see me later, her manager added.

Swallowing my irritation at the brush-off, I ordered a steak, grudgingly conceding its excellence. I was finishing the meal off with an espresso when a member of her staff approached.

'Mr Mortimer, Miss Nolan has asked me to escort you to the refurbished suite.'

We exited the main hub of the hotel and travelled a series of well-lit stone pathways to the east wing of the sprawling hotel. The suite was on the fifth floor, down a beautifully decorated hallway.

But the decor was the last thing on my mind when we arrived.

Neve was talking with Tyler outside the door.

In the most casual way I'd seen her dressed, in black denim that moulded to her hips and firm arse, and a scoop-necked fire-red T-shirt that clung to her breasts, with her blonde hair piled carelessly high on her head, she was every inch a delectable and fuckable sight.

A short sharp bite of acrid jealousy threw itself into the volatile cocktail swirling inside me as Tyler raised his hand to make a point and left it hovering near her cheek. Whatever he said made her laugh, the sound beautiful and sexy, just like the woman.

My stomach knotted uncomfortably. 'Tyler, I think I saw your sister heading to the restaurant. Are you supposed to join her?'

He started, looking a little flustered as he glanced my way. 'Uh…yeah.'

'Best not keep her and the chef waiting.'

Tyler grimaced. 'Sam's intolerable when she's hungry. But I'm used to it because she's always hungry. I was just telling Neve—'

I interrupted. 'Nothing that can't wait. I have other business matters to attend to, so if you don't mind?'

Tyler tensed. 'You don't want one of us around when you inspect the room?' he asked Neve.

With one dismissive glance at me, she shook her head. 'I'll come find you in the morning to give you feedback. Go and enjoy your dinner.'

He summoned a smile. 'Okay. Sure, no problem. We'll...catch up tomorrow.'

I gave a tight nod and he left.

Neve turned to me, her face pinched and her eyes glaring. Somehow that eased the knot inside me. I was shallow enough to accept that was because her attention was on me.

Jesus. You're bordering on pathetic, Mortimer.

'Shall we?' I suggested when she remained frozen in front of the suite.

'Was that really necessary?'

I wasn't going to pretend I didn't know what she was talking about. 'Good evening to you too. And yes. It was.'

Her mouth dropped open.

I reached behind her and nudged the door open. 'Close your mouth, darling. You'll catch flies. Besides, I think I made my stance pretty clear last night.'

She stumbled backwards into the room, her gaze fixed on mine.

'You didn't exactly say the words.'

'Well, I'm saying it now. I intend to be the guy

who takes care of that ache between your legs. Is that bloody clear enough for you?'

'I think—'

The rest of her response never came. Her gaze shifted away from mine, widened, and I lost her again. This time to the splendour of a suite transformed into a nineteenth-century masterpiece.

'Oh, my God.' Her voice was hushed. Reverent. Filled with the kind of pleasure that had filled my ears one long night two years ago and not for long enough last night.

I stepped inside, kicked the door shut and reluctantly dragged my gaze from her face to the room.

It was impressive. The attention to detail alone was exceptional.

'Indeed. Not what I expected,' I conceded.

She turned to face me. 'Let me guess, you anticipated a French boudoir to be a clichéd blood red and black silk?'

I shrugged. 'Isn't that what our clients will expect?'

'They'll be required to fill in a questionnaire on their wants and desires but if they're open to suggestions, why give them a tired old truism when they can have a fresh original?'

As she talked she wandered away from me, trailing her fingers over the heavy-silk-draped walls and gold brocade curtains. The mint-green and gold bedspread complemented the furniture right down to the gold bows holding back the filmy gold muslin material draping the four posts of the bed. When she fingered the fringe of an embroidered pillow, something hot and heavy thudded in my groin.

'You like it, I take it.'

She glanced over her shoulder, unabashed pleasure in her eyes. 'From the first glance it looks great, don't you think?'

I nodded. 'It's impressive.'

Her gaze roved contemplatively around the room. 'They've done a fantastic job, but...' She paused, her gaze locking on mine. Slate-blue eyes fell to an alluring half mast, her lips parting to suck in a delicate breath.

'But?'

'But... I think to fully appreciate it, it needs to be truly experienced,' she murmured sultrily.

Me. Pick me.

My hand itched to shoot up into the air like an eager schoolboy intent on impressing his hot teacher. I curbed the urge by shoving both hands into my pockets. 'What exactly do you have in mind?'

She held up a long manicured index finger, strolled over to the bedside table and picked up the phone. 'Whitney, can you reschedule my meeting with the spa managers for Monday? Great, thanks. And can you get catering to send a bottle of Dom Perignon to the Willow Suite, please? And canapés. I want everything in here in one hour. And I'm not to be disturbed. Thanks.'

She put the phone down, eyed me for a minute, then walked to an antique closet and pulled it open.

'What are you doing?

She wistfully caressed the period costume hanging in the closet. 'Right now, I'm heading back to my place to take a long bath, then I'm going to return to this room, and make full and, hopefully, rewarding use of it. If I'm fully satisfied, I intend to get my lawyer to expedite drafting the partnership papers with Sam and Tyler.'

I arrived in front of her without being aware I'd moved, slid my fingers around her nape and tilted her chin up. I was a little relieved she was letting me touch her after how we'd parted earlier. 'Specifics, Neve. Tell me *how* you intend to test the room out.'

A wicked smile curved her lips. 'Why? Imagination is a powerful thing. For example, I imagined a different life for myself than the one I was born into and look at me now,' she murmured, almost to herself.

I slotted that little piece of info away because my more urgent question burned harder. 'Stop playing games with me. Tell me.' My gruff tone had everything to do with the erection tenting my pants.

She swayed towards me, her belly brushing my uncomfortable thickness. I smothered a groan as she mimicked my gesture and curled her hand around my nape to nudge my head down until our lips were a half-inch apart. 'I'll tell you this, Damian. Whatever I do it'll be amazing, and it may or may not involve my favourite gadgets. But if you want to find out…' She inhaled slowly.

God, she was a cock-tease. And I was fucking lapping it up. 'Yes?'

'Then be here at eight. Not a minute later or the door gets locked. Is that understood?'

It was another subtle dig at my tardiness to our first production meeting. 'I'm so hard for you I can't see straight. Your pupils are already dilated with the thought of being fucked hard and fast on every surface in this room. If you think anything's going to keep me away from that door, think again.' I brushed my lips over hers in a butterfly kiss—because anything else would've ignited the raging need coursing through me—and stepped back.

I left the suite wondering how I was going to fill my time for sixty whole minutes without going clean out of my mind.

CHAPTER EIGHT

Neve

HE KNOCKED AT seven fifty-five.

Firm. Bridled impatience. Too self-assured. Just like the man.

No. Not totally true. I'd seen another layer of Damian today at lunch and that'd thrown me for a loop ever since I'd walked away from the table. Granted, I'd been more than irritated too.

But that brief glimpse into his life, relayed with a whole host of new, bleak demons in his eyes, had planted something inside me I couldn't shake off. It came uncomfortably close to compassion. Because that meant I risked seeing him in a different light. One that might lead to a further softening, even understanding the man.

Even if he hadn't shut me down, I didn't want to deal with another facet of a man I found far too fascinating. Besides, I should be used to getting shut down. My mother had done that my whole life, perpetually sabotaging the link I'd promised to keep alive, one that still felt vital to me, even after all this time. Even after common sense dictated I should write it off as a failed venture and move on.

The knock came again, more insistent.

I took a breath, reminded myself that this was about teaching Damian a lesson in the most basic way possible.

Sex. That was all.

Nevertheless, my stomach flipped in excitement, mockingly contradicting my level-headedness. I pulled the full-length robe tighter around my body and secured it with the long velvet belt.

One last glance in the mirror, and I answered the door.

He stood square, tall and spectacular in the doorway, his brooding hazel gaze latching onto mine. It stayed for a tense minute before drifting over my shoulder into the room to probe the corners of the suite.

'Looking for something?' I knew what he was doing but enjoyed toying with him.

'Just making sure you didn't settle for an alternative while we were apart.'

As if I would've wished for anything but exploring the torrid promise in his eyes after that wickedly thrilling reminder last night of what he could do with his mouth and fingers.

I wanted him desperately. But where was the fun in letting him know that?

'The night is young and I've learned that it's wise to keep my options open.'

The fire in his eyes morphed into something dangerous. A warning not to test his limits.

'I'm not great at sharing, Neve. Once I step through

this door, you'll have to agree to let go of some of those options.'

Why did I get the feeling we were talking about more than just my sex toys?

At my lack of response, his lips flattened and he inhaled long and hard, his gaze moving slowly, feverishly in a head-to-toe scrutiny. 'Invite me in,' he requested thickly.

'On one condition.'

One eyebrow rose.

'You come in, you abide by my rules.'

After a charged silence, he nodded. 'Fine.'

I stepped back and gestured him in. An hour ago, the suite had looked incredible. Now, with strategically lit lamps highlighting the best features of the suite, it looked magnificent.

Damian strolled inside, taking in every inch of the room before he paused in front of a green velvet chaise longue that invited the decadent relaxation I had in mind.

Desire sizzled in my blood as I watched the suite through his eyes. Imagined him spreading me on top of the silk-covered bedspread, sweat glistening on his glorious skin as he rammed deep inside me while the moon rose high in the sky.

The room was having an effect on him too, judging by the rapid rise and fall of his chest as he faced me again.

We stared at each other across the space for a full minute before I reached for the remote control. It wasn't exactly authentic but this was my fantasy, and frankly the presence of a harpist would throw a dampener on what I had in mind for Damian tonight.

Strains of Maria Callas's haunting tones eased through the room as Damian prowled towards me.

'I'd like a glass of champagne, please.'

He paused, that now familiar hard-edged look flitting over his face before he altered his course to where the silver bucket stood next to the chaise longue. Expertly, he worked the foil, twisted the cork until it gave a sophisticated pop.

He poured one glass, set the bottle back into the bucket and approached me.

I took it from him. 'Aren't you having one yourself?'

'No.'

Curiosity ate at me and this time it wouldn't stay down. 'You keep refusing my drinks. A more fragile person would have a complex by now. Care to elaborate?'

His jaw clenched once. 'No. I prefer to get you off in some other way than satisfying personal curiosity.'

'Even if that's my specific fantasy right now?'

'Your fantasy is to dissect my life?' The question was sharp, his face drawn into lines of displeasure.

'You could've answered differently if you didn't want me to probe.'

'You asked a question. I gave you a truthful answer. Let's move on to your next fantasy. Preferably one that involves discovering what's beneath that robe.'

I smiled despite the curious ache digging inside me. 'It's a secret I intend to keep a little while longer.'

A terse smile lifted the corner of his mouth. 'As long as it's my hands doing the revealing, I'll be patient. Just about.'

Renewed heat in his eyes dissipated the little blip

in our discourse. The crescendo of the music rose. I swayed towards him, swivelling my hips in a sensual dance as I savoured the champagne. When nothing but stark arousal remained in his eyes, I presented my back to him and continued to dance to the haunting tune.

When I moved, he followed. By silent command he knew not to touch me. I liked that.

As the music grew to a close, I headed for the chaise, hyperaware he tracked my every move.

One hand clutching the train of my robe and the other my champagne, I reclined against the headrest and tucked my legs to one side, careful not to reveal too much skin.

Even still, Damian made a rough sound as his eyes devoured the little skin I exposed.

Discarding the champagne, I reached for the platter of canapés. 'You won't drink with me. Will you at least eat something or am I wasting my breath there too?' I plucked a grape, popped it between my lips and held it there for teasing seconds before biting into it. The juices exploded on my tongue. I held in my moan, sure it was the fierce arousal burning through me responsible for my heightened senses.

I resented Damian a little for inciting the unquenchable flames so it was a little gratifying when he stumbled forward, his movements uncharacteristically jerky as his gaze switched from my legs to my mouth to the platter and back again.

'I see your fantasies include copious amounts of torture,' he stated roughly.

I feigned wide-eyed innocence. 'I'm just offering sustenance. How is that torture?'

'You know exactly what you're doing.'

I shrugged. 'Are you not enjoying yourself?'

His gaze rushed over me once more. 'The entertainment is…stimulating.'

I laughed and watched his eyes darken.

'I like the way you laugh.'

His compliment took me by surprise. 'Do you?'

He nodded. 'The problem is so far I've been denied it.'

'Ah.' I smiled. 'You don't like things not going your way, huh?'

His mouth firmed. 'It's a curiously novel experience. Which I don't want to ruin the mood with.'

'Then try these French tarts. They're to die for.'

I picked one and held it against his lips. He caught it with his teeth, chewed and swallowed without taking his eyes off me.

I was a thirty-one-year-old woman in control of a multimillion-dollar business, and yet having Damian Mortimer eat from the palm of my hand was a heady experience that made me as giddy as a schoolgirl.

In the background, Maria Callas wailed in guttural French. 'I love Maria Callas. Don't you?' I asked, toying with my belt.

Damian sauntered to the bottom edge of the chaise and lowered himself onto the seat. 'She'll do. Personally I prefer something a little older.'

His hands curled around my ankles and lifted my feet into his lap.

My breath caught when my instep connected with the hard ridge in his trousers. 'How much older?'

Warm fingers trailed up my silk-covered calves. 'Puccini holds my attention. Vivaldi equally so.'

'Ah, you're the *stuffy* opera-loving type.'

His smile was a touch warmer but he didn't look up from where his thumbs gently dug into my calves. 'Something that lifts your soul can't be stuffy. I'm also equally moved by a Bowie song.'

His magic fingers reached the backs of my knees and lingered. I couldn't help my gasp as heat lanced my body.

When his gaze stopped pointedly at where I held the robe closed at my thighs my fingers tightened. I fought the urge to open myself up to him. Instead I wanted to dig deeper beneath *his* surface even though he'd clearly stated that he'd prefer me not to.

'What else moves you?' I asked, ignoring the breathlessness in my voice.

'You. You move me, Neve, even when I don't want to be.'

The terse, unfettered confession strangled my breath.

I cautioned myself against being taken in by it. We were living a fantasy. Closed off in a bubble of searing desire that had no substance outside these walls. It would be foolish to get carried away by anything that happened here.

Anything that didn't feed my goal to have Damian at my mercy.

'Show me,' I commanded. 'Show me how much I move you.'

His nostrils flared as I tugged on my belt. The hands cupping my knees tightened and his fingers dug in, adding another searing layer of lust to my already rampant arousal.

His gaze fixed at the opening to my robe, probing as his hand trailed back down to ease off one heel.

Firm hands caressed my foot, then raised it to plant a soft kiss on my instep. He trailed his lips over my ankle bone, up the inside of my leg to my knee before repeating the intoxicating course with my other leg.

Damian shifted, hitched one knee onto the seat and arranged my legs on either side of his body. Then he prowled forward until his upper body was draped over me. Catching the sides of the robe, he slowly eased them apart, swallowed thickly as his gaze hungrily raked over me.

My lingerie was authentic French lace and expensive satin, bought as a birthday present to myself. The moss-green material formed a corset that cinched in my waist and blatantly emphasised my curves with the tops of my breasts almost spilling free of it.

'Jesus,' he rasped hoarsely.

'Do you like what you see, Damian?'

'Bloody hell, yes,' he replied in a strained voice, whispering his hands over the satin in a light dance over the tops of my breasts before rising to caress my neck.

After a moment, his fingers dipped beneath the robe, slid it from my shoulders and down my arms before lifting me free to toss it away.

He sat back on his heels.

No longer restricted, I draped my arms over the chaise, and moved one foot towards his lap, shamelessly rubbing his rock-hard erection.

His eyes squeezed shut, a pained grimace lancing over his features before he speared me with a sizzling stare. 'Tell me what you would've done if I hadn't come.'

The unexpected question threw me, as did the possessive throb in his voice. I hadn't quite taken Damian to be the possessive type.

'Why?'

'Because I intend to make it better than you could ever have managed on your own.'

'That's a bold boast.'

'Tell me,' he insisted.

'I was going to listen to music, enjoy the champagne and canapés. I may or may not have had a reading of E. E. Cummings in mind. Then I was going to relish this chaise for a while before moving on to other things.'

'What other things?' he demanded gruffly.

I bit the corner of my lip, hesitant to reveal my private fantasy. I didn't plan on telling him that most of them had revolved around him so I made it up on the fly. 'I had every intention of using a few of my toys to make myself come. But now you're here...you get to participate. But first...'

Eyes blazing with carnal heat hooked on mine. 'Hmm?'

'I want you to kiss me, Damian.'

He didn't need a second invitation.

Hot, demanding lips fused with mine, his tongue breaching my mouth to slick erotically against mine. There was an edgy hunger to his kiss as he gorged on me. I started to reach for him but paused. There was something decadent and arousing about delaying the gratification of putting my hands on him.

But that didn't stop me from digging my heels in the seat, raising myself up and shamelessly rubbing my body against his. One arm banded my waist, effortlessly holding me against his rock-hard body as we simulated everything we intended to do to each other.

Heat exploded in my pelvis as my hips ground against his. He groaned against my mouth. 'God, you taste so incredible.'

Sharp teeth nipped the corner of my mouth then licked it until I was moaning. He drew away and stared down at me for a terse little stretch before swooping down to plant hard, urgent kisses along my throat to the tops of my breasts.

He levered up again, his eyes devouring me as his fingers moved determinedly to the corset fastening. With a hungry growl, he hooked his fingers into the cleavage and scooped out my breasts.

'I'm not going to take this off. You look way too sexy in it, so I'm going to fuck you while you're wearing it,' he said, his eyes latching onto my tightly furled nipples.

The need to touch him grew unbearable. I started to reach for him but he stopped me. 'Stay there for another minute.'

'Why?'

He flashed me a surprisingly pleading look. 'I can barely think straight right now, darling. I want this to last a little longer before things get a little too…crazy. I still have fucking blue balls from last night.'

I mock-pouted and shamelessly arched my back. 'Aww, poor you.'

'Are you enjoying your torture, Neve?'

I smiled a wickedly feminine smile. 'You're not allowed to ask me that.'

One eyebrow lifted. 'Another rule?'

'Yes.'

His head dipped to my cleavage and my smile disappeared. Eyes fixed on me, Damian drew the flat of his tongue over one nipple in a slow, decadent lick that lit a fuse in my pelvis.

Before I could catch my breath, his fingers moved to my untended breast and caught the tight peak between his thumb and forefinger.

And the real magic began.

He teased and licked and tortured until my heart threatened to beat itself into exhaustion. My fingers were digging into the delicate fabric of the chaise and I didn't even care. With my body exposed so blatantly to him, letting him feast on me fed my pleasure in a way I'd never imagined. Perhaps it was the room and the fantasy.

No. It was all of that *plus* this man who was delivering the kind of pleasure I'd never known with any other. He bit down on one nipple, causing the tiniest explosion between my thighs.

'Oh, God.'

Hazel eyes blazed with ferocious intent as he blatantly absorbed my pleasure, his tongue flicking in rapid succession over my heated flesh. 'Good?'

My head bobbed eagerly. 'Yes. More.'

A very satisfied, very male smile tugged at his lips and he delivered pleasure for another minute before withdrawing.

Sitting back on his heels, he curled his fingers into my French knickers and dragged them down my thighs. His gaze latched onto the trimmed hair between my legs, then darted up to my face as he tossed the panties over his shoulder. 'Are you glad I came, Neve?'

I opened my mouth to deliver a flippant answer

but only one unguarded word emerged. 'Yes,' I confessed raggedly.

His answering smile was filled with poignant pleasure, then his expression grew serious. 'Before this goes any further, I have a condition of my own.'

Again my challenging response fell apart before I could utter it. 'Okay.'

'This isn't a one-way thing. I expect you to play a role in my set-up when the time comes.'

My heart skipped several foolish beats despite my self-admonition for common sense.

'Agreed?' he insisted.

The anticipation of reliving this again, of sex with Damian in the near future, filled me with a kind of dangerous pleasure I didn't want to admit. 'Agreed,' I replied before I could stop myself.

It would be another opportunity to teach him a lesson, I told myself.

Satisfaction blazed in his gaze before it dropped to my wet, throbbing pussy. Immediately the feverish hunger returned. 'I've craved another taste of you since last night. It's been driving me fucking insane,' he muttered thickly, almost to himself.

Need seared every cell in my body. 'Then what are you waiting for?'

He gripped my thighs, pushed them roughly apart and dropped his head to my heated core. A cry ripped from my throat as his firm mouth latched onto my clit.

No longer capable of keeping my hands away, I speared my fingers in his hair, my nails grazing his scalp as I held him in place.

I was terrified of what he was doing to me and terrified that he would stop. Damian toyed with my clit for mindless minutes, then sucked the swollen nub into his mouth. Over and over, he rolled it between his teeth and tongue, tortured me until I was on the brink of insanity.

Heat gathered in my pelvis. Tingles danced up and down my spine. I sucked in a deep breath, ready to let go. But then, he eased away.

'Don't stop,' I cried urgently.

'Just for a minute, darling.'

God. 'No,' I insisted, my fingers tightening in his hair.

Firm fingers pried mine free, and, with casual strength that robbed me of what little breath I had, he flipped our positions, draped me over him, and let loose a wicked smile.

'Judging by the decor of this room you get off on decadence. Don't you, my dirty little thing?'

I couldn't stop myself from blushing. 'Damian…'

His fingers brushed my mouth. 'Tell me what will get you off harder than me kneeling between your thighs. We can do that if you want but I get the feeling that's a little too conventional for you tonight.'

As if his invitation had opened a door, searing hot fantasies exploded in my brain. Fantasies I'd craved while reading my favourite erotic romances but had never given in to crowded my mind and delivered sizzling anticipation to my pussy. I could set them free now.

And why not?

Two years ago he used me. It was my turn to use him.

I ignored the guilty little catch in my chest as his

hand tightened insistently on my waist. *'Qu'est-ce que tu veux, mademoiselle?'* he demanded gruffly.

I gasped, my pussy getting unbelievably wetter. 'You speak French?'

'Parfaitment,' he replied, his accent flawless.

I hadn't imagined I could be more turned on a second ago but he'd just achieved the impossible.

Thrilled with his avid, almost worshipful gaze, I braced one hand on the top of the seat and swung my leg over him to rest my knee beside his head.

Exposed to him, I expected to feel a little vulnerable, a lot self-conscious. But Damian's thick, ragged groan infused me with more feminine power, although I almost disgraced myself by climaxing at the image of my pussy hovering three inches above his succulent lips.

'Is this what you want, Neve? To sit on my face?' he asked gutturally.

'Yes. *Oui*,' I breathed.

Rough hands clamped onto my thighs. 'Hold on tight,' he advised, then drew me down to meet his lips.

In a flash I was back at breaking point, this time with my arousal sharpened by a secret fantasy brought to life and at the point of fulfilment.

Wracked in pleasure, I threw my head back and flagrantly rode Damian's lips. His groans grew thicker and more urgent as I soared towards my climax.

'Look at me, Neve,' he instructed gruffly.

Heart hammering, I met his turbulent hazel gaze, and, amazingly, that searing connection tossed another layer of pleasure onto the already blazing fire, as I watched Damian eat my pussy with unfettered eagerness, his growls of pleasure shoving me over the edge.

With a scream, I tumbled headlong into orgasm. White-hot stars exploded across my vision, my body gripped with uncontrollable shudders as I came with a force I'd never known before.

I was vaguely aware that he was supporting my weight as I helplessly convulsed above him. At some point, my back reconnected with the chaise and gentle kisses drifted over my face even as a litany of French words drifted over me.

Dear God, Damian Mortimer speaks French.

I should've been disgusted by the man's accomplishments but he'd just given me my best orgasm yet. Complaining felt petty.

Still drifting on a sea of bliss, I sighed as he rolled my stockings down my legs. When he lifted me up, I opened heavy, sated eyelids to watch him walk purposely towards the bed.

He set me down long enough to pull back the bedspread and toss away a few excess pillows before placing me in the centre of the king-sized bed.

My languor evaporated and renewed hunger spiked as I watched him unbutton his shirt and shrug it off.

His trousers quickly followed and the sight I'd yearned for while quietly hating myself for two long years, the sight of a naked, gorgeous Damian, was exposed to me. A thick sound left my throat. His gaze dropped to my hands and I realised I was clutching the bedspread in an unguarded reaction to the sight of his body.

'Christ, you're so fucking sexy. You're not even touching me and I'm ready to explode.'

Intoxicated by his rabid stare, I drew my hands up my body, cupped my breasts and teased my nipples.

'Fucking hell, Neve. What the hell are you doing?'

What was *I doing?*

Supposedly driving him to the brink. And yet here I was riding the edge with him. Wasn't there a saying about revenge and digging two graves? Was I in danger of falling into the same pit I was creating for him?

I pushed the thoughts away. This afternoon, when he'd spoken about his parents, I'd made the mistake of feeling sorry for him. Until he'd harshly turned on me.

Whatever lurked in his past had moulded him into a hardened, cynical man who felt no qualms about the cruelty he spread around. Worse, he'd happily closed himself off from any sort of emotion, preferring to exist as an entity unto himself.

I would be foolish to give into empathetic emotions. This was about sex. Nothing else.

'If you want the torture to stop then come here and stop it.'

He toed off his shoes and socks, grabbed a stack of condoms from his trousers before shucking them off.

About to rip one condom open, I reached for it and set it to one side. I wasn't ready to have him inside me. Not until I'd tasted him as thoroughly as he'd tasted me.

Hunger building, I crawled to the edge of the bed and crooked my finger. Two long strides brought him within touching distance.

My gaze rested on his gorgeous face, his square jaw, the sensual lips reddened by his sublime oral dexterity. The hard six-pack beautifully delineating his stomach made my mouth water as I took in the V grooves bracketing his hips, dovetailing to his thick, beautiful erection.

'I want to suck your cock,' I blurted. 'Damn, I wish I could say that in French.'

With a groan, he muttered something beneath his breath.

He'd probably just translated but my need to have him in my mouth surpassed the need to hear him repeat it.

Braced on my hands, I dropped an open-mouthed kiss in the groove between his pecs. With tiny flicks of my tongue, I trailed kisses to his navel before reversing direction. A nip of one hard, flat nipple earned me a pained hiss that delivered fresh wetness between my thighs.

He jerked harder into my caress as I lavished equal attention on the twin nipple. By the time I made my way down his body to my mouth-watering destination, he was panting.

My mouth closed over the head of his cock and his stomach muscles rippled in reaction. 'Fuck, that's incredible,' he groaned.

I sucked him deeper, swirling my tongue over his swollen crown. Urgent fingers gripped my hair, bore me down until he hit the back of my throat.

Clad in just the corset, with my bare bottom high in the air, I felt shamelessly sexy and erotic. Damian confirmed it a moment later by boldly gliding his hand over my rump to my soaking wet pussy. 'Do you have any idea how fucking magnificent you look right now?'

Moaning, I sucked him enthusiastically, gliding my tongue down the underside of his shaft.

It wasn't enough. I wanted more. So much more.

But my intentions scattered to the wind as Damian slid two fingers inside me.

'I licked you dry moments ago but you're soaking wet again. I want it, Neve. I want that hot pussy around my cock.'

Since it was exactly what I wanted, I released him and sat back onto my knees.

His eyes were fevered, devouring pools. 'Top or bottom, I don't care. I just need to be inside you.'

Barely able to think straight, I glided on the condom, stealing a moment to revel in his length.

'Now,' he snapped impatiently.

Smiling, I reversed positions, and, with my back to him, met his gaze over my shoulder. 'Fuck me, Damian.'

He exhaled harshly and stepped between my legs. 'Like this?'

'Yes. Just like this. Hard and fast.'

His hands glided over my bottom, gripped my waist hard before he leaned forward to growl in my ear. 'Then that's exactly how you're going to get it.'

'One more thing,' I said in a voice I barely recognised as mine. 'In French. You fuck me in French until I come.'

His low laugh dissolved into a heated groan when I widened my stance. *'Comme tu veux, ma chérie.'*

He notched the head of his cock against my core and rammed in deep. My scream drowned his groan as he gripped my hips and seated himself fully inside me.

We both froze, frantically catching our breaths. *'Mon Dieu, tu te sens incroyable.'* As the words tumbled from his lips, he ground his hips into my ass, the head of his cock nudging almost painfully at my end.

My fingers convulsed in the sheets. 'God, yes!'

Triggered by my pleasure, Damian began to thrust, deep, hard strokes that tapped into hedonistic bliss.

He fucked me like the ravenous beast I'd turned him into and I welcomed every single inch of him, turned inside out by the thrill of living out this fantasy.

Decadent words tumbled from his lips and I fleetingly regretted the command for him to speak in French because I wanted to understand what he was saying. Nevertheless it added another dimension to the pleasure, and before I knew it the sizzling fire building inside exploded into an inferno. 'I'm coming. Oh, God, I'm coming.'

He grunted words I took to be encouragement, his speech slurring as he pistoned harder inside me.

Bliss tore through me. I tumbled over the edge. A moment later, Damian followed, his harsh pants filling the room as he emptied himself inside me.

When I collapsed onto the bed, he followed. I welcomed his weight, a small part of my brain craving that contact, that need not to feel so alone. And when he rolled us and caught me in his arms, I gladly went.

Even though I knew that moment was fleeting, this intimacy only imagined.

CHAPTER NINE

Neve

GENTLE HANDS BRUSHED the hair off my face, tucking strands behind my ear.

'So now you've fully experienced it, do you love it?' The low, growly voice whispered.

For a moment my mind blanked.

He was asking about the suite. Talking business. Whereas I was firmly back in bliss-land.

'Water. I need water,' I croaked through a throat sore from having screamed so many orgasms I could barely count. Thirst aside, an urgent need to avoid the eyes probing mine, sinking beneath my skin, powered through me. I attempted to dislodge him under the pretext of reaching for the crystal carafe of fresh water placed on the bedside table.

'Wait. I've got it.' Damian curled his fingers around my wrist, and even that gesture felt too intimate. Which was ridiculous after every debauched thing we'd done to each other since he walked into the suite.

I tugged myself free, avoiding his slight frown as he moved away, poured a glass of water and handed it over.

I drank deeply, aware of his eyes on me.

'You want some? Or something stronger? You look thirsty.' I'd meant to tease, but the abrupt shake of his head told me the joke had missed its mark.

'I'm fine, thanks.'

I frowned. 'You're set on giving me that complex, aren't you?'

His lips flattened. 'It's not you. It's me.'

My fingers tightened around the glass. 'Seriously?'

He grimaced. 'I can't… I don't want to talk about it.'

The thinnest blade of anguish sliced through the terse reply, making my insides tremble and threatening to disintegrate that stone of retribution I was so desperate to hang onto.

It scared me. But it didn't shake the need to understand him.

'There's nothing wrong in admitting a drinking problem, Damian.'

His bark of laughter was pure bitterness. 'I'm not an alcoholic, darling. Not even a recovering one. In fact I have zero problems with booze.'

'Then what is it? Did something happen?'

'Jesus, you're like a dog with a fucking bone, aren't you?'

I flinched. He saw it and sighed. 'Neve—'

'It's late.' I set the glass down with a loud click. 'It's time we call it a night.'

'You're not staying here till morning? Or are you kicking just *me* out, again?' Grim amusement twisted around his bitterness.

But I was done laughing. Somehow Damian kept

hurling me back to a default setting of compassion and caring I couldn't control.

Despite all my reservations.

Despite all the hard, harrowing rejections I'd been subjected to from my mother.

I slid towards the side of the bed opposite to where he now stood, gloriously naked and infinitely jump-able. 'I have an early start in the morning,' I stressed, probably more for myself. Because my heart was doing that lurching, clenching thing again. The one that re-sembled *loss* and *missing* even though this man wasn't mine in any way. Even though this was meant to be a clinical exercise.

I stood. And wobbled like damn Bambi on ice. Da-mian was on me before I could take a step.

'You okay?' His hands drifted down my arms to cup my elbows.

That compulsion I couldn't fight made me glance into his too-handsome face. To the concern etched in his eyes. Dear God, he was a master at playing hot and cold.

'I'm fine,' I snapped.

Concern only deepened. 'We don't have to leave, Neve.'

I hesitated, seduced by the idea of sliding back into the warm bed, with an even warmer promise of hav-ing Damian slide in with me, holding me close into the night, falling asleep in a boneless heap with him. *Waking up with him.*

A deep yearning for all the above shook through me further, unseating my goals. 'The hotel is at ninety per cent capacity. This suite needs to be converted back to its original state, ready for new guests on Monday. I need to vacate so that can happen.'

Despite us both knowing that wasn't the main reason, he didn't argue. After a short stretch he nodded and stepped back.

My limbs felt shaky and drained as I headed to the closet, conscious of his gaze sliding over me. Despite my many orgasms, my body started to heat up again, my clit swelling at the thought of sex.

With more than a little desperation I pulled on my clothes and slipped my feet into heeled sandals. A quick glide of my fingers through my hair to mitigate the mess, I turned around.

Damian was dressed, although his shirt was only half buttoned. In his hands he held my French bustier, robe, stockings and shoes. The blaze in his eyes as his gaze met mine nearly flayed me. Slowly he advanced towards me. 'You'll need these back, I think, unless you want to scandalise Housekeeping?'

I rescued the tote bag containing the toys I never got around to using from the closet and snatched the clothes from him. About to shove them away, I noticed one vital missing piece. 'Where are my panties?'

'No idea.'

For some absurd reason, his shameless pilfering made me want to smile. 'Seriously?'

He held his arms aloft. 'Feel free to frisk me,' he invited.

The temptation to do just that, in the most thorough way possible, made me grip the tote harder.

God, what was wrong with me? I was grappling with answers I didn't want to when he tugged the bag out of my hands.

'Shall we?' He nodded at the door.

Protests rose and died on my lips as warmth suffused me. The feminist inside me wanted to vehemently deny that I needed him to do something as mundane as walking me out of a hotel room.

But for once, I wanted to experience the art of walking out with Damian, rather than watching him exit.

In silence we walked out of the east wing, down the winding stone paths that led to the main building separating the three parts of the hotel. My feet slowed as we reached the diverging paths. We'd never parted on cordial terms. I wasn't even sure this counted as cordial but I cleared my throat nonetheless to dispel the awkwardness assailing me.

'Umm… I'm headed this way.'

Expecting him to walk away, I froze when he nodded and adjusted his course.

'Your suite is that way, Damian.'

He placed his hand on my back and nudged me forward. 'I'm aware. I don't care what your safety record is around here. It's after midnight. I'm walking you home.'

Again I opened my mouth to protest. Again I closed it.

Because I liked Damian's hand on my waist.

Because I liked the warm body so close to mine that smelled of aftershave and sweaty sex.

Because I am a raving sex maniac who needs her head examined?

'So how come *you* inherited this place from your grandparents?'

I jumped, startled by the direction of the conversation. 'What?'

He shrugged. 'I had a little time on my hands after you kicked me out last night. I did some research. There were a couple of paragraphs about your grandparents on the history of this place. It mentioned one child, a daughter, so I'm guessing they were your maternal grandparents?'

I frowned. 'Yes.'

'It's not a secret, is it?'

A little dazed by his interest, I shook my head. 'No.'

He nodded and we walked in silence until, 'So why not your mother?'

Maybe it was the warm hand in the small of my back. Maybe it was the smooth, deep interest in his voice. Whatever it was, I found myself replying.

'Because she hated this place. Told me she couldn't wait to leave when she turned eighteen. She never looked back, didn't bother to get in touch with her parents unless she needed something. She didn't even tell them when she had me. I think that's what hurt them the most. The first I knew of them was when she packed a weekend bag one Saturday and told me we were coming up here to visit my grandparents. It was the best weekend of my life. After that, whenever she'd had enough of me—which was often—she'd dump me here.' I stopped, the dull pain of rejection still potent enough to leaden my heart. Damian's hand squeezed my waist and I wanted to lean into him, draw on his solid strength.

This time brushing that need away was more difficult. 'Anyway, my mother and grandparents were back to being estranged by the time we left, but I'd fallen in love with this place. With how much my grandparents loved it. They poured their hearts into that little

B & B. So…suddenly I had family I never knew about and a clear idea of what I wanted to do with my life. It was win-win for me.'

I could feel his stare boring into me, his interest almost too intense, but I kept my gaze on the path.

'How did your mother feel about you getting this place?'

Pain scythed through my warm feeling. 'She was far from thrilled. She still hates it here. But I promised my grandparents I would look after it…and her…so…'

He nodded. As if he understood. As if he empathised.

I quickened my step, almost afraid of accepting his compassion. Of giving into that softening again. I breathed a sigh of relief when we skirted the north wing.

Beyond that, up on a little rise, was my house.

The cottage my grandparents had lived in for over forty years was straight out of a Norman Rockwell painting by day. By night it was even more magical, with soft lights glowing from the windows, a wraparound porch and a white picket fence promising tranquillity.

I stopped in front of the gate, reluctant to go any further. Reluctant to invite Damian into my sanctuary. The only place I'd known love and acceptance. He stared down at me for a long moment before he glanced over at the house.

'Charming place.'

'I like it,' I said, a little too defensively.

He merely smiled. 'You never answered me earlier. Did you enjoy your Fantasy Room experience?'

My head spun with yet another change of subject. 'Yes.'

'Good. Then you'll come to France.'

I froze, which was a curious reaction because everything inside me wanted to scream, *yes*. Perhaps my self-preservation was kicking in. *At last*. Except not a single part of me rejoiced.

At my continued silence, Damian's eyes narrowed. 'We have an agreement, Neve.'

Something heavy in my chest sagged in disappointment.

Agreement. Business.

Reminders that should've put me back on an even keel. Yet all I wanted to do was stumble away, hide out in my house and dissect my confusing feelings.

'The only way you get this deal done is after I give my seal of approval, Neve,' Damian pressed.

As much as I wanted to think I had the upper hand, I would have no hand at all if Tyler and Sam decided I wasn't a good bet. And a sure-fire way of ensuring that was to stall for no apparent reason other than I was terrified of how much I wanted to experience another Fantasy Room with Damian.

Firm fingers cupped my nape, then spiked into my hair. His thumb brushed my jaw before nudging my chin up. Our gazes clashed. His fiery expression warned he was prepared to fight me on this.

I surrendered because…because…

'I'll clear my schedule for France.'

Triumph blazed bright and unabashed in his eyes. He pulled me forward and I fell into his torrid kiss, unable to help myself. Hell, I more than fell. I drowned, clinging to him for what little stability I could find

as he devoured me right there on my Norman Rockwell doorstep.

I was moaning when he lifted his head. 'I'm dying
to push my luck and ask you to invite me in but I'm
going to quit while I'm ahead.' He stepped back and
handed over my tote. 'Goodnight, Neve.'

I'd lost the power of speech, so I nodded.

He waited until I climbed my porch and unlocked
my front door.

Then Damian walked away.

He'd left by the time I arrived in my office at eight
a.m. I flatly refused to accommodate the spiky disappointment knotted in my gut as I sipped my coffee
and perused my emails.

My foolish heart leapt when I saw one sent half an
hour earlier from Damian.

Returning to the city to take care of a few urgent matters. The producers think two full days of shooting will
wrap up Raiders so I've arranged for us to fly out to
Bordeaux on Wednesday morning.

Clear your schedule for four days. Separate travel
arrangements will be made for our business partners.

See you on Monday.

Damian

Straight. To the point. Yet I found myself rereading
it, dissecting every word. Was there something to be
gleaned from the way Damian kept referring to Sam
and Tyler as *our* business partners when in essence he
was merely a consultant? And why did that word no
longer grate as sharply?

Also…separate travel arrangements for them meant we would be alone, with no distractions for over eight hours… I slammed my laptop shut before the rush of giddiness storming my system could shame me.

But it was too late. I already craved him with a need bordering on rabid and an emptiness inside me I wasn't sure just sex would fulfil.

The scary thought propelled me out of my office.

Tyler and Sam were at a table in the dining room enjoying their breakfast.

They looked up with expressions of anxiety and hope as I approached. Smiling, I put them out of their misery. 'The demonstration was everything I hoped for. You did a brilliant job. I'm on board.'

A quick toast later, I outlined my vision.

It quickly became clear that Sam, although a design major, was more the brains of the business, while Tyler was the artistic heart.

His passion shone in his expression, his ideas effusive and robust. As a team, they were an excellent pairing and I concluded our meeting even more excited for the future.

'Mr Mortimer wants us on a flight to France tonight with our team. We hit the ground running tomorrow,' Tyler said.

I blinked. 'But we won't be in France till Wednesday night.'

'He's sending us the specs later but I get the feeling it's more than one room,' Sam said, unable to stem her excitement.

We parted ways shortly after, my intrigue building through the day. Many times I was tempted to call Damian, find out what he was up to. Instead I buried myself in work, thankful that I employed the kind of manager I could leave in charge with zero anxiety.

My heart was thumping wildly in my chest when I walked into the *Raider's Den* production warehouse on Monday morning.

As usual, Damian was already in despite my arriving half an hour early. It was as if he couldn't resist showing off. I tried to summon irritation and failed. Instead my gaze raked feverishly over him, and in a rush of surrender I accepted that I'd missed seeing him.

After a mere twenty-four hours…

Dear God.

He lifted his head and pierced me with hot hazel eyes.

I'd chosen another suit with a tight but flirty skirt and I watched his hungry gaze linger on my legs before rising. 'Morning, Neve.'

'Did you get whatever it was taken care of?'

The light in his eyes dimmed. 'Not all of it. But it'll get done by hell or high water.'

My breath caught at the brusque pledge but before I could comment, he tapped my chair. 'The others are arriving. Let's get this show on the road, hmm?'

I wasn't sure whether to be thankful or disappointed he'd made no reference to our night together. Once filming got under way, it was all business.

Sadly the pitches that rolled in were less than stellar.

The Auto-Waiter app programmed to mix sixty-nine different cocktails in your hotel room drew a raised eyebrow from Damian and ribald jokes from Gary I was sure would be cut during editing.

I was relieved when we broke for lunch, tucking into my sushi as Damian chatted with the producers. Afterwards, I headed to the bathroom to refresh my make-up and was at the vanity when the door opened.

Damian entered, his gaze darting to the empty cubicles before he nudged the door shut with his foot. My heart leapt into my throat when he turned the lock.

'You can't be in here,' I said a little too breathlessly.

'I can if you promise not to scream when I make you come,' he replied, reaching for me. He parted my jacket and cupped my breasts, mercilessly teasing my nipples before he began tackling my buttons.

'Damian—'

'Shh.' He pinned me against the vanity and kissed me hard and fast. 'We can waste time arguing about this or you can shut up and let me fuck you. Which would you prefer, Neve?'

I looked into eyes blazing with desire, at the flare of colour across his cheekbones, before taking in the rapid rise and fall of his chest.

He wanted me, just as badly as I wanted him. Why deny it?

'I want you to fuck me.'

'Bloody good choice, darling,' he responded gutturally.

Words ceased as he hiked up my skirt and dragged my panties down my legs. The moment I stepped out of them, he dropped to his knees and yanked one leg over his shoulder. I bit my lip to stop from making a sound as he buried his face in my pussy and drew my clit firmly into his mouth. Flicking and rolling his tongue over the nub drove me from zero to a hundred in seconds. I scrambled to stay upright as my leg gave way. Damian wrapped his hands around my thighs, supporting me easily as he continued to eat me with unapologetic alacrity.

I came in a fierce rush, my fist jammed against my mouth to smother my screams. Through the haze of my orgasm, I felt Damian rise to his feet, pull his zipper down and free his cock. I had only a moment to blindly reach for him, caress his thick length before he was knocking my hand out of the way and sliding on a condom.

Demanding hands jerked my hips to the edge of the vanity, and this time he used his mouth to smother my scream as he impaled me in one ferocious thrust. I threw my legs around his waist, eager to get him closer, deeper for the next thrust. When it came, I cried out again.

'Christ, do you know how much I've been dying to fuck you again? I think I'm getting seriously addicted to you,' he groaned against my lips.

My heart lurched, filled with a buoyant sensation that threatened to carry me away to a thrilling and dangerous place. A place with pitfalls and minefields all pointing to emotional danger.

And yet... 'Show me,' I whispered urgently. Recklessly. Because I was desperate to know that I wasn't alone on this slippery slide to somewhere other than just sexual gratification.

He grunted something incoherent, curled his hands beneath my bottom and lifted me clean off the vanity. With his gaze fused with mine, Damian fucked me with raw, unfettered urgency that emptied my mind of everything but him, possessing me, turning me inside out.

Making me…different. Somehow.

'God… Neve.' His voice was tinged with that same bewilderment slithering through me. But that couldn't be, because it would mean…

That single thought shattered as he slammed home one more time and held himself deep inside me. My muscles clenched around him as I felt him pulse within me.

'Come for me, darling,' he ordered in his perfect English accent.

I came with a long, tortured moan he devoured for endless seconds before he threw his head back and hissed his own release.

Damian's head dropped to my shoulder and I held him to me as we caught our breaths. All too soon he pulled out, then set about adjusting my clothes before taking care of his. When he was done, he brushed a soft kiss on my lips, his gaze searching my face.

'I missed you. Did you miss me?'

I shrugged. 'Maybe.'

He laughed, the sound low, pleased and *pleasing*. 'I'll see you outside in five minutes, okay?'

Still caught in a post-orgasm haze, I nodded and watched him saunter towards the door. Then I scrambled to my feet, frantically searched the floor and came up empty. God, he didn't… 'Damian!'

He paused with one hand on the door. 'Yeah?'

'Give me back my panties,' I demanded in a fierce whisper.

He raised one haughty eyebrow. 'I have no idea what you're talking about, darling. Now shift that delicious arse or you're going to be late.'

He stepped out with the easy confidence of a man

who didn't give a damn who saw him walk out of a ladies' restroom.

And I knew I was in deep trouble when I turned around and caught my wide, bright smile in the mirror.

Filming wrapped up late evening on Tuesday, a high-spirited post-production meeting marking the end of the segment. When the senior producer indicated that he would love for me to return for the next season, I politely declined.

My objective had been achieved—Damian Mortimer under my sexual control.

He might be his own man in every other area of his life but with every look, every subtle touch, he was mine sexually.

But for how long…?

This project was almost over. I'd landed the deal that with careful, clever marketing would put Nevirna on the international map.

After France, there would be no valid reason to keep seeing Damian. No reason to keep him in my bed.

This time the pain in my heart was sharp. Acrid.

Altered in a way I couldn't pinpoint exactly but felt deep inside.

The helicopter ride from Bordeaux-Merignac Airport to Damian's chateau on the edge of the Garonne valley was swift and exhilarating. And passed in almost as much of a blur as leaving Manhattan and experiencing Damian's incredible private jet and all the extravagance that both had to offer.

'We're flying over the property now,' Damian said through the mic attached to his headphones.

The view below was breathtaking. Rolling green hills, farmland and endless copses of trees were intersected by a large winding stream. But none of it compared to the majesty of the classic rectangular French chateau standing proudly on its own hill. Set on three floors and made of stone that gleamed white gold in the bright sunshine, the frontage boasted arched windows, with two slate-roofed turrets jutting out from each corner.

'Welcome to Chateau des Nuages,' he said as the chopper set down gently on its own helipad.

I stepped out, looked around and the scene was so magnificent, I was almost afraid to breathe. Almost afraid to fall in love with a place that wasn't Westport, Connecticut.

Almost afraid to…fall in love.

No. *No, no, no.*

'*Nuages* means…?' I asked hurriedly as if words would halt the chaos happening inside.

'Clouds.' He pointed to the west turret almost ablaze in the setting sun. 'On stormy days it feels like you're floating on a bed of clouds when you're up there.'

For a single moment I wished we weren't surrounded by clear dusk. That the sky was filled with fat fluffy clouds so I could experience that magic with Damian.

I shook myself free of the fantasy as we headed towards the chateau. 'How long have you had this property?' I asked, just for something practical to drag my head out of the clouds.

'A few years. I look in on it once or twice a year.'

'Other than that it just sits idle?'

He shrugged.

I looked at the spectacular structure looming up before us. 'How many rooms?'

'Twenty bedrooms. Nine reception areas. Assorted outhouses and stables.'

'That seems…excessive.'

He gave me a tense little smile as he opened a set of French doors and ushered us into a vast hallway with gleaming herringbone parquet floors and two immense stone fireplaces. 'I'm a Mortimer. I'm conditioned to do everything with my family in mind, whether I want to or not. Right this minute Gideon is buying an almighty great yacht big enough to fit the whole Mortimer clan even though we all hate each other.'

'Because like you, he hates failing too?'

He tensed, then faced me at the foot of a grand, sweeping staircase. 'Perhaps I'm practising what has been ingrained in me since I was old enough to understand.'

My heart banged against my ribs, fleeing whatever he was about to say. 'Which is?'

His eyes were hard. Piercing. 'That everyone has an agenda. And that it's rarely selfless.'

A chill crawled over my skin, sank deep into my blood. I wanted to reject that allegation but…how could I? I wanted to demand what *his* agenda was, but again…how could I?

We were here because I had an agenda of my own. One that seemed to grow more nebulous by the second.

Confused emotions roiled inside me, rending me speechless.

Footsteps approached, as if summoned by some

unknown signal to interrupt that exact moment. The slim elderly woman who appeared was simply but impeccably dressed. Damian chatted to her in flawless French before he turned to me.

'This is Margret, the housekeeper—' He stopped when his phone buzzed.

He pulled it out, stared at the screen and exhaled angrily. The gaze he flashed me was distracted. 'I have to take this, Neve. Margret will show you to your room. Feel free to explore on your own but stay away from the second floor. I don't want the surprise ruined.'

I realised I was staring at his departing figure when Margret cleared her throat. 'Would *mademoiselle* like a quick tour?'

I wanted to say, no, *mademoiselle* would like to know what had just happened. Instead I summoned a smile. 'Yes, please.'

Then came the progression through stunning room after stunning room, each with an identity of its own but somehow melding in perfect symmetry with the whole. Crown mouldings blended seamlessly with hand-painted mosaics. Stone archways invited exploration of beautiful rooms with spectacular views.

By the time I was shown into my suite on the third floor, Chateau des Nuages owned a piece of my heart.

Just like its owner?

I leapt back from the question, but it haunted me into sleep and still lurked, insidious and terrifying, when I woke from my nap an hour later.

The more I tried to push it away, the faster my weighty emotions churned. Going where I didn't want them to go. Towards Damian Mortimer, and the suspicion that the plan I'd hatched during the pre-production meeting two weeks ago had indeed *altered*.

That I wasn't in complete control.

Margret's arrival with a tray of the most exquisite seafood bisque and crusty bread I'd ever tasted, followed by a mouth-watering crème brûlée, distracted me for a blessed half an hour.

I was fresh out of the shower when she returned to clear away the dishes, and I stopped in surprise as she wheeled in a clothes rail on which hung an expensive-looking garment bag. '*Monsieur* asked me to give you this.' She handed me a note.

I waited till she left before I opened it and read Damian's bold scrawl.

See you in an hour. Wear the red ensemble. My fantasy. My rules.

I'd accepted that Damian's fantasy might require its own unique accoutrements. The evidence of it sent decadent shivers down my spine as I went to the rail and slowly pulled down the zip of the garment bag.

The red dress was stunning, complete with a plunging neckline and an honest-to-God sweeping train. Sky-high strappy red-soled shoes with sparkling diamanté buckles winked at me from the bottom of the bag. I was so absorbed with the shoes I almost didn't spot the black satin bag hanging to the side.

With fingers that trembled like a schoolgirl's, I opened the bag. A pair of long red silk gloves spilled out. The bag still felt weighted. I reached in and gasped as my fingers encountered cold stone.

The diamond necklace was beautiful, its sparkle flawless.

I sucked in an uneven breath, not entirely sure why this fantasy I wasn't even fully aware of intensified my heart's tremble. Attempting to ignore the puzzling sensation, I reached into the bag for the last items. Bra. Garter belt. Stockings. No panties.

Shaky laughter ripped from me as I started to dress.

I was securing the necklace when he knocked. With a quick exhale, I swayed to the door and opened it.

No other man looked better than Damian in a tuxedo, I was convinced. I forgot to breathe as I took him in from slicked-back hair to shiny handmade shoes.

It took him longer to return the scrutiny, and the heat in his eyes made me tremble all over again. 'Neve. You look…' he stopped and visibly swallowed '…breathtaking.'

'You don't look so bad yourself,' I replied huskily.

After another heated appraisal, he held out his hand. 'Shall we?'

I slipped my gloved hand in his, noting the ease of the action, the giddy lightening of my heart, the fit of our fingers.

He kissed the back of it before tucking it into the crook of his arm.

Our progress down the hall to the grand staircase was unhurried, giving me time to study him, to note that he wasn't as relaxed as he made out. There was an edgy set to his jaw and a little strain around his eyes.

'Is everything okay?'

He turned his head and I glimpsed a stern little light in his eyes before he visibly shook it off. 'I won't let anything ruin our evening,' he replied cryptically.

We'd reached the top of the grand staircase by then. I needed to concentrate before I fell on my ass so I let him guide me down the stairs to the second floor and along the west hallway.

The room we entered was immense, a grand ballroom transformed into a miniature early century opera house, with elegant drapery on the walls and a raised platform for a performance.

A large mezzanine overlooked the ballroom.

'I wanted to see what Sam and Tyler could do with a larger area than just a suite—to see if there are more possibilities to the business plan. We're going up there.' Damian led me up a spiral staircase to the mezzanine where two elegant armchairs had been placed near the balcony. It gave a perfect view of the stage and on each chair lay an embossed programme. At the far end, something large and shrouded stood at the back of the room.

I didn't ask what it was, sure it would be revealed in time. I sat down, then froze as Damian lifted a bottle of champagne from a nearby ice bucket. His gaze met mine as he manoeuvred the cork, popped it and poured out two glasses.

'Why now?' I asked when he handed me a glass.

His lashes swept down for a long moment before he exhaled. 'Because…it's you,' he said simply.

That shifting and shaking inside me intensified. Almost too late I recognised it for what it was. An emotional earthquake, shifting my axis, rearranging my preconceptions and goals in a way that shocked and awed.

'Ready?'

With a nervous swallow that had nothing to do with

what was about to happen and everything to do with the metamorphosis occurring inside me, I nodded.

He sat down and pressed a button.

The stage lit up as the area around our seats dimmed.

CHAPTER TEN

Neve

I DIDN'T RECOGNISE the handful of people who streamed onto the stage, but I recognised their musical instruments as they took their places.

I picked up the programme and opened it. Six short lines were written in curly font.

On the menu tonight:
Beethoven's Silence
A solo from La Bohème
Vivaldi's Four Seasons
A surprise
Most importantly...you

'You did all this because I called your choice in opera stuffy?' I murmured, attempting to divert my focus from that last item.

His bright smile lit up the semi-darkness. 'Haven't you noticed that I relish proving you wrong? By the time we're done, I guarantee you'll change your mind about me, Neve.' The words were easy and offhand but his gaze was solemn. Weighted.

He clinked his glass against mine and I watched him take a sip. His gaze locked on mine as he swallowed and I felt intensely moved by that simple but profound action.

The music started up.

Within minutes I was lost. Converted. Reborn.

I glanced at Damian and saw he was equally enthralled. He turned his head and our gazes met. Something shifted in his eyes and he reached out and caught my fingers in his.

The link was tenuous, easily broken. And yet it snagged and locked onto something deep inside me.

I'd never stopped to appreciate classical music. But seeing its effect on Damian, hearing it for myself, I was thrilled and humbled by how it moved him. Moved *me*.

So much so I did the unthinkable and disregarded the insult to my dress as I left my chair, stood in front of him for one long minute before I slid into his lap.

Surprise lit his eyes but he didn't say a word. Probably because neither of us wanted to ruin the exquisite music with speech. When I rested my hand on his chest he immediately covered it with his.

We stayed like that, eyes on each other as the music transported us. Every now and then, he raised his champagne glass to my lips, then took a sip himself, his fierce brooding eyes fixed on me, searching, reading my every expression.

I raised one gloved hand and traced my fingers over his cheek, jaw. His sensual mouth. His eyes dropped to half mast but remained locked on me. Parting his jacket, I trailed my hands down his chest, over his hard six-pack to his waist, then laid my head on his shoulder.

Damian exhaled, thick and heavy, then discarded his glass to curl his hand over my hip.

Warmth I shouldn't have craved suffused me and when he brushed a kiss against my temple, I shut my eyes against the wave of emotion racing towards the heart I knew was under serious siege.

'I understand now,' I murmured.

He nudged my chin up until our gazes met. 'Understand what?' he asked, his deep voice a little gruff.

'Why this music moves you.'

Something shifted in his eyes, again probing, searing. 'I thought I did too. But I'm learning there are many more ways to be moved.'

A tremor shook my body...one he couldn't have missed considering our proximity. I wanted to ask. Wanted to delve beneath his surface and pry the meaning I wanted from him. Fear made me silent. The corners of his mouth curved in a serious little smile, as if he understood, before he brushed his knuckles over my cheek.

'Neve.' My name was a solemn whisper on his lips.

I threw my arms around his neck, felt his groan resonate inside me as I offered my lips.

He took them, scooping me up in his arms and standing to stride to the back of the room.

The shrouded object turned out to be a large divan, draped in heavy silk. A tug revealed an opening.

Damian stepped through and laid me on the bed. Shrugging off his jacket, he lay down next to me. My breathing turned choppy as he stared at me with a fierce intensity for a long spell.

Then he started to undress me. Unable to remain still through the thick gravity of whatever was happening, I reached for his clothes. The moment my dress was off, he was sheathed and crouched over me, his face a rigid mask of desire and need, the force of his fingers digging into my hips as he stared deep into my eyes and thrust, hard and deep, into me.

My muffled cry was lost in the crescendo of the aria as I shook from head to toe. Firm hands held me still as he buried himself to the hilt and let out a thick groan.

Filled to capacity, brimming with sensations that baffled and awed, I surrendered to the sensual riptide Damian created. Even as I met him thrust for thrust, even as the crescendo rose around us, I knew I wouldn't emerge from this experience the same.

But I did nothing to stop the drowning. Far from it.

I threw myself into it, letting go completely as Damian dropped his forehead to mine; sharing my air, he drove us both relentlessly to the edge.

He pounded into me as the aria ended and the beautiful sound of violins filled the room.

I came with a scream, not caring who heard, and he followed close behind, his cry thick and affected as he emptied himself inside me.

We collapsed onto soaked sheets, our bodies glistening with sweat as the ballroom fell silent.

'So what do you think of Vivaldi?' he muttered hoarsely in my ear after my breathing was back to somewhat normal.

'He's…amazing.'

'Yeah, Spring wasn't bad but Winter is definitely my favourite.'

My laughter triggered his. When he nudged me

into his arms I went freely, draping myself over his chest and splaying my hand over where his heart beat in steady rhythm.

Time ticked by with lethargic sweetness.

Damian picked up my hand and kissed my palm. 'Are you hungry?' he asked after a few minutes.

'No, but I could murder a glass of champers,' I replied in a posh British accent.

'Hmm, that's not a bad imitation for a Yank.'

I slapped his chest. 'A half Yank. I'll have you know I have English blood running through my veins.'

He froze. 'You're half English?'

I nodded. 'I was born in England and lived there until I was five. My mother didn't like it there either so my father relocated us to Connecticut.'

'Is he still around?' he asked with a note in his voice I could have sworn was wistful. When I looked up, his expression was interested but guarded.

As I recalled his spiky tale of his own parents my heart squeezed. This time I didn't stop the flood of compassion. Or fight the tide of pain for my own loss. 'No. He died a few years after he returned to England.'

'So he left you?' he said tightly.

'I don't think he had a choice in the end. My mother wasn't exactly easy to live with. And...' I stopped when I couldn't exhale around the ache in my chest.

Damian cupped my chin. 'And?'

'He drew the line at her infidelity. He filed for divorce and custody. He won the first and lost the second.'

Damian's eyes darkened and the kiss he placed on my lips and the arms that drew me closer were gentle. And I was weak enough to embrace both.

'Do you visit England often?' he asked after a long stretch.

'Not for a while now. I've been busy running Nevirna.'

'What about your plans to expand Nevirna overseas?' he probed.

'It was my intention two years ago. In fact I was all set to open new branches of the resort in three countries across Europe.'

Thick silence fell between us but Damian's hand didn't stop caressing my hip. 'Nothing to stop you now, is there?' he finally murmured.

I searched a little desperately for that well of bitterness I was used to tapping into. I only got dregs. 'I guess not,' I replied.

And when he spread his fingers in my hair I eased my head back, didn't stop him as he lowered his lips to mine.

After a thoroughly decadent kiss, he rose from the bed. 'First champagne, then the next fantasy.'

Something kicked hard inside me. 'There's more than one?'

He looked over his shoulder as he crossed the room, gloriously, mouth-wateringly naked, to retrieve the chilling champagne. 'There are three. The final one is not till tomorrow afternoon, though.'

'Do I get to find out what it is?'

He returned with the drinks and passed me one. 'Nope.'

I mock-frowned. 'What will I do with myself for the rest of the time?'

'Relax. Unwind. Fuck me.'

And then what?

The question hit me hard. Enough that my hands shook. Enough that I dipped my head and avoided his piercing gaze as he slid back into bed.

'Neve—'

'Do I need a different outfit for the next fantasy?' I asked hurriedly before he could probe my unguarded moment.

'Not if you don't want to.'

I sipped my drink. 'Hmm…intriguing.'

His gaze moved over me, lingering on my breasts. As I watched, he dipped his fingers into his glass, then held his wet fingers over one nipple until a fat drop of champagne dripped onto my puckered flesh.

At my gasp, he smiled, then swooped down to tug my nipple into his mouth.

'If you like, we can just stay here, do more of this?' he muttered as he repeated the decadent action with my other nipple.

'Shame to let the twins' hard work go to waste, don't you think?' I managed through a lust haze. But the part of me that was terrified I was addicted to Damian needed a little distance.

He swirled his tongue around my nipple one last time, then reluctantly pulled away. He tugged up his boxers and trousers but held out his shirt to me. Sliding off the bed, I shrugged it on, unable to help myself from inhaling his scent as he did up a few buttons. My stockings and garter had stayed on during the undressing and I felt decadently sexy as he caught my hand in his and led me downstairs.

Halfway down the hallway, he stopped before a set of double doors. The grin he threw me was downright boyish, giving me a glimpse of a Damian Mortimer free of the demons snapping at his heels.

The deep yearning to slay those demons, to restore whatever had been taken from him, struck me harder than the question I'd asked myself minutes ago.

So I was in a semi-daze when I walked into the room. Filled with life-size posters and memorabilia of David Bowie.

'Oh, my God.'

Damian laughed, hit a button and disco lights strobed into the room as the thumping beats of 'Let's Dance' pounded.

He caught me around the waist, twirled me around, then began to move.

Later, I would recognise that I fell in love with him in that moment, with unfettered delight in his eyes, killer moves to make a girl swoon and his hands reaching out to me. Time ceased to exist as we danced, fucked and danced some more.

As I ignored the ache in my feet and the building terror in my heart and gave myself to Damian in every way I could imagine.

When he swung me into his arms and carried me to his bedroom beneath the east turret, I wanted to scream my happiness to the world. Instead, I slid into bed with him and let him wrap me in his arms.

'So I take it you enjoyed your Fantasy Room experiences?' I mimicked his words.

'I finally realised a teenage dream. What's not to like?'

I pulled back to look into his eyes. 'A Bowie party for two was what you dreamt of?'

His expression tightened. 'I would've taken *any* sort

of party. That just happened to be on a list of many things I never got to have.'

'Why not?' I asked, tentatively because I didn't want him to clam up again.

His lips firmed for a moment. 'You know about my parents.'

I nodded. 'I know they left you behind when they went to Greece—'

'Not just me. My sister, Gemma, was seven and my brother, Jasper, was six.'

'Who looked after you?'

'Like any wealthy, dysfunctional family, we were conveniently shipped off to boarding school. During the holidays we were looked after by a procession of nannies and occasionally visited by the odd uncle or aunt when they remembered we existed.'

'So you never saw your parents?'

'My aunt Florence attempted to guilt my parents into behaving like responsible human beings at one point.'

He gave a half-smile, despite the pain searing in his eyes.

'What did she do?'

'She organised a lavish party for my thirteenth birthday. Bowie was on the list somewhere if I recall correctly.'

'And she invited them?'

'No. She had the event planners and caterers fly everything—from the dozen race-car simulators I'd been bending everyone's ear about, to the birthday cake I didn't want but she insisted I have—to my parents' island. She flew my cousins and everyone I'd so much as nodded to at boarding school and their parents to Greece. Close to a hundred people turned up. Besides my own relatives, I only knew about a hand- ful of the rest. But I bet every single one of them never forgot what happened.'

Concern welled inside me. 'What happened?' My question was little more than a hushed whisper.

'My mother ordered her household staff to throw us off the island. When Aunt Flo refused, she threatened to have us all arrested for trespassing.'

My heart lurched in pain and sympathy. 'Oh, my God.'

'It was fascinating,' Damian said, his tone almost conversational. But I heard the flatness layering it. The distance he sought from his pain. It was the same way I'd dealt with my mother all these years.

'Fascinating?'

His smile was humourless. 'Yes. I found it fascinat- ing that a mother could feel nothing for the children she'd brought into the world. That she would hate me so much she'd threaten me with jail just so I'd be taken out of her sight.'

'Damian—'

He pulled away, cutting me off before I could speak. 'Save your pity, Neve. I learned a valuable lesson that day.'

Hurt darted through me. I smothered it, reminding myself that we all needed coping mechanisms. This was Damian's. 'What did you learn?'

'That it was stupid and pointless to get swept up in someone else's agenda. That I was the only who con- trolled my path to wherever I wanted to go. Success. Failure. Happiness or contentment or whatever label you want to slap on what drives you. It all comes down to me and me alone. My mother couldn't have made it plainer that I was no longer part of her life. Aunt Flo, as well meaning as she was, shouldn't have swayed me into going along with her. She wanted to shine a spotlight on my parents' irresponsibility, guilt them into loving or, at the very least, acknowledging that their children still existed. And I went along with it.'

'You were only thirteen years old.'

'Old enough to accept what I'd known since I was nine, or, hell, even before then.'

'You had hope. There's nothing wrong with that.'

He spiked impatient fingers through his hair, throwing me a *wise up* look. 'There's everything wrong with it when it's useless. When your very existence is built on greed and lies. I didn't know it then, but my great-grandfather had stipulated in his will that every Mortimer who produced an heir would receive a lump sum or shares for every child. He was very big on family. My father wanted to have six. My mother drew the line at three. They cashed in their fund when Jasper turned five. By his sixth birthday, they were gone. So you see, for me and my siblings, having *hope* was like banging your head hard enough against a concrete wall believing it would yield when you know all you'll get is a fucking cracked skull.'

Damian

It didn't make sense for me to expose the parts of my life that were important to me. Talk about leaving myself wide open the way I swore I'd never do. But the strange little kinship I'd felt walking her back to her little house on the hill had lingered long after I'd left Neve in the early hours of Sunday.

I'd shrugged it off as the after-effects of spectacular sex but that feeling had only intensified with her appearance on Monday morning, along with that feeling of wanting to be with her.

So despite my better judgment I'd commissioned a fantasy around my most precious cravings, the things I thought would bring me joy. Was it any surprise that it'd led to this…unholy confession? This unburdening that drew sweet touches and soft sympathy, even as she flinched from the horror of it.

I hated that part. But I couldn't look away from the sympathy. So I absorbed it, let it soothe jagged parts inside I refused to acknowledge.

I took one breath, then another to calm the raging inside me when she remained silent.

My relief that we were getting off a subject I shouldn't have started in the first place was short-lived. Neve Nolan had sent me off-kilter since that first night in Boston. I suspected it was a sensation I needed to get used to.

Still, there was no excuse for this. My parents were a subject I didn't discuss, full stop.

But Neve opened her mouth and I knew she wasn't done. Just as I knew I wouldn't be able to deny her.

'You've only mentioned your mother. Where was your dad when all this was happening? Wasn't he there?'

A chill invaded my system, tingeing my bitterness with sharp icicles that defied the heat of the sun. 'Oh, he was. But if my mother cared little, he cared even less. Aunt Flo wouldn't have fared any better if he'd let her into the house.'

'He didn't?'

'My father didn't even come outside. He watched the whole ungodly spectacle unfold from the comfort of his bedroom window. Truth be told, I've never seen Aunt Flo so apoplectic as when she was shouting at her brother from the front lawn. It was positively operatic.'

She inhaled sharply. 'Damian…'

I brushed my fingers over her plump lips, ignoring the curious fracturing inside me.

'Shh, it's okay. If nothing else, you turned a bad memory into a good one tonight, Neve. Thank you.'

She blinked rapidly, as if holding back tears. Her hands framed my face, her fingers stroking my wounded places, her eyes questioning, probing. Seeing too fucking much.

'What about Gideon? Is he connected to the not-drinking-in-public thing?'

My insides froze, even as the urge to spill that too overpowered me. Was I ready to risk this…whatever had made tonight special? Sure, it was a moment out of time. But what if it all…went away?

I slid my hand down her back to cup one supple buttock, eager to distract myself from the conflict raging inside me. Her lips were parted, swollen from my kisses, welcoming with their sweetness. It would've been the easiest thing in the world to lean in, lose myself in her.

And yet I felt them…the dark, turbulent words of my confession rushing from its hidden place, dooming the moment I wanted to hold back with everything

I had. 'I had a bad experience the last time a woman bought me a drink.'

She tensed, her eyes widening. 'Who?' she asked softly.

'She was my cousin's fiancée. I thought I could trust her. Turned out she was a manipulative bitch who'd broken his heart over and over. She turned up in the bar I was drinking in and sold me a sob story about how hard she was trying to make Gideon happy. How she was failing and needed my help. I let her buy me a drink. And I lost the next six hours of my life to a black hole.'

Neve gasped, her fingers digging into my arm as confusion clouded her eyes for a moment before clarity dawned. 'Are you saying...?'

My insides clenched tight. 'She roofied me? All the signs point to that. I've never been a heavy drinker, certainly not enough to black out. But it took me a while to accept that as a possibility. I've had investigators looking into it since then.

'The night you and I met was exactly one year after it happened. I'd spent the better part of it trying to get Gideon to listen to my version. He flatly refused. And why the fuck should he? I wouldn't listen if I found my woman in bed with my cousin either.'

She froze. 'Oh, my God, Damian...'

Her voice contained shock. Sympathy. *Horror*.

Icicles coated my veins as she stared at me. She started to remove her hands. To withdraw.

I tightened my hold on her, aware that the years' long bitterness had been overtaken by something else. Something that skated far too close to fear of the rejection I'd experienced on a vivid green lawn on a

Greek island a thousand years ago. 'You pushed for this, Neve. Now you know, you don't get to scurry off in horror.'

Her breath caught. 'I wasn't… You…' She stopped, drew her tongue over her lower lip. When she finally met my gaze the horror still stained her eyes. 'I just… get you a little more now. And perhaps I'm stating the obvious but you're not to blame. You were wronged, not the other way around. This wasn't your fault—'

The laughter that ripped from my throat was harsh. Acid-sharp. 'Of course it was. She caught me at a weak moment and I fell into her trap. She knew how close Gideon and I were. She'd been around us long enough to see that he was the only person I trusted to have my back in the viper pit that is my family because his parents fucked him over too. She tracked me down with a clear agenda and I let her play me like a damn instrument.'

Neve curled her hands against her chest, her subtle withdrawal scraping my senses. 'What was her end game?'

'She wanted to marry a Mortimer. Either Gideon or me. She wasn't fussy about which one of us she trapped.'

I watched her gaze sweep down, felt her tremble as she attempted to ease away again.

'Neve.' My voice emerged sharper than I'd intended.

She tensed, lifted stormy blue eyes to me. 'Not everyone has an agenda, Damian,' she said, her voice wary and hushed.

A rough chuckle squeezed out. 'That's bullshit. I

tried, just that once, to believe that and got fucked over for my troubles. So guess what, darling?'

She exhaled slowly before answering. 'What?'

'It's never going to happen again.'

She opened her mouth. I slanted mine across it, delving deep until I drew a moan. 'No more talking. Right now, I want back inside that snug little pussy. Are you going to deny me, Neve?'

Her gaze shadowed, but a moment later she slid her hand up my chest and over my nape. I let her draw me close, taunt me with possibilities I didn't deserve but wanted to grab with both hands anyway.

And as I lost myself inside her once more, I dared to contemplate reaching out. Holding on. For a while.

Neve

I woke up alone to a room bathed in streaming sunlight, in the wide four-poster that screamed expensive antique in every inch. The whole suite boasted the type of furniture I would've spent hours rhapsodising over had my attention not been directed inward.

Very deep inward.

To a place I'd never visited before. Simply because I'd never experienced what I'd felt with Damian last night.

There were parts of him that remained an enigma. But his revelations had thrown him into a different light. One that made me understand him better. See past the self-assured man to the wounded soul who believed everyone had a malevolent agenda.

I rolled over and grabbed his pillow, my heart aching for him as I breathed in his scent.

Damian Mortimer wasn't an unfeeling bastard. He was the product of the worst type of rejection from his parents and treachery from someone he'd trusted. Both resonated deep within me.

It threw light on how bad the timing had been the first time around.

The first time around?

The path of my thoughts startled me out of bed. Even if I wanted longevity of any kind with this… thing with Damian, there was absolutely no guarantee that it was the same for him. We'd made no plans beyond a handful of days. Our only connection was via Fantasy Rooms.

But there could be something. You can heal each other. Be partners.

I rushed into the shower, almost afraid of a solution so simple. So…tempting. But it wouldn't go away, wouldn't drown under the forceful jets of water.

Possibilities grew as I shrugged back into Damian's shirt and left the room. Intending to return to my own to get dressed, I paused at the top of the stairs when I heard voices.

Well, one voice. Damian's. Talking heatedly on the phone in what appeared to be a study. The door was ajar. I had every intention of walking past, every intention of giving him privacy.

But the raw, savage pain in his voice, echoes of last night, slowed my steps.

'No. Enough is enough. Does he know what Penny did to me? Did you tell him?'

He paced back and forth in front of a marble fireplace, the phone glued to his ear, listening. After a minute he exhaled sharply. 'You're right. This is between me and him. It's my story to tell and he'll bloody well listen to me. Why? Because someone intelligent and compassionate has reminded me that this wasn't my fault. Gideon and I are *both* the injured parties here. He needs to hear that so tell him I'm on my way to see him now.'

My heart threatened to melt into a puddle. I held it in place with a hand to my chest as I listened, hope and warmth filling me up.

'I won't let him stand in the way of my rejoining the board, Flo. It wasn't enough that I exiled myself at your recommendation. They wanted me to hunt and gather. I've toed the fucking line. And if they're not bloody satisfied with that, I'm in the final stages of closing one last venture. No, it's not Fantasy Suites. It's Fantasy *Rooms*. I'm not even going to ask how you know about it. I signed on as consultant but I won't be for much longer. It's too good an investment to take a back seat on.'

My heart iced over and dropped stone cold to my feet.

He stopped for another minute, pinched the bridge of his nose as he let out a weary laugh. 'No, Aunt Flo, don't tell me about your fantasies. And while we're at it, I'd like you to stay out of this.'

He listened for another moment. Nodded. 'Thank you.'

I watched as he tossed the phone into the nearest chair and paced to the window, raking both hands through his hair.

I knew I needed to move. Either towards him or far, far away. Fight or flight. But unlike two years ago, the fury building inside me felt different. It wasn't sharp and evangelic.

It was gloomy and sad and wretched. And when my feet finally moved, I wasn't surprised when they retreated backwards, away from a battleground I'd unwittingly approached with no armour or strategy.

In my room, I perched on the edge of the bed, holding the numbness inside with the utmost care. I hadn't fully worked out what would happen if I didn't. I just knew I didn't want to let it spill here. It could wait till I got home.

Home. Westport, Connecticut.

Pack. I needed to pack.

I staggered upright, surprised my feet weren't leaden weight. The sound of rotor blades starting up redirected my path from the dressing room to the window.

Damian was striding purposefully towards the helipad. With detached surprise, I watched him hop into the cockpit next to the pilot. A minute later, the helicopter took off.

I watched until it was a speck on the horizon, until my senses screamed at me that he'd truly gone.

Slowly, my fury sharpened, galvanising my sluggish senses awake. Part of me just wanted to leave. Put him behind me.

Like you did two years ago?

The mocking question sparked my fury anew.

No.

The other part of me didn't want to retreat. Didn't want another two years to pass by before I spelled out exactly what I thought of him. I wanted to look him in the eye and tell him I'd fallen in love with him and he'd broken my heart.

I was going to take back control I wasn't even aware I'd handed over until it was too late.

A sob caught the back of my throat as my brain finally caught up with my heart. The clash was ugly. Mean and dispiriting. Enough to propel me from the breathtaking salon, outside and down the rolling lawn.

I walked until I came to the stream I'd spotted from the chopper, followed its winding path until I reached a natural boundary. Seeing a flat rock, I perched on it, willing my churning emotions to settle. But I knew it was a futile wish. Despite all the self-warnings, I'd fallen hard for Damian, lulled in by our kindred rejection and a wounded soul too damaged to sustain the weight of my love.

But even in the depths of my despair, I wanted to reach out as he'd reached out for me last night. I wanted to heal him.

I gave a hollow laugh, right there on that barren rock, and called myself every kind of fool as time passed in an excruciating trickle, steeping me in my heartache.

By the time the helicopter returned, I'd retreated into a deep state of irretrievable anguish. Which was a blessing in disguise, my brain insisted, as I trudged back to the house.

Margret was waiting when I stepped into the living room. '*Monsieur* asked me to give you this.' She handed over a note, and, with a curious glance at my pallid face, disappeared.

Every instinct screamed at me to rip up the paper

and toss it in the trash. But of course my foolish heart needed to know. I opened it. Read the five short lines.

Final fantasy
The study on the second floor
Fifteen minutes
No peeking
My rules

I crumpled it, smashed it in my fist until pain overcame hope. Because I knew deep down Damian wasn't planning a seduction in his study.

That spark of fury reignited, propelling my feet to its destination.

But it wasn't Damian who sat at the end of the polished oak table. It was an elderly woman in elegant clothes, with stylish blonde hair, sipping tea as she perused a stack of documents in front of her.

At my entry, piercing blue eyes locked on me.

'Ah. You must be the reason my nephew is bristling like a wet hedgehog. Sit down, my dear,' she invited, although her voice wasn't all that welcoming.

'No, thank you.'

She eyed me for a taut stretch. 'What's your name?'

'Neve Nolan.'

'Mine is Florence Mortimer. Now that we're acquainted, would you care to tell me what has you so het up?'

The urge to tell her to mind her own business tripped to the edge of my tongue. But then I remembered what she'd done for Damian. 'Your nephew isn't who I thought he was.'

Her lips pursed. 'No one is, my dear. We all wear masks.'

'Well, his masked slipped. And I don't like what I see.'

Her blue eyes attained a hard glint. 'Watch it, young lady. That's my kin you're disparaging.' She sighed. 'Damian has a good heart. Whatever it is you think he's done, surely it's forgivable?'

'I thought so…the first time. But fool me twice?'

She set her cup down with a sharp click. 'Neve… may I call you Neve?'

I gave a jerky nod.

'I don't want to be here, Neve. But I get the feeling he's about to do something reckless. Do I need to stick around to pick up the pieces? Or can I convince you to have this thing…whatever it is…out with him another day? He's been through the wringer already today.'

'Because he's been to see Gideon about Penny?' I asked with a heavy dose of bitterness. 'How did it go, by the way?'

Surprise sparked her eyes. 'You know?'

'Know what?' Damian asked from behind me, rough tension in his voice.

I took my time to face him, guarding my every exposed surface. But it was no use. The sight of him singed and flayed me, sparked every cell to roaring life, while shrivelling a heart that wanted to open wide in welcome.

My senses absorbed him greedily, certain this would be the last time they had a chance.

And in the time we stood there staring at each other, Aunt Flo rose and approached. 'You sure know how to pick 'em, dear boy. Good luck.'

He barely acknowledged her departure, his hazel eyes fixed on me. 'What was that all about?'

'Tell me why I'm here, Damian.' I struggled to keep my voice even and barely pulled it off.

'Neve—'

'Is it this?' I indicated the two stacks of papers on the table.

He stared at me in rigid silence before he sighed. 'This wasn't how I intended to present this.'

'Let me guess, you were going to set the scene, mellow me out with some more sex before you attempted your nice little takeover?'

He froze, a chill turning his eyes frosty. 'Excuse me?'

'Everyone has an agenda. Those were *your* words. Did you plan all of this just so you'd get the leverage you need to cement your place on your precious board?'

'Neve, you've got this wrong.'

'Have I? Then tell me what's in the document,' I challenged.

His lips firmed and he exhaled hard before approaching. 'It is a bid for The Mortimer Group to absorb Nevirna but—'

'You bastard.'

'Dammit, hear me out.'

'Why? So you can chop me up and sell me off like you did with Cahill Hotels nine months after you partnered up with him?'

'That was *his* proposal. He wanted out of the hotel business.'

'Well, I don't! God, to think I was beginning to trust you. To think I imagined we could be...'

'Be what?' he asked sharply, his eyes ferociously intent.

I swallowed my vulnerable words. 'You should set your aunt straight on a few things.'

'Why? What did she say to you?'

'She seemed to be under a few misapprehensions about us.'

His nostrils flared. 'Don't give me broad strokes, Neve.'

'She thinks I have some sort of power over you. That I'm capable of hurting you. I didn't get round to telling her you were incapable of being hurt because you have a rock where your heart should be. That sex was all you really care about so she had nothing to worry about.'

'You think I'm incapable of being hurt?' The words were tersely spat out.

'I think you gave two strikes, once with your parents and once with Penny, and decided you were out. No more chances for anyone else. Everyone else is used, then written off before they even have a chance to crack that fortress you've placed around yourself.'

His face turned to stone. 'You think I used you?'

I somehow managed to summon a smile. 'Are you or are you not planning on leveraging Fantasy Rooms with your board, Damian?'

'Well, you got me. But what about you, Neve?' His voice was a sharp scythe.

'What about me?'

'Tell me what your grand plan was. Or should I guess? Sex was your weapon of choice, wasn't it? Get me to the point of obsession. Make it so I wouldn't see bloody straight by the time you were done with me?'

My deep flush gave me away before he was done talking. But I still shrugged. 'What does it matter now? You're going to leave and I'm going to go back to being the forgettable screw who amused you for a little while.'

He laughed, a scraping, scary sound. 'You think you're forgettable? You think I didn't wake up this morning knowing I had to make changes if I wanted—'

A throat cleared at the door, and Margret appeared. '*Pardonnez-moi, Monsieur*, but Madame Mortimer wants to know if you're ready to leave.'

Damian didn't answer. Not right away. He stared at me as if he wanted to say something more.

His silence cut me open, freed the burning question blazing through my heart. 'If you wanted what, Damian?'

His face tautened into an impenetrable mask. 'Nothing I'm going to get from you. I see that now.' He turned to Margret. 'Tell my aunt I'll be right there. I'm done here.'

I knew that last bit was intended to wound. And it found its mark so accurately, I could do nothing, not even breathe, as he walked out of the room.

The sound of the rotors spinning in preparation for take-off tore through me as surely as if the blades had struck my skin.

CHAPTER ELEVEN

Damian

IT WAS AMAZING how much could happen in four short weeks. A person could come out of the wilderness and be enfolded back into his family—or reinstated on the board by a slim majority, as was my case. Amazing too how that same board could fall apart after a short absence of its CEO and convene an emergency meeting to instate me as interim CEO. At least until Gideon returned from his extended sabbatical and we could co-CEO together as we'd planned many years ago.

Most amazing of all was how none of that mattered a damn to me any more.

Gideon and I had patched things up before he went after the woman he had fallen in love with. Our bond had bent out of shape and would require a hell of a lot of work, but it hadn't broken.

Neve, on the other hand…

I tried to take a breath and tensed at the lance of pain in my gut.

Fucking hell, what hope did I have of living anything resembling a normal life if I couldn't take a breath without her?

I whirled in my comfy CEO seat, stabbed my keyboard and waited impatiently for the laptop to flare to life.

A sharp tap of the refresh button showed an empty inbox.

Same as five minutes ago.

Same as every day that dragged by without a response. Every single email arrived at its destination—I'd co-opted a nerd from IT to monitor it—and every email was immediately trashed.

Who could blame her?

She'd seen the demons I carried, and had still given me the time of day. Hell, she'd given me more than that. She'd listened without judgment. Given me comfort where I hadn't received any for a long time. Hell, she'd even given me that last push I'd needed to confront Gideon, set things straight once and for all.

She'd wanted to do more. I'd seen it in her eyes, felt it in her touch.

But I was the fucking bastard who'd turned away from it all.

I wanted it back. All she had to give and more.

She might be trashing my emails but she was still connected even though her manager claimed she didn't know where Neve was.

In a last-ditch effort, I picked up the phone. Ten minutes later, I had a plan in place.

Neve

My finger hovered over the delete button, as I wondered how much more of this I could take before I succumbed and cried wolf. Or how much more I could take before the broken pieces inside me fossilised into permanent scar tissue.

Every day felt worse than the last. And every day he sent me a message.

Why was he doing this?

Damian has a good heart.

Of all the words we'd exchanged, why did the ones uttered by his aunt haunt me the most?

I pushed away from the desk, pacing to the window in a futile hope that the glorious Surrey countryside would overcome the temptation to open the email. But even the short distance from the computer flayed me alive. I withstood the agony for a pathetic minute before I succumbed.

The message was short. Succinct.

Fantasy Rooms. Special Edition
Mortimer Royal, London
Tonight or any night that suits you. 8 p.m.
My fantasy. Your rules.

Did he know I was in England? I'd sworn my manager to secrecy while I explored a possible new hotel site.

But Damian was a billionaire with unlimited resources. And somehow he knew I was close enough… to what?

It was the *what* that saw me alight from a taxi two nights later outside Mortimer Royal, the latest in the illustrious hotel chain.

The doorman doffed his cap and held the door open. As I walked across the stunning atrium it occurred to me that the email hadn't given me a suite number or specific location.

Before I could complete the thought, a tall, striking man approached. His badge announced him as Head Concierge.

'Miss Nolan, welcome. If you don't mind following me, the lift you need is right this way.'

Biting back the questions that rose, I followed him to a lift marked *private*. He accessed it with a black key card, before handing it to me. 'Please use it if you need to come down. Enjoy your evening.'

The doors slid shut, throwing back my reflection at me. My cheeks were pale and I looked…wide-eyed and terrified. I dropped my gaze, straightened my red cocktail dress and silently willed my insides to stop shaking.

The worst that could happen was another unpleasant confrontation.

Yes, one that could decimate what's left of your broken heart.

My fingers tightened around the key card as the lift slowed. The carriage stopped. Pain and uncertainty sliced me in two.

When I'd boarded the helicopter he'd sent back for me in Bordeaux, I hadn't thought I could be capable of loving with my heart shattered in a thousand pieces. And yet I had.

Still did.

I can't do this.

I lifted the key card, aimed it at the electronic panel. And stopped.

You've come this far.

Shaky and tentative, I stepped out and looked

around. Plush carpeting rolled towards a single solid door that stood ajar. I approached slowly, nudged it open.

The air evaporated from my lungs.

The bar, and the bartender mopping the shiny counter, looked achingly familiar. In fact, the whole scene looked familiar, right down to the chairs grouped near the window that showed night-time Boston. Except this time, there were no other guests.

Heart thumping wildly, I approached and slid into the farthest seat.

The bartender sauntered towards me with a smile. 'What can I get you this evening?'

'Umm…whiskey sour, please,' I managed past a throat clogged with roiling emotions.

He nodded. 'Coming right up.'

I took the drink he set before me a minute later with trembling fingers, not even a little ashamed that I was fortifying my wild tremors with liquid courage.

Damian slipped into his seat just as I finished my drink.

This time I didn't glance his way. I knew every inch of his body, knew what looking at him would do to me. But from the corner of my eye I saw him reach for the bottle of water set before him.

The bartender approached. 'Want another?'

'Yes.' I paused, cleared my throat. 'And a shot of your best whiskey for him too, on my tab.'

The bartender nodded. He returned with my drink, then, unable to stand the agony any longer, I turned and watched him slide a shot of whiskey towards Damian.

He stared into the amber liquid for a nerve-wracking stretch. Then ferocious hazel eyes pierced me from across the bar as the bartender slipped through the door and shut it behind him, leaving us alone. 'There's only one woman I trust to buy me a drink.'

My heart lurched wildly. 'Why?'

'Because she's the only person in the world I trust implicitly. The one who helped *me* learn to trust again. Helped me accept a part of myself I thought I'd lost.'

My mouth twisted. 'She sounds like a saint.'

His eyes locked on me, pleaded with me. 'She is. A saint. A vixen. A sharp, intelligent businesswoman. Most of all, a compassionate human being who deserves nothing less than abject worship from a fool like me.'

I remained frozen, my shattered heart unable to pick itself up from the crater it'd fallen into weeks ago. Not even to acknowledge the pain rushing through his eyes.

'Abject worship sounds...tedious. Don't get me wrong, I'm sure it'll be fun for a while. But then... what?'

'Then she can have whatever she wants.'

'What if she has an agenda?'

He grimaced, agony flashing across his face. 'I'm learning that not every agenda is bad. Some of them are pursued with integrity and compassion as the end game. Mine going forward is to love, cherish and, yes, worship too.' His eyes met mine, his gaze pleading. 'If I'm given the chance.'

I shook my head. 'I can't.'

His jaw tightened. 'God, don't say that, Neve. I'll do anything. Just don't close the door on me. On us. I fucked up in France, I know I did. My plan was to propose an affiliation deal like the one you wanted with Cahill two years ago. I know I should've heard you out in Boston, maybe we could've worked something else out that didn't involve jeopardising your company. Don't get me wrong, that's not why I was offering it in France. Simple truth is you're a brilliant business-woman, an asset I didn't want to get away. And yes, a large part of it was that I was terrified of you walking away from me for good. But I want... Fuck, I'll jump through whatever hoop you want so long as you con-sider giving me a chance.'

Shame lanced me. 'You were right, Damian. I kinda had my agenda too.'

He shook his head. 'You were reacting to what I did. I was a little too brutal with my assessment. You weren't ready. But I could've framed the whole thing much better.'

'I worked hard for everything in my life. *Every-thing.* I learned to keep quiet and make myself un-obtrusive so I didn't upset my mother when she was having one of her pity episodes. I fought for a rela-tionship with my father after my mother drove him away and tried to keep us apart. And guess what, you were right. I hated failing at both but I still persevered with miserable results. My business was the only area I thrived in. So for a long time I hated you for turning Cahill against me. But looking back now, I'm glad you did. I would probably be bankrupt now or sold off in pieces. So, in a roundabout way, you saved me.'

He continued to look pained. 'I hurt you. Attacked you to save myself the pain of hearing the truth. I know that's not a great pedigree to align yourself with, but

I'm selfish enough to hope that I can learn from you, Neve.'

'Your pedigree doesn't define you. I've learned the hard way that not everyone who can have children should. As much as it hurts, my mother is probably one of them. You can't bring a child into the world only to turn around and blame it for everything that goes wrong in your life.'

'Or in my case use it as a bargaining chip for money.'

We fell silent, absorbing our shared pain for a moment before he rose. 'I don't want to dwell on the past. The reason my rift with Gideon hurt so much was because we vowed that we would be different from our parents. That we would be better. You showed me that it was possible, that I could rise above the bitterness. I want to be that person, Neve. But only with you.'

My lungs flattened. 'I... What are you saying?'

'That I regressed into shitty behaviour that last day in France. I told myself it would be a pleasant surprise for you but I was desperately trying to find a way to hold onto you. I didn't want our time together to end. I was hooked on you.'

'Hooked?'

He ventured closer, until he was within reach. 'Fuck it, okay, I was in love with you. I fell in love with you the day I walked into the pre-production meeting and you tore strips off me. Only I didn't know it then. All I knew was that I wanted you in my life. The night I walked you home and you didn't invite me in I knew I couldn't live without you. You drew me when I didn't want to be drawn. You reached inside and touched me deeply and I knew I'd never be the same again. I talked to Tyler and Sam this morning. I've withdrawn my consultancy deal. They've agreed to partner with you exclusively if that's what you want.'

'No. I don't want.'

His forehead twitched. 'What?'

'I don't want a deal that doesn't include you.'

'But…'

'You want to worship me? Well, I'll give you a chance. But only if you let me love and worship you too, Damian.'

A visible tremble went through his body and his eyes turned black. 'Bloody hell, you know how to bring a lovesick man to his knees, don't you? You do realise I intend to stay there for ever for you?'

I laughed. 'That was kinda my plan from the beginning. Such a shame I had to fall in love with you that night two years ago when you sat down at the bar with a world of pain in your eyes.'

'God, I never thought I'd be thankful for Gideon being an arsehole and refusing to listen to what I'd found out from the investigators that day. If he had I'd never have flown to Boston.' He shuddered with the rush of unwanted might-have-beens. 'I'd never have met you.'

'But he was. And we did.' My smile seemed lit from within. 'We'll have to send him a very large gift basket.'

He moved closer, his gaze devouring me. 'He can wait. Tell me more about how you felt that first time, please.'

'I wanted to soothe you like I've never wanted to soothe anyone. I wanted to take you home to Westport, feed you, take care of you. And yes, fuck you blind every chance I got.'

Hoarse laughter barked from his throat.

'But most of all, I wanted to love you.'

The hand he lifted to rub over his jaw shook wildly. 'I don't fucking deserve you,' he said gruffly.

'I have ways to remedy that.'

'I'm all ears, sweet love. Tell me,' he commanded.

I left my seat, made my way to where he stood. Leaning up, I wrapped my arms around his neck, breathed him in and filled myself with everything I'd missed for long, harrowing weeks. 'First, you drink that shot I've paid good money for.'

He immediately threw back the drink and tossed the glass on the bar. 'Next, please.'

'Next, you let me throw you a party for all the birthdays you've missed.'

Another tremble shook him from head to toe and the eyes that blinked at me were suspiciously damp. 'Neve, darling, you don't have to—'

I sealed his mouth with mine. He groaned, pulled me close and deepened the kiss. When we parted we were both breathing hard. I rubbed my belly against his erect cock and smiled when he groaned again.

'You were saying?'

'Yes, Neve. Whatever you want.'

'What I want is for us to be each other's safe place, Damian. Always.'

He lowered his forehead to mine and slowly exhaled. 'For as long as I live, I'll always be yours. You have my promise.'

I blinked back tears and forced myself to look around. 'Where exactly is this place?'

'My penthouse.'

'And the bar? I can't believe you made a replica of the bar where we met.'

He smiled slyly. 'It's not a replica. I had the whole thing dismantled and shipped over from Boston.'

I gasped. 'You didn't!'

'I had no idea how to get you over there but I hoped I could tempt you to come here since you were in England. So I took a gamble. The bar at Hotel M is closed until further notice for refurbishment.'

I stepped away from him, ran my hand over the smooth, shiny countertop. 'So this belongs exclusively to you now?'

'It belongs to *us*, Neve,' he said, stepping up close to wrap his hands around me.

'Hmm.' I nudged my bottom into his groin, revelling in his thick groan. 'In that case I have a fantasy or two of my own.'

He leaned close, caught my earlobe between his lips. 'I'm way ahead of you, darling. And I guarantee you won't need panties for a very long time.'

* * * * *

ENEMIES WITH BENEFITS

To authors everywhere who have to deal with a
'birthing-a-pineapple' book every once in a while.
I took one for the team with this book.
You're welcome.

CHAPTER ONE

'I CAN TRUST you to behave yourself, can't I?'

Shit.

I dragged my gaze from the statuesque brunette weaving her way through the one-hundred-plus guests sipping vintage champagne on a chilly autumn evening. The five heating towers positioned around the terrace and immediate lamplit grounds of the Surrey mansion were doing their damnedest to warm up the abysmal temperature and failing, but I, for one, didn't need their help.

My body had heated up the moment I spotted Wren Bingham, wearing a clingy jumpsuit that lovingly followed every curve of her spectacular body. Fringed, shoulder-length jet-black hair brushed the frilly-looking scarf wrapped around her shoulders. Stilettos on her feet and a diamond bracelet circling her wrist completed her outfit. Her guests wore double and triple layers but she was obviously nowhere near cold, either.

I didn't mind one bit because she looked fuckable in the extreme—

'Jasper?'

I reeled myself in at Aunt Flo's sharper tone. An apologetic glance her way showed pursed lips and a disapproving glint in her eye. I was usually more circumspect but being in the same vicinity as Wren Bingham always scuppered my concentration.

I cleared my throat. 'Of course I'll behave. Scouts' honour.' The woman who'd been more of a mother to me than my own living parent snorted her disbelief.

'As if they'd have let you anywhere near a Scouts camp. You'd have scandalised them all within an hour.'

I grinned at her no-nonsense reply because her tone was couched in familiar, reassuring warmth. Warmth I let wash over me to disperse the soul-shrivelling chill that came from thinking about my birth mother, which inevitably led to thoughts about my father. Specifically, their arctic wind of rejection, far more brutal than any winter I'd experienced since their desertion. No, tonight most definitely wasn't the time to dwell on that noxious period of my childhood and how it'd ruined not just me but my siblings, too.

Tonight was about bringing recalcitrant business partners to heel. Mostly…

After another search failed to reveal my elusive prey, I focused once more on Wren, that compulsion since Aunt Flo and I had walked through the impressive double doors of the Bingham mansion in Esher forty-five minutes ago pulling at me.

So far I hadn't spotted Wren's brother, Perry Bingham, my primary reason for being here. Sure, I'd nodded and reassured my favourite aunt that accompanying her to this soirée was my pleasure and the right Mortimer thing to do. Also because, on some weird rota only Aunt Flo was privy to, it was apparently my turn to escort her to another social function. What I'd failed to mention was that I was on the hunt for Perry Bingham, CEO of Bingham Industries, who had stopped answering my calls for nearly two weeks, thereby threatening to throw one serious spanner into my latest project.

With my patience wearing thin, I'd grasped the opportunity to track him down at his family estate. Except it looked as if he was a no-show here, too.

But Wren was here, and I intended to drill his sister about his whereabouts. My choice of words brought an inner smirk I wisely kept off my face as I downed my whisky and turned to my aunt.

'Can I get you another drink?' I indicated her half-empty glass of sherry.

Several waitstaff circulated with trays of drinks but I didn't plan to grab one from them. Not when Wren stood next to the bar, chatting with two of her guests. As I watched, she threw her head back in laughter, her smooth, swanlike neck thrown into perfect relief.

Immediately, I imagined my lips there, beneath her jawline, tasting her silky skin, then lower, tonguing her pulse. Would she cry out in delight or moan with pleasure?

'We both know that's an excuse to get away from me. Go on, then. Just don't do anything we'd both be ashamed of come morning, would you? I could do without a Mortimer tabloid scandal before Christmas,' Aunt Flo said.

Brushing a kiss on a well-preserved cheek, I muttered, 'You've taught me the importance of not making promises I can't keep. Don't make me start now.'

She rolled her eyes but her smile deepened.

I grinned again as I made a beeline for the bar, and I wasn't one little bit ashamed to admit that I was hard as stone.

I made sure to wipe the smile off my face, my eyes settling in the middle distance to prevent business acquaintances engaging me in conversation. A few feet from Wren, I paused to ponder why this woman, amongst so many others, had fired me up ever since she'd crossed my path five years ago.

Perhaps it was discovering that, far from being a superficial heiress and supermodel flitting around the globe between the ages of nineteen and twenty-three, she'd attained a master's degree in business while slaying the runways of the fashion capitals of the world. More besides, she'd graduated top of her class and was, at twenty-eight, now on course to become one of the youngest power executives in the city. Or perhaps it was some twisted attraction born from our family being embroiled in a generations-old feud, which dictated we should hate each other on sight like some pathetic Roman tragedy.

Whatever. All I knew was that Wren had intrigued me with increasing intensity over the past few years.

Intense empire-building in order to establish my role in my family's company as President of New Developments in Europe, Africa and the Middle East, and perhaps even the arrogant belief that our chemistry was a passing whim and wasn't worth turning my family upside down for, had so far kept me from pursuing Wren, but each encounter only deepened whatever this phenomenal chemistry was that stopped me from seeing any other woman but her whenever we were in each other's orbit.

Lately, I'd accepted that it simply wasn't going to go away by itself, as I'd assumed. Not until I did something about it.

I realised my motionless state was drawing curious attention from nearby guests, not to mention Aunt Flo's disapproving glare from across the terrace.

Discarding my glass, I stepped beside Wren. 'Good evening, Wren. You look incredible.' I said, my voice pitched low.

She tried not to stiffen, but didn't quite succeed, nor could she disguise the flare of awareness in her vivid green eyes when she turned to me. She didn't reply immediately, instead she scrambled for the jaded expression that had been her trademark in her modelling days.

I stifled the urge to tell her not to bother. Witnessing a demonstration of her fiery passion and stiletto-sharp business acumen five years ago across a boardroom table for an unforgettable fifteen minutes had etched a different Wren Bingham in my mind from the façade she wore for the public.

'Jasper Mortimer.'

The way she said my name, striving to be curt when different textures sizzled beneath, ramped up my temperature. I wanted her attempting to say my name just like that while she was tied to my bed with silken restraints, naked and wet.

'I don't recall seeing your name on the guest list.'

Pausing just as long as she did before answering, I snagged a glass of champagne from the bar. 'Because it wasn't there. I'm privileged to be my aunt's plus one. What I haven't had the privilege of is being acknowledged by the hostess since my arrival. I'm feeling sorely neglected.'

She tried to look through me, as if that would stop the arc of electricity zapping between us. As if she hadn't performed a quick once-over of my body as I got my drink. I planted myself in her line of vision until she had no choice but to focus on me, her nostrils flaring slightly as her green eyes—alluringly wide and sparkling with an interest she was trying to hide—connected with mine.

I barely heard her guests murmur their excuses and drift away, leaving us in a tight little cocoon.

'Perhaps I would've already greeted you, if you hadn't arrived half an hour late.'

I curbed a smile, inordinately pleased she'd noticed my arrival. 'I'm willing to make amends by doubling my donation to tonight's cause.'

One elegantly shaped eyebrow arched. 'Name it.'

I frowned. 'Name what?'

'The beneficiary of tonight's cause. What's this mixer in aid of?' she challenged.

Crap. I'd tuned Aunt Flo out when she'd mentioned it in the car, my frustrated attention on the echo of the ringing phone Perry was—yet again—refusing to answer. 'Something to do with pandas in Indonesia?' I hazarded.

Sparks gathered in her eyes. 'Why am I not surprised you don't know?'

Heat surged through me. 'That suggests a curious level of personal knowledge. Have you been attempting to get to know me behind my back, Wren?'

She gave the smallest gasp, then tried that bored look again. 'I've no idea what you're talking about. I can't help it if others feel the need to gossip about you Mortimers.'

'Oh, yeah? What else do they say about me? What else has that brilliant brain of yours retained?'

Her nose wrinkled in distaste. 'Nothing worth repeating.'

Unable to resist, I stepped closer. 'Are you sure? I'm happy to hear you out, set a few things straight if you get anything wrong.'

She didn't reply. After an age of trying to decipher which I liked more on her skin—the scent of bergamot or the underlying allure of crushed lilies—I looked up to catch her gaze on my mouth.

Hell yes, that insane chemistry was still very much alive and well—and sizzling, as usual.

'Stop that,' she said in a tight undertone.

I raised my glass, took a lazy sip before answering. 'Stop what?'

'That extremely unsubtle way you're looking at me,' she hissed in a ferocious whisper, then glanced around. Thankfully, the music was loud enough for her words to reach my ears only. 'The way you look at me every time we meet.'

I laughed under my breath. 'And how do I look at you, Wren?'

'You might lure some women with those come-fuck-me eyes but I'm not one of them so stop wasting your time.'

My laughter was a little louder, genuine amusement reminding me how long it'd been since I'd enjoyed the thrill of a chase outside the boardroom. 'Come-fuck-me eyes? Really?' I didn't bother to keep my voice down.

Several people stared but I watched Wren, keenly interested in her next move.

She flashed the patently false smile she'd been doling out all evening but I caught the strain beneath the thousand-watt beam. Taking in the rest of her, I sensed tension in her lithe frame, in the fingers that clutched her glass a little too firmly. For reasons I suspected went beyond our conversation, Wren was wound extremely tight tonight.

And I was curiously concerned about it. 'Is everything okay?'

'Of course. Why shouldn't it be?'

I shrugged. 'You seem a little…stressed.'

Her chin notched upward. 'You don't know me well enough to make that assessment.'

'Ah, but I've attended enough of these shindigs to see when the hostess is fretting about the vegan-to-carnivore ratio of her canapés, and when it's something more. This is something more.'

Her delicate throat moved in a nervous swallow, but her gaze remained bold and direct, swirling with a deep, passionate undercurrent I craved to drown in. 'Even *if* it's the latter, it's none of your business. Now, if you'll excuse me—'

'Where's Perry?'

She froze mid-brush-off, her eyes widening fractionally. 'What?'

No, she wasn't as carefree as she pretended.

The rumours that Bingham's was in trouble had been circulating for a few years now. The veracity of those rumours was partly why I'd initially been reticent about joining forces with them. But, hell, call me a sucker... I'd always had a thing for the underdog.

Maybe it was a hangover from my daddy issues. Or a tool I used to my advantage when idiots underestimated me. Either way, my instincts hadn't failed me thus far.

There were certain family and board members who considered me, at thirty-one, too young for the position I was in, notwithstanding the fact that my older brother, Damian, and my cousin Gideon had been wildly successful in their newly minted co-CEO positions of the entire Mortimer Group despite being only a few years older. Or that my cousin Bryce was acing his similar position as President of New Developments in Asia and Australia. Even my sister, Gemma, and my cousin Graciela, who'd both resisted joining the board until recently, were excelling in their chosen areas of expertise.

I was damned if I'd let Perry Bingham's antics prove them right. Especially after going against all my business instincts and signing him onto my deal.

'There's nothing wrong with your hearing, Wren. Where's your brother?' I steeled my voice because, however much I enjoyed this erotic dance with her, Perry was at risk of tanking everything I'd worked for during the last eighteen months.

Several expressions filtered through her eyes—alarm, worry, irritation, mild disappointment. She finally settled on indignation. 'Is that why you came?'

'I told you, I accompanied Aunt Flo—'

'A ruse to hunt down my brother,' she interjected.

'That implies awareness that he's hiding. Is he?'

A look flickered across her face, gone too quickly but revealing enough to intensify the unease knotting my belly. 'Tell me where he is, Wren,' I pressed. 'He's been avoiding my calls for almost two weeks and it's getting really old.'

'I'm afraid you'll have to do your own hunting. I'm not Perry's keeper.' Her tense reply gave her away. As did the minuscule tremble in the fingers that held her glass. Both intrigued and disturbed me but before I could push for more, she added, 'You've monopolised me quite enough. Enjoy the rest of your evening, Jasper.'

Just for the hell of it, and because something wild and reckless yearned for another demonstration that she wasn't immune to me, I brushed my fingertips down her arm. 'This isn't over.'

She attempted to cover her tiny shiver of awareness with a wide sultry smile that diverted my attention to her luscious lips. 'How can something be over when it didn't start in the first place?'

With that, she sailed away, her hips swaying in that unique way that'd held male and female gazes rapt during her modelling days. Since then, Wren had gained even more confidence in her womanhood, and left a swathe of admirers slack-jawed in her wake. I wracked my brain, trying to recall if she had a current boyfriend. The gut-tightening rejection at the idea of her being attached made me grimace into my champagne.

Until my gaze fell on the woman who placed herself directly in Wren's path before manoeuvring her away from the nearest guest.

Agnes Bingham—Wren's mother and powerhouse socialite in her own right.

The tall, slim woman was what Wren would look like in thirty years. Except where Agnes's beauty was classically cool, Wren was vibrant, passionate, even though she seemed hell-bent on suppressing it.

Why?

None of your business.

But I wanted to make it my business. I wanted Wren in my bed and damn all the consequences to hell. And more and more I suspected I wouldn't get over this fever in my blood until I'd had her.

Tension of a different kind raced up my spine when mother and daughter glanced my way. The touch of rebellion in Wren's gaze made me raise my glass in a mocking toast, even while I observed the animosity emanating from Agnes Bingham.

Bloody hell.

Family feuds, Perry Bingham going AWOL and now Agnes Bingham. Three stumbling blocks in my intent to have Wren. But despite the damning words my father had taken pleasure in decimating me with as a child, I wasn't afraid of a challenge.

All the same, my gut twisted as I made my way back

to my aunt, the thought of broaching the subject of my father making my stomach curdle.

'Everything okay?' Aunt Flo asked, after smiling an excuse to the guest she'd been chatting to.

I let her fondness wash over me for a moment before I pulled myself together. Wishing her warm concern came from a different female voice had been fruitless when I was a child. It was even more foolish now. The woman who'd given birth to me wasn't interested in taking up her maternal role. Not for her first or second born, and certainly not for me, her third child. My arrival had spelled the end to her obligation and she couldn't get away fast enough. Years of hoping, of saving my allowance in a childish hope of enticing her financially had been laughed off. I was no longer ten years old, fighting to stop myself from crying as Damian advised me to give up my foolish hoping.

'George Bingham. I need to know the full story,' I said to Aunt Flo, my low voice brisker than she deserved.

'What's brought this on? You've never wanted to know before,' she said after eyeing me in frowning silence.

I shrugged, moving her away to the more private edge of the terrace. 'I've never cared enough about the finer details. Now I do because whatever happened all those years ago is endangering an important deal and I've just about had it.'

'Dear boy, money isn't—'

My bitter laugh stopped her. 'Do me a favour, please, and don't finish that sentence, Aunt Flo. We both know

money is definitely everything to any red-blooded Mortimer.'

She harrumphed. 'Well, I don't agree but, since you
seem to have a bee in your bonnet about it, I'll let it go.
To answer your question, it was your father's last deal
before he and your mother stepped away from the company, and the family. He and George Bingham were supposed to go fifty-fifty but George messed up somehow
and could only come up with a fraction of the investment by the deadline date. There was a clause in their
agreement that it was fifty-fifty or nothing and that
loophole gave your father the right to cut him out regardless of how much money he'd pumped into the deal
up to then. He didn't take it well. He wasted money he
didn't have trying to sue your father. But Hugh was a
brilliant, if somewhat ruthless, businessman.'

There was no *somewhat* about it. I'd come across
some of his deals while my father had actively worked
in the family firm. His cut-throat antics were legend-
ary. If you liked blood and gore with your negotiations.

A memory shot through my head. 'Was closing that
Bingham deal part of my father's walking-away package?'
I asked.

Aunt Flo sighed. 'Yes, it was. Back then, every deal
closed by a member of the board came with a ten-per-cent
profit bonus. Cutting out Bingham and making it an exclusive Mortimer deal meant Hugh received a bigger bonus.
About two hundred million.'

And he was probably in such a hurry to walk away
from his family that he'd been unflinchingly ruthless.
'I see.'

'What's going on, Jasper?' Aunt Flo asked curiously.

The cocktail of bitterness, anger and arousal swirled faster inside me as I looked over her shoulder to find Wren watching me. 'It's just business.'

'No, it's not. You're not cut-throat like your father. But you're just as dogged. I had my reservations when I heard about your deal with Perry, considering his problems,' she murmured. 'But knowing you, you'll move mountains to make it work.'

'Forgive me if I don't welcome the comparison to Hugh,' I rasped.

Her eyes clouded with momentary sadness. 'His blood may run through your veins but you're your own man where it counts, Jasper. Whatever you're getting involved in, just…protect your heart. I don't want to see you hurt again.'

Another harsh laugh bubbled up, but I swallowed it down. And just about managed to stop myself from telling her that, while I'd struck a deal with Perry Bingham in a moment of madness, perhaps even a sting of conscience and despite Perry's rumoured drinking problem, somewhere in the mix was the reasoning that it would put me in a good position to strike a better deal with Wren in the near future. Business-wise and in other ways, too.

'You have that gleam in your eye, Jasper. Am I wasting my breath by telling you to be a dear and spare my nerves?' Aunt Flo asked.

I couldn't promise that. Hell, I *knew* there would be plenty more fireworks between Wren and me in the future. 'I can promise dinner at The Dorchester as soon as my schedule lets up a little. I know how much you like their new chef. We can check out the competition in the process.'

She smiled. 'Cecil is a culinary genius. And very easy on the eyes. I'll hold you to that promise,' she said, just before another acquaintance snagged her attention.

Briefly alone, I tried to suppress the tangled emotions churning through me.

I don't want to see you hurt again.

As much as I wanted to put my parents out of my mind for ever, to rub them from my existence as much as they'd rubbed me from theirs, the ten-year-old boy's anguish from relentless rejection, which I'd never been quite successful in smothering, wouldn't let me. But it was a good reminder not to count on anyone but myself. Not to let frivolous emotion get in the way of business.

I wanted this deal with Bingham because it was sound and profitable.

I also wanted to fuck Wren Bingham, once she got over the pesky family-feud thing. The two were mutually exclusive enough not to cause me to lose any sleep.

Which was why when Wren hurried away from her mother, her shoulders tight with barely-harnessed emotions, I followed.

She was heading towards the far end of the grounds, her heels sinking soundlessly into the grass. She didn't hear me until I was six feet from her.

'Wren?'

Her head whipped around. 'Are you following me?' she asked sharply. But then she trembled. A tiny reaction, but, coupled with the slight wobble of her mouth, it hastened my steps, the peculiar punch in my chest unsettling me.

'What's wrong?'

'Other than the fact that you're stalking me now?'

'Hardly. You just seem—'

'There's nothing wrong. Just leave me alone, please?'

I looked beyond her to the high hedges of what looked like an elaborate garden. 'If everything's fine, why are you running away from your own party?'

'I'm not running away. And it's not my party—' She caught herself and snatched in a deep breath. 'Why the hell am I explaining myself to you?'

'Because sometimes it helps to vent.' Not that it'd done me much good. Ever. All my good intentions had ended in disaster, the repercussions of which I still lived with. But this wasn't the time or place to examine old scars. 'Or so I've heard, anyway.'

'Do you go around dishing out inexperienced advice?'

I shook my head, unwilling to drag my far from delightful childhood into this moment. 'We're not talking about me.'

'You're right, we're not. In fact, I'm going to pretend you're not here at all. Feel free to make that a reality,' she suggested, right before she turned on her heel and marched away from me.

And since I was far too intrigued to heed her brush-off… I followed.

If she gave even a hint of needing comfort, I'd offer her a shoulder, and other parts of my body, to cry on.

Bloody hell. I cringed at my own crassness. Then

shrugged it off. *I am who I am.* And that person wanted Wren Bingham any way he could get her. Besides that, though, I was here on Mortimer business. Technically.

She ignored me until she reached a bricked pathway. Then she turned and stared at me for several seconds without speaking. For a moment, a deep yearning flitted over her face, then her expression blanked. 'You're really not going to leave me alone, are you?' she murmured.

'Not until you tell me what's wrong.' Before she could reply, I jerked my chin at the hedge. 'What's behind there?'

Her eyes narrowed, her fingers twitching against her thighs. 'Nothing interesting. Just the garden. A pool. Gazebo. The usual.'

She was lying. Or at least holding something back. 'What else?'

'Why do you want to know?' she demanded, then flinched as someone laughed loudly nearby.

'You look like you need a breather. What's out there?'

'A maze,' she confessed with reluctance. 'I go there sometimes…to think.'

Before my brain could growl its warning that this was a bad idea, I stepped closer. 'Show me.'

She tensed. 'Excuse me?'

'I'd like to see this maze. A quick tour. Then, if you still insist, I'll leave.'

Something flickered in her eyes, undercurrents of lust zinging between us. Her gaze dropped to my lips and I almost wanted to crow in triumph. 'Fine. Let's go.'

She wrapped her scarf tighter around her neck and

I stopped myself from mourning the loss of the sight of her satiny skin.

Even in the cold, my libido was racing feverishly. I cleared my throat. 'So, what was that with your mother?'

Stubborn fire lit her eyes. 'I'll allow you to stay on condition we don't talk about my mother. Or any member of my family.'

I didn't protest her condition. Families like mine were complicated and she didn't need to vocalise her feelings towards hers for me to get it. Why that little commonality turned me on, I refused to contemplate.

In silence we walked along a dark red-bricked pavement until we reached a tall iron gate set into a walled-off section of the garden. Pushing it open, we followed the path until we reached a tall hedge the size of a barn door that remained full and thick despite the low temperatures. Wren's hand disappeared between the leaves and a section of the hedge sprang open.

With another glance at me, she stepped inside. I followed and stepped onto two diverging paths. She took the left one, her footsteps barely making a sound on the grass as we walked between tall hedgerows. Further chunks had been cut out intermittently and lower hedges transformed into shapes of animals, with a large space transformed into a picnic area with benches and seats.

We went deeper into the maze, her head bent forward as if weighed down by her emotions. I wanted to reach out and cup my hand over her nape, test the suppleness of her skin, feel that electricity between us. Instead, I shoved my hands into my pockets, willed the urge to pass. Jumping her right now would be the wrong move.

Eventually her steps slowed. 'We're almost at the centre,' she said, her voice low, as if she didn't want to speak.

'How big is this place?'

She shrugged. 'Big enough when you're a child seeking adventure. Not big enough when you're a teenager, attempting to flee from your demons.'

I wanted to ask about her demons but her pursed lips suggested she already regretted her revealing statement. I tried a different tack, hoping to take her mind off whatever was bothering her. 'Tell me one good memory you have of your maze.'

She didn't speak for several seconds, and I watched as she trailed her fingers over the tall green foliage. 'That's easy. I had my first kiss in here.'

Envy knotted my stomach. 'It was that good?'

She shook her head. 'It was that bad. It's what happened afterwards that makes it a good memory.'

'Tell me more,' I said, intrigued by the barely there but infinitely more genuine smile tugging up the corners of her full lips.

'I told Winslow Parker I didn't want to be kissed.' She shrugged. 'Call me shallow but I didn't want my first kiss to be from a boy named Winslow with a wet nose and clammy hands. He went ahead and stole a kiss anyway. So I blocked the exit to the maze and left him to freeze his arse off for three hours. When I came back to rescue him, he was crying.'

My lips twitched, a wicked part of me enjoying hearing that her first kiss had been less than memorable. 'So you enjoy making boys cry?'

We reached a dead end and she turned to face me. 'If they deserve it? Absolutely.'

A compulsion I didn't want to fight pulled me closer until I towered over her. Until she had to raise her head to meet my gaze. Despite the darkness around us, every inch of her stunning face and graceful neck was exposed to my keen gaze. 'What else do you enjoy making boys do?'

'I'm not nine years old any more. I'm a grown woman and I prefer grown men to boys now,' she murmured, her gaze fixed boldly on mine. A shiver caught her a second later and I drew closer, locking my fingers in the trellised hedge, caging her in.

'And what do you want this grown man to do for you?' I asked, aware my voice was gruff with the lustful urges running rampant through my bloodstream.

She stared at me for a minute, then cast her gaze around her, looking a little lost for a minute. 'Is it bad to say I don't want to be here? That if I could leave right now, get on a plane and go far away, I would?'

'Because of your mother?'

Her eyes darkened and she didn't repudiate me for ignoring her condition. 'Amongst other things.'

I got it. A long time ago, I'd accepted that it was better my parents lived in another country. Out of sight… out of mind…out of heartache… 'There's absolutely nothing wrong with wishing to be elsewhere.'

'But I can't, can I?'

I didn't answer because there was no right answer to that. I was born into a family where bullshit and dysfunction were the norm but where conversely fierce loyalty and absolute dedication to duty were the cornerstones that held most of us together. I suspected the Binghams were the same.

'Tell me what you want, Wren,' I said instead.

I watched a hot, determined look slowly fill her eyes. She shivered again and my gaze dropped to where her nipples had turned into twin points of succulent torture. Whether her body's reaction was from the cold or the arousal gathering heat in her eyes, I wasn't completely sure. Still, I shrugged off my jacket, draped it over her shoulders, wrapped my hands around her trim waist.

And waited.

Slowly, she slicked her tongue over her bottom lip. I bit back a groan as blood gleefully rushed south.

'Distract me,' she said, a mixture of challenge and pleading in the low, thick words that hardened my rousing cock. 'I don't want to go back to the party. I don't want to make stupid small talk. So just…make me stop thinking about all the crap I have to deal with now that…' She stopped and took a shaky breath.

Despite the flames licking through my veins, I hesitated. 'Are you sure?'

Her gaze grew defiant. 'Are you a boy or a man, Jasper Mortimer?'

I gave a low laugh. 'You don't want to ask me that, even as a challenge.'

'Why not? Will you punish me?' Her voice was breathless, edged with sexual anticipation.

My cock leapt to full attention. Jesus. 'Is that what you really want, Wren? For me to turn you around against this hedge and spank your tight little rump red for daring to question my manhood?'

Her eyes darkened, her mouth parting on a hot little pant. When her hips jerked forward a fraction, I yanked her the rest of the way, until our groins connected. Until she felt the hard, eager rod of my cock against her soft belly.

Hunger exploded over her face, her hands rising to grip my neck. 'Do your worst,' she invited with bite.

I fused my mouth to hers in a rough, carnal kiss powered by every single filthy fantasy I'd had about this woman. And there were hundreds. Thousands.

She opened for me immediately, her tongue gliding against mine in an erotic caress that weakened my knees. I tasted it, sucked on it, bit the tip and felt her shudder. Deepening the kiss, I trailed my hands up her flat belly and midriff to cup her soft, heavy breasts. Another moan escaped her, crushed between our lips as the kiss grew even more frantic.

She tasted intoxicating. Like the shot of adrenaline that brought every sense into vivid focus. I brushed my thumbs over the hard peaks of her nipples, then, giving into the wild clamouring, I nudged her zip halfway down her belly and pushed aside her bra. Before her gasp was fully formed, I swooped down and drew the exposed tip into my mouth. I suckled long and deep, then flicked my tongue rapidly over her burning flesh.

Her fingers bit into my nape. 'God…yes!'

Frantically, I freed the other breast, caught the tip between my fingers and teased. Her fingers gripped my nape, her breathing erratic as she held me to her breasts. After delivering equal amounts of attention to each, I pulled back, again wracked with the need to see her face.

She looked even more spectacular than before. Defiant. Aroused. Wanton.

'You're so fucking gorgeous,' I groaned.

An impatient sound escaped her, intensifying the heat in my veins. Dragging my hands from her breasts, I cupped her bottom, using the firm globes to pull her harder into my erection. She rewarded me by grinding her pelvis against my length, drawing needy sounds from both of us.

'I really, *really* want to fuck you, Wren,' I confessed, my voice a hot mess. 'I've wanted you since you stepped into my boardroom five years ago.'

She gave a cheeky little laugh, her eyes lighting up for the first time tonight. 'You mean when I turned down your internship offer?'

My fingers tightened on her bottom. 'I'll freely admit, I'm still a little salty about that.'

Her smile widened. 'Poor Jasper. Not used to hearing no?'

I smiled in return. 'I'm only sore at losing when what I want goes to a less worthy competitor. We both know why you turned me down.'

She licked her lips, her eyes lingering hungrily on mine. 'Pray, enlighten me.'

I wasn't going to ruin the moment by mentioning our family feud. 'Because neither of us likes to mix business with pleasure,' I said instead, running my thumb over her lower lip. Immediately her teeth nipped at my flesh, drawing a deep groan.

'I'm not going to confirm or deny that assertion.'

'Have it your way. I still want you. Badly.'

Eyes wild with defiance, she nodded eagerly, sucking my thumb into her mouth for a few seconds before she released me. 'Yes. *Now.*'

I planted a long kiss on her mouth as I lowered her zip. Only to groan when shocking reality hit me. For ten long seconds I remained paralysed. 'Shit.'

'What?' Her voice was beautifully slurred, her gaze hazy with arousal as she stared up at me. I wanted more of that look. Wanted to watch her shatter completely. Wanted to feel her pussy grip my cock as waves of ecstasy rolled over her.

'I don't have a condom,' I confessed through gritted teeth.

She stared at me blankly for a few seconds before disappointment drenched her beautiful face. 'Oh.'

I clenched my jaw tighter, unwilling to let go of this unique moment. 'Are you on the Pill?' I asked with more than a little hope. It wasn't my usual practice. I liked to be in complete control of my sexual fate. But just this once I prayed for a *yes*.

'No,' she replied, pained resignation in her voice.

'There are other ways, Wren.' I pulled her closer, trailed my lips over her jaw until I reached her ear. 'Let me make you come with my mouth. I want to taste you on my tongue. Lick you dry. You want to be transported? I can't do it with my cock but I can give you a little relief. Don't you want that?'

For a moment, she wavered, on the verge of calling quits on this madness. Selfishly, I didn't want to let her.

'I will eat you out for as long as you want me to. Think about how much I'll suffer while you do. You get to ride my face while you torture the hell out of me,' I invited.

Her fingers clenched harder into my skin. 'Yes,' she responded breathlessly. 'Please. Yes.'

Satisfied that I had her back in the moment with me, I caught the soft fabric of her jumpsuit between my fingers, careful not to wrinkle the material. Normally I wouldn't care but she had to return to a party filled with gossip-hungry guests and a mother she was clearly locked in tense disagreement with. I didn't want to draw any more attention to what we'd been doing than necessary.

I trailed my lips back to hers and kissed her hard before releasing her. 'Take this thing off for me,' I instructed.

Soft hands drifted down my forearms and wrists and covered mine for a second before she complied. I stepped back, eager for a snapshot of her leaning against her favourite hedge, undressing for me.

When she stepped out of the jumpsuit, I re-draped my jacket over her shoulders to keep her warm.

Call me primitive but the sight of her in my clothing threatened to undo me. With her hair loose and straight and falling around her face, her upper body almost lost in my coat and her lower half almost exposed to the elements, she was breathtaking. Her legs alone were worth an extra minute of worship. But it was cold, and we couldn't stay out here for ever.

With more than a throb of regret, I stepped forward and trailed the backs of my hands up her inner thighs. She gave a soft gasp and quivered. My gaze raced up from her thighs to her face, unwilling to lose a second of her reaction. Her lips were parted, her eyes hooded but not shut. She watched my hand draw closer to where her pussy was hidden behind a layer of sexy black lace.

'Open your legs wider.'

Her gaze rose and caught on mine for a second before she obeyed, widening her stance until I could fit my closed fist at the juncture of her thighs. Slowly I dragged my knuckle lightly against her flesh; from where she was hot and sodden to the swollen nub pushing against the fabric.

She gasped again, thicker, louder, her breath a puff of vapour in the air between us. I repeated the action. She caught her lips between her teeth and moaned.

'You like that?'

She gave a jerky nod, her gaze once again dropping to follow my hand. On the next turn her hips rolled, her body chasing the exquisite sensation. I felt her grow hotter, wetter with need.

'More,' she moaned on the next pass.

'Look at me, Wren.'

Her gaze rose. Defiant fire and deep arousal. God, what a combination. I cupped her chin to hold her gaze, then I slipped my fingers beneath her panty line.

A wet, decadent sound wrapped itself around her gasp as I inserted two fingers inside her. She was hot.

And wet. And so damned tight. For the first time in my life I wondered how it would feel to fuck a woman bareback. To replace my fingers with my cock and experience that snug channel sucking me in.

Her hips moved and she gave a greedy little moan. Slowly, I withdrew and pushed back inside her. Her mouth dropped open and her eyes glazed.

'You're gorgeous when you're lost in pleasure. Do you want more, Wren?'

Without replying, she shifted her stance wider, wrapped her hand around my wrist and directed my movements, pressing my fingers inside her.

'I'll take that as a yes?'

Despite the rampant arousal coursing through her, her eyes flashed at me, reminding me that beyond this temporary haven of her maze our families detested each other. That she was using me simply because I was here. That any man who happened to be in her vicinity at the right time would probably have done?

No. Every cell in my body rejected that idea.

'Either you're too turned on to speak or you're attempting to make this a party for one.' I resisted her when she attempted to hasten my movements. I slowed down, then pressed my thumb against her engorged clit. She shuddered hard, and a hoarse cry broke from her lips. 'Which one is it, Wren?'

'I… I…'

I moved my thumb again and another cry ripped free. 'Do you want me to make you come, baby?'

She hesitated for a mutinous second. Then nodded frantically. *'Yes,'* she hissed.

'Then I want to hear exactly how you want it. And I want you to say my name when you do.' I hoped she wasn't dating anyone, but hell if I was going to be a replacement for some absent arsehole.

I circled my thumb and her head jerked back, pushing into the hedge. 'I want it deeper, Jasper. Faster.'

I smiled in unashamed triumph and increased the tempo. Immediately, she got even wetter...

Bloody hell. Any more and she would blow the top of my head clean off. Or more likely make me blow my load in my pants like a damned schoolboy. But I couldn't stop fucking her with my fingers any more than I could stop breathing. The sounds she was making from both sets of her lips were driving me insane.

'Slide two fingers into your mouth for me, baby. Make them nice and wet.'

Her eyes widened but she obeyed my instruction. The sight of her sliding her digits slowly into her mouth was almost too much to bear. Unable to resist, I swooped down and added my tongue to the play, licking her fingers as she withdrew them. Her pussy clenched around my fingers, a sign that she'd enjoyed that little action. I filed it at the back of my mind for next time as she rested her wet fingers against her lips.

'I have a few ideas of what you can do with those fingers. But I'd love to see you play with your gorgeous nipples.'

Her breath caught then released, and her fingers dropped to one exposed, beaded nipple. Slowly, she circled the bud, gasping as sensation piled high. Then she transferred her attention to the other peak, her breath coming faster as she pleasured herself.

Her pussy began to tighten around my fingers, making pushing inside her both a sizzling thrill and a torture. She wetted two more fingers, then, with both hands, tugged and tortured her nipples as I pumped inside her.

In under a minute, she started to unravel. And it was the most stunning thing I'd ever seen.

'Don't stop. Please... I'm close. So close...' Her hips jerked as she chased her bliss. With a sharp cry, she started to come.

Driven by lust, I dropped to my knees and replaced my thumb with my mouth. Gripping her thighs to hold her open, I sucked her clit hard and long.

A keening cry surged up her throat, the sound tormenting me as I groaned and sucked her harder. Rolling convulsions slammed into her, fresh wetness dripping over my lips.

'Jasper!'

Frantic fingers gripped my hair and her whole body shook wildly. I cupped her bottom to hold her steady as her knees weakened and her body sagged. I wanted to eat her pussy for ever, but her frantic whimpers turned a little urgent.

The kind that suggested reality was returning.

I stayed an extra minute, licked her clean with gentle laps of my tongue as her trembling quieted and the hold in my hair loosened. And just for the hell of it and because she was too addictive to resist, I shoved my fingers inside her one last time as I kissed my way up her body to her mouth. Our lips fused and our tongues tangled for another minute while I committed her taste to memory before removing my fingers from her.

Still watching her, I brought my hands to my mouth and licked the last of her taste off. When I was done, I readjusted her knickers and helped her redress.

Silence throbbed between us as she furiously avoided my gaze. I suppressed a sigh and shoved my fists into my pocket to stop myself from reaching for her.

'Are you okay?'

She stared at me for a handful of seconds before she nodded. 'Yes.' Another several seconds drifted by. Then, 'Thank you.'

'My pleasure,' I replied, my voice more than a little gruff.

Her gaze dropped tellingly to the raging hard-on tenting my trousers. I laughed around the agony of my erection. 'Believe it or not, watching you come was a pleasure. Maybe we can—'

The words dried in my throat as her expression altered. Within a blink of an eye she was no longer the sated siren at one with the foliage around her.

She was a cool and collected princess, dispensing rejection. 'This was a one-time thing. Gratefully received but something I intend to forget at the earliest opportunity.'

Disappointment—and, yes, blistering anger because I'd hoped this could be the start of…something—unravelled through me. 'You think I'm that forgettable, sweetheart?' I asked, modulating my voice to that deceptive pitch that always confused my opponents. They weren't sure whether I was pissed off or indulging whatever mood they were in.

Fleeting uncertainty chased across her face before she marshalled it.

'I do.' She handed back my jacket, her lips once again curved in that fake, dismissive smile. 'Because it's already in the past,' she said.

'Like hell it is. We're going to fuck, Wren. I'm going to make you come many, many more times. It's simply a matter of when.'

I gave her props for attempting to fight her excitement. She fussed with her hair, rearranged her scarf and tugged her zip another fraction upwards. And when she achieved that facade of outrage, I allowed it. I intended to disprove it at the very next opportunity.

'I allowed a moment of temporary madness, Jasper. Don't hold your breath that it'll happen again.'

She started to walk away. I shrugged on my jacket and followed. 'Wren.'

She paused without turning.

I stepped around to face her. 'I still want to know where your brother is. This time I'm not taking no for an answer.'

The eyes she lifted to mine were haunted, filled with the tension I'd sensed in her all evening. For a handful of seconds, she pressed her lips together. Then her gaze shifted away from mine. 'I don't know.'

Instinct suggested she wasn't lying. 'When was the last time you heard from him?'

A shaft of pain crossed her flawless features. 'My mother spoke to him a week ago.'

Her mother. Not her. Was that the reason for the tension between them?

'I need to reach him, Wren.'

Her face tightened. 'Is that why you followed me here? To pump me for information?'

I bit back my irritation. 'We both know what just happened has been a long time coming, pun intended. Don't demean it.'

Her eyes flickered and I could've sworn she blushed. Slightly mollified, I trailed my knuckles over her warm cheek. 'Doesn't change the fact that I still need to hear from Perry, though.' I dropped my hand. 'When you do get in touch with him, tell him it's in his interest to contact me, asap.' Knowing I needed to leave before I gave in to the urge to re-enact that heady episode again, I stepped away.

'That sounds like a threat,' she challenged.

I turned back to the woman I intended to have, again and again, in the very near future, and smiled. 'You can see it as such if you want. It's a simple statement that says I'm done playing games. He's fucking around with something important to me. Sooner or later, he's going to have to answer to me. How much mercy I show him is entirely up to him.'

CHAPTER TWO

THE FILES ON the desk in front of me had increased three-fold in the last three weeks. Each one was flagged with a red Post-it note that indicated it required urgent attention.

Except three weeks ago, I'd been in *front* of the desk and Perry behind it. My brother had been the CEO with the full backing of the board of directors at Bingham Industries. Whereas I'd had to fight my way into an *acting* CEO position, even after Perry finally resurfaced a few days ago and accepted that he needed help.

Unfortunately, it'd been too late to stop the tabloids from splashing his alcohol-fuelled downward spiral on the front pages, plunging the company into a stock-market nightmare and me into a fight to protect my own family firm from ruin.

Bitterness soured my mouth as I inched my chair closer to the desk. I'd been here for fifteen minutes and was yet to reach for the first file.

I couldn't. Not because I was scared. Far from it. I couldn't reach for it because everything in this office reeked of my father. With strong undertones of Perry, the son and heir he'd treasured above everyone else. Including me.

Both hard, intransigent men with firm, ingrained views about a woman's place. Perry had tried to disguise his beneath brotherly concern, but that conceit had been there, inherited from the man he'd looked up to. A man who'd taken reckless risks with the Bingham name and died bitter and broken when those risks had shattered his family.

With hands I refused to let shake, I reached for the phone. My PA answered on the first ring. 'Alana, can you find me a replacement desk asap? Ideally today?'

'I...yes, of course. Right away, Miss Bingham. What do you want done with the old one?'

'Have it couriered to the house in Esher. They can put it in my father's study.'

I set the phone down, took a deep cleansing breath. My position as Acting CEO might well be temporary if I lost my fight against the Big Boys Establishment that were my uncles and cousins. But I intended to do things my way for however long I was here.

And before my stint ends, I'll show them...

That silent vow echoing through me, I picked up the first five files, rose and moved to the chesterfield sofa situated beneath the window. Everything in the office was stuffy and old-school but the chair and coffee table would have to do as a working area until the new desk arrived.

Setting the files down beside me, I opened the first one. Then immediately shut it when the name on the letterhead jumped up at me.

The Mortimer Group

My breath rattled around in my chest, echoing the sensations in my body. Mainly of the hot and bothered kind. Mainly between my legs. All because of Jasper Mortimer and what I'd let happen in the maze a week ago.

I'm done playing games.

The words might have been aimed at my elusive brother, but they resonated deep within me. Probably because Jasper and I had been playing a game for the better part of five years, ever since I walked into the boardroom at the internship fair and first experienced his dynamic magnetism. Heat flared up my body and I fought a squirm as total recall plunged me into that lustful state that never failed to materialise whenever I thought of him.

That searing, dangerous attraction had partly fuelled my decision to decline his internship offer. That and my family's abiding hatred for everything attached to the Mortimer name.

I tossed the file away. I wasn't ready to deal with him. Or the Mortimer Group. Nor did I want to think of how hard he'd made me come. How wanton he'd made me feel.

How much I'd craved a repeat performance ever since...

That madness in the maze was a shameful episode I'd intended to put out of my mind. If only it'd been that simple—

I jumped when the second office phone, positioned

conveniently on the coffee table, rang. I didn't want to picture my brother in this chair, drinking himself into a stupor when he should've been safeguarding our family. Unfortunately, so far all evidence pointed that way.

To stop thoughts of the brother I'd never really got on well with, despite my desire to, I snatched up the phone. 'Hello?' I said, then grimaced at the lack of professionalism. Must do better in future.

'Congratulations on your official instatement as Acting CEO.' The deep voice of the last person I wanted to talk to filtered through the handset.

Shock rippled through my body. 'How do you know about that?' The board meeting had only ended at ten. It was barely noon. 'And how did you get my direct number?'

'I have my ways,' Jasper Mortimer said.

'You mean you have a spy in my company,' I deducted.

He chuckled, a rich, indulgent sound that threw me back to the maze. To his very male groans of satisfaction as I lost my mind. 'Let's not start our relationship with accusations.'

'We don't have a relationship.'

'Yet,' he countered smoothly.

'We never will. I suggest you accept that now.'

'Thanks for the suggestion. But how are we going to work together on this Morocco project if we don't have even a basic rapport?'

My gaze flitted to the file I'd flung away. Something inside me shook. 'Why are you calling me?'

'To set up a meeting. The sooner the better.' The

lazy indulgence had left his voice to be replaced by a crisp, uncompromising tone. 'Now that you're officially the head of Bingham's, we need to get this deal back on track.'

The ambitious deal that had, by all accounts, driven Perry over the edge. The thought hardened my resolve. 'No.'

'Excuse me?'

'You heard me. The official Bingham position is that we won't be going ahead with the Morocco deal. You'll receive our official statement shortly.' I hung up before he could reply. Then stared at the silent phone, my heart banging against my ribs.

After five minutes without it ringing, my stomach started churning.

Had I been too reckless? The board I'd battled to win over—the same board who'd expressed their wish to remain leaderless until Perry returned from his six-month rehab stint in Arizona—would love to be proven right that I wasn't suitable for this position. Had I, with my very first act as CEO, played right into their hands? Tentatively, I reached out towards the phone. To do what? Admit to Jasper that I'd been too rash? Give him an opening to gloat? I snatched my hand back.

He'd waited for a week. He could wait another day.

Resolute, I opened the second file, putting thoughts of Jasper, his masterful fingers and wicked, orgasm-giving tongue out of my mind.

By five p.m. I'd resolved a third of the issues contained within the various files, and unfortunately received even further insight into Perry's true state of decline— they'd been drastically neglected for months.

My chest tightened the more my thoughts dwelled on my brother. According to the family doctor who'd examined him, he'd been dangerously close to alcohol poisoning, a fact my mother had actively denied even though it'd been an open secret that Perry—like most Bingham men—had harboured a drinking problem for years.

And just like my father, Perry had refused to admit he even had a problem. The board had turned a blind eye to his addiction since he'd managed to keep Bingham Industries above the red line since stepping into Father's shoes seven years ago.

My heart ached as I mourned our deteriorated relationship. Our interaction on the occasions we'd been forced to socialise had been stilted to the point where we'd been relieved to be largely out of each other's orbit for the last three years. Still, his chilled silence when I'd accepted a junior marketing position at another firm had hurt.

Ultimately, he'd been as dismissive of my ambitions as my father had been; he'd fully supported my mother's and aunts' view that I should marry into some wealthy investment family, with guaranteed connections and endless resources, instead of striving to make my own way in the world.

Tears prickled my eyes and I blinked them away.

The bottom line was, Perry was getting the help he needed and I was in charge of steering Bingham's away from bankruptcy.

Frankly, I was surprised the corporate sharks hadn't started circling already.

My gaze dropped to the royal-blue Bingham's logo on the file I held. Once a powerhouse in its field, my family's logistics and hospitality supply reputation had dropped several rungs in the last decade, forcing us to make poorer business choices that'd led to an even steeper decline.

Was that why Perry had joined forces with Jasper Mortimer? Because while Bingham's had faced significant fiscal woes, the Mortimer Group had grown exponentially, expanding its initial construction arm into several other industries at a breakneck rate that I'd watched with secret awe and, admittedly, a little resentment. How could I not, when a part of me wondered if some of that fortune had been achieved at the cost of my family's decline?

I tossed the file away, irritated with myself for my unhelpful thoughts. Whatever the reason for my family's current situation, nothing would be achieved by dwelling on the past. And especially not thinking of the incident in the maze!

My intercom sounded and I pressed the button with guilty relief. 'Yes?'

'I have a message from a Mr Jasper Mortimer for you.'

My pulse leapt. 'Is he on the phone?'

'No, he just wanted me to tell you he'll call again at six. And that you should make sure you're all read up on the project.' The hint of nerves in Alana's voice made me wonder what else he'd said. And why a sensation a lot like disappointment twisted in my stomach that he hadn't asked to speak to me.

'Thanks, Alana. I'll see you tomorrow.'

I hung up, cursing the untrammelled excitement fizzing through me, then my complete inability to slow my heart's crazy racing as the clock approached six.

Wren picked up on the first ring, and even before she spoke my pulse had rocketed to ridiculous levels. Then came her incredible voice.

'I'd appreciate it if you didn't disturb my assistant with unnecessary messages or me with ultimatums.'

'You made going through her necessary by hanging up on me earlier. I simply used her to let you know we'd be skipping the foreplay this time and getting straight to business. Unless, you specifically want the foreplay?'

'I don't want anything from you, Jasper,' she said briskly.

'Are you absolutely sure?'

'Yes, I'm unique like that, you see.'

I laughed a touch incredulously under my breath. 'You think I don't know that? Believe me, Wren, I do.'

I could've sworn I heard her breath catch, but her voice was curt when she replied, 'Trust a man like you to make allusions.'

I laughed harder, knowing it would irk her more. Cool, calm and collected Wren was intriguing, but I'd discovered I preferred the fiery, passionate woman in the maze who'd lost control, if only for a brief time. 'A man like me? And here I thought, like you, that I was one of a kind...'

'Sadly, you're not as rare a specimen as you think you are.'

I gave a dramatic sigh. 'That just makes me want to prove you wrong.'

'You can't. You won't be able to.'

I gripped the phone tighter, felt myself drawn in deeper into the compulsion I couldn't fight. 'Why not? Because every guy you've been with has made you come as hard as I did in that maze?'

'Seeking validity of your male prowess? How predictable. You disappoint me, Jasper,' she said, her voice a touch huskier.

Despite the curious throb in my chest, I smiled. 'I'm wholly satisfied with my strengths, thanks.' *But you weren't always, were you?* I pushed away the taunting voice. 'As for seeking validity, the end result in that maze is all the validity I need where you're concerned.'

'Can we get off that subject, please?' she whispered fiercely. 'I don't have time for personal conversation.'

'Do you despise me as much as you pretend to, or is this you simply toeing the family line?' I taunted, a sudden restlessness prowling inside me.

She inhaled sharply. 'You'll never get the chance to find out. Goodbye, Mr Mortimer.'

'Before you dramatically hang up on me again, let me remind you that your continued failure to engage with me only brings Bingham's closer to being in breach of contract.'

'I've read the file. Nothing in there remotely suggests a breach,' she said tightly, and I got the feeling I'd upset her by that family comment.

Bloody hell.

I tried to get my head back into business mode. 'May I suggest that you read the paperwork again. Carefully.'

Silence greeted me and I imagined her bristling, those eyes flashing with low-burning anger. I wondered what she'd look like in full blaze. God, it'd be glorious.

'I graduated university at the top of my class. You know this because you came sniffing around, trying to headhunt me, remember?'

'I remember you turning me down flat and accepting an internship at a much more inferior company.' That still grated, but it'd been the first inkling for me that, all these decades later, the Binghams were still as bitter about the fallout between our families. Now I knew the depths of my father's ruthlessness, I wasn't surprised. 'Do you regret that decision?'

'Not for a single moment. So I can only conclude you're trying to insult me by insinuating I would've missed something as crucial as a break clause in a contract.'

I took a beat to formulate my reply because this was where it got tricky. Saying anything negative against Perry might backfire. And as much as I liked tussling with Wren, the project I'd worked my arse off for needed to be kept on track. 'No offence intended. But the clause is there, I assure you. I can courier over a copy if you'd like?'

'Now you're implying I'm sloppy with paperwork. And blind, too?'

'You seem hell-bent on taking offence no matter what I say. A meeting will resolve this quickly enough, don't you think? Even if it's so you can put me in my place?'

'Inviting me to prove you wrong won't work, either. I don't need my ego stroked.'

It was time to pull out the big guns. 'I suggest you make time in your schedule. I'm not losing this deal because of some chip you've got on your shoulder. I expect to see you in my office tomorrow.'

'Or what?'

'Or I'll have no choice but to make good on my promise. You're already mired in unwanted publicity. Divorcing yourself from this deal at this late stage is going to bring nothing but unwanted attention to Bingham's.'

'Are you threatening me?'

'I'm laying out the course of action I'll be forced to take if you remain intransigent. The ball is in your court, sweetheart.'

She hung up.

Despite the two-nil score against me, I wasn't overly disgruntled. She hadn't earned her position by being dismissive of a potential lawsuit. Not that it'd come to that. For starters, I wasn't champing at the bit to become *the* Mortimer incapable of closing my division's biggest deal yet. The labels my father had callously and frequently branded into my skin were enough.

No, I was willing to bet my very treasured vintage Aston Martin that Wren would make contact. And if not…

I smiled grimly to myself as I swivelled in my chair to enjoy my multimillion-pound view…

If not, I'd take delight in becoming a very significant pain in her delectable backside.

The break clause wasn't in the contract.

Jasper's insinuation that I'd missed something had spurred a wild need to prove him wrong. After a two-hour search, I'd given up and headed home. Nothing in the electronic or paper files showed Perry had agreed to an early break clause. Sure, there were several clauses—all dishearteningly skewed in favour of the Mortimer Group—peppered within the contract but nothing that stated what would happen if Perry changed his mind about proceeding with the Morocco deal. Because he hadn't planned on it? Like my father, had he gone into this with unshakeable hubris, only to fall?

My heart twisted in dull pain and a little shame for assuming his culpability. He wasn't here to defend himself. And for all I knew, Jasper had twisted his arm into agreeing to this deal. The man was clever enough.

And not just with his words.

My heart skipped a beat and shame deepened, but for a completely different reason. Our heated verbal exchange had sparked something to life inside me. Something that, hours later, made me feel restless. *Needy.* I'd been spoiling for an argument. Then ended up spoiling for something totally different. Something to ease the ache between my thighs.

Like his mouth. His fingers.

His cock.

I pressed my fingers into my eyes, hoping to erase the image of him looking far too handsome for my sanity at the party. But the images simply reeled…of him caging me against the maze hedge. Of him on his knees, enthusiastically bringing me to an insane climax. Hell, even watching him suffer with that incredible hard-on had turned me on. God, what the hell was wrong with me?

You need to get laid.

I dropped my hands in frustration. If only it were that simple. Despite my short, rebellious modelling stint, I was a Bingham, cognisant of my ever-increasing family responsibility. The tabloids would love nothing better than to splash the front pages with details of whatever brief hook-up I indulged in for the sake of getting my rocks off. Especially now I was Acting CEO of a once multimillion-pound company now on the brink of collapse.

While my last two relationships hadn't worked due to lack of chemistry, behind it was the same resentment that had led me into modelling at nineteen. Resentment and rebellion stemming from my mother's attempt to orchestrate those relationships.

Unable to control either my father or Perry, she'd turned her attention to me the moment I reached puberty. Attention I'd mistakenly believed was affection I'd sorely missed in my childhood years when I'd needed her most. Discovering that she was simply using me to while away her time until her husband or son needed her, whereupon she set me back on my isolation shelf, had hurt long before I'd reached maturity. Of course, it didn't stop the foolish hope that sprang inside me whenever she turned her attention on me.

Not until lately. Not until her indifference—identical to Perry's—to my announcement that I'd accepted a marketing position at a different company had forced me to accept that true affection or acknowledgement from her would never happen. I was merely an ornament to be displayed when it suited her.

More fool me...

Exhaling through another tide of hurt, I padded over to the window, while parsing Jasper's parting words. He wanted Bingham's to hold up their end of the deal, agree to a three-year plan to supply the hospitality infrastructure for the four luxury hotels and casinos he was building in Morocco.

On the surface, it sounded like a deal made in heaven, but the reality was that Bingham's would be operating at an eighty per cent loss for the first year with possible gains coming only in the second and third years. Perry had tried to push for a five-year contract. Jasper had refused. Because like a typical Mortimer, he wanted to keep the initial financial gains for himself.

Well, I wasn't going to let the past repeat itself. The maze incident and our phone call tonight had proven two things: this insane attraction between us that made me want to tear off his clothes when he was within touching distance was untenable, and working with Jasper would be a nightmare.

The man was too full of himself. And I was woman enough to recognise that not all battles needed to be fought. Besides, I had several ideas of how to put the resources Perry had earmarked for the Mortimer deal to better use.

Striding over to my phone, I checked my schedule for the next day, then slotted a half-hour to deal with Jasper. It wouldn't take more than that to send the message home.

And if my belly somersaulted and my pulse raced at the thought of tangling with him again…it was only because I looked forward to emerging the victor.

Nothing else.

I strode through the doors of Mortimer Tower after business hours the next day, power-suited and determined not to be impressed with my surroundings. The reminder that all of this had been built by cut-throat Mortimers helped me focus as I entered the executive lift that serviced the upper floors where Jasper's office was located.

A part of me regretted leaving this meeting until last thing on Friday. If I'd tackled it first thing this morning, I'd already be free of this disquieting…*thrumming* in my veins. My brain wouldn't keep flashing scenarios of what could happen when I saw him again. I wouldn't have wasted precious stretches of time replaying his promise that '*We're going to fuck, Wren*' and '*I'm going to make you come many, many more times*'.

I sure as hell wouldn't be riding the empty lift with trembling hands and panties slightly damp from that memory of him going down on me in my family maze.

Enough, already...

The self-admonition worked for the thirty seconds it took for the lift to spit me out into the pristine, ultra-sleek reception area. The whole building had been redecorated recently at huge expense by Bryce Mortimer, the award-winning architect in the Mortimer clan. I might have ignored the impressive atrium downstairs, but I couldn't avoid the burst of bold colours softening the sharply angled steel and dark grey surfaces.

A smartly dressed receptionist smiled as I sucked in a breath and approached her.

'Hi, I have a meeting with Jasper Mortimer. He's expecting me.' Half true. Jasper might have summoned me here today but I hadn't bothered to inform him when I would be making my appearance.

Her smile slipped. 'Is he? Only, he went into a meeting ten minutes ago.'

'We didn't agree on a specific time. Just show me to his office. I'll wait.'

'Of course, Miss Bingham. Right this way.'

The greys were more pronounced than the steel in Jasper's office and the colours came from art rather than flower arrangements, but the effect was the same—sleekly professional, contemporary and elegant. But what made the space different was his lingering scent in the air, coupled with the aura of power I couldn't dismiss as I stared at the immense dark-wood desk and black high-backed chair, and I couldn't help the shiver that coursed down my spine. A throat cleared beside me. Composing myself, I glanced at the receptionist. 'Thank you.'

'Can I get you anything?'

I started to refuse, then changed my mind. 'Coffee with cream, no sugar. Thank you.'

She nodded and glided away. I returned my gaze to

my surroundings, noting the absence of files or paper-work. Either Jasper was naturally meticulous in maintaining a paper-free environment or he'd anticipated my arrival. My instinct suggested the latter, eroding a layer of that upper hand I'd hoped to gain by my unexpected arrival.

After the receptionist served my coffee and left, I sat on the wide grey velvet sofa facing the spectacular view of the Thames and attempted to immerse myself in Bingham business. I wasn't sure where the notion of how to handle Jasper came from. All I knew was that it happened somewhere between sipping the excellent java brew—purportedly supplied to every Mortimer establishment by Graciela Mortimer—and when the door suddenly sprang open to reveal Jasper Mortimer in all his breathtaking glory.

Perhaps I sensed the moment I saw his face that walking away wasn't going to be as easy as I'd convinced myself. Here, in this space, in his *domain*, I realised my first mistake—we should've met on neutral ground.

Because the man striding towards me teemed with quietly ferocious purpose. And yes, regardless of how late it was, he'd *known* I would come. 'Sorry for the wait. I couldn't get out of the meeting as quickly as I wanted. Do you mind?' He pointed to the coffee on the tray.

I shook my head. 'Go ahead.'

He poured himself a cup, added a dash of cream, and took a seat next to me.

Immediately, his dark woodsy smell engulfed me.

The strong, visceral urge to breathe him in made me lift my own cup, hoping the coffee smell would dilute the potency of his scent.

That particular quest became redundant because my gaze was on a mission of its own. It took in the strong fingers lifting the cup to his lips for a large gulp, then followed the lines of his throat as he swallowed. The play of his powerful thighs as he crossed his legs and set the cup and saucer on his knee.

'First things first, did you come across the clause we talked about?'

His assumption that I'd gone looking set my teeth on edge. But I answered anyway. 'No, I didn't. We must be looking at different documents because there's nothing in my copy of the contract to support what you're saying.'

Jasper's hazel gaze narrowed on me for a tight, long stretch. Then he set his cup down, rose and crossed to his desk. When he returned with a sleek laptop, my heart lurched, then dropped to my toes as he fired up the machine. A few taps and he turned the screen to face me.

'Perry signed this document down the corridor in my conference room three months ago. It was duly witnessed, and I couriered him a copy for his records. The break clause in question is on page forty-seven.'

With not quite steady hands, I placed my cup on the coffee table and took the laptop. I wanted to blurt out that the presence of the break clause didn't change anything. But I couldn't delude myself. Break clauses were notoriously costly and I suspected Bingham would end up shouldering the burden if I didn't play my cards right.

That outlandish idea that struck me five minutes ago returned, more forcefully, as I read the document. It looked similar to my copy except for the crucial page missing from mine.

'Why is this one different from mine?'

Jasper didn't answer immediately. He drained his coffee before glancing my way. 'Negotiations with your brother weren't…smooth. He insisted on renegotiating several contracts before things were finalised.'

Given Perry's debilitated state, I wasn't surprised. But a question had been gnawing at me since I became aware of this deal. 'Why Bingham's? There are literally thousands of companies out there you could've partnered with. Why us?'

His lips firmed. 'You mean considering our family history?'

He wasn't beating about the bush. I didn't see why I should. 'Yes.'

'Would you believe me if I said that ultimately didn't factor into my decision?'

Who was he kidding? 'No, I wouldn't.'

He sighed. 'Didn't think so. Wren, if you're asking then I'm going to presume Perry didn't tell you.'

'Tell me what?'

Hazel eyes locked on to mine, pinned me in place. 'That he begged me for this deal. He pretty much stalked me for the better part of three months before I even agreed to meet with him. I was all set to go with someone else.'

A flush of shame crept up from my belly and soon engulfed my whole body. I'd seen the books. We were in a precarious financial position. But we weren't crawling-on-our-bellies desperate. Yet. Not enough for Perry to beg for scraps from our sworn enemy. 'I'm not sure why he did that—'

'Aren't you?' Jasper's expression was entirely cynical.

Pride swarmed through me. 'No, we're not destitute. I'm not going to lower myself to prove it to you. You'll have to take my word for it.'

He frowned. 'No need to be so defensive. I'm simply relating things as they happened. For whatever reason your brother wanted this deal to happen.'

'Then why did he drag his feet?'

Jasper's lips twisted. 'At least you're admitting he did.'

I handed him back his laptop. 'Clearly he wasn't satisfied with something. I've looked at the projections. We supply you with everything from gambling tables and staff to tea towels and garden fertiliser but see very little profit for twelve months? Why the hell should I come on board with something like that?'

His gaze hardened and I caught a glimpse of Hugh Mortimer, the adversary my father had faced—and lost to—decades ago. Was Jasper his father's son in every sense of the word? Whatever. I didn't intend to stick around to find out.

'Because he signed on the dotted line. It's too late to back out now. This project has been delayed by months already. I won't let it suffer another setback,' he said grimly.

I rose from the sofa, gathered my tablet and briefcase as calmly as I could, despite the roiling in my stomach. I'd seen the books. Our company was haemorrhaging money, yes, but we still had substantial assets to hold back the dam for a while. 'I'll look over your papers and get back to you.'

He rose to join me. Despite my above average height, he towered over me, made me feel small and delicate in a way very few people could. And… I didn't exactly hate that feeling. Which was totally absurd. I turned away as he glanced at his watch.

'Let me take you out to dinner. We can discuss this over—'

'No, thanks. I only eat with people I trust.'

His eyes darkened. 'Ouch,' he drawled without a hint of the purported affront. 'You really are determined to make this adversarial, aren't you?'

For some reason, the softly voiced accusation niggled, striking me with a wild urge to apologise. *Stay strong.* 'I'm just looking out for my family's best interests.'

That brought a wry, twisted smile to his lips. 'Can't say I blame you, but I'm really not the enemy here, Wren.'

God, the way he said my name—that name I'd hated for so long—somehow sounded pleasant on his lips. 'If you're not the enemy, then agree to end this amicably,' I replied.

His smile turned edgy, delivering another glimpse

of the true man beneath the suave exterior. 'I haven't made it this far by being sentimental over business, Wren. I'm a little disappointed you would play that card. Your brother signed an agreement. I expect you to honour it. Starting on Monday, you'll devote the required time and energy into progressing this deal.'

'Or what?' I dared, even though my stomach dipped wildly. There was something raw and primal in that command, something that incredulously turned my blood hotter, my skin more sensitive. With a compulsion I couldn't deny, my gaze dropped to his lips. Mine tingled, a need to taste him almost overpowering me. It was enough to make me take a step back. But I wasn't totally out of his reach. So when he raised his hand and slowly extended it towards my face, there was absolutely no reason not to take another step away. Out of the path of temptation. Except I didn't.

His knuckles brushed my cheek, slowly caressing down to my jaw. Electricity charged up my thighs, making me bite back a gasp. Why the hell was I getting so wet? *Dear God...*

'You say you're looking out for your family? Then what was that in that maze last week? Was it a touch of much-needed self-indulgence? One you wouldn't be averse to repeating?'

'I...no.'

'Try that once more, with feeling. But before you do, remember my promise. I intend to fuck you, Wren. Very hard and very thoroughly. In every position you desire.'

My clit throbbed and fresh flames shot through me at the thick drawled words. Suddenly, I was very aware of the sofa nearby. That all I had to do was say the word and I'd have him.

But then what? He would be just another temporary act of rebellion that could go nowhere when I should be concentrating on dragging my family's company out of the quagmire. Perry was in rehab. The last thing I should be doing was adding flames to a roaring scandal-hungry fire by embarking on a tryst with the enemy.

'Business,' I insisted, even as a thick coil of regret unravelled inside me, reminding me of how many times I'd denied myself for the sake of family. 'I'm here to discuss business. Nothing else.'

That overconfident smile returned, turning his far too gorgeous face even more spectacular as his hand dropped. 'Good. Then do the right thing. Or you'll leave me no choice but to fight your hot little fire with flames of my own,' he answered, a growl of anticipation in his voice that hastened my heartbeat.

'You don't want to go to war with me, Jasper.'

'To get this deal done, I'll take you however I can get you, sweetheart.'

Much too late, I took that vital step back. Then another. 'Goodnight, Jasper.'

'Would you like me to walk you out?' he asked, right after his hooded gaze circumvented my body, leaving me even hotter than before.

'I can manage on my own, thanks,' I replied, aware my voice was a little hoarse when I needed it snippy.

'Okay. I'll see you on Monday for the phase two meeting at nine a.m. Don't be late.'

I turned and walked away without answering. In

the lift, I sagged against one wall, a traitorous little tremble seizing my body as snippets of the conversation scrolled across my brain. Nothing had gone as I'd smugly predicted. If the agreement he'd shown me was valid—and I didn't see why it would be fabricated—it meant Perry had agreed to a deal that would be impossible to walk away from without seriously crippling Bingham's. So why had he signed it? And why had he left it out of the file?

My phone pinged as the lift reached the ground floor. I stared at the text, my heartbeat hammering as I saw the familiar-looking number. Jasper.

I've emailed you a copy of the agreement for your records.

I checked my email and, sure enough, the agreement was in my inbox. I tapped out a reply as I walked through his stunning atrium, once again determined not to admire its grandeur.

Email received. Thanks.

I discovered other hidden bombshells once I was back home in my maisonette in Fulham, showered and dressed in my favourite pyjama shorts set. The glass of red wine was forgotten in my hand as I read and re-read the agreement, tiny waves of shock building into a tsunami as I absorbed just what Perry had committed Bingham's to.

Besides the supply agreement, which would eat heavily into our cash reserves, Perry had agreed to being on hand, day or night, to troubleshoot any problems that arose either in London or on sites in Morocco for a minimum of twenty hours per week. To 'help' with that particular clause, Jasper had offered the use of his empty office in London or a suite in the Morocco hotel.

Even before I'd taken up the mantle at Bingham's I was working long hours. Hard work had earned me a fast track from junior to senior executive in my last firm. Adding a few more hours to my workday didn't faze me. What disturbed me was the thought of being that close to Jasper. Because when he'd touched me tonight, every cell in my body had roared to life in a way that shocked me.

I downed the rest of the wine, set the glass down and reclined on my sofa. I had the rest of the weekend to figure a way out of this.

For Perry's sake. For my family's sake, I couldn't fail.

Eyes closed, I tried to work out how to best the man with the wicked tongue and clever fingers.

I'll take you however I can get you…

Why did those words make me so hot? Why the hell couldn't I get his voice out of my head?

I'll take you…

I was flushed and panting as my hand crept down my belly. I bit my lip, hating myself a little for succumbing to the lust trickling through my blood. My nipples beaded as sensation unfurled in my pelvis, heating my pussy and engorging my clit. Uncustomary anticipation fired me up, my fingers tingling as I spread my legs and slipped my fingers beneath the waistband of my pyjama shorts.

A hot little gasp left my lips when I touched myself, shivering when I noticed how wet and slippery I was.

I'll take you...

Need and lust built. My fingers worked my clit in desperate circles, the realisation that, for once, I didn't need the assistance of my trusted vibrator, ramping up my desire. Working my clit with my thumb, I slipped my middle finger inside my wet heat, finger-fucking myself while I imagined thicker fingers filling me. Or a cock... Jasper Mortimer's cock.

Inside me.

Pounding me.

Making me scream.

My orgasm curled through me, arching my back off the sofa as liquid bliss drowned me from head to toe.

It was as I came down from that intense high, my heartbeat roaring in my ears, that a line from the agreement suddenly flashed across my mind.

I jackknifed off the sofa, almost knocking over the wine glass as I reached for the laptop. And there, on page fifty-one, was my answer, my saviour, in black and white.

I read and reread it for good measure.

> *The Mortimer Group has the right to terminate this agreement, with due notice, in the case of non-performance by Bingham Industries. This includes, but is not limited to, continued disruption of services...*

I smiled.

For now, Jasper Mortimer had the power. I was going to take it from him by simply doing…nothing.

Even while I blew his mind *out* of the boardroom.

CHAPTER THREE

WREN WAS FORTY-FIVE minutes late. Irritated, I hit my intercom button again.

'Yes, sir?' my PA answered.

'Try her mobile again. If she doesn't answer, call her office. I want to know where she is,' I growled.

'Of course.'

Why I expected Trish to succeed when my own numerous calls had gone straight to voicemail was a mystery but it beat just sitting around fuming because Wren was a no-show. I'd hoped providing her with the valid copy of the agreement would make her see sense but, clearly, I'd overestimated her.

Jaw gritted, I acknowledged that my disappointment in her was more acute than it'd ever been with her brother. Yes, I loved a challenge and I'd known getting involved with Bingham's, all things considered, would be difficult, but I'd convinced myself I could handle it.

Handle *her*.

When the hell was I going to learn my lesson? Bitterness rose up to fuse with my annoyance. I tamped down both emotions. I wasn't dealing with my father's scathing remarks, disparaging me about wanting peace when we Mortimers were a proudly bloodthirsty lot.

I was dealing with an intelligent, if extremely stubborn, woman. I needed another way to deal with her.

Immediately my mind flew back to the maze, as it had been doing increasingly over the past week or so, but especially since Friday night. It'd taken every ounce of willpower not to kiss her in my office. But I'd needed to prove to her that I wasn't driven by my desire.

Succumbing to the urge to keep touching her, to kiss those luscious lips, would only convince her I was driven by base instincts. Yet I couldn't deny that she only needed to flash those green eyes to trigger a fever in my blood.

I laughed under my breath. I'd had my share of women, some more beautiful than Wren. This rare phenomenon where she was concerned was inexplicable. Why the hell did she trigger this strong reaction in me?

I shook my head, growing more annoyed when I clocked that I'd wasted almost an hour waiting for her. About to open one of the many files that needed my attention, I paused when my intercom buzzed.

'Yes?' I responded, a little too eagerly.

'I'm sorry, Mr Mortimer, I couldn't reach her. Her secretary says she's in a meeting.'

'I know. She's *supposed* to be in a meeting, here, with me.' Aware that I was snapping at my PA, I throttled down my emotions. Christ, she drove me crazy. 'Thanks, Trish.' I collapsed in my seat, forcing calm into my bones.

I'd always been a strategist. A planner. Favouring

dialogue over conflict. But I was a Mortimer, as my father had taken delight in reminding me every time I'd displayed what he'd termed my *weakness*. Did Wren really want war with a Mortimer?

Especially when Bingham's, according to trusted sources, was one ill-judged deal away from complete collapse? She couldn't afford to take me on in a corporate battlefield. So why the hell was she trying? Perry had been equally hard-headed but evidently his intransigence had been mostly fuelled by alcohol. Wren was simply stubborn.

And loyal. Perhaps blindly so, but loyal.

It was a stark reminder that my family was acutely different. Mortimers—my father especially—didn't do blind loyalty and, as he'd proven with his callous desertion, wouldn't fight to the death for anyone else but himself.

But wasn't that what had made us who we were today? Successful. Feared. A global powerhouse with immeasurable clout. Sure, we wouldn't win any Family of the Year prizes but there was a lot to be proud of. I wasn't going to let a woman with brains, beauty and fireworks in her green eyes convince me otherwise—

As if I'd conjured her up by my imagination, my door opened and there she stood.

My annoyance didn't recede as I stared at her, but several new sensations crowded in. First, the jolt of electricity just the sight of her rammed through my body. I attempted to control it by taking another deep breath. And failed.

The second was utter shock as I took in the state of her.

She looked as if she'd stumbled in from a night of hard partying. And even harder fucking. Her hair was dishevelled as if some lucky bastard had won the privilege of running his fingers repeatedly through it. Her lips were faintly bruised and smeared as if someone had eaten off her lipstick. Then came her smudged make-up. Dark jealousy spiralled through me as my gaze dropped lower and my gut tightened against the inevitable hard-on heading my way as I took in the rest of her.

Holy hell, she was wearing a trench coat. Not necessarily a fashion *faux pas* considering the time of year, but it was tightly belted at the waist in that highly suggestive *sexual* way that screamed she was wearing very little or nothing at all underneath. Fire lit through my groin as she took a step towards me and justified my suspicions by flashing a bare leg.

Jesus, she wouldn't. Would she?

'Good morning, Jasper.' Whether that husky greeting was deliberately exaggerated or the result of long hours of screaming in ecstasy wasn't something I particularly wanted to dwell on. Either way, it threw another gallon of flammable fuel on my libido. I clenched my gut as I grew even harder.

'You're late,' I bit out, watching her strut across my office in sky-high heels.

With each step, I caught a glimpse of her leg, and nothing else. My nape heated and I desperately scrounged around for every scrap of willpower not to drag my fingers over my jaw and stop myself from salivating like a pathetic dog. I tried to remain pissed off, but my mind fixated on one thing.

Was Wren Bingham totally naked under that coat?

She reached my desk, laid her hands flat on it, and leaned towards me. I kept my eyes on hers, determined not to be drawn into whatever game she was playing.

'Am I? You said the meeting was at ten. It's now…' she paused, glanced around the office before reaching into her pocket for her phone '…nine fifty-nine. Oh, look, I'm a whole minute early.' She waved her phone at me and I caught a glimpse of her home screen.

It featured a picture of her, head thrown back, laughing into the camera. The image only showed her from bare shoulders up but it was again suggestive that she was naked. Arousal attacked my body, leaving me with a serious urge to fidget. I steepled my fingers on my belly, thankful my suit jacket and desk hid my compromised state from her.

'I told you the meeting was at nine o'clock. I've had to put off the Moroccan team twice already.'

'Heavens! In that case I can only apologise. There must have been some sort of mix-up.' She slipped the phone back into her pocket, the movements exaggerated enough to make her coat gape wide. I saw the curve of her breast and swallowed hard.

'What the fuck are you doing?' I bit out.

Her eyes widened. 'I don't know what you mean, Jasper.'

'Do you attend all your meetings dressed like that?'

'You don't like what I'm wearing?'

I gritted my teeth, knowing I was getting close to the danger zone. 'We abide by a dress code here.'

Her smile. 'Ah, but then I don't work for you, do I, Jasper?' she asked softly, but there was a hard glint in her eye, a stubborn flame flaring to life.

Before I could answer, my phone rang. I allowed myself a small smile as I met her gaze. 'You're right. You don't work for me. But we're working together and I expect professionalism, like being on time. I'll let it slide just this once.' I reached for my phone. 'Yes?' My PA relayed the information I wanted to hear, and I hung up. 'Are you ready?'

She tensed. 'Ready for what?'

'I told you I rescheduled the videoconference. The Morocco team is waiting for us in the conference room. Since you made the effort to come all this way despite being late, I'm assuming you'll join me?'

I watched her jaw drop, her whole act vanishing for a second before she composed herself. 'Of course, lead the way. I hope they're just as accommodating as you about my tardiness,' she said, her voice saccharine sweet.

I managed to stop my teeth gritting as I rose, buttoned my jacket and rounded the desk. The last thing I wanted to do was to walk her through my open-plan office floor dressed as she was. Call me a chauvinist but having every guy out there wondering what she was wearing under that coat made my blood boil.

But…business was business. And I wasn't about to let this deal fall apart over yet another hurdle.

I stepped out of my office, keenly aware that she was

following, those sky-high heels perfectly displaying her spectacular endless legs with every step. Of course, as I'd feared, seemingly every male in the vicinity suddenly needed to be in the hallway leading to the conference room right at that moment.

Avid eyes gravitated to Wren, her sexily dishevelled state triggering more than one male fantasy. I hurried into the conference room, barely stopping myself from snarling at my own employees as I shut the door behind us.

Strolling to the head of the table, I grabbed the remote and flicked it on. The four women and three men who made up the Moroccan executive team stared back at us. Then, one by one, they switched their attention to Wren. Eyes widened, and wild speculation flickered across their faces.

I cleared my throat, rearranging what I suspected was a scowl into professional neutrality. 'Ladies and gentlemen, my apologies again for the delay. Let me introduce you to Wren Bingham. As of today, she'll be taking over Bingham Industries' side of the project.' I glanced at Wren, who'd taken the seat across from me.

She was staring at the screen with a sultry, faintly challenging smile. As I watched, she swivelled her seat towards the screen, dragging one hand slowly through her long hair before flicking it over one shoulder. With her other hand she waved at the team. 'Hi, it's lovely to meet you all,' she murmured, right before she crossed her mile-long legs.

I didn't need to be on her side of the table to know she was flashing more than a hint of thigh. The expressions on the screen—especially the male ones—telegraphed her effect on them, plain as day. Silence reigned in the room as their gazes flicked between Wren and me.

Bloody hell.

'Wren?' I prompted, aware of the bite in my voice.

She slanted green eyes at me and blinked slowly. 'Yes, Jasper?'

'Are you going to give the Bingham briefing? The team is pretty much on page as to where the Mortimer side of things stand. They need you to confirm the various timetables for delivery of phase two. You did get up to speed on where we are, didn't you?'

Her eyes flashed irritation at me but she maintained her bored expression. 'Oh… Right. Phase two…' She didn't say anything else, just continued to stare at me with those eyes.

'Yep. Phase two. Don't keep us in suspense,' I taunted, ignoring the stares from the screen as our intrigued audience watched our silent battle, suddenly enjoying this tussle with her.

She shrugged, indicating she was going to do just as she pleased. That she was going to enjoy watching me twist in the wind.

After another stretch of mutinous silence, I swivelled my chair towards the screen. 'My apologies, but I didn't quite make a full introduction, did I? I should have mentioned that Wren has a master's degree in Business from Oxford University.'

I felt her gaze sharpen on me. 'She was recently featured in Business Tomorrow's Young CEOs Under

Thirty. She's too modest to tell you herself, but she graduated at the top of her class and, according to one of her professors, she has one of the most brilliant business minds of her generation.'

'Stop it,' she hissed under her breath for my ears only.

I ignored her. She wasn't going to win this game. 'I tried to poach her even before she'd finished university but, alas, I lost her to another company. So I guess you can imagine how stoked I am to finally have her on board?' I flicked a mocking smile her way before returning my gaze to the team. 'The reason she doesn't have any files with her this morning is because she doesn't really need them. All the facts and figures she requires are right up there in that exceptional brain of hers. On top of her many accomplishments, she also possesses a photographic memory. I haven't seen it in action myself but I'm dying to. Wren?' I prompted again, finally focusing on her, the gauntlet writhing on the table between us.

Hellfire erupted from her gaze as her hands balled into fists.

I smiled inside, satisfaction eroding my irritation. She'd meant to test me by pretending lack of interest, boredom, even apathy. But the one thing Wren Bingham couldn't do was let our audience walk away with the impression that she was dumb. I suspected, like me, she'd fought too hard for her accomplishments and her true place in her family to let herself be so easily dismissed.

When she swallowed, surreptitiously pulled the lapels of her coat together and slowly uncrossed her legs, I allowed myself an inner fist pump.

Uncurling her hands, she glanced at the screen. 'What do you need to know about phase two?' she asked, the sexy seduction in her voice gone.

At my nod, the team launched into their questions. As I'd suspected, Wren knew the project inside and out. She answered every query concisely, offering alternatives when needed without once requesting information from me or consulting the electronic documents I'd emailed her yesterday.

When the meeting ended and the screen went blank forty minutes later, she surged to her feet. 'You think you're very clever, don't you?' she snapped.

I reclined in my seat, taunting her with a smile. 'Don't throw a hissy fit just because your little game backfired on you, sweetheart,' I drawled.

Luscious lips pressed together as she raked her fingers through her hair, immediately making my imagination run wild about the array of sexual things I could do with every strand of that hair. 'This isn't going to work.'

I waved a hand at the screen. 'You just proved otherwise. It'll work even better if only you'd stop playing these silly games.'

Her eyes flashed. 'What makes you think I won't just let you list my accomplishments then show you up anyway next time?'

I shrugged. 'I don't. But I can guarantee that I'll keep coming up with different ways to ensure that you don't get away with whatever you have up your sleeve.'

She threw up her hands in exasperation, the closest

I'd come to seeing her lose her cool. 'Why don't you do us both a favour and just end this?'

I exhaled slowly. 'I don't get it. Going ahead with this deal will benefit both of us.'

She performed a perfect pirouette and headed for the door. 'Keep telling yourself that,' she threw over her shoulder. 'In the meantime, I'm going to make it my business to make sure that you regret this.' She reached for the door handle. Started to turn it.

Everything inside me clenched tight. 'Wren.'

Fingers frozen, she glared at me over her shoulder.

'Please tell me you're not naked under that coat.'

That slow, cock-stroking smile returned, deadlier than before. 'I'm not naked under this coat, Jasper,' she echoed with a siren voice that transmitted straight to my groin. Then to taunt me further, her fingers dropped to toy with the loops of the belt. 'Would you like me to show you?'

Lust rushed through my blood, making me steel hard in moments. But I remained silent, swallowing down the *yes* that clawed at my throat. Without shifting her gaze from mine, she tugged on the belt. Her coat loosened and gaped. From where I sat, I couldn't see, but anyone who chose to enter in that moment would.

My stomach knotted and I lost the ability to breathe. 'Fucking hell,' I muttered under my breath.

'What was that?' she asked with false, wide-eyed innocence.

'I said keep that damn door closed, Wren.'

'Ah, I could've sworn you said something else.'

'Jesus, what are you doing?' I rasped, forgetting that I was meant to keep my cool.

'I'm going back to my office. I'm assuming we're done here?' she asked, one shapely eyebrow quirked.

My gaze dropped down the coat, fighting the urge to stand, rush over to her to see for myself what she was baring to the door. 'You know what I'm asking. What are you doing with all that?' I jerked my chin at her attire.

Her smile deepened. 'Why, nothing. Not yet, anyway.'

Her hand dropped from the door. My throat clogged with tension as she slowly retied the belt, cinching it even tighter so her trim waist was fully displayed. My fingers itched with the need to capture that waist. I bunched them to stop myself from acting on the feelings rampaging through me.

'I need you back here tomorrow to discuss the casino outfitting.'

'I have a full day tomorrow.'

'Then we'll meet after you're done,' I countered, and watched her nostrils flare.

'I work pretty long hours. Are you sure you want to wait up for me? I wouldn't want to disturb your beauty sleep.'

'Thanks for your concern, but my beauty won't suffer too badly from a few extra hours of work. And, Wren?'

She cocked an eyebrow at me.

'Don't make me come after you. My patience won't hold out for ever.'

One corner of her lips lifted and she all but vibrated with the *Bring it on* she didn't utter.

I sighed under my breath. This game wasn't over, regardless of my daring her into displaying her intelligence just now. I watched as she opened the door and threw me one last look over her shoulder.

'Until next time, Jasper.'

I collapsed into my seat the moment she left, dragging my fingers through my hair as the rush of adrenaline drained from my body.

Maybe she had a point, damn it. Maybe the Mortimers should avoid the Binghams at all costs. Because even this small taster of what I suspected she had in store for me would wreck my concentration for the rest of the day.

Of course it will. Because you're just that weak, aren't you? Are you going to shy away from another fight, give in that easily? Debate your way through another fight with an opponent? Maybe you should change your name, then. Because that is certainly not the Mortimer way.

Arousal receded as my father's pitiless, unwanted voice echoed in my head. My jaw clenched as I fought a different kind of discomfort. But those disparaging words, branded into my soul from childhood, continued to echo through me, followed by bitterness for how long I'd let it rule every corner of my life.

But I'd done something about it…eventually. I'd taken control.

By letting Perry Bingham convince me to allow him to sign on to my deal? Knowing deep down it would probably piss my father off when I proved the genera-tions-long feud meant nothing to me?

I shrugged the suggestion away. Regardless of the reason behind it, I was going to see this thing through. This project was my baby, the biggest deal I'd ever ne-gotiated. I wasn't about to let it fall to pieces now.

Because Hugh Mortimer was still alive and well. Re-gardless of the fact that he'd removed himself from the immediate sphere of the clan, I knew he kept an eye on what happened within the company. And the last thing I was about to do was to prove him right. Even if I had to fight and wrestle Wren and her whole family under my control, I would bring this deal home.

Just to prove my father wrong about me.

Again.

CHAPTER FOUR

'WHAT KIND OF time do you call this?' I growled at the woman who stood in my doorway, thankfully wearing more clothes than yesterday. That moment of gratitude was fleeting though. On account of her succeeding where I was sure she'd fail at annoying me even more.

She sashayed into my office, looking stunningly immaculate, despite the very late hour, tossed her stylish briefcase on the sofa and shrugged. 'I'm pretty sure I warned you.'

'Working late is one thing. Turning up for a meeting at almost midnight is just taking the piss. How did you get here, anyway?'

'I took a cab. Why, were you worried about my safety?' she asked, one hand braced on her lean, curvy hip as she stopped in front of my desk.

Damn it, yes, I'd been worried. And increasingly vexed about it. I'd succumbed and called her office an hour ago, only to be blocked by her security who rightly wouldn't give out details of their boss's whereabouts. Not knowing whether she was going to turn up or not had kept me rooted in my office, tackling work that could easily have waited till tomorrow with dwindling concentration.

I shook my head as I stalked over to my liquor cabinet, poured myself a stiff Scotch. I toyed with being inhospitable for a few seconds before fixing her the mineral water with lime I'd seen her drinking at her party.

I offered the drink, daring her with my eyes to refuse. She glanced at the glass, a hint of surprise lighting her eyes before, frowning, she accepted it.

'I reread the contract today. The break clause might be skewed in your favour, but you realise I can simply do nothing for six months and watch you crash and burn?'

I tensed at her opening salvo. 'You'd really do that and lose close to half a billion pounds in profits?'

She hesitated for the tiniest revealing moment. 'Yes.'

'Are you sure? Don't you want to run that by your board first?'

Her chin went up and she boldly met my gaze. 'The board will stand behind any decision I make. Perry already had their backing to get out of this deal.'

Shit. That was news to me. 'After going to all that trouble of begging me for the partnership?'

Her lashes swept down and stayed down for a long time. 'His reasons are none of your business. Same goes for mine.'

'Wrong, sweetheart. They are exactly my business, since we're effectively joined at the hip.'

She shook her head. 'You left him no choice. Not after you bought out the previous company Perry was supposed to partner with.'

I frowned. 'What are you talking about?'

'The Morocco deal. Isn't it true you only intended to go with two hotels?'

'That was the initial plan, yes. But—'

'But then you got greedy and bought up four more adjoining sites? Just because you could?'

'It wasn't a matter of greed, it was a matter of good business. And yes, because I damned well could. I'm failing to see what your point is here, Wren.'

'My point is, Perry came to you only after you became the new owner of the contract he was trying to secure. He didn't want to, but he'd been working on that deal long before you came on board. He…he was forced to come to you.'

My fingers tightened around my glass. 'Unless your family derives some macabre pleasure from hanging on to this shit even after twenty years, he could've walked away. Why didn't he?'

Her gaze rose and I caught a shaft of pain in her eyes. 'Perry hates losing. And some wounds run deep.'

Frustration bit through me. 'What about you? I'm not asking for a family reunion or even a suggestion that we bury the hatchet. All I'm asking for is a business deal where we both stand to profit for a very long time.'

Her lips twisted. 'Money isn't everything.'

I snorted. 'Then what are you doing in that office half a mile away? Running a charity?'

'I meant money isn't everything, *every time*.'

'Maybe not. But is that a strong enough reason to risk everything? For God's sake, who I am shouldn't matter in the grand scheme of things.'

'To my family, it does.'

I approached her until we were a foot apart.

She stayed her ground and that defiant stance made me instantly hard. Surprise, surprise. I leaned forward until her alluring perfume tortured me mercilessly. Until my thoughts began to fracture under the weight of the need to pull her close. Kiss her. Vent my frustration on anywhere she'd let me touch.

Starting with the silky skin of her neck. I'd work my way down, ridding her of that pristine cream shirt, which clung to her body. My gaze dropped to her chest, saw the faintest outline of her nipples. Sweet heaven, what I'd give to suck on those succulent nubs.

My eager mind strayed deeper into erotic realms.

I'd take off every single item of clothing except those red-soled heels, bend her over my desk and ram myself so deep inside her that we'd both see stars. Unlike last time, I had a condom nearby this time. Several, in fact. I'd taken to carrying the things with me wherever I went now. In case Wren Bingham happened to be there and begged me with her alluring mouth and eyes to service her as she had that night in the maze.

I leaned closer. She twitched and shuddered as my mouth brushed her earlobe. I wanted to catch the delicate flesh between my teeth, hear that control-destroying gasp she gave when she was caught in pleasure, but I restrained myself. Barely. 'Then they need to get over themselves, and fast. Because I'm not letting this one go. Now, shall we get on with this meeting? My casino isn't going to fit itself and, I promise, the longer you make me wait, the less reasonable I'll get about accommodating your behaviour.'

She froze, then jerked back a step. Whatever she read in my eyes made hers widen before it narrowed. 'This is your last chance, Jasper,' she said, her voice throbbing with an emotion I didn't want to examine.

'No.'

She stared at me for an age, then nodded. 'Fine. Let's discuss the casino.'

An hour later, I watched her walk out ahead of me—because I wasn't letting her catch a cab home at one o'clock in the morning, despite her protests—her sexy arse and endless legs an erotic sight that made my mouth water.

Just like last time, she'd come fully prepared. I had a set of approved timetables and proposed delivery of top-of-the-line gaming equipment in my briefcase, ready to green light in the morning.

I was buzzing with quiet excitement at her sheer proficiency while she'd grown increasingly despondent as the meeting had progressed. It was clear she wasn't happy about my insistence on our partnership continuing.

She reached the lift and shot me a look filled with venom. And despite a low warning hum at the back of my head suggesting that it wasn't too late to ditch Bingham's, I found myself smiling as I stepped into the lift with her.

I wasn't smiling two weeks later when I slammed my phone down after another failed call to the number that had risen to the top of my speed-dial list.

She didn't answer.

It was time to pull out the big guns.

I typed out a quick text.

I'm calling you in one minute. I suggest you pick up or the next call will be from my lawyers. Trust me, you don't want that.

The speech bubble that said she was answering rippled for several seconds—while I held my stupid breath—before it died. Exactly one minute later, I dialled her number.

'Hello?'

'What the fuck do you think you're doing, Wren?'

'Good afternoon to you, too, Jasper. How's your day going?'

'You know damn well how it's going. You went behind my back and cancelled our meeting with the advertising team. Yesterday you didn't bother to show up for the VIP guest hospitality meeting. The day before that—'

'If you're going to list everything I've done or not done in the last two weeks, do you mind if I pour myself a drink? I have a feeling I'll be thirsty by the time you're finished.'

'This is absurd. You're costing us both a lot of money.'

'Nothing earth-shattering I can't recoup eventually.'

'At the risk of sounding egotistical, I can withstand the losses way longer than you can. Have you thought about that?'

She hesitated for a split second. 'Maybe. But just as

you've done your research on me, I've done mine on you. You have a board to answer to. And I dare say not everyone is thrilled about you hanging on to this deal when cutting me loose makes better sense. What do you tell them when they ask, Jasper? That you're holding on, on the off chance you'll get to fuck me as part of the deal?'

My stomach muscles knotted. I wasn't going to deny it. But it wasn't my *entire* reason. 'They trust my judgement, which is more than I'm guessing you can say for your own board.'

'Clearly you don't know as much as you think you do.'

'Enlighten me, then.'

'For starters? My board approved the list of willing partners who have indicated they'd be happy to buy out Bingham Industries' interest in this deal and they know you're refusing to entertain that idea on the basis that you're being a pig-headed—'

'Watch it, Wren. I won't be spoken to like that.'

To her credit, she didn't offer a scathing comeback.

'Has it occurred to you that prolonging this battle leaves you progressively exposed, not to mention in danger of ruining your personal reputation?' I asked.

'What are you talking about?' she replied, her voice tight.

'It's no secret that Bingham's is facing financial issues. Have you wondered why the corporate sharks haven't started circling yet?'

'Because we're not as weak as you think.'

'Bullshit. It's because of your association with the Mortimer Group. For now anyone with a lick of corporate sense knows not to mess with you because you've partnered with me. That protection erodes the second you give the impression we're not on the same page on this.'

'It's not an impression.'

I pinched the bridge of my nose and exhaled loudly. 'Christ, Wren, you're an intelligent woman. Don't let emotion cloud your judgement. I'm reaching the point where I won't feel inclined to keep the wolves from storming your door.'

'I beg your pardon?' she said sharply.

'Frankly, I'd rather have you begging for something else. But more on that in a while. For now, I want you to think hard about what you're doing.'

'I may be wrong, but I swear you just called your-self my saviour.'

'Take the advice or don't. And just so we're clear, the meeting has been rescheduled for tomorrow morn-ing. If you're not in my office at eight a.m., I'll start playing dirty, too.'

I hung up before I lost it. Or let that sexy voice of hers wreak even more havoc on my self-control.

For the third time, I picked up the phone, this time to my assistant. 'Trish, reschedule the meeting with the advertising team for eight a.m. tomorrow and tell them Miss Bingham will attend. Then send her an email to say I want the boutique contracts I sent her last week reviewed and couriered over by close of business today.'

'Right away, Mr Mortimer.'

I replaced the handset and sat back, the throb of an-ticipation firing higher.

At five past five it'd turned to irritation. By five-thirty, I was pacing my office, my jaw locked in burning annoyance.

Striding to my desk, I hit the number for my assistant. 'Anything?'

'No, sir.'

'The courier is still there?'

'Yes, sir, he's still waiting at the Bingham Industries reception. Should I tell him to leave?'

'No. He stays there until I say otherwise.'

'Okay. Um… Mr Mortimer?'

I paused. 'Yes?'

'Don't forget you have the Art Foundation's Annual Gala at seven-thirty.'

I smothered a curse. I'd forgotten about my next social obligation while indulging in games with Wren. Thankfully, I'd prepared my speech weeks ago. 'Thanks for the reminder.'

'You're welcome. I've sent your new tux up to the penthouse and arranged for the car to be downstairs at seven.'

About to hang up, I tossed in one last question. 'How many more to go until gala season is over?' I asked, praying she'd say this was the last one.

'Another two, and your cousin Graciela sent an email today about the next Mortimer Quarterly launch party.'

'Thanks.'

After hanging up, I took several deep breaths. I was in danger of letting Wren unbalance me. As patron of several art foundations, I had a duty to attend this event. That it'd slipped my mind so completely made me grimace. The grimace intensified when I realised I'd been all set to track Wren down wherever she'd disappeared to instead of tackling the other time-sensitive deals I had piled up on my desk.

She was becoming an obsession.

Becoming?

I smothered the mocking inner voice and resisted the urge to call Trish again and find out whether the contract was on its way back to me. Instead I picked up a random file.

The knock on the door interrupted my focus an hour later. My pulse leapt but it was only Trish poking her head through the door. 'It's six-thirty, sir. And before you ask, no, the courier is still at Bingham's.'

My lips flattened. 'Tell him to leave. I'll deal with Miss Bingham myself.'

Several ways of dealing with her reeled through my head, all of which were most definitely NSFW.

Three hours later, the speeches were done, I'd handed over a very fat cheque and worked the room twice to ensure all present and future donors were appropriately satisfied with my attention.

Then I called the number I'd been hoping not to use any time soon. It was answered on the first ring. 'I need an address,' I said.

'Of course, sir,' my head of security answered.

Twenty minutes later, I leaned on the doorbell of the ground-floor maisonette in Fulham. Enough lights blazed within to make me comfortable she was home. Still, she kept me cooling my heels for a couple of minutes, during which time I wondered whether she was alone. What I'd interrupted.

'Who is it?' she said, her sexy voice coming through the solid wood.

'You know who it is. I just saw you looking through the security glass. At least you're not reckless about your safety.'

'It's almost midnight, Jasper,' she replied after a short pause.

The possibility that I'd caught her off guard pleased me. Which went to show how pathetic I was in gaining this tiny upper hand. 'Isn't that your favourite time of day to talk business? I'm merely obliging you. Open the door, Wren.'

'What could we possibly have to discuss that can't wait?'

Her sheer gumption drew an incredulous laugh from me. I dragged my fingers through my hair. 'I'm going to throw some names at you. Let me know if you're interested in discussing them. Palmer Jones Plc. Winlake Hotel. Morpheus Tech—'

She yanked the door open, her eyes wide with alarm. 'What did you do?'

'Do I have your attention now?'

Her jaw clenched and alarm morphed into a scowl.

'Invite me in, Wren,' I suggested softly.

Her fingers tightened on the door for a few stubborn seconds before she nudged it open.

I entered, walking down polished floorboards and Venetian wallpapered walls into a large sitting room decorated in white with splashes of warm, earthy colours. Exotic artwork featured majorly and I fought the urge to ask about her taste in art. This wasn't a social call.

'I said what did you do?' she repeated.

I turned to face her, noting for the first time what she was wearing. Her black satin, lace-edged top—clearly a nightie set designed to drive men insane—clung to her full breasts. The shorts skimmed her upper thighs, and even in the lamplight I saw enough bare skin to ramp my arousal through the roof. I dragged my gaze up past her face to the hair piled haphazardly atop her head. So far, I'd only seen it down, but she looked even more delectable in that slightly dishevelled, ready-for-bed state.

I tried to reel myself in. What the hell did she just ask me? Oh, yeah… 'So far? Nothing. But I know they're three of your top five clients.'

Her green eyes snapped with fire. 'So what? You've proved you have a spy in my office. Bravo, Jasper. And what exactly are you accusing me of? I sent your boutique contracts back an hour ago. Did you check your email before you came storming over here?'

'Yes, I did. And while I'll forgive the odd typo or two, which wasn't in my version, what the hell do you think you're playing at, allowing your sub-contractors the option to trigger an extended delivery clause?'

She shrugged. 'What can I say? I'm a generous boss. And that option was in exceptional circumstances only.'

'Which every single one of them will take advantage of! Here's a free tip, since you haven't been CEO for long—soft-balling your contracts like that is a sure-fire route to driving Bingham's out of business. Hell, even

Perry knew that.' I mentally kicked myself the moment her brother's name fell from my lips.

She sucked in a quick breath and her lips flattened. 'Don't you dare say his name.'

I exhaled slowly. 'I'm done fucking around with you, Wren. This nonsense stops now or, come tomorrow morning, I'm going after your top five clients. You don't need me to tell you that I have enough personal resources to scupper every deal of yours, or, at the very least, stall it as much as you're trying to stall mine.'

Her fists balled. 'Get the hell out of my flat, Jasper.' The words were low but pithy, her eyes burning with anger and pain.

'I will, as soon as you give me your word that these shenanigans are over.'

Her chin went up. 'Agree to a five-year deal instead of three and I'll think about it.'

I considered it for half a second. 'No. As much as you won't like to hear it, it's for your own good as much as mine.'

'How utterly condescending of you,' she tossed back at me.

I didn't realise I'd been walking towards her until I caught the scent of her shampoo. Until I saw the tiny gold flecks in her eyes reflecting the lamplight. Her head was tilted up and I couldn't help visually devouring the creamy smoothness of her skin.

'I may not deem it good business sense to renegotiate now but I won't deny you the option of doing so at a later date.'

She rolled her eyes. 'Please, stop trying to wrangle

yourself into those sheep's clothes when we both know you and your family are wolves.'

Dear God, but she tested me. 'You know something? I regret not giving you that spanking you begged me for that day in the maze.'

She sucked in a quick, betraying breath. I enjoyed watching her nonplussed expression before her features closed. 'Your memory must be faulty. I never begged you for anything.'

'Not with your mouth. But we both know what you wanted that day.'

Her nostrils fluttered delicately, her eyes growing that shade of moss green that betrayed her. 'You have a vivid, and very flawed, imagination, Jasper.'

'I agree with the vivid part. I'm very happy to demonstrate just how flawed you think my memory is. Right now if you want.' I gestured at the wide sofa behind her and for the tiniest moment heat flared in her eyes.

'I don't want, thank you. Not that. Not any of this.' There was a desperate note in her voice. 'When are you going to accept it and end this?'

End our association? Watch her retreat behind that glass building half a mile away from my office that might as well have been a continent away for all the access I'd have to her? Not if I could bloody well help it. 'You know the terms of the deal as well as I do. So far I have zero incentive to give you what you want. Until such time as that changes…' I shrugged '… I want you to accept that and work with me.'

'I won't. And you'll be wise not to push me.'

'Or what?' I challenged.

'Remember those accolades you generously listed for the benefit of your Moroccan team? It's only a matter of time before I succeed.'

And as absurd as the feeling was, a part of me relished that fight with her. Glancing down at her, I drawled, 'It turns you on to fight with me, doesn't it?'

She snorted. 'Now you're just being plain ridiculous.' But her words lacked the punch of conviction.

'Am I?' I murmured. 'Then why are your nipples hard? Why's your skin flushed? I bet you'd be too proud to admit you're hot and wet right now.'

Her nostrils flared. 'Haven't you learned the futility in attempting reverse psychology with me by now?'

I smiled, enjoying myself for the first time today. 'I don't hear a denial, sweetheart.'

'Don't call me that,' she admonished. 'I'm not your sweet anything.'

'You're right. You're like a stiff shot of Scotch whisky, raging and burning all the way down. Problem is, one taste just triggers a need for another. And another...'

She stiffened. 'I wouldn't know. I don't drink.'

The tastelessness of my analogy hit home a second too late. 'Hell. I'm sorry. That wasn't meant—'

'You're still here, Jasper. Why?'

'Because your nipples are still hard. You're breathless and I know it's not because you're offended. Or annoyed with me. You want another taste, too, don't you, Wren?'

She opened her mouth, but I placed a finger on her

lips. 'You can take the high road if you want, but I'm not ashamed to admit that I'm dying to kiss you. Can I?'

One perfectly sculpted eyebrow arched, and, God, even that was beyond sexy. 'You didn't bother to ask last time. Why ask now?'

'Last time was...different. Yet you did invite me to do my worst, as you put it. You needed me to take control. You wanted the fastest route out of your head and I provided it.'

She continued to glare at me. 'You think this makes you some kind of noble knight or something?'

I shrugged. 'Or something. So can I kiss you, Wren? Or do you want me to take the decision out of your hands again, give you the chance to tell me off later and claim it was all a mistake?'

The faintest flush of guilt stained her cheeks. 'You think you know me?'

'Not well enough. Not as much as I'd like. But we'll get around to that soon enough. For now...' I inched closer until mere millimetres separated our lips, until her sweet breath washed over my top lip. Until I craved her so badly it was a physical pain not to just let the lust lashing us take over. But she was right. I wanted her to see me in a better light. Wanted her to want me without the speed bumps of our corporate skirmishes in the way.

Just when I started to give up hope, her beautiful eyes locked on mine. Still challenging. Still vexed. But also aroused. Interested. Hell, even craving.

Her gaze dropped to my mouth. And she swallowed hard. 'For now...you have one minute. Then I'm throwing you out.'

The words were barely out of her mouth before I was on her, intent on not missing a single second. Memories of kissing and touching her in the maze had haunted me for weeks and *finally* I was reliving them. My fingers in her hair held her steady as I stroked her tongue with mine. Yeah, I was a little forceful, but, hell, she'd driven me steadily insane and I wasn't in the mood to play gentleman.

She squirmed, fighting an internal battle, then, with an impatient moan, she gripped my shoulders. She rose on tiptoe, her movements increasingly demanding as she pressed her body against mine and opened wider for me.

Yes! I grabbed one hip, pressed her against me as I walked us back towards her sofa. Seconds later, she was on her back and I was on top of her, devouring her for all I was worth.

Sweet Jesus, she tasted even more sublime. Just as brazen with her needs as in the maze, she spread her thighs, accommodating me as I palmed one breast and toyed with her nipple. Her hips undulating, seeking the iron rod of my cock. We met, strained and groaned at the exquisite intensity of it. In slow, torturous rhythm, we writhed against one another, while the kiss turned hotter, wetter, simulating everything I wanted to do to her, and vice versa.

But through it all, I was keenly aware of the seconds ticking down, aware she could kick me out at any moment.

So I chose to play dirty.

On the next roll of her hips, I pressed hard against

her, holding my cock tight against her satin-covered pussy, urging her to feel what I could do for her. What we could do to each other.

I bit back a smile when an involuntary spasm shuddered through her body. 'Let's renegotiate,' I rasped against her lips. 'One minute isn't going to cut it.'

She laughed a little unkindly, even while her fingers dug painfully into my biceps to hold me in place. Why did I love that she wasn't afraid to show me her fire? 'Poor Jasper.'

I growled. 'Give me ten minutes.' It was nowhere near enough for what I craved to do but it was a starting point.

She raised her head a fraction and bit my lower lip, making me shudder. 'No.'

'Christ, Wren. You're a ballbreaker, you know that?'

She stiffened slightly but didn't pull back. 'Five,' she countered after another round of furious kissing.

I yanked down one strap of her nightie top as she eagerly unbuttoned my shirt. Her fingers delved down to caress my chest and abs as I swooped onto one eager nipple. She hissed her appreciation and I feasted, groaning at her silken skin, the mouth-watering taste of her. Her back arched, offering more of herself.

'God, you're beautiful,' I rasped. 'Maddening but breathtaking.'

Against my temple, I felt her faint smile as she raked demanding fingers through my hair. Then, taking my head between her hands, she redirected me to her neglected breast. I teased, tortured and suckled until she was a glorious rose-pink. Only then did I trail one hand down, beneath the elastic of her shorts.

The brazen discovery nearly blew my head clean off. 'You answer your front door not wearing panties, sweetheart?'

'My home, my rules.'

I smiled, deciding to enjoy this particular gift before it was taken away. Spearing her with my gaze, I slid my hand lower, down over that silken strip of hair until I encountered hot, slippery flesh.

'God,' I muttered, a red haze passing over my vision. 'You're so wet.'

Expecting a smart retort, I watched as she sucked in a slow breath, her eyes not leaving mine as she chased my touch. 'Yes, I am. And your five minutes are almost up,' she said a little unsteadily.

'I'm aware, sweetheart.' I pressed my middle finger inside her and her hips jerked, her inner muscles clinging as she whimpered. 'Thing is, do I use that time for you or shall I be selfish and use it all for me?'

Her eyes widened a touch but she remained still, her hands gripping me tight. I was sure she wasn't aware of how her nails dug into me, and I bit back another smile.

Who the hell was I bluffing? I was going to use this for her. When I got around to fucking Wren, I intended to be inside her longer than whatever seconds I had left in this ridiculous game.

Bending low, I flicked my tongue over one ripe nipple as I speared her with my fingers. Her head started to roll, those insane sounds erupting from her throat again. I squeezed my eyes shut to regain some control.

But soon, much too soon, I was at that point of ravening lust, where my mind threatened to cease to function. She did this to me. Every single time. Even before we'd ever had a proper conversation, she'd pulled at me on some level. First with her brilliant mind and now, with her glorious body. The way it softened and moulded beneath my hands, the way she fought the groan tearing through her before finally letting it free to vibrate its feminine power through her body. The way those hips rolled so perfectly into mine.

Every. Single. Time.

But…hold on a sec. How long was I going to keep buckling? Sure, I might have started this, hell, *begged* for this, but she'd ended up dictating the terms anyway.

Because you're weak…

I gritted my teeth against Hugh Mortimer's damning words. Against the growing din of the clock counting down while I was getting lost in my own head. Against the even dirtier game I suspected I had to play if I was going to win this thing. Win her around.

Slowly, I raised my head. 'Wren.'

She ignored me, nibbling on my jaw before sinking her white teeth into my throat. I jerked back before I lost complete control.

'Wren. Stop.'

CHAPTER FIVE

I'VE ALWAYS HATED my name, ever since Perry let slip when I was nine that my father had given it to me as a cruel joke. George Bingham had possessed a rather dark sense of humour. Humour he'd often directed towards me in the rare times I was allowed in his vicinity.

He'd chosen a name with no softness to it, apparently, because he didn't want a soft child. Particularly, he hadn't wanted a daughter. So in his bitter humour and disappointment, he'd named me Wren. Nondescript. Forgettable. All hard angles and far too close to *wrench* for my liking. At school I'd been teased about it. *Wren the Wraith* because of my thinness, my paleness and my height. Coupled with the oppressive cloaks we'd been required to wear at my equally oppressive Hampshire boarding school, the name had fitted all too well.

But now, hearing it groaned from the depths of Jasper's arousal, it sounded…different. Not ordinary. Definitely lusty. Erotic and potent. A name uttered as if he couldn't help himself. As if he had to say it…or die.

Even as I dismissed my thoughts as a stupid flight of fancy, I leaned into him, silently pleading for him to groan it again, to fan the flames of my own arousal to that mindless place he'd taken me that chilly evening in my family's maze.

No, not back to that place.

I wanted a new place. One I could claim wholly for myself, without the spectre of my judgemental family looming over me.

As much as I hadn't wanted to let him into my personal space, now that I had him here, it wasn't so bad. My sofa would be a good starting point. Maybe eventually my bed…if we could drag ourselves there—

Except…he was already pulling away.

Far too quickly, painful reality rushed back in. Dear God, I was literally cavorting with the enemy. And even worse, he was about to leave me hanging moments away from another mind-shambling orgasm. Dazed and more than a little confused, I glanced down at myself, sprawled out with my breasts on display and my shorts pulled up tight enough to frame my crotch, highlighting the need coursing through me.

Somehow my fingers were caught in his and even though he'd rejected me, he still held on to me. Which made my exposed state even more humiliating.

I yanked myself out of his hold, face flaming as I pulled up the straps of my top until my shamefully erect nipples were covered. Jasper was still wedged between my thighs and despite his withdrawal, the outline of his erection pressed behind his fly. The sight of it reminded me of what I'd been grinding up against moments ago. His glorious thickness, the very masculine way he rolled his hips. The promise of how he would feel deep inside me…

Hunger and frustration threatened to overshadow my humiliation. But the very thought that I was considering, even for a millisecond, talking him into finishing what he'd started forced me to locate my elusive outrage.

'Can you get off me, please?'

His lips firmed. 'Wren, we need to—'

'Now, please,' I interjected, infusing my voice with necessary ice.

For several seconds, his hazel eyes narrowed, eyes that seemed to see beneath my skin, examining me intently before, thankfully, he rose from the sofa.

He crossed to the window and stared out onto the street. Whether to give me time to compose myself or because he needed a minute himself, I didn't question as I jumped up. I yanked my passion-tousled hair out of the band securing it, letting the strands fall around my shoulders and partly obscure my face in the vain hope of a shield. I contemplated going to retrieve my dressing gown out of my room and decided against the revealing move. The last thing I wanted was to lose further ground to Jasper Mortimer.

I sucked in a deep breath, exhaling slowly as he turned to face me. His stark hunger was throttled back and the eyes that stared at me held only iron resolution.

'Believe it or not, that wasn't how I wanted this to go,' he rasped.

Something fairly substantial lurched with disappointment inside me. 'And by this you mean what exactly?

Storming into my flat or that half-baked seduction on my sofa?'

For some reason, my snippiness amused him. I hated myself a little for liking his smile. 'I didn't storm in and I may have stopped short of the full five minutes but there was nothing half-baked about it, sweetheart.'

Again, something lurched. It was the *sweetheart* I'd outwardly objected to but secretly didn't...hate. While I wasn't about to examine why, I knew it had something to do with the lack of softness and warmth in my life, both in childhood and now. And yes, I feared for my own gullibility at being taken in by a common term of endearment.

I crossed my arms over my chest, stingingly aware my erogenous zones were still on fire and one particular area was announcing it to the world.

'Whatever. You're going to use those extra minutes to leave, aren't you?' I said, striving for boredom.

This time his whole face hardened. 'Not until we've cleared up a few important things.'

'And what would those be?'

'You'll find out in the morning. In the meantime, fix the contract. Bring it with you tomorrow.'

I chose a silent glare as my answer.

He crossed the room to where I stood, gazed down at me long and contemplatively enough to make me tense against the urge to fidget.

'We both know you're better than this, Wren,' he murmured. 'There's absolutely no shame in proving me right. And who knows? You might get a nice surprise when you turn up tomorrow.'

When…not *if.* His confidence would've been insulting had I not spent the last two weeks and most of today confirming what I knew in my gut but hadn't been ready to admit.

I held my breath as he raised his hand, trailed his finger from my jaw to the lower lip that still tingled with the need to repeat that kiss. His eyes burned hot and heavy into mine for another moment before, gritting his teeth, he walked out of my living room.

A moment later, I heard the door close behind him. A breath shuddered out of me. I didn't exactly call it relief because that knot of hunger was still lodged in my belly, intent on reminding me how long it'd been since I'd had good sex. Or any kind of sex, for that matter.

It was only when I realised I was listening out for the sounds of his car leaving my quiet street that I sank onto the sofa. Head buried in my hands, I tried to breathe through confusion and need. Through all the reasons I'd allowed Jasper into my personal sanctuary. I wasn't melodramatic enough to fear that I'd never sit on my sofa without imagining him there wreaking sweet havoc on my body, but I suspected the experience wouldn't be easily dismissed.

Growling with impatience and frustration, I jumped up again, resolutely keeping my gaze averted from the wide expanse of the sofa as I left the room. Half an hour later, I conceded that I wouldn't get to sleep without expelling the sexual energy coursing through my blood.

As I reached for my vibrator, I cursed Jasper Mortimer loudly and succinctly. Then ruthlessly used his image to find a quick, semi-satisfactory but thankfully mind-numbing release.

I stepped out of the cab and paused on the pavement, tilting my head up to stare at the majesty that was Mortimer Towers. During my previous visits I'd used the barrier of righteous indignation to ignore its grandeur and, while I couldn't predict what would happen in the next hour, I instinctively felt today was...different. That it wouldn't be so bad to admit the masterpiece building that had won a clutch of accolades was worthy of them.

Or perhaps it was because I'd accepted on some level that the man I was dealing with was a lot more powerful than I'd given him credit for, and that power could irreversibly impact Bingham's.

Certainly, my visit to my company's archive department yesterday had uncovered the worst of my fears. Perry had been playing fast and loose with several contracts and had 'misplaced' important documents that could have severe repercussions on our business relationships.

That shocking discovery was the reason I'd buried myself in the basement of Bingham's till late last night. I was still staggered by how much Perry had been allowed to get away with by the board.

But truly, when it came right down to it, I wasn't surprised. The board was made up of the extended Bingham relatives and cronies who'd trusted Perry simply because he was male, and a Bingham. There'd been little to zero oversight and no one had dared to question his way of doing business. Just as long as he'd managed to keep the company just above the red and they collected their fat bonuses come Christmas.

Which reminded me…no Christmas bonuses this year.

I sucked in a deep breath, lowering my gaze to the glass doors that led into Jasper's domain. After a restless night that my vibrator had done very little to cure, I'd given up on sleep at five o'clock. The boutique contract was fixed and an email sent to the subcontractors apologising and withdrawing the clause I'd inserted in the last-chance hope that it would frustrate Jasper into releasing me from the contract.

We both know you're better than this…

Perhaps more than anything else that had happened in my flat last night, those words had made the most impact. Because Jasper was right.

Despite my attempts to aggravate him into dropping this deal, a significant part of me had cringed at the depths I was sinking to; the mockery I was making of my own hard-won achievements.

I hadn't quite decided what the new course of action in fighting him would be but I most certainly wasn't going to lie down and let him walk all over me.

Heat caressed my neck and flowed up into my face at the sexual connotation of my thoughts. I'd been more than prepared for him to do exactly that on my sofa last night. Firming my lips, I attempted to push the memory out of my head as I strode towards the lift.

His receptionist greeted me when I stepped out on his floor.

'Good morning, Miss Bingham. Mr Mortimer is waiting for you in conference room six. He says you're to go straight through.'

I told myself my escalating heartbeat was because I was irritated that he'd assumed I would turn up this morning. Not because I wanted to see him again. Not because the smell of his aftershave on my skin and the rasp of his stubble burn on my inner thighs had made me groan into my pillow more than once last night.

And most definitely not because he knew that two of the three company names he'd thrown at me last night were threatening to pull out of their deals with us.

Struggling to empty my mind of the challenges that awaited me back at Bingham Industries, I took a few calming breaths. I'd need optimal mental dexterity to survive this meeting with Jasper.

Running a hand over my stylish skirt suit, I strode down the wide hallway, pinning a cool, professional smile on my face as I passed his executives. I was absolutely not going to wonder how many of them had seen my trench-coat-and-promiscuous-heels performance. I'd been forced into a corner, and doing something was better than doing nothing and letting Jasper win.

What if it was all for nothing?

I mentally shrugged, gritting my teeth when I noticed that conference room six was the last one down a long hallway. Had Jasper orchestrated this walk of shame so his employees would see me? Was he that petty?

A flash of anger whipped through me, threatening

to wipe away my smile. I fought to keep it in place as I pushed the door open.

He stood at a long cabinet that bordered the far wall, helping himself to a cup of the same java blend his secretary had offered me that first visit. As I breathed in that mouth-watering hit of caffeine and watched the ripple of broad shoulder muscles encased in another immaculate suit, I wondered whether I would associate this particular brand of coffee with him for ever.

He turned just then, a small smile playing around his lips as his gaze tracked me from head to toe and back again. As he noted my attire his smile widened, what looked dangerously like triumph gleaming in his eyes.

I forced my gaze away, partly because I didn't want to confirm it and partly because in the morning light, with the sun streaming in, he looked far too delicious for my sanity. Reminded me far too vividly of how thoroughly I'd explored his body last night.

How I craved more?

'Can I get you anything? Coffee? I've had breakfast laid out for us if you're hungry.'

I shook my head. 'I'll take the coffee, but I don't want any breakfast. I've already eaten.' He didn't need to know it had only been a couple of bites of toast, hurriedly wolfed down because I'd got caught up in another woefully mismanaged Bingham file and almost missed leaving on time to get here for his eight o'clock deadline.

He nodded and poured a second cup, then added a dash of cream. When he reached me, he stared at me for a handful of seconds before holding out the cup. 'Good morning, Wren. You ready to begin?'

His voice was a low rumble that travelled through me, reminding me how his lips had felt trailing the sensitive skin of my neck. The sweet abrasion of his stubble against my breast. The filthy decadence of his tongue capturing and swirling around my nipple.

I accepted the cup without answering. Saying yes would be deemed surrender and I couldn't give in, not until I'd exhausted every avenue. Because while I could rightly claim that Perry had been the one to agree to this deal, it wouldn't stop another confrontation with my board, another round of questioning my decision and intentions. Another call from my mother under the guise of checking in on me but really to lament about the path I was taking.

Shaking my head, I approached where the papers were laid out.

'Wren?'

Refocusing on him as he joined me, I glanced at him. His expression was just as resolute as last night, but his eyes held the gentleness that conveyed understanding of my predicament. My guts tightened against the need to sink into that gentle look. It was the opposite of what I needed.

I set down my briefcase and coffee and pulled out a chair. 'I have a long day ahead. Shall we get on with it?' I said crisply.

His gentle expression evaporated, and his face hardened but he joined me at the table, pulling out the chair for himself before settling into it.

'I checked with the subcontractors this morning. Looks like this morning you withdrew your magnanimous offers?'

I wasn't going to give him the satisfaction of admitting my impetuous mistake. 'Is that a question?'

He smiled. 'Just an observation. And an offer of thanks for one less pain in my arse.'

I'd gripped that taut arse last night. Heat tunnelled through me and I moved my gaze to the papers in front of me. 'Sure. Shall we move on to the next item on the agenda?'

He nodded, then took a sip of coffee.

I tried not to let my gaze drop to his lips. I really did. But a mere eight hours ago those lips were devouring mine, and, as much as I hated to concede it, he was one hell of a kisser. Combined with the knowledge of how much sweet havoc he could wreak with those lips between my legs, surely I could forgive myself for five seconds of indulgence?

'Do you need a minute, Wren?' he asked, a thread of amusement in his voice.

My gaze shot up to meet his and he was smiling knowingly. Without breaking eye contact, he nudged the agenda sheet towards me. 'I went to the trouble of printing it out in case you didn't check your emails this morning. So we can be on the same page, as it were,' he added with a definite smirk.

I picked up the paper and quickly scrutinised it. There were twelve items on the list, mostly spelling out in black and white the tasks I was supposed to perform. I already knew the hours I was supposed to devote to the project but one item in particular made me glance up sharply.

'You expect me to go to dinner with you on Wednesday?'

He nodded briskly. 'A tequila producer I've had my eye on for a while is in town this week. He has a new specialised brand coming out around the time we open the first hotel. I want you with me because technically this should have been your job but I'm hoping you'll help me convince him to supply exclusively to us for at least three months before he rolls it out to the general market.'

I frowned. 'I already had a supplier lined up for you.'

'Did you?'

The tight edge to his question made me pause for a second before answering. 'Yes, I did.'

'That's curious. Because I'm sure there's an email in my inbox telling me we'd lost our potential liquor supplier due to non-communication with Bingham Industries.'

The throb of shame was more powerful this time. I tried to hide it by taking a sip of my own coffee. Slightly more composed, I set the cup down. 'I've had lot on my plate, as you know. This project with you isn't the only thing occupying my time.'

He stared at me for another stretch of time before he nodded. 'I'm not too fussed about losing that supplier, to be honest. His product was great but not spectacular. This new one promises to be rather exceptional. That's why I don't want to lose it. So, you'll come with me on Wednesday, yes?' he pressed.

A business dinner with him to secure a supplier wasn't a complete concession. I'd been in this business long enough to know contractors came and went for any number of reasons. Even if Bingham Industries managed to pull out of the contract, I could at least help Jasper secure this small part of his project.

I shrugged. 'Sure, I can do dinner. What time do you want me?'

His eyes darkened. 'I'll pick you up at seven at your place,' he said, his voice deep and raspy.

It would've been far more professional to arrange to meet him at the restaurant. And yet, I found myself answering, 'Okay.'

His smile grew warmer, his gaze several degrees hotter as it dragged over my face to rest on my mouth. Time stretched taut and charged with far too much sexual intensity, before he stared down at the paper. 'What's next?'

We worked through the next few items, and with each one I reassured myself that nothing was set in concrete. Sooner or later, once Jasper realised the futility of a Mortimer-Bingham deal, replacing me would be a simple matter of snapping his fingers.

And if he didn't?

I dismissed the question. Just as I attempted to suppress the quiet excitement that was building inside me as we went down the list.

My head snapped up as Jasper abruptly rose. 'More coffee?'

A small bolt of surprise went through me as I re-

alised I'd finished mine. I nodded as he walked over
to the buffet cabinet, glancing at me over his shoulder.
'Are you sure I can't get you anything?'

I was about to refuse, but my gaze went to the clock
and I noticed we'd been working for an hour. As if on
cue, my stomach rumbled. It wasn't enough to get his
attention but I knew it would eventually if I carried on
working without eating.

Setting my pen down, I rose, rounded the conference
table and joined him. Trays of warm, mouth-watering
pastries were set out next to platters of fruit, juice ca-
rafes and assorted condiments.

Jasper grabbed two plates and handed me one.

Our fingers brushed as I took it from him. He heard
my sharp intake of breath and stilled, staring down at
me.

For several, electrifying seconds, we stayed frozen.

Then, as if pulled by invisible strings, I swayed towards him. At the very last moment, I caught myself,
veering away towards the food.

Dear God, what is wrong with me?

He'd gone down on me in the maze and, somehow,
I'd managed to work on and off with him for two weeks,
but one little tumble on my sofa last night and my concentration was shot to hell?

A little bewildered, I randomly selected food while
desperately attempting to downplay how badly Jasper
affected me. How badly I wanted to lean into that strong
column of his neck, breathe in the aftershave that had
so tantalised me last night.

Of course he'd put the brakes on then, though. Which meant, like me, he probably didn't think it was a good idea—

My thoughts stumbled to a halt when he laughed. 'That's the spirit. I love a woman with a healthy appetite.'

I blinked, then glanced down at my plate. My very full, very heaped plate of food. I cringed, aware of the flush creeping up my cheeks.

Then his words registered. Who was the last woman with a good appetite who'd occupied his attention? Did he have a girlfriend? It suddenly struck me that we'd had two sexual encounters without knowing the basics about each other. An uneasy, wholly unwelcome sensation tightened my chest. Surely, he wouldn't do the things he'd done to me if was seeing another woman?

He's a Mortimer, isn't he?

The twisting sensation inside me intensified.

'I guess you were pretty hungry, after all?' Jasper continued.

I dragged my focus from his imaginary harem to the embarrassment of my heaped plate. 'God, there's enough to feed an army here. I don't need all of this. Not really. I was just…'

Just wondering who else you were going down on when you weren't turning me inside out with your tongue…

As I shook my head free of the thought, he stepped closer. 'Here, I'll take a couple of those off your hands if you want.'

I watched, a little annoyed for being so easily distracted by him as he transferred a bagel and croissant from my plate to his. He left far more than I needed on my plate but somehow I didn't protest as his free hand landed in the small of my back, scrambling my brain as he guided me back to the table. 'Come on, let's get back to it,' he said.

In between watching him take healthy bites out of his food and attacking the next item on the agenda, I demolished several pastries, mentally promising myself another twenty minutes on the treadmill at my next gym session.

I didn't object when he returned to the buffet table and brought back a bowl of fruit, only squirmed stealthily in my chair as I watched him toss a grape into his mouth.

God, what the hell was so fascinating about watching this man eat? Whatever it was, I couldn't stop myself from watching him swallow, the movement of his Adam's apple curiously erotic enough to shoot arrows of desire into my pelvis.

'Are we done?' I asked, more out of desperation than anything else.

'More or less,' he replied.

'What else is there?'

For the longest time, he didn't reply. When he reacted, it was to reach into the fruit bowl and pluck out a ripe, juicy strawberry. Then he rolled his chair around the table, breaching the gap between us. 'There's something else I want to talk about.'

Something dark and decadent in his voice made my

thighs tingle, my breath rush out in a lustful little pant. 'Oh?'

'I feel the need to apologise for the way I left things last night.'

The reminder reduced the tingles but didn't demolish them altogether. 'You came to deliver a message and I received it loud and clear.'

'I'm not talking about business, and you know it.'

'Do I?'

He leaned forward, held the fruit against my bottom lip then trailed it lazily from side to side. 'I left you hanging,' he murmured throatily. 'I'm not in the habit of doing that.'

Curiously compelled, I licked the fruit before answering, 'I'm a big girl, Jasper. I can take it.'

His nostrils flared in arousal. 'Not if you don't have to.'

I sucked in a breath, the scent of the strawberry and his aftershave a potent mix that rendered me strangely breathless. 'You don't owe me anything…'

'Okay. But you still owe me one minute, possibly two.' He pressed the fruit harder against my mouth. 'Open,' he instructed gruffly.

My lips parted and I took the fruit. His gaze dropped to my mouth as I held it between my lips for a moment then bit into it. Sticky juice trickled down one corner of my mouth. His gaze latched on to it for one tight little second before, groaning, he lunged forward.

He devoured half of the fruit as he sealed his lips to mine.

As if a switch had been thrown, feverish electricity

consumed us as we consumed each other. He rose, his urgent hands landing on my waist to yank my body into his. My hands flew up his broad shoulders, explored for mere seconds before spiking into his hair.

Jasper's tongue delved into my mouth, licking away the last of the juices before tangling with mine. Desire shot through me, lifted me onto my tiptoes as I strained against him. Wanting more.

My vibrator last night had come nowhere close to satisfying the need clamouring anew inside me. The thought that Jasper was equally ravenous for me thrilled my blood as he deepened the kiss.

The faint sound of a ringing phone momentarily reminded me of where we were, the possibility that someone could walk in on us at any moment.

With a monumental effort, I broke the kiss and laid my hand on his chest as I fought to catch my breath. 'Jasper, I…the door…'

Without letting go of me, he walked us a few steps to the middle of the conference table and snatched up a small remote. Aiming it at the door, he clicked a button and I heard the distinct sound of it locking.

Burnished eyes pinned me where I stood. 'No one will disturb or hear us now. The room's soundproofed.'

My breath shuddered out, my fingers tightening on his nape even as I questioned my sanity. 'Jasper…'

He dropped his lips to my jaw, trailing little erotic bites before he caught my earlobe between his teeth. 'I regret not making you come last night. I sure as hell regret missing the chance to be inside you, even if it was only for one minute.'

My laugh emerged shakily. 'You're assuming I would've let you.'

Just like last night, his lips explored the pulse in my neck. Shivering in delight, I angled my head, granting him access.

'My negotiating skills are exceptional, Wren. I'm sure we would've come to some agreement had I stayed. But no matter. I have a new proposition for you. One I'm sure will satisfy us both.'

My arsenal was depleted. I had very little to fight him with. But he didn't need to know that.

'What is this proposition?' I asked, my insides dipping alarmingly at how much I wanted to know. How much I hoped it was something I could agree to.

Yeah, my head definitely needed examining.

He held on to me but eased his torso away from mine. 'You're brilliant and sexy. You've driven me insane thus far but I don't think I've hidden the fact that I want you. Hell, at this point it goes beyond want.' His eyes burned into mine as he inhaled slowly.

My throat dried at the raw, potent need in his voice. A tremble commenced inside my belly as he continued.

'Don't think I haven't noticed you still haven't given me a clear-cut answer as to whether you intend to work with me or not. But I have a way I think we can co-exist for the immediate future. A way that might make working with me a little more bearable?'

I didn't think there was any way forward that wouldn't incite my family's disapproval but I held back from mentioning it. Somehow, discussing family feuds in this moment felt…wrong. 'I'm listening,' I said.

He dropped his forehead to mine. 'You know I'm dying to fuck you. And I know you're not completely immune to reciprocating.'

I couldn't deny it. 'I think you got your answer last night.'

He gave a lopsided smile. 'Even though you also invited me to leave several times?'

I raised an eyebrow. 'You annoyed me. And I'm complicated.'

'Well, maybe this is one thing we can agree on. I'm great at giving you orgasms, despite withholding one last night.'

A husky laugh left my throat. 'Are you seriously tooting your own horn?'

He shrugged, an arrogant gesture that was so completely natural I wouldn't have been surprised if he'd been born with it. One hand trailed up from my waist to rest beneath my chin. His thumb rubbed my lower lip and I felt his erection jerk against my belly. Heat arrowed between my legs, making my core wet and needy as I waited for him to elaborate.

'Okay, here's the deal. For every six hours you devote to this deal, you get an orgasm.'

My mouth sagged open. 'I...what?'

His head dropped and delivered a hard, quick kiss before drawing back. Hazel eyes stayed on mine, his easy manner belied by the fact that every word out of his mouth held fierce determination, a promise to deliver on what he was offering. 'I think it's a better way for us to relieve our frustrations, if you like. Why scream with anger when you can scream with pleasure?'

I refused to examine why I wasn't completely outraged, why, contrary to every scrap of common sense I possessed, I was held rapt and completely aroused by his proposition. 'Let me get this straight. You want to buy my cooperation with orgasms?'

That wicked little smile tilted one corner of his mouth again. 'I want us to make love, not war,' he offered.

I raised an eyebrow. 'Wow, are you sure you're not on some two-for-one deal on clichés?'

His fingers dug into my waist to pull me closer still, ensuring I felt his hard cock against my belly. I shuddered, unable to help but push back, revelling in the power and promise of him. I was racked with mounting need; my gaze darted to the shiny expanse of the conference table.

Jasper followed my gaze and laughed. 'We can christen our new agreement right there, if you want, sweetheart.'

I swallowed, unable to believe that I was contemplating this absurdity. The excuse was that I'd arrived here with very little option but to continue to work with Jasper for the time being. Loyalty to my family dictated that the prize of working with the Mortimer Group was forbidden to me as a personal career choice, but while I was contract-bound to work with him, was it wrong to help myself to the cherry on top when he was freely offering it?

Between the mess Perry had left the company in and pressure from my mother, I didn't plan on dating anyone soon. Jasper's proposition ensured that we could work relatively friction-free, while enjoying a side benefit we both wanted.

The promise of sex lit a fuse in my blood. Before I got completely carried away with it, the question that'd niggled at me for the last hour rose again. 'Is this suggestion of yours inconveniencing anyone else?'

His brow knotted. 'What?'

'Are you dating anyone, Jasper?'

His frown cleared but his eyes remained mildly accusing. 'I'm not sure how to interpret you believing I would give you orgasms while seeing another woman.'

I tried to stop the wild relief flowing through me. 'Is that a no, you're not seeing anyone else?'

'It's a no,' he confirmed with gritted teeth. 'You may not have a very high opinion of me, but I do have some standards, sweetheart.'

His censure shamed me a little, but I brushed it away.

'I'm waiting for an answer, Wren. You want me, I want you. Are we going to do this, or not?' he pressed.

He was still doing that thing with his hips that drove me insane. Just as it had last night. That knot of need I thought I'd dampened with my vibrator came roaring back, stronger than before. The thought of walking out of here nursing that ache suddenly became unthinkable. Unbearable.

Keeping my gaze on his, I reached between us and unbuttoned my jacket. Slowly, I shrugged out of it, then tossed it on the nearest chair.

Jasper followed the action with eyes ablaze.

Next, I reached for his tie, loosening it before snapping it free of his collar. He swallowed, and I smiled.

Leaning forward and trailing my lips up to his throat, I whispered in his ear, 'I accept your proposal, Jasper.

And I'd very much like to christen your conference table. Now, please.'

He hoisted me up as if I weighed nothing, and between one frenzied heartbeat and the next I was laid out flat on his conference table and he was staring down at me with eyes that promised mind-altering passion.

CHAPTER SIX

I'D CHOSEN MY attire specially today because I'd needed the confidence boost; and because I'd accepted that the way I'd been handling things the past two weeks needed to change.

And perhaps—okay, extremely possibly—I'd also chosen my underwear because, deep down in a place I didn't want to examine too closely, I'd hoped *this* would happen.

Between frenzied kisses and the need to explore every inch of his sleekly muscled body, I wasn't certain which one of us undid my silk blouse. But I was certain which one stopped in their tracks, mouth hanging open at the sight of the sea-green lace bra I wore beneath it.

I hid a pleased smile as Jasper growled beneath his breath, his eyes rapt on my chest.

My lingerie was the indecently expensive kind, concocted of gossamer-thin scraps of lace, strings and silk, bought on a slightly tipsy whim while late-night online shopping, then shoved deep into the underwear drawer with much chagrin after the hangover wore off and the package arrived on my doorstep.

But in this moment, I patted myself on the back as Jasper's hands hovered reverently over my breasts, as if he wasn't sure whether to worship me or devour me.

'Jesus Christ, Wren. You're exquisite,' he breathed, his eyes darting from my chest to my face and back again.

'Not too exquisite to touch, I hope?'

He started to reach for me, then paused. 'Tell me you weren't wearing this underneath that damned trench coat when you came into my building two weeks ago?'

'Why would I want to stop torturing you by satisfying your curiosity?'

He raised an eyebrow, even while his frantic gaze dropped to latch onto my peaking nipples. 'Because we just agreed to call a truce?'

Trailing my finger down over the firm, tanned skin covering his clavicle, I decided to give a little. 'I wasn't wearing this exact same set, no. Now, are you going to unwrap me or make me wait?' I demanded softly.

With effortless ease, he divested me of my blouse. It landed on the floor, but I didn't care. Because my busy fingers had done some unwrapping of their own, exposing the most perfect set of abs I'd seen outside a magazine. I touched his skin, almost moaned at how warm and firm and utterly delicious he was. About to put my mouth where my hands had been, I whimpered in protest as Jasper pushed me back firmly.

Reading his intent, I relaxed, reclining on the table as he stepped back, took me in, then groaned. 'I'll never be able to take a meeting in this room without picturing you like this.'

'You'll get through it somehow, I'm sure.' I arched my back, the cool surface momentarily chilling my skin; making my nipples harder. He saw the reaction and charged forward with another animalistic snarl.

'I don't like being the only one without a shirt on, Jasper.'

Cracking a taut smile, he jerked off his jacket and tossed it away. A crook of my finger and he was leaning over me. Strong hands framed my hips, trailed up my ribcage as I attacked his remaining shirt buttons. The moment I bared his chiselled torso, I dragged my fingernails over his taut, smooth skin.

'Fuck, that feels good,' he groaned, his gaze latching on to the lace doing a very poor job of hiding my arousal from him. 'As much as I'm dying to get you naked, I don't want to risk ripping anything off...this time. We both need to walk out of here with as many of our clothes intact as possible.' He cupped my lace-clad breasts, squeezing with an urgency that telegraphed his need. 'Help me out?' he requested hoarsely.

I wanted to tell him to rip it off, if only for the novelty of experiencing such raw passion for the first time in my life. But I bit my tongue. There were other ways to achieve the mindless state his eyes promised. Trailing my fingers back up his torso to his neck, I dropped my other hand to the first strap and slowly lowered it. 'Like this?'

His head jerked in a nod. 'More,' he commanded.

I tugged down the strap another fraction, bearing the top of my breast and exposing the smallest hint of a nipple.

'More, Wren. More. Show me those perfect breasts I tasted last night.'

'Hmm, how do I know you're not going to leave me hanging again?' I teased.

A dash of hectic colour highlighted his cheekbones. He nudged my hips to the edge of the table, until there was no mistaking his hard, potent ridge. 'I promise, this time I'm not stopping until every inch of my cock is buried inside you. Now, please take that damn bra off before I rip it off with my teeth.'

A shiver coursed through me, pooling heat between my thighs. I felt myself getting wetter and sucked in a deep breath to compose my erratic heartbeat. I was dying for him to take me, and, though I suspected this would be more memorable than my previous sexual encounters, I still wanted him to work for it. My instincts warned me that giving in too easily to Jasper Mortimer was the absolute wrong tactic to take.

With a saucy little smile, I abandoned the bra and reached for the hem of my skirt. He watched me, his face tightening with every passing second as I nudged the material up my thighs until my panties were exposed. A projection in my mind's eyes of how I looked—semi-naked and sprawled out, open to his gaze—sent a hot rush through me, followed swiftly by a pulse of feminine power as I caught his expression. He liked this. Hell, he more than liked it. In a fight where it seemed I was losing at every turn, it felt good to reclaim some ground.

'Take my panties off, Jasper,' I instructed, my voice a husky mess. 'The bra stays on.'

He didn't need a second bidding.

He dragged my panties off with a smooth move that made my heart miss several beats. And in the flip of a switch, I sensed a shift in the power balance. Firm hands grasped my thighs, parted them boldly so he could stare down at my damp flesh. A deep breath expanded his chest as he passed his thumb over my engorged clit. My whole body jerked, a spasm of pleasure rippling through me at that smallest touch.

Lust-dark eyes darted to my face and then back to my core. 'I'm going to enjoy fucking you, Wren,' he declared with gruff anticipation.

His dirty words made me hotter; more impatient. I tried to grasp him with my thighs, nudge him closer, to get this show on the road. Jasper merely smiled, put his thumb to his lips and decadently sucked off my wetness as he looked into my eyes.

'You want it hard or slow?'

Again, I felt my face flaming, even as excitement fluttered in my belly. No other man had ever asked me that. And how pathetic was that? Or had I not been interested enough before to vocalise my own needs?

'Do I have to choose? Can't I have both?'

His smile widened, the confident stamp of a man who knew how to wield his sexual prowess. 'You can have whatever you want, sweetheart.'

I swallowed at his thick promise; watched him reach into his back pocket for his wallet. He plucked out a condom, tore it open and gifted me another erotic sight of watching him slowly lower his zip.

I already knew he was thick and long, but I wasn't

quite prepared for the beautiful sculpture of Jasper's cock or the pleasure I took in watching him glide on the condom.

Then he was reaching for my thighs, dragging me even closer to the edge of the table. Breathing harshly, he teased his length over my hot, wet core without entering me, his eyes on my face as he tormented me.

Wrapping his hands around my waist, he tilted his hips in one smooth movement and thrust deep inside me. A curious little sound left my throat, a cross between a muted scream and sheer delight at how deeply, completely he filled me. Then for the longest time he held still, his eyes shut and jaw locked tight.

'Again, please,' I gasped.

Exhaling, he withdrew, slowly...and repeated the penetration. Fiery desire shot up my spine, my hands scrambling for purchase on the table. 'Oh, God, again. Please,' I begged.

He gave a low, ragged laugh and started to thrust in earnest. My breath shortened, panted as he fell into a steady, mind-bending rhythm. My eyes drifted closed as pleasure collected deep in my pelvis but after a moment, I prised them open, the need to watch Jasper too overwhelming to deny.

And he was a glorious sight. His hooded gaze was rapt on my face, a lock of hair draped over his forehead as he shuttled in and out of me. Dear God, he was beautiful. An animal. One concentrated fully on me. The fierce light in his eyes said he would deliver on every single sexual promise he'd made.

'Tell me more, Wren,' he urged thickly. 'I want to hear everything you're feeling.'

I wasn't sure why that demand rattled something inside me. When was the last time anyone had asked me what I felt? All my life I'd been subjected to what everyone believed was good for me without considering my input. I knew this was just sex, that he'd set himself a goal he was determined to achieve, but something inside me still lurched as I scrambled around for adequate words to describe this unique experience. 'It feels good. So good.'

'What else?' he demanded, a touch harshly.

'The way you're holding me down. I like it.'

His fingers convulsed on my waist, tightening briefly as he pulled me into another thrust. A tiny scream left my throat, the sensation sharper, even more exquisite. 'Yes! More of that. Faster.'

'Fuck yes,' he breathed, as if I'd delivered the very thing he wanted. He dragged me lower until my bottom hung off the edge of the table. Arranging my legs up until they were curled around his neck, he leaned forward, plastered his lips over mine in a dirty, carnal kiss; a brief but frantic duelling of the tongues before he surged back up. His breath emerging in harsh pants, Jasper widened his stance and slammed even harder inside me. A louder scream left my throat, my back arching off the table as sublime sensation curled through me.

'Come for me, sweetheart. I need to feel you come all over my cock.'

Needing somewhere on his body to anchor myself,

I wrapped my fingers around his forearms. Moments later, I smashed through the barrier of no return.

'Oh, God, I'm coming,' I whispered, a strange transcendental sensation washing over me as I was thrown headlong into my climax. It arrived as a forceful tsunami, threatening to rip me apart from the inside. My nails dug into his arms when bliss crashed over me, dragging me deep, deeper than I'd ever been before in my life. Longer than I'd ever experienced.

When the storm abated, when I could again prise open eyes I couldn't remember closing, it was to find Jasper propped on his elbows over me, his incisive eyes absorbing my every twitch and gasp.

A half minute passed before I realised he was still hard and solid inside me. Shock must have registered because he gave a tight smile, his face a mask of deep arousal, ruthlessly controlled.

'Did I leave you hanging?' I attempted to tease, although the shifting emotions inside me left me wildly unsettled in the aftermath.

'That one was for you. Watching you come was a pleasure I wasn't about to deny myself.'

'But?'

He didn't answer immediately. His head dropped a few inches, his mouth taking my nipple and sucking hard before, at the sensitive shiver coursing through me, he raised his head.

'But now I get to experience what it feels like to come inside you.' His voice was a raw throb of anticipation that tingled every nerve in my body.

Before I could draw breath, he snatched me off the

table. He disengaged long enough to flip me around and repositioned my legs, until my feet met the floor, and then bent me over the conference table.

Then, as if he had all the time in the world, Jasper ran his fingers through my hair, over my neck and down my spine. He unclasped my bra, trailed kisses where his hands had been, and cupped my breasts. As if he knew how sensitive I was, he merely squeezed and fondled them for another minute without teasing my nipples. Then he nudged me upright; my back to his hot, muscled chest, he wrapped one arm around my waist. 'Raise your arms, Wren. Wrap them around my neck,' he whispered in my ear.

Wearing my heels and stockings with my skirt around my waist and my arms angled backwards around his neck, I felt dirty and decadent. Apparently, he thought so too because his breathing grew frantic and rapid. 'You have any idea how long I've imagined you like this?'

I smiled. 'Hmm, roughly about two weeks?'

He laughed. 'Try a whole lot longer, sweetheart.'

With that, he thrust upward inside me.

Every single thought dissolved from my brain as Jasper began to fuck me again.

With his free hand he explored me, from chest to thighs and in between, and when I began to lose my mind again, and his thrusts grew erratic and much deeper than I thought possible, his fingers delved between my folds, expertly strumming my clit in exquisite motions that sent me surging into the stratosphere once again.

His head aligned with mine, I heard his low growls as I started to come. 'Christ, Wren. You feel fucking amazing. So tight and hot and beautiful. *Yes, yes, yes,*' he hissed in sync with his thrusts as we drowned in our mutual orgasm.

Coming down from the second high was just as surreal, and when he pulled out of me and perched me on the table, a twinge of loss staggered me. Watching him stroll to the cabinet, I felt weirdly unmoored, turned inside out as I struggled to get my emotions under control.

None of my previous encounters had affected me this much. But this was still just sex. Great sex. It was the height of stupidity to get emotional or evangelical about it. I repeated those words feverishly to myself as he returned. Striving for composure, I lifted my head, meeting his gaze with a cool smile as he set down the stack of tissues on the table. 'May I?' he asked.

What little poise I'd scrambled together threatened to evaporate at his request.

Stop it. This didn't mean anything. So he cared about my comfort. Big deal. About to tell him I was a grown woman and he didn't need to attend to me, I found myself biting my lip and nodding.

The gleam in his eyes said my answer had pleased him but in the next moment the expression was gone. Surrealness engulfed me again as he cleaned me up, then, plucking my panties off the floor, he sank low and looked up at me. Our gazes connected, I stepped back into my underwear and he pulled it up my legs slowly, his gaze dropping once to rest on my pussy for a long, prolonged moment before sliding the underwear back into place.

Perturbed by how unnerving his aftercare was, how needy it made me feel, I jerked upright and cleared my throat. 'I need to get going.'

Jasper rose calmly, stepped forward and spiked his fingers through my hair. Tilting my face up, he dropped a soft, brief kiss on my lips.

With every cell in my body, I wanted to prolong the kiss. I sucked in a breath when he stepped away, the loss echoing inside me.

God, what the hell is wrong with me?

A little desperately, I retrieved my bra, slipped it back on before reclaiming my blouse. I kept my back to him as I buttoned it up and slipped on my jacket. On slightly firmer ground, I passed my own fingers through my hair and then gathered my papers off the table.

And turned around to discover Jasper was fully dressed, too. Hell, he was so immaculately put back together, it was as if he'd had way too much experience at this.

Nope. I most definitely wasn't going to think about how often he'd done this. I'd never been possessive or jealous about sexual partners in my life. I wasn't about to start.

'Are we good?' he asked, walking towards me.

My head shot up. 'Of course.'

His gaze raked my face before, nodding, he reached for the control and unlocked the door. 'Good. I'll walk you out.'

I tightened my fingers around my briefcase. This

was stupid. I should welcome the chance to escape this room, to regroup. Nevertheless, when his hand arrived in the small of my back, I couldn't help the shiver that coursed through me. I had a long hallway to traverse before I got into the lift; a long hallway where his employees would probably catch a glimpse of my dishevelled state.

'Are you sure everything's okay?' Jasper asked, a frown between his eyebrows.

I started to nod, but then paused.

He leaned down, trailing his lips over my cheek before kissing the corner of my mouth. 'There's a quicker way out of the building if you prefer?'

I looked up, hating myself for the relief bursting through me. Then a thought scythed through the feeling. I glared at him. 'Do you sneak all your lovers through the back door?'

His eyes narrowed. 'Believe it or not, this is the first time I've done it in here. I don't intend it to be the last time though. With you.'

I hated the spurt of excitement that sprang up in my belly. 'The front door will be just fine.'

He smiled, and again I got the funny feeling that I'd pleased him. Mentally, I shook my head. I really needed to get out of here.

Thankfully, the office floor was less busy. And Jasper in calm, professional mode as he walked me to the lift eased my nerves. About to utter a brisk, professional goodbye, I looked up in surprise when he walked into the lift with me. 'What are you doing?'

He didn't answer until the lift doors shut. Then he stepped into my space again, one hand cupping my nape.

'I need one last kiss,' he said gruffly. He sealed his mouth to mine, tongue curling round mine in a kiss so possessive, so hot and sexy, my toes curled. All too soon, the lift reached the ground floor and the doors parted. With clear reluctance, Jasper released me. But not before he caressed his knuckles down my cheek.

'Have a good day, Wren.' And then, as I shakily stepped out of the lift, he added, 'I'll see you back here tonight at six.'

Before I could ask what he was talking about, the doors slid shut.

A little breathless and a whole lot flustered, I stumbled out of his building then paused on the pavement to check the email that had pinged into my inbox. Jasper.

Six hours until your next orgasm. We can use up three of those hours working tonight. Don't be late.

I tried to summon all the righteous indignation I could think of. But as I hurried to my office, all I could think of was how good he'd felt inside me. How the day was going to absolutely drag until I saw him again. How quickly I could make up the extra three hours I needed.

How much I feared—with addiction stamped into my family's DNA—that I was already way too obsessed with Jasper Mortimer's sexual prowess.

CHAPTER SEVEN

THAT BRACING, TERRIFYING thought turned out to be the impetus I needed to block Jasper from my mind for the better part of the morning, despite my phone pinging intermittently with text messages from him. Even the perfectly valid reasoning that answering his texts could be deemed work and therefore contribute towards my six-hour accumulation terrified me a little when my heart leapt at the idea.

Perhaps fate thought it prudent to deliver me from my increasingly frantic Jasper-induced withdrawal symptoms. Because just before midday, when the door to my office swung open, my heart lurched for one giddy moment at the thought that it was him, before plummeting at the sight of the woman framed in the doorway, dressed from head to toe in designer white, complete with radiant pearls.

I couldn't help but wonder if my mother's inability to feel affection for me was because she resented me for choosing to earn my living rather than marry into it, as she had.

Stifling the bruising thought, I looked past her to

a visibly flustered Alana who mouthed *Sorry* before hurriedly closing the door. 'Mother. Did we have an appointment?'

'You're not senile, Wren, you know we don't. Just as you know the reason I don't have an appointment for this meeting is because you've been avoiding my calls. You've left me no choice but to chance this visit. And you know how I feel about impropriety.'

I gritted my teeth, wondered for a wild moment if one of Jasper's texts had included an invitation for a working lunch. And whether I should've accepted it.

No.

If my mother was the frying pan, Jasper was most definitely the fire. Regardless of how pleasurable it'd been to dance in the flames this morning, I needed to pace myself or risk being incinerated. Inhaling calm, I rose from the desk, approached where my mother was pulling off stylish winter gloves to drop them along with her designer handbag on the coffee table. My spirits sank lower at the sign that this wasn't going to be a quick visit.

'I'm sorry, I've been busy. What can I help you with?' I asked, keeping my voice even.

Eyes a shade lighter than mine studied me with cool assessment. 'There's something different about you.'

Oh, Christ.

I sucked in another calming breath and reminded myself I was a grown woman, not a child terrified of chastisement or one desperate for her mother's approval. Or, heaven forbid, her mother's love or whatever dregs remained after she'd already given the lion's share of it to her husband and son. 'I'm not sure I know what you mean, Mother.'

One well-plucked eyebrow rose. 'Don't you? Maybe not. But you were definitely more…flappable the last time I saw you.'

I wasn't going to admit, even to myself, that the skirmish with Jasper had helped me tap into confidence and determination reserves that had been in danger of dwindling recently. Perhaps it wasn't even the sex. Maybe it was accepting that negotiating a better deal with Jasper was better than opposing him and letting Bingham's go down in a fiery blaze. Whatever. For now, I was keeping the wolves away from the company door and I wasn't ashamed about it. 'Perhaps it was because you knew where Perry was and what he was up to but decided not to share it with me?'

My mother was too cultured to roll her eyes but not averse to pursing her lips and delivering a frostier stare. 'Your brother is in Arizona now, getting the help he needs. Let's be thankful for that and not drag him into this, shall we?'

'And what exactly is this?'

She took her time to sit, crossing her long, shapely legs. I thought about offering her tea, then suppressed the urge. Instinct warned me that the reason for her visit wouldn't go down well, tea or no tea. And I wasn't going to prolong it more than necessary. 'You've been seen colluding with that Mortimer boy again, Wren.'

Several protests rushed to the tip of my tongue. Firstly, that Jasper wasn't a boy but very much a man, in every sense of the word. Secondly, that I couldn't wait to *collude* with him again. In various positions I hadn't been able to stop myself from imagining all morning. 'Again?' I echoed, buying myself a little time.

'Anyone with decent eyesight saw you two at the party. And you've been seen at the Mortimer building, too.'

'Because we're partners in a business deal, Mother. A business deal Perry signed with him, which you already know about. Even if you didn't before, I know you have eyes and ears on the board now.'

'And you assured that same board that you would fix any tiny lapses your brother committed while he wasn't quite himself. Or did I get that wrong?'

My heart hammered against my ribs, this time with anger and pain. 'You may not want to hear it, Mother, but the problems Perry left behind are a lot more than *tiny lapses*. I'm just trying to make the best of the situation we now find ourselves in.'

Her face hardened. 'Is that your way of telling me you're about to let this family down? Need I remind you that it's exactly because of *that* family that we find ourselves in this situation in the first place?'

The vise tightened around my heart. 'I'm sorry you think I'm letting you down by doing everything I can to save our company. Would you prefer a complete stranger take over, one without the family's best interests at heart?'

She waved me away with a flick of her wrist. 'Now you're just being overdramatic. If your father or Perry were here—'

'But they're not!' The sharp rebuttal stopped us both

in our tracks. A flash of pain crossed her face and I swallowed the sudden lump in my throat. 'They're not, Mother,' I repeated firmly. 'But I am. And I'm doing my best. I promise. Please trust me?'

The plea earned me nothing but a colder stare, which in turn hardened the edges of my pain. 'And I hate to say this, but regarding the feud—are we really blameless?' Was Jasper right? Maybe we needed to lance this boil once and for all, give the wound a chance to heal.

Or maybe not; judging by the paleness of her cheeks and the tightening of her jaw, my mother wasn't of the same mind. 'How dare you?'

I pressed a hand to my eyes. 'How dare I? Maybe I'm tired of fighting, Mother. Maybe I just want to use my energies to save this company rather than perpetuating a ridiculous fight that should've ended decades ago.' I dropped my hand.

She surged to her feet, her eyes flashing disappointment that shouldn't have eviscerated me, but did. 'Your father would be ashamed of you.'

Pain lacerated deeper, enough to drive my fingers into the back of the sofa opposite where she sat. 'Just as you are?'

Her delicate nostrils flared, the exquisite cheekbones standing out in relief as she stared at me. 'Excuse me?'

'Nothing I've ever done has been good enough for you, has it?'

Her mouth worked but no words emerged for several seconds. Then, 'You've known since you were a child what I expected of you—'

'What about what I wanted for myself? Did that

count for anything at all?' I blurted, aware my emotions were in danger of running away with me.

'What counts, my dear, is that you seem determined to do the opposite of what's expected of you. I've never understood that about you.'

As usual I was getting nowhere. My mother was entrenched in her thinking where I was concerned. No amount of talking would sway her. So I shook my head. 'I don't want to do this now, Mother.'

'I should think not. I'm not sure what's got into you, but you need to remind yourself where your allegiances lie. Your brother most certainly did.'

For a moment I experienced a resurgence of that searing jealousy I'd tried to suppress for so long. My mother's blind love for my brother and father had made me wonder what I lacked that her love couldn't extend to me. For so long, I'd hated that I couldn't answer the question. In my weakest moments, I still did.

But I'd learned to survive without that emotion in my life, hadn't I? Surely in time I'd learn to do without altogether? The hollow inside me mocked that forlorn hope. If I could live without it, then why had Jasper's gentleness affected me so much? Why did I, even now, yearn for it when the probability of it being ephemeral—like my mother's regard—was the true reality?

Just sex. Given and taken. That was all I had to give Jasper. It was delusional to believe I *could* give anything more when my reservoirs had never been filled.

'Is that all? I have work to do, Mother.'

Her lips pursed, then she snatched her gloves and bag off the table. 'If my feelings and opinion are worth anything to you, Wren, then you'll think harder about distancing yourself from the Mortimer boy. His family have brought us nothing but grief and if they've done it once, they'll do it again. Nothing you say will convince me otherwise.'

She sailed out without deigning to deliver the air-kiss she normally dispensed when we were in public. I told myself I was glad, but the searing realisation that I craved even that small show of false affection made my gut twist in mild sorrow.

God, was I really that needy?

I was still mired in that maelstrom of anguish and anger when my phone rang minutes later. I reached for it without stopping to check the caller. And experienced a different emotion entirely when Jasper's deep, sexy voice flowed into my ear. 'Sushi or Greek food?'

I scrambled to focus. 'Umm...what?'

'Your choice for lunch.'

'Neither.' My appetite was non-existent after dealing with my mother. 'I wasn't planning on eating lunch. I had a very big breakfast,' I replied, then felt heat swelling through me at the double entendre.

The wickedly sexy man on the other end of the phone laughed, sending electrical currents along my nerve endings, making a mockery of my effort to keep him at arm's length. 'Hmm, so you did.'

'Wow, seriously?'

His laughter deepened, surprisingly numbing a layer of my pain. 'Your fault, sweetheart. You teed that up nicely for me.'

I felt a smile playing at my lips and immediately killed it. 'Thanks for the offer of lunch, but no, thanks.'

Jasper went silent for several moments. 'What's wrong?' he asked.

My fingers tightened on my phone. 'What makes you think anything is?'

'Don't play games with me, Wren. We're past that.'

That suggested a new level of relationship I wasn't sure I was ready for, even business-wise. And yet, I found myself answering, 'I had a disagreement with… someone.'

'A board member?' he pressed.

'No.'

'Your mother?'

A gasp left my throat before I could stop it. 'How do you know?'

'Wild guess. With Perry temporarily out of the picture, I'm thinking it could be one of three problems— board, family or lover. And since I'm your lover and I'm being on my best behaviour…'

The remainder of his deductive reasoning melted away, his words eliciting a fizzle of warmth.

Jasper Mortimer. *My lover.*

Lover. Love.

The smile evaporated.

No.

'Wren?'

I snapped back into focus. 'Yes?'

'Tell me what's wrong.'

God, why did that occasional gentleness from Jasper erode every ounce of my resistance? Why did I want to bask in it, roll around in it until I was covered head to toe in warmth?

Because you've never experienced a bona fide version of it. Surplus recycled affection has never been enough for you. Never will be.

But was it wise to accept it from Jasper? Was fate really that twisted as to show me a glimpse of what affection looked like from the very last person I could accept it from? Of course, it was. Because wasn't karma that cruel? I inhaled a settling breath, but he spoke again before I could will common sense into our interaction.

'Before you tell me it's none of my business, know that I've been in your shoes,' he said, again in that calm, even voice. 'More or less.'

Curiosity swallowed me whole. 'How?'

His laugh was a little sharp. A little edgy. 'What's worse than a parent who tells you how to live your life?'

I frowned at the puzzle. 'I'm…not sure how to answer that.'

'Try parents who don't care at all.'

My heart squeezed, this time for the hardened bite of pain he didn't hide. 'I… I'm…' For whatever reason, the *sorry* stuck in my throat. Probably because, freshly bruised from my run-in with my mother, a part of me felt as if it was a betrayal to my family. Or maybe I didn't want even a sliver of softer feelings to slither through my cracks in case the floodgates tore wide open? Either way, bewilderment kept me silent.

'It's cool, Wren. Loyalty is a big deal to me, too, even when the people we're loyal to don't deserve it,' he murmured and, absurdly, tears prickled my eyes.

Jesus, I was pathetic. Determined to wrestle my feelings under control, I cleared my throat. 'Well. This has been fun and all, but I really need to get back to work.'

Expecting him to convince me otherwise, or at the very least remind me I was beholden to him via our contract, I was a little stunned when he said, 'Okay. Bye, Wren.'

Disappointment seared deep as I ended the call and set the phone down. Then spent an absurd amount of time analysing our conversation. What had his parents done to him? As far as I knew, Jasper's parents lived overseas. According to the grapevine, they hardly involved themselves in Mortimer businesses any more. Had their reclusiveness extended to their own children? Did I have more in common with Jasper than I wanted to?

Realising I was spending way more time dwelling on Jasper's phone call than I had my mother's visit, I fought to put both out of my mind. Until a knock on my door revealed yet another surprise, this time a smiling Alana holding a white takeaway box bearing a well-known exclusive Greek restaurant logo.

'This just arrived for you. It smells amazing,' she said, placing the box on my desk before departing.

The giddiness in my heart bloomed as I reached for the note taped to the side of the box. Opening it, I read the bold scrawl.

They may take your good mood, but never let them take your appetite.
Jasper

The note was so absurd I burst out laughing. On wild impulse, I grabbed my phone and sent a two-word message.

Thank you.

The speech bubble started immediately. Breath held, I waited for his reply.

My pleasure. Oh, and just for clarity, not answering my earlier texts doesn't mean it didn't count as work. I make that sixty-five minutes so far. Call me when you're ready to make up some more time.

I knew I should resist, that I was straying far too close to liking our skirmish-banter-tiny-moments-of-emotional-synchronicity, but I couldn't help reaching for my phone again as I opened the box and groaned at the heavenly smelling moussaka, feta cheese salad and tiny bites of grilled lamb. Helping myself to small portions of each dish, I went through his earlier texts, answering each query between bites.

He didn't answer until the last text and email was sent and I was stuffed to the gills after a final sinful bite of baklava.

Mood improved?

Eyeing the half-empty boxes, I smiled and answered.

Much. Thank you.

Any time. See you tonight.

I sailed through the rest of the day, surprisingly focused after my turbulent emotions, and when I arrived
at the Mortimer building to find Jasper caught up in another meeting, the idea that had been mushrooming at
the back of my mind on my way over sent me wander-
ing into the empty office next to his. He found me there
twenty minutes later, with my copies of the Moroccan
deal spread out on the desk while I pored over equip-
ment-delivery schedules and personnel management.

'Would it be totally sexist to say you look good behind that desk?' he drawled, leaning casually against
the doorjamb.

I bit my inside lip to stop myself from smiling. To
stop my insides from melting at the sight of him, tie
loosened, hair slightly dishevelled, his long legs and
spectacular body framed in a bespoke suit that highlighted his masculine perfection. 'Yes, it totally would.'

Hazel eyes glinted as he rounded the desk I'd appro-
priated and perched on the edge, his muscled thighs a
tantalising touch away. 'You should punish me for my
heinous crime, then,' he said in a low purr.

I sat back in my chair, futilely willing my racing
heartbeat to slow, while blatantly eyeing him from head
to toe. 'Hmm, I think I will. Just give me a few seconds
to devise an adequate torture.'

A sexy smile lifted the corners of his mouth and I
tightened my gut against the punch of need that threatened to leave me breathless. His eyes left mine to cast a

look around the room. 'I take it you've decided to make use of the office?'

I shrugged. 'Since the contract says I need to spend time here, I thought this was best.'

His smile widened. 'I agree,' he said, then those sinful eyes dropped to scrutinise my body just as I did his. He swallowed when his gaze reached the hem of my pencil skirt. Desire spiralling through my veins, I deliberately crossed my legs, allowing the hem to ride higher.

When his eyes met mine again, flames blazed high and dangerous. 'Two hours, forty minutes,' he murmured, reminding me of how much time we'd spent on work so far.

A rush of heated anticipation to my core almost made me groan. Correcting him to say he was off by a vital thirteen minutes felt a little too needy so I let it go. 'I have a bit more to catch up on, so I suggest you leave me alone.'

His gaze dropped to my lips, lingering for an indecently long time. 'Can I get a little bit of that punishment first?' he asked thickly.

No. Say no.

Of course I didn't. Because this morning already felt like a lifetime ago. And damn it, he'd fed me and made me feel better after that argument with my mother. What was wrong with a little give?

Relaxing even further in my chair despite wanting to jump him, I crooked my finger. Hunger deepening in his eyes, he gripped my arm rests, his face hovering over mine. Slowly, I wrapped my fingers around his loose tie and tugged him closer until he was a whisper away. Then I slowly licked my bottom lip.

With a deep groan, Jasper breached that last inch between us, yanked the chair close and fused his lips to mine. Decadent minutes of sliding tongues, playful nips and frantic groping later, I pushed him away.

'I really have work to do, Jasper. And you're wasting my time.' I cringed at the breathless mess of my voice.

He stayed where he was for another handful of seconds, his throat working, his eyes fixated on my kiss-bruised lips, savage hunger and a clear reluctance to end our entanglement pulsing from him.

And yes, it pleased a deeply needy part of me to see him fighting his own need for me. Battling to get himself under control. And when I spotted the thick bulge behind his fly, I fought a hard battle of my own. But ultimately, I knew this was for the best. That I needed this vital distance to control my needs. Before they escalated out of my control.

CHAPTER EIGHT

TWO HOURS, THIRTY-NINE MINUTES.

That time was emblazoned across my brain as I guided Wren into the exclusive restaurant in Fitzrovia on Wednesday evening to meet the tequila supplier.

The ambient lighting and tropical atmosphere of the Spanish fusion restaurant suited my mood and I watched the lights play on Wren's flawless skin as we approached our table. I'd been unable to take a complete breath since she stepped out of her front door wearing the sleeveless, thigh skimming, butt-hugging moss-green dress. The soft material clung to all the right places and I'd barely been able to keep my eyes on the road on the drive over.

I wasn't entirely sure whether to squander the entire time wining and dining this potential business partner and making her wait as payback for the way she'd tortured me for the last two days, or devote exactly two hours and thirty-eight minutes on Paolo Alonso and spend the last minute locating the nearest flat surface to rip Wren's panties off and drive myself into her snug pussy the way I'd been dying to do ever since the lift doors had shut between us on Monday.

Within fifteen minutes of us being seated, I sensed it would be the former, and not because of the need to torture Wren. Our guest seemed hell-bent on a different type of torturing of his own. Paolo was in no mood to discuss business. The Mexican businessman was only interested in regaling us with tall stories of his journey from simple farmer to multimillionaire tequila manufacturer.

Every attempt to steer the discussion back to business was merrily lobbed away.

I was hiding gritted teeth behind a sip of wine halfway through the main course when Wren leaned her elbows on the table and smiled at Paolo.

'La Tromba, the name of your tequila brand. That means whirlwind, doesn't it?' she asked.

Paolo grinned. 'It does, *sí*. I named it after my wife,' he mused. 'From the moment I met her until now, she has never stopped making my life…interesting.' A faraway look entered his eyes, private enough that Wren looked away. Straight into my eyes. I stared right back, not bothering to hide the depths of my hunger for her.

Her eyes widened a fraction, but, sweet heaven bless her, she didn't shy away from what I was projecting. Which was that I wanted her more than I'd ever wanted another woman. That I intended to have her the second our six-hour deadline was up.

She matched me look for look, her nostrils flaring slightly as she brazenly acknowledged my intent.

A throat cleared. Paolo. Had he asked a question?

Or merely narrated another anecdote? When I looked his way, he raised his glass in a silent salute, which I answered. 'To feisty women and all the exciting ways they keep us on our toes—eh, *amigo*?'

'Sure,' I responded, then grabbed the bull by the horns. 'So, are we doing business, Paolo?'

'It's probably prudent for me to take a day to think on it.'

'But come tomorrow you'll be saying yes, right?' Wren pressed. 'Because otherwise you'd be disappointing me greatly for misjudging you for an astute businessman.'

Shrewd admiration flickered in his eyes. 'Ah, the very fine art of complimenting and challenging that women seemed to have honed over the ages. How can I resist?'

Wren's gaze met mine and we both silently acknowledged that he still hadn't said yes. 'I've sent you all the paperwork. What will it take to convince you tonight?' she asked.

Another flicker of respect, then he set his shot glass down. 'For La Tromba to be the signature drink you serve on the opening night and for the next seven nights. You can throw your vintage champagne and whatever else you like at your guests, but I want my tequila to be the showpiece. Dare I say even base the whole event around it?'

'You aren't trying to hijack my launch by any chance, are you, Paolo?' I asked, my voice firm enough to reflect my seriousness.

He laughed. 'I'm striking a good business deal by

getting myself as much of the action as I can. You would do the same, my friend.'

'Seven days is out of the question. But I think we can make something work, can't we, Wren?'

She nodded. 'I'll speak to the event organisers, come up with something to show you by Monday. Provided you give us your agreement tonight,' she said, her eyes steady on his, her smile replaced by steely determination.

Paolo smiled. 'I understand why you brought her along, *amigo*. She drives a hard bargain.'

Wren's challenging gaze slid to mine, and I fought the urge to squirm in my seat. 'You have no idea.'

Paolo grinned and smacked his hand on the table. '*Bueno*, we have a deal.'

Wren smiled in triumph. She looked so stunning in that moment, I wanted to climb over the table and taste the beauty of it. The urge intensified as she snuck a glance at her watch. We'd been here close to two hours but Paolo was only halfway through the extensive tapas he'd ordered. At the very least we were looking at another forty-five minutes until this ordeal was over.

I forced myself to finish my steak and salad, my temperature skyrocketing with every sultry glance Wren slid my way.

I almost groaned in relief when the waiter arrived to clear away our plates. Only to glare at Wren when she smiled and asked, 'Would you like some coffee, Paolo?'

Before I could utter the strenuous objection firing up my throat, her left hand landed on my knee. Without glancing my way, she toyed with her small diamond pendant with her right hand as her left slowly caressed up my thigh.

Was she really about to stroke me into a frothing frenzy beneath the table? *Fuck yes*, my senses shrieked.

Paolo contemplated the tequila bottle with longing before he shook his head. '*Sí*, I'll take an espresso.'

I watched in frustration as the waiter hurried away to fetch the beverage, then I bit back a tight groan as Wren's clever fingers landed on my steel-hard cock. She stroked me through further small talk as we waited for the espresso, and then under cover of observing the waiter set out the coffee, her fingers slowly lowered my zip, reached inside the opening in my boxers and wrapped her hand around my hot length.

Sweet holy hell.

Stars burst across my vision as she stroked me harder, all the while smiling through another Paolo anecdote. When she toyed with the head of my dripping cock, smoothing the liquid over me in an expert pump, I gripped her wrist, terrified for a second that I would disgrace myself in the restaurant.

'Another nightcap, amigo?' Paolo asked, once he'd finally finished his drink.

'No!' I stopped, cleared my throat. 'I mean, I need to call it a night. I have an early morning meeting.'

He looked from my face to Wren's, a smile twitching at his lips before he nodded. 'You're right, I better get back to my hotel, too.'

As I reached for my wallet, I wrapped my fingers over Wren's, allowing her to stroke me one more soul-searing time before easing her away. And then she threatened to blow my head clean off when, under the guise of fixing her hair, she flicked her tongue over the fingers that were wrapped around me a moment ago.

The knowledge that she was tasting me, right there in front of our guest and restaurant patrons, was so shockingly arousing I knew I'd need five minutes to get myself under control before standing. As if she knew the havoc she'd created, she rose. 'I just need to dash off to the ladies. Shall I meet you at the front entrance, Jasper?'

'Sure,' I croaked.

She smiled, turned to Paolo. 'I'll be in touch in a few days, and I look forward to seeing you in Morocco at the launch.'

'If I didn't think you would do me bodily harm, my friend, I'd think of poaching that one from you,' Paolo said as Wren walked away.

My grin was all teeth, no humour as I stared him down. 'Yes, I would. So don't even think about it.'

He laughed and rose from the table. Jaw clenched and thankful for the low lights in the restaurant, I joined him as we headed for the door.

Once he left, I eyed the ladies' room, every cell in my body straining to storm through the doors, find the nearest empty stall and fuck Wren into a stupor. And damn the consequences. Before I could give in to the urge, I saw her walking towards me.

Bloody hell, she was gorgeous. I wanted her so badly, everything inside me ached with it. The novelty of it all stunned me for a moment, made me wonder if there wasn't something…*more* to all of this.

Then her perfume was filtering through my senses and I was cheerfully stepping back from examining that peculiar feeling. This was about sex. And business. Nothing more.

Yeah, right... That's why you told her about your rubbish parents. That's why you've been thinking about her non-stop for weeks. That's why something inside you tightened with unfamiliar concern when you heard the pain in her voice on Monday.

I pushed the mocking voice away and held the door open for her. In lust-charged silence we headed for my car, our strides picking up speed. It was past eleven at night and the street was quiet and dim. Enough for a torrid little quickie. But I didn't want that. Nor did I want to risk someone capturing us on camera. I wanted a feast. I wanted to gorge on Wren until this stark hunger inside me was assuaged. Then I wanted to feast some more.

Nevertheless, for a single moment when we reached my car, we stared at one another across the low hood, her eyes projecting everything we intended to do to each other.

The beeping of her phone wrenched us from the lust trance. When mine pinged five seconds later, the spark in my chest sent fireworks through my blood.

'You set your alarm for the six hours, too?' I asked, inordinately pleased that I wasn't caught in this madness alone.

She shrugged, although a bashful look crossed her face before she composed her expression. 'No need to work overtime if I don't have to.'

'Of course not. You're nothing if not super-efficient, right?' I teased.

The tiniest smile quirked her lips as she slid into the car. I gunned the engine, aiming the car towards the nearest main road when she asked in a low, raspy voice, 'Where are we going?'

My fingers tightened on the wheel. The moment I'd dismissed a quickie on the hood of my car, my mind had zeroed in on the next quickest option. Still, I forced myself to list them all. 'We have three choices. Your place. Mine. Or the penthouse suite at a hotel four minutes away.' My breath locked in my throat, praying she would choose the last option.

'Which hotel?' she asked, her gaze boring into me.

Mentally crossing my fingers, I answered, 'Mortimer Mayfair.'

Perhaps we weren't past the hurdles of our family history but surely she wasn't going to let that get in the way of what we both wanted?

We reached a traffic light and I turned my gaze on her. The look in her eyes was a cross between apprehension and rebellion. It was that same rebellion I'd seen during her interaction with her mother. Wren Bingham wasn't a woman who toed the line. I freely admitted it was partly what drew her to me. Was she going to throw caution to the—?

'Okay.'

Scarily heady sensations rushing through me, I caught her hand and pressed a kiss to her knuckles. 'Excellent choice.'

I shaved half a minute off our journey time. Using

the allocated private parking reserved for my family in the underground car park would add at least five minutes to our trip so I pulled up to the front of the hotel, tossing the keys to the valet the moment I stepped out.

A minute later we were in the private lift. To preserve that little bit of my fraying control, I parked myself in the opposite corner from her, but I still couldn't keep my eyes off her.

'You're looking at me with those caveman eyes again, Jasper,' she mused, reaching up to free her bound hair in one sexy little move.

Far from being offended, I laughed, then gripped the railing as her hair tumbled down around her shoulders. 'I can't help it, sweetheart. I'm going insane pondering where to start with you.'

Alluring green eyes on me, she reached into her clutch. I wanted to tell her refreshing her make-up was unnecessary since I intended to besmirch it all in the next five minutes. But she chopped me off at the knees by extracting the tiniest, laciest thong I'd ever seen, dangling it right in front of my face. 'Maybe this will help.'

'Fucking hell, Wren,' I croaked, every drop of blood rushing south until I was terrified I was actually going to pass out. 'You left the ladies' room without panties on?'

She stepped forward, raising the scrap of lace higher. 'I was a little too wet to keep wearing them, you see.'

My jaw dropped as the lift doors parted. I stood frozen as she closed the gap between us and tucked the panties into my handkerchief pocket, then sauntered out of the lift, her mile-long legs making short work of the hallway that led to the suite's double doors. She tossed her clutch on a nearby console table, then, with a saucy look over her shoulder, grasped the handles and pushed the doors open. 'Are you coming, Jasper?'

Sweet Lord in heaven, was I ever? I stumbled after her as she crossed the vast living room to stop in front of the floor-to-ceiling glass window. Below us, London was spread out in a carpet of lights. In the darkened room, all I saw was Wren's stunning silhouette as she braced her hands on the glass.

Before I reached her, I'd wrenched off my jacket containing the panties I was definitely going to keep and unfastened the first few buttons of my shirt.

'I like this view,' she said, casting another wicked look over her shoulder.

'Then stay there. Take it all in,' I suggested, intending to do some sightseeing of my own. I reached her, curled one hand over her plump buttocks as I swept her hair aside and dragged my lips along her elegant neck.

Her shudder and soft moan went straight to my cock. My hand tightened on her soft, rounded arse. 'I should spank this naughty little bottom for walking around with no panties on.'

Her shiver said she liked that idea. Very much. 'Do it,' she muttered, her hands spreading wide on the glass, even as her hips rolled into my groin.

'Fuck, Wren,' I groaned, the indecent thought of reddening her behind punching a fresh bolt of lust through me. With fingers that weren't quite steady, I tugged up her dress as my tongue licked up the side of her neck. The moment she was exposed, I delivered a light slap to her derriere.

A hot little gasp left her lips. 'Oh!'

'You like that?' I growled.

'Yes. Again,' she commanded.

My fingers delved into her hair, gripped her lightly and turned her head to receive my kiss as I spanked her again. I swallowed her next gasp, devouring it the same way I wanted to devour her. Two spanks later and we were both so excited I was in fear of this getting out of hand. Releasing her, I undressed, then reached for the condom. Before me, Wren wriggled out of her dress and bra and tossed them aside, her eyes green flames of need as she watched me.

'Hurry up, Jasper.'

I tugged the condom on, then froze for a moment, arrested by the spectacular sight before me. 'Not yet, baby. I need to look at you.' Despite our previous dalliances, this was the first time I was seeing Wren completely naked. My mouth dried as I took in every inch of her silky smooth skin, the graceful arch of her spine, trailed my fingers from her nape to her tail bone. 'Fuck, you're so beautiful.'

Her head dipped a fraction, another bashful look fleeting across her face before the siren returned, her eyes commanding me to grant her wish. 'I need you inside me, Jasper. Right now.'

And since that was exactly what I wanted, I braced both hands on her hips. 'Open your legs wider for me,' I rasped.

The moment she did, I positioned myself at her heated entrance. Then, volcanic need threatening to rip me to pieces, I thrust inside her. Her scream echoed my gut-deep groan. I lost all sense of time and place, the only sensation the tightness of her sheath as she welcomed me in. 'Fuck, Wren. Fuck!'

'More, Jasper. Give me more.'

I kept thrusting until sweat coated both our bodies, until her final hoarse scream ended in convulsions that milked my own release from me. Bracing one hand on the glass to keep me upright, I planted kisses on her neck and shoulders as we caught our breaths.

Something inside me tightened when she reached back and trailed one hand over my thigh. The idea that she needed to touch me as much as I yearned to caress her kept me at the window far longer than I would've done if she weren't touching me.

I wasn't one for post-coital cuddling, and yet I couldn't find any reason to move away. When my kisses trailed to her jaw and she turned into my kiss, my insides continued to sing and twist and sizzle in a way I wasn't too keen on exploring. And when she gave another soft moan, I knew I was gone.

'We did leave it open-ended as to how many times we fucked once the six hours were up, right?'

Her sultry little laugh went straight to my balls, making me hard all over again. 'I believe we did.'

Bending low, I scooped her up in my arms and strode for the bedroom. 'Wonderful. Let me know when you've had enough.'

'Let me know when you've had enough.'

Jasper's words reverberated through my mind as I packed for the week-long trip to Morocco a week later.

Far from experiencing the emotional apathy I had with my two previous relationships, I felt…alive. Quietly unfettered. As if something inside me were straining to break free.

Perhaps it was all the glorious sex.

Perhaps it was the inroads I'd made into renegotiating the terms Perry had initially tied Bingham's to.

Paolo had signed on the dotted line to be the exclusive tequila supplier for one year in not just the Moroccan resort but in all Mortimer hotels. And as of last night, I'd received a firm *maybe* from Jasper to shorten the one-year profit-margin projections to nine months, a term that I fully intended to reduce to six months before we touched down in Marrakesh.

Success on that front would mean, by summertime, Bingham's could well see a healthy profit from our association with the Mortimer Group. Not that my board was in the mood to heap accolades on my head. Nevertheless, the blatant grumblings had…lessened in the past week. At least from the board members.

My mother on the other hand…

As if summoned by thought, my phone rang. It took a moment to locate it beneath the mountain of clothes I was sorting through, on account of sudden nerves over which clothes Jasper would prefer to see me in.

The thought that I was even remotely interested in pleasing him made me pause for a shocked moment before answering the phone. 'Mother, I'm afraid I can't talk for long—'

'Why? Because you've decided to publicly draw a line in the sand, show me where your true loyalties lie?'

My breath caught at the acid in her voice. 'What are you talking about?'

'You were seen, Wren. Coming out of the hotel with the Mortimer boy last week. And don't bother to convince me it was business.'

My teeth gritted, the urge to demand she stop calling him a boy bubbling up in my throat until I swallowed it down. That insult was minor in the grand scheme of things. As, I was further stunned to realise, was the revelation that I'd been spotted leaving the Mortimer Mayfair. The sharp bite of remorse I expected to feel never arrived. And when I exhaled it was with a certain…pain-edged freedom that made my throat ache when I answered, 'Okay, then, I won't.'

It was her turn to gasp. 'You're not going to bother denying it?'

'Why should I, Mother? It's true. I was in the hotel with Jasper. And it wasn't business. Is that what you called to condemn me about?'

She went silent for a frozen moment. 'Of all the men in this town, Wren,' she asked bitterly. 'Why him?'

I shut my eyes, a wince catching me hard inside because I'd asked myself the same question at least a half-dozen times since that moment in the maze. And every answer had only deepened my bewilderment. Because not even once had I considered simply… walking away, regardless of the fact that I'd demanded he release me from our business deal. 'No explanation I give is going to satisfy you, so why put ourselves through it?' My question emerged solemn and reserved, directly opposite to the churning in my belly.

Something was happening with Jasper. Something I seemed powerless to stop.

'I guess there's nothing more to discuss, then, is there?'

The finality in her tone unnerved me. Enough to make my answer rushed. 'Mother, can you trust me for once? Please? I'm trying to salvage this for all of us.' The worrying thing was, I wasn't sure if the business was the only thing I was attempting to salvage.

'You want me to trust you when you've openly thrown yourself into the enemy's bed? Oh, sweet girl, don't you know this will only have one unfortunate ending for you? Don't you know that's what they live for?'

Jasper's face materialised before my eyes, the ruthless and dogged determination in getting his way. I couldn't deny that so far things had worked in his favour. Mostly. But I planned on changing that. 'It... won't,' I replied, then...stronger when my voice wobbled, 'It won't.'

My mother sighed. 'Your father deluded himself about getting into bed with vipers once upon a time, too.'

Before I could reply the line went dead.

I hung up, hurt and incensed. And when tears filmed my eyes, I dashed them away with an impatient hand. Wasn't there a saying that history repeated itself only if we didn't learn from it? Why was my mother so determined to write me off?

The answer shook through me, terrifying me into blindly throwing random items of clothing into the suitcase. Who the hell cared what Jasper preferred? I would dress for myself and no one else.

Still, my senses jumped into sizzling life when my phone pinged with a message from him.

Be there in ten.

I was waiting by my front door when he pulled up in his Aston Martin. When he started to get out, I waved him away, wheeling my suitcase towards the boot. 'I'm fine. Just pop the boot, please.'

A frown twitched across his face as he flicked the button. I stymied another flare of unease when I saw his suitcase—a top-of-the-range designer exclusive with his name monogrammed in neat letters.

Get a grip, Wren. You're now annoyed because the billionaire you're sleeping with has nice luggage?

'Whoa, did you wake up on the wrong side of the bed, sweetheart?' he enquired dryly when I got into the car.

I shut the door with a tiny slam and yanked on my seat belt. 'What if I did?'

He stared at me for a moment, then nodded. 'Right, you're itching to pick a fight with me. Fine. Go ahead. As long as we get to make up properly afterwards.'

That should've angered me more. Instead, part of me leapt in excitement while the painful knot in my belly expanded. I shook my head, my thoughts bewildered. 'Can we just go, please?'

He set the car in motion and stayed silent for the first few miles.

Far from the silence easing my churning emotions, I grew even more unsettled.

After another few minutes, he sighed. 'Can I take a wild guess at what's eating you up? You're raging at fate for matters that aren't in your control? That had nothing to do with you but in which you're fully embroiled somehow? And the more you think about it, the more it pisses you off, and the more ridiculous guilt eats you up?'

I shifted in my seat, a little riled and lot bewildered by his acuity. 'Don't shrink me, Jasper.'

A wry, cynical smile curved his lips. 'I'm not. But have you considered that I'm stuck in the same situation? My nightmare of a father did something to yours and now the sins of our fathers are being visited upon us.'

'Don't you mean the sins of *your* father?' I snapped.

He flinched. 'Since we're talking about Hugh Mortimer, renowned bastard and destroyer of lives, then yes, maybe I am willing to take full responsibility on his behalf.'

A touch mollified, if a little unjustly since I suspected my father also bore some of the responsibility, I breathed through the easing of the knots inside me. 'Careful there or I'll take you up on that *mea culpa* you're bandying about.'

He shrugged. 'Take it, sweetheart. It's all yours.'

The peculiar thickness in his voice made that curious little hook catch once more in my midriff. Only this time it was positioned higher, dangerously close to where my heart hammered an erratic tattoo. He switched lanes in a suave move, increasing our speed. He said nothing more after that and I gladly welcomed the silence, a chance to contemplate how best to deal with my mother.

When we pulled into the private-jet section of the airport just outside London forty minutes later, it was with the acceptance that it would be better to let things play out, show her the proof of my success when I accomplished what I meant to. Anything else would be akin to banging my head against a stone wall.

What if it's not enough?

That bleak little question echoed through me, threatening to dull my enjoyment of my surroundings long after I'd boarded the seriously opulent Mortimer jet.

But with the even bleaker thought that this was a cycle I'd found myself repeating with my mother, and that, like before, I needed to snap out of it, I forced myself to look around. To steep myself back into the present as the plane taxied down the runway and rose into the sky with a smooth take-off.

The inside of the 747 private jet was worthy of its own spread in a premium airline magazine. I'd flown in enough such jets in my modelling days to recall that the general layout meant the bedroom suites were located at the back.

Back then, I'd done nothing more than sleep to mitigate jet lag, but I grew hot and needy at the thought of changing that on this trip. The flight to Morocco would take a little over four hours. The possibility of stepping off the plane as a member of the mile-high club made me tingle.

On the tail of that thought, Jasper stepped out of the cockpit where he'd gone after take-off. And just like that, my breathing bottomed out.

In my unsettled mood, I'd failed to clock what he was wearing and as he strolled down the aisle towards me it struck me that I was seeing him in less formal clothes for the first time. Then came the more potent acceptance of how devastatingly handsome he looked in whatever attire he wore. Today's selection of white polo shirt with raised collar, coupled with khaki chinos that hugged lean hips and hard, muscled thighs, lent him a charming swagger and assured sophistication that made my mouth dry and my chest palpitate like a hormonal schoolgirl the closer he got.

And when he was close enough to touch, those distinctive eyes piercing mine, it was all I could do not to launch myself at him. Because being in Jasper's arms was a guarantee that every other thought would be pushed out. That I would only be consumed by him. Which was a scary thought in itself…

Don't you know this will only have one unfortunate ending? Don't you know that's what they live for?

'You still have war and pain in your eyes,' Jasper murmured, a thoughtful observation forged with a little steel and a lot of contemplation. 'Will you permit me to find a way of combating that?' he asked.

The shiver that went through me was a warning against embracing that offer. It was strong enough to make me shake my head. 'I'll pass, thanks.'

If my answer displeased him, he hid it well. In a blink, the steel was gone from his eyes and he was taking the seat next to mine. 'Something else, then? Champagne? Or shall I order us something to eat?'

With my mother's warning still echoing through me, I lifted a leather briefcase from where I'd dropped it next to my seat.

'I'm not hungry. And the champagne can wait for a while.'

I pulled out the newest version of the contract and placed it in front of him. We'd been dancing around with a parry and thrust that was frankly a little too thrilling. But the bottom line was that I had to secure Bingham's business interests regardless of whether I shared Jasper's bed or not.

'You said you'd consider a nine-month profit-sharing clause. I've changed my mind. I think a six-month contract is a more viable option.'

He remained silent for almost a minute. Then his shrewd gaze flicked over my face. 'Convince me.'

'Hobbling Bingham's into working with one hand behind our backs stymies your productivity, too. We need money to make more money. With an earlier profit-sharing contract, you make half a per cent more than you would in the next six months. I've done the figures.' I rose from the chair. 'I'll go and freshen up while you look it over.'

Instead of concentrating on the file I'd placed before him, his eyes travelled over my body. 'Or we can look it over together and I'll help you freshen up when I'm done?'

I smiled even while my pulse leapt wildly. 'No can do. I wouldn't want to ruin your concentration.'

'Too late for that,' he responded, his voice hoarse with arousal.

I leaned over and tapped a finger on the file. 'Deal with this, Jasper. It's important to me that we're on the same page by the time we land.'

While we'd been embroiled in enough sexual tension to break a few records, business had never been muddied by sex. This deal, for better or worse, meant too much to both of us to allow that so I was confident, once I left the room, he'd give it his full attention. Still, I basked in the sizzling heat of his regard as I headed for the rear of the plane. When the stewardess directed me to the bathroom, I thanked her, then, unable to resist, glanced over my shoulder.

As I suspected, Jasper was engrossed in the file, eyes slightly narrowed as he digested the facts and figures I'd painstakingly put together.

I took my time in the well-appointed bathroom, splashing cool water over my wrists and touching up the very light make-up I'd worn. My unbound hair didn't need much attention, but I ran a brush through it all the same. Then, with nothing more to do, I left the suite.

To discover Jasper had moved from the living area into the business area and spread out more papers on the desk. He looked up as I entered.

'I've read your contract. There are a couple of issues that need ironing out.'

'Oh?' It wasn't a flat refusal. I could work with that.

'I think you're underutilising manpower on the ground. At least three per cent of the staff members can double up on other tasks without affecting quality or productivity. Here, take a look.'

I joined him at the table and within ten minutes I was admitting the sheer genius of Jasper's input.

'Give me an hour and I'm sure I can find other areas to increase productivity,' I countered.

He gave an appreciative smile. 'Do that and we have a new deal.'

My breath caught. 'Really?'

'Really. And once we're done with that, we can get down to what's bothering you and the reason why you haven't kissed me since I picked you up.'

CHAPTER NINE

HER FEATURES TIGHTENED and I knew she was about to shut me down. 'I don't need you to fix my problems, Jasper.'

An expected response. One I fully intended to smash through. 'When that problem directly impacts me, I think I'm entitled to a basic understanding of what's going on.'

Her eyes flashed with annoyance. And I admitted quietly to myself that it was way better than the bitter, silent pain I'd seen there before. That kind of pain was acidic, had a tendency to eat away inside you until only a husk remained. The last thing I wanted to see was the woman I was growing increasingly attached to stripped of her vibrancy. Of the passion that blazed through everything she did.

'Impacts you in what way?' she challenged.

I raised my eyebrow and let her read the answer on my face.

'You mean sex?' There was a tight edge to the question that made me wonder if the surface answer wasn't what she wanted. And fuck if that didn't thrill me. I wasn't sure how much of myself I could give but if she wanted more, I would oblige. Up to a point. Because I was a Mortimer, after all. And we were renowned for the amount of dysfunctional baggage we tended to lug around.

'Not necessarily. But I expected the trip thus far to be a little more…stimulating.'

She stiffened, her back going ramrod straight. 'I didn't throw myself into your arms like an overeager teenager when you rocked up in your fancy car, so I must be defective somehow?'

'Stop. You're deflecting.' I hardened my voice.

She opened her mouth, about to snap my head off, but then swallowed and looked away. The weight of that action sat uncomfortably in my gut. Wren never shied away from confronting me. Added to that weight was the realisation that I would fix it, regardless of what it was. Regardless of my suspicion that this would hit close to my own parental issues. Issues I'd happily placed in a vault my whole life.

I cupped her chin and redirected her gaze towards me. 'Tell me what's bothering you, Wren. I may not have crystal-clear answers for you but, much like this contract here, we can figure our way through it, even if it requires several iterations before we're satisfied with it.'

Her eyes grew suspiciously filmy, then she blinked them clear. 'It'll take much longer than a few weeks of hard negotiations to unravel a lifelong conundrum.'

Her voice was solemn, much more subdued than I'd ever heard it, and that unnerving weight in my gut grew.

I rubbed my thumb over the smooth-as-silk skin of her jaw, felt her pulse leap beneath my touch. 'I get that. But conundrums remain that way if you leave them alone. Shove them into the light. Show them to me, Wren. I want to see.'

'Why?' she asked, her voice a little bewildered.

Why indeed? I could've given her the flippant answer, told her I was a ruthlessly determined Mortimer who despised secrets and wanted full disclosure for the sake of our business dealings. But since I hid fat, ugly secrets of my own...

I shrugged. 'I've seen you in business mode and I've seen you content with a well-put-together meal. I've watched you wow a room full of corporate sharks and had you aggravate me with a trench coat I'm still determined to burn the first chance I get. Your many facets fascinate me. This sad version of you irks me. If helping you work through your pain is the only way for you to free yourself of it, then it's a task I'm volunteering to undertake. No strings attached.' Yeah, that last bit was a white lie. I wanted a few strings. The kind of strings that made me want to feed her when she was hungry. Tear a few arseholes to shreds when they upset her. Bask in her smile when she was happy.

She swallowed, and I caught another sheen of tears in her eyes. Then, determinedly, she dragged her chin from my loose grip. 'I won't be deemed weak by divulging things that trouble me, Jasper,' she said, her voice low but stern, her warning clear.

'Believe me, Wren, you're the last person I'd consider weak.'

Green eyes locked on mine, probing for several moments before, satisfied by whatever she was looking for, she nodded. 'Let me get this business out of the way. Then I'll let you feed me champagne and whatever delights your chef has in store for us.' Her gaze flicked past me to the double doors that led to the master suite. 'I might even let you experience that other facet of me you enjoy so much. Then...maybe I might tell you a thing or two about...stuff. Agreed?'

The weight shrank in direct proportion to my expanding relief. 'Agreed, but with one tiny addendum.'

One perfect eyebrow rose. 'Yes?'

'Since you'll be working full-time on Mortimer business, shall we dispense with the six hours nonsense?'

Her smile slowly grew, banishing a few shadows in her eyes. And the reappearance of my vibrant, gorgeous Wren made something unnervingly vital shake loose and free inside me. Instinct warned me that it might be irretrievable. For the moment, I didn't scramble to chase after it. Because her smile was knocking me for six and I wanted to bask in it until I passed out.

'You have yourself another deal, Jasper Mortimer.'

It was a good and bad thing that Wren was a meticulous businesswoman. It meant that she came up with the goods eventually. But it also meant that we were left with only forty minutes to eat and fuck by the time she presented me with the promised solution. I happily signed on the dotted line of the new contract while the stewardess poured the celebratory champagne. The moment she left us alone, we wolfed down the succulent array of canapés and finger food the chef had prepared before we stumbled into the master suite.

'Bloody hell, we only have thirty minutes,' I grumbled against her lush lip as my fingers dived beneath the light pink cashmere sweater she'd worn to combat the cool English weather.

Her laughter was sultry and musical, her earlier mood finally evaporated as she tackled the zip to one ankle-high boot. 'I'm confident you can make me come at least…twice before we land.' She drew back, teasing in her eyes. 'I'm not overestimating your prowess, am I, Mr Mortimer?'

I chased after her cheeky mouth, playfully biting her lower lip before I growled against it. 'Challenge fucking accepted.'

We tumbled into bed in a tangle of half-undressed frenzy, laughing and growling our frustration until, gloriously, she was naked, her sinuous body warm and welcoming beneath my eager caress.

Knowing I had to wait a few hours more to discover what was bothering her threatened a return of that unease, but then she was rising above me, a siren with her willing captive, the look on her face ethereal and breathtaking as she sank down, taking me inside her tight, hot channel. Then she rolled her hips in a sensual claiming that had my breath hissing out.

'I love it when you do that.'

Hands on my chest, she smiled wider until I was certain I would get lost in it. I didn't give one little damn. Instead I focused on rising to her sensual challenge, my own smug smile appearing when she threw her head back and screamed her first orgasm. Then a second. And just for the hell of it—and probably irritating the hell out of my pilot for ignoring his announcement to return to our seats and fasten our seat belts—a third.

She was locked in my arms, light shudders wracking her beautiful body, as the wheels touched down in a smooth landing in Marrakesh.

From the many hours of work I'd poured into the project, I knew the resort was situated on the outskirts of Marrakesh, midpoint between Essaouira and Agadir. What I hadn't known was that we would be travelling there by helicopter after disembarking Jasper's plane.

A further surprise arrived when he slid behind the controls of the sleek and powerful-looking aircraft with discreet lettering announcing it as a property of the Mortimer Marrakesh Resort.

'You're piloting this thing?' I asked when he donned the headgear and passed me a smaller set.

His teeth flashed in a boyish grin that tunnelled straight into my chest. 'Don't worry, sweetheart, I've had a pilot's licence since I was twenty-one. I think it'll come in handy when I have to step in to ferry VIP guests to the resort. And who knows? It might even knock a quarter per cent off your staffing streamlining.'

Two things struck me just then, the first being that Jasper would most likely spend a great deal of his time here to ensure the resort got off to the good start the projections predicted. And secondly that his absence would…devastate me.

Because…*because*…

My mind seized up, unable to grapple with the emotions mushrooming inside me.

'Wren?'

I heard the frown in his voice but couldn't summon the nerve to look him in the eye. In case he read the very thing I was unable to accept myself? Still feeling tasered by emotions I wasn't ready to deal with, I answered, 'Yeah, sure, I think we can manage that.' Aware that my answer was spacey at best, I forced myself to rally and smile his way as I slid on my head gear and buckled up.

Hazel eyes bored into mine for an extra few seconds before his large hand squeezed my bare thigh. 'You good?'

Perhaps because he was inside me less than twenty minutes ago, or because I was really losing my mind, I dropped my hand on top of his. 'Yes. I am.'

His answering smile hit me square in the solar plexus but even though I was braced for it, it still took my breath away. As did the arid but incredibly stunning landscape as we took off and headed west.

I basked in the beauty of Morocco, happy to play tourist as Jasper pointed out various landmarks. But the most breathtaking of all was the distant but majestic vista of the endless, snow-capped Atlas Mountains, a watchful range of giants dominating the horizon.

'The resort is coming up now, on your right,' Jasper said after fifteen minutes, his voice intimate through the headphones.

Sliding up sunglasses I'd worn to protect against the mid-afternoon sunlight as he went low enough for a close view, I was awed all over again at my first sight of the hillside resort.

Rather than one giant building, it was a sprawling collection of sand-coloured mini castles, joined together by long interconnecting walkways, which would offer spectacular views of landscaped gardens and the Atlas Mountains on either side through elegant Moorish archways.

After landing and an introduction to the general manager in the cool, marble-floored interior of the staggering beautiful reception, I discovered on the tour that followed that those archways had been painstakingly hand-painted in swirls of gold and bronze and turquoise.

Each mini castle contained four luxury *riad* penthouses, complete with private pools, hammam suites and endless sources of pampering and relaxation facilities, a true desert oasis unlike any other.

While I'd seen it all laid out in one report or another in the past few weeks, experiencing it in person was a thrill that drew increasingly loud gasps from me as we toured the extensive grounds. At my latest one, Jasper turned to me, a wide grin splitting his exceedingly handsome face.

'Am I blowing your mind a little bit, sweetheart?' he drawled, assured in that fact even before I answered.

'You're blowing my mind a lot,' I replied. And not just with the architecture. More and more, it seemed as if getting on the plane and leaving England behind had lifted a layer of tension off us despite our little charged conversation.

His smile widened, then slowly morphed with sexual heat, increasing in temperature until that space between my heart and stomach tightened with a new kind of tension. The one that warned the addiction I'd feared I was succumbing to had probably passed the point of no return.

When he caught my hand in his and brushed his lips across my knuckles, I experienced an even harder kick. And when he kept hold of my hand for the remainder of the tour that once again led us outside, I let him, that fiercely intimate connection of palms gliding together a sensation I suddenly didn't want to do without.

Outside, a long rectangular pool was banked by a palm grove, offering the perfect balance of sun and shade that meant guests could linger for hours, the inviting water sparkling in the sunlight.

A little further on, amongst fig and citrus trees that sweetly scented the air, giant awnings resembling the wings of a Bedouin tent offered more stations of shade, with plump cushions and beaten leather pouffes laid out on Persian carpets. It was a seductive and decadent invitation to lounge and indulge, to free up one's senses to the pleasures the resort provided.

I felt the last of the tension leave my body as we meandered back into the resort.

'Ready for the *pièce de résistance*?'

'There's more?'

His hand tightened around mine. 'The jewel in the crown. You'll like it, I think.' He stopped to order a tray of mint tea and refreshments at the concierge desk before ushering me into a discreetly tucked away lift that didn't jar with the blend of traditional and contemporary gold and turquoise decor. Pressing a button that only had a star next to it, he pulled me into his arms as the lift doors shut, content to simply hold me as we were whisked seven floors up.

We stepped into the foyer of what was clearly the largest of the mini castles. A discreet plaque announced it as the Tower Suite and I soon discovered why when, after a jaw-dropping tour of the decadent master suite housing the largest four-poster bed I'd ever seen, I stepped out onto an equally vast terrace. No, to call it a terrace was a gross understatement.

The tennis-court-sized space came complete with turrets, parapet and three-hundred-and-sixty-degree views, the interior accommodations perfectly centred and smaller versions of the whole resort repeated in the vast space.

'Oh, my God, this is incredible! You can experience everything the resort has to offer without leaving the tower if you don't want to.'

He nodded. 'That was the general idea. Even the desert sand can be brought to you if you wish it.'

Stopping at the rectangular bathing pool fashioned from the same coloured turquoise tiles accenting the decor, I trailed my fingers through the cool water. 'I've never felt the need to be clean the way I do right now.'

Strong arms wrapped around my waist, his voice a husky rasp in my ear, 'Hmm, I can't wait to watch you bathing under the stars, with just moonlight covering your skin. Well…moonlight and me.'

My laugh felt as unfettered as the contentment seeping into my bones. Then, his words sinking in, I turned within the confines of his arms. 'Wait, I don't get my own suite?'

He looked a little startled, then mutinous before he quirked one brow at me. 'Do you want your own suite? I'm sure I can organise one for you if that's what you want?' His tone said he would do so reluctantly.

But it was a moot point anyway because it wasn't what I wanted. I yearned to spend every spare moment with him. 'No. I'd love to share this suite with you.' Why not go all out and embrace this temporary insanity?

The shadows left his eyes, that almost conceited confidence drenching his smile. 'Brilliant answer.'

The wind-chime doorbell went and Jasper excused himself to answer it. A sharply dressed waiter wheeled out a silver trolley, positioning it under one of the four awnings where a traditional floor seating of rugs and cushions was laid out.

'Thank you, Azmir. I'll take care of the rest,' Jasper said.

The waiter left with a huge tip and a wide smile and when Jasper held out his hand, I joined him, happily kicking off my platform shoes that went with the orange and white polka-dot sundress I'd hurriedly changed into before disembarking the plane.

Reclining against one thick cushion, I accepted a plate of sandwiches, which I finished in record time. With my second cup of mint tea, I sighed my pleasure at my surroundings.

Everything I'd experienced so far impressed a bone-deep belief that I was doing the right thing by not walking away from this deal, regardless of what my mother wanted. It had every promise of becoming the kind of exclusive, six-star resort reserved for the elite. Even without the Mortimer name attached to it. And with Jasper fronting it, I wouldn't be surprised if there was already a mile-long waiting list.

No wonder Perry had bent over backwards to grab a piece of this.

Thoughts of my brother made my mind veer down a different path.

'Hey, why the frown?' Jasper asked.

About to give an evasive answer, I surprised myself by blurting out the truth. 'I was thinking about Perry. I'm wondering whether he'd think I've stolen this project from him. It was his baby, after all.'

It was a testament to the kind of family we both came from that he didn't think the question absurd considering Perry and I were siblings, supposedly working for the same team.

'Have you heard from him?'

I shook my head, a wave of concern and sadness washing over me. 'I don't expect to even if places like that allowed contact with family. Things weren't that great between us even before all of this.' I waved my hand at the resort.

Jasper nodded. 'You think he'll be angry because he'll believe he teed it up for you to hit the winning shot?'

I frowned, knowing he was making a point. 'You don't think he did.'

He snorted. 'Absolutely not. And I'll be happy to

set him straight on that score. Sure, you and I have had a few ups and downs but think of the progress we've made in the last three weeks. It sure beat the months I was chasing him around to stop this project from suffering a catastrophic and costly setback.'

The praise was welcome but the hollow feeling inside remained. 'Telling him is one thing. Getting him to accept it might be something else.'

'And you believe it's that something else that might drive a deeper wedge between you?'

Feeling a mournful little lump climbing into my throat, I took a hasty sip of tea. 'I don't know. On the one hand it seems inevitable that he'll resent the progress I've made. On the other, I'm hoping I get lucky and he comes out of rehab, all goodness and mercy, champing at the bit to end our...estrangement.'

Jasper only frowned deeper. 'Were things really that bad?'

My lips twisted, my inner voice mocking the hope of my latter statement. 'You sound surprised. I got the impression your family wasn't sweetness and light, either.'

His lips twitched sardonically. 'We aren't but our dysfunction is curiously programmed to infect the parent-child bond rather than the sibling one. Don't get me wrong, Damian only recently emerged from some self-imposed secondment in New York and Gem is busy with her own family.' He shrugged. 'I don't see much of them, anyway.'

'And let me guess, you prefer it that way?'

The flash of disconcertion on his face told me I'd hit

the nail on the head. For some reason, that deepened the chasm yawing inside me.

Before I could ask him more questions about his family—mainly to deflect from answering painful ones about my own—his eyes speared me again. 'Was that what was bothering you this morning? The friction between you and Perry?'

Staring into the leafy green depths of my tea, I answered, 'No, it was the parent-child part. I'm lucky enough to have it from both sides.'

'Tell me,' he encouraged, much as he had on the plane this morning.

'My mother saw me leaving your hotel last week. Amongst my many other failings, that apparently makes me an irredeemable traitor to my family.'

His jaw clenched tight, his face a gathering thunderstorm. 'Wren—'

'Which is rich, considering they barely acknowledge my existence ninety-nine per cent of the time. I've been barely a Bingham since before my father died.'

This time my voice did break the smallest fraction. He heard it. Abandoning his tea, he slid his fingers over my nape and pulled me into a tight embrace. Unfortunately, that only reminded me of every other embrace I'd been deprived of for as far back as I could remember. I dissolved into Jasper's arms, tears I seemed to have battled all day resurging, this time spilling down my cheeks as I buried my face in his chest.

I felt…cherished. Protected in a way I'd never done before in my life. As unwise as everything indicated, I wanted to hang on to it. Absorb it into myself until it became a part of my soul. Until I could look back on it some time in the dismal future and bask in its afterglow.

'I'd love to say fuck them all but it's not as simple as that, is it?' he rasped, a deep understanding in his voice that spoke of his own demons.

Tears welled faster. 'No, it's not.'

His chest heaved in a long sigh, then I felt his lips brush the top of my head. 'Our inability to kick them permanently out of our lives doesn't mean they get to control us, though, correct? Only you have the power over you. No one else.'

The depths of bitter conviction in his voice said this was as much about him as it was about me. I looked up and his jaw was set in iron, his gaze on a faraway point I suspected didn't involve me. And yet, I still felt...wanted.

The earlier need to probe his own family situation rose again but I was a little terrified and a lot selfish to lose the warmth and security of his arms. So I bit my tongue, closed my eyes and breathed him in.

After an eternity, I felt his gaze on my face. 'Are you glad you came? And don't say yes because this is work,' he tagged on gruffly.

Raising my gaze, I met his. 'Yes, I'm glad I came,' I replied, my voice a husky mess. We were crossing an invisible but dangerous line and yet, I was...exhausted with resisting its magnetic pull.

Jasper dropped his head slowly, and I held my breath until his lips sealed over mine. We kissed with slow languor, allowing the heat to build between us until we were both breathless.

He raised his head in torturous increments and when he spoke, his lips still brushed mine. 'The sunsets here are quite spectacular. Want to experience the outdoor bath tonight?'

I shook my head. 'Too tired to appreciate it,' I replied, just as a yawn caught me unawares.

He stood and held out his hand. 'I think an early night is on the cards. We have a full day tomorrow.'

I frowned, trying to remember the itinerary and realising…there was none. 'What exactly is happening tomorrow?'

That boyish grin, totally lethal to my state of mind, flashed into life as I let him help me up. 'Everything.'

With that ominous declaration, he tugged me back into the *riad*, to the master suite. Then, catching my hem, he freed me of my dress and panties, and nudged me into the bathroom. Bypassing the Jacuzzi bath, he switched on the jets in the shower, then made short work of undressing himself. All the while watching me with an expression that made my breath catch and my heart squeeze.

To mitigate the erratic mess that was my pulse and my emotions, I reached for an apple-shaped bottle with an exquisitely carved stopper top in the shape of the M'Goun Valley rose, the national flower of Morocco.

Jasper stopped me with a soft grip. 'No, let me.' He took the bottle, uncapped it, poured a decent measure into his palm, then motioned for me to come closer. I watched him rub his hands together, that simple act so intensely erotic, my nipples beaded and my thighs clenched hard with desperate need. 'I've dreamed of at least two dozen ways to do this.'

Swaying towards him, I lifted eyelids that were curiously heavy to meet his gaze. 'We've showered together before.'

'Hmm, but always when one of us had to rush off somewhere. Or when one of us needed to fuck the other super urgently.'

Heat rose up my body. Yes, so I'd attacked him the last time we'd been in the shower together. 'No need to rub it in my face.'

'Oh, I intend to rub it in all right. All over your body.'

Laughter caught me completely unawares, a peculiar strain of joy fizzing through me. It died in a sigh as Jasper's hands proceeded to wreak exquisite magic on my body. I didn't bother to hold back my moans of pleasure because it felt disingenuous in this place. Instead, I closed my eyes and gave myself over to him. And by the time he swung me into his arms and carried me to the four-poster, I was a boneless, mindless creature, ready to receive everything he had to give.

Like the kiss before, the lovemaking was indulgent, decadent and slow, tapping into the rhythm of the land.

And just like before, I blinked back tears when it was over. Then gasped with a different sort of pleasure when, with a touch of a remote, the doors slid back to reveal the insanely gorgeous sunset he'd promised.

From the perfect vantage point of our bed, it felt as if we were being treated to the creation of an extraordinary oil painting. The world itself seemed ablaze, streaked with the richest scarlet, vibrant orange and saffron yellow.

'My God, that's beautiful,' I whispered.

Jasper pulled me tighter against him. 'Yes. And just in case I didn't mention it before, I'm glad you came, too.'

Later, when it all went wrong, I would remember this moment.

The moment that last sane string unmoored me from reality as I knew it and gaily wove its way through the air into the hands of the last man I should've trusted it to.

The next day, rested and sated from glorious early-morning sex, we set off on dune buggies to a desert encampment half a mile away that formed part of the resort. The objective of the visit was to judge the experience as a possible business retreat and relaxation exercise. The twelve Bedouin tents were each large enough to host up to thirty guests and, as evidenced by the signals from our laptops as we got down to work, the business facilities were more than adequate.

By lunchtime we'd pronounced it a success and moved on to the next item on the agenda. Thrilled at the rate we were checking things off our extensive to-do list, we didn't stop until after the sun had gone down.

Dinner was an exquisite lamb and vegetable couscous cooked in an authentic tagine, followed by a creamy locally made dessert of sugared almonds and crushed dates served over a baked yoghurt. Over rich, cream-laced coffee, Jasper regarded me with heavy-lidded eyes. 'I'm getting you in that bath tonight.'

Since the stars were shining bright and I'd had exactly the same idea, I smiled. 'You have my full cooperation.'

With a heart-stopping smile, he reached for the tablet next to his coffee cup. I'd discovered to my delight that most amenities within each suite could be operated digitally and when I heard the sudden rush of water hitting the cavernous bath, my temperature rose. I set my coffee down as Jasper reclined back in his seat, his eyes promising everything he intended to do to me. But I intended to flip the script on him tonight.

'How long do we have until it's ready?'

'About eight minutes.'

I smiled. 'Hmm, that's long enough.'

Telltale heat scored his cheekbones. 'For?'

'For me to drive you a lot crazy.' I crooked a finger at him. He rose, prowling over to me in a way that made every cell in my body sing. When I made space between my knees, he stepped into them, hands hanging loose at his sides.

Slowly, teasingly, I placed my hands on his calves, then dragged them up. Arousal darkened his eyes as I explored muscular thighs for several seconds before heading north. He hissed out a breath when I brushed my knuckles over his very prominent erection. Keeping my eyes glued on his, I unbuttoned his chinos and drew down the zip. Another slow but firm tug freed his beautiful, engorged cock.

I gripped him, revelling in the hot smoothness of

him, while attempting to contain the wildfire hunger rushing through me.

Still keeping my gaze on him, I pumped my hand once…twice. 'Would you like me to taste you, Jasper?'

His fists clenched convulsively. 'Holy hell, yes,' he rasped.

Moaning in anticipation, I leaned in close and wrapped my mouth over his broad head. A thick groan left his throat and I felt a light tremor wash through him. Ravenous, I took more of him in my mouth, my tongue shamelessly circling and licking as pleasure swelled through me.

'Ah, that's so good, Wren.'

I explored his cock from root to tip, licked and sucked and teased until he was panting, one hand firmly lodged in my hair as he fucked my mouth. I was so absorbed by the filthy and beautiful act, I protested when he started to draw away.

'I'd love to come in that gorgeous mouth of yours, sweetheart, but the bath's waiting.'

The bath I'd forgotten about. A little drunk on him, I watched him tear off the rest of his clothes, then tackled mine. Together we stumbled to the immense rectangular bath that could easily have accommodated a dozen.

Jasper paused long enough to tug on a condom before stepping into the warm water and helping me in. Dropping down onto the last step, he stared up at me, his eyes blazing. 'Do it, Wren.'

With a needy moan, I braced my hands on his shoulders. Then slowly, my eyes locked on his, I sank down, taking him deep inside me. Shudders of bliss wracked us both as I fucked Jasper into a panting frenzy. Lips bruised, nails raking over flesh as our simultaneous orgasms swept us under.

And when it was all over, he carried me deeper into the water, making space for me between his thighs so I could recline against him. Soft lingering caresses followed, my dreamy gaze on the stars above our heads as minutes drifted by.

Perhaps it was that sense of being untouchable by life's cruelty in that special moment that made me speak up just then. 'Can I ask you a question?'

His answer was a contented rumble, his lips trailing kisses against my bare shoulder. 'Sure.'

'Your father. You called him a destroyer of lives. Why?'

Jasper stiffened behind me, the hand caressing my thigh freezing. 'Bloody hell, Wren,' he replied. 'I have the most beautiful woman in the world bathing under moonlight with me. The last thing I want to talk about is my father.'

I said nothing, leaving him with the option to answer or not.

Another minute drifted by. 'Fine. Yes, he was.'

'Why?'

Another long pause. 'He called me weak for trying to be the peacemaker of the family. For as long as I could remember, he butted heads with Damian. Even Gem, to some extent. But I was the boy who wouldn't fight the bullies in school; the one who happily gave away his pocket money to the poor kid I felt needed it more.' Bitterness coated the laughter that punctuated his words. 'He particularly hated that when my teachers mentioned it to him, thinking they were doing me a favour and praising me for it. What they didn't know was that Hugh Mortimer was all for anarchy in the name of dividing and conquering.'

It was my turn to stiffen, the evidence of his father's ruthlessness the very thing that had created our feud in the first place. But as I heard his clear opposition my soft heart felt for him.

'He would've been prouder of me if I'd thumped everyone who eyed me the wrong way. And he didn't pull his punches by keeping that shit to himself.'

I twisted in his arms, my shocked gaze searching his. 'He hit you?'

Relief poured through me when he shook his head. 'No. Weirdly enough, he had a line he wouldn't cross. Apparently. But he wasn't shy about delivering emotional bruises.' He laughed again.

I cupped one taut cheek. 'Jasper, I didn't mean to bring it all up—'

'It's fine. He's no longer in my life. And I may be many things now but weak I'm definitely not.' The harsh proclamation sent a cold shiver over me.

No, Jasper Mortimer wasn't weak. I knew that firsthand.

And when he dragged his lips over my jaw and unerringly claimed my mouth again in a ruthless kiss, I wondered whether there was a warning in there for me, too.

CHAPTER TEN

'MORNING, SLEEPYHEAD.'

The miniature roller coaster that had taken residence inside me over the last three days since our arrival in Marrakesh performed a deep spiral at the sound of the sexy voice in my ear. Despite the sensation, I grinned, rolling over to find Jasper perched on the side of the bed, completely naked and looking gloriously virile in the morning light.

'Sleep well?'

I nodded, sighing at the memory of what felt like the best three days and nights of my life. Days filled with work that didn't feel like work at all and nights of transcendental sex.

'Good.'

Hoping I'd get a good-morning kiss, I silently grumbled when he turned away and reached for something on the bedside table. 'Pick one.'

I glanced down at the two envelopes stamped with the Mortimer logo in one corner. The wicked gleam in his eyes made me glance suspiciously at the mysterious offering. 'I don't think…'

'Do you trust me?' he murmured.

The right answer was…no. Perhaps love and affection were conditional but I'd discovered that even after jumping through hoops the way I'd done for my family for most of my life, they'd still let me down. And while cloud nine felt like pure heaven, my instincts shrieked for me to beware. Or, at the very least, take it down a notch the way I'd been utterly unable to since we arrived.

'Don't overthink this, Wren,' he said, his voice a low rumble. 'It's all good, I promise.'

Stupid tears clogging my throat, I plucked the nearest envelope and tore it open to distract myself before I blubbered in front of this man. Again. The words blurred for a minute. When I blinked and they came into focus, my stomach dropped to my toes.

'No way. I want the other one.' I lunged for it.

He held it out of reach, his hazel eyes dancing with humour. 'No, you picked that one, so we're doing that. Unless you're afraid of heights?'

'I never agreed to abide by your rules. And no, I'm not.'

A glimpse of steely ruthlessness surfaced in his eyes. 'So are you going to back out or are you going to trust me?'

Like before, I felt as if he was testing me, weighing me up for something more profound than…sweet heaven…*paragliding* in the desert. Again, the urge to say no pummelled me. Again, I held it at bay. Then I responded with a compulsion pulled from deep within me. 'Okay, fine. I'm going to trust you. This once,' I added, drawn by a desperate need to protect myself, emotionally and otherwise, despite the growing suspicion that it might already be too late.

An hour later, after a succulent Moroccan breakfast of yoghurt, dates, rich coffee and muesli, we left the resort.

I was pleasantly surprised when we arrived at the adventure camp set several hundred metres high up in the High Atlas Mountains. The makeshift camp I'd expected turned out to be a first-class, well-run outfit, with different groups for different levels that put me slightly at ease. The safety lesson further eased my nerves, enough to spark excitement. But not enough to fly solo when given the option.

The smouldering looks Jasper sent me as we suited up said he was pleased I'd chosen to double up with him; the intimacy of being strapped in tight against him only underlined that fact.

Regardless of all of that, my nerves nearly gave out as we stepped closer to the cliff edge.

'Jasper...wait, I don't think I want to do this—'

'One small step, Wren. That's all it takes,' he whispered in my ear. 'One small step and the belief that you're not alone. That I won't let anything happen to you.'

Dear God, what was he doing to me? I glanced back at him, saw the unshakeable promise in his eyes, and just like last night I wanted to open myself up and fill my soul with it. For however long it lasted.

With that assurance cloaking me, I swallowed, stepped forward into nothingness and felt my belly drop away from my body.

For the first five seconds, sheer terror gripped me, my scream searing my throat. But over the strong rush of air, Jasper spoke again. 'Sweetheart, open your eyes. See what your bravery has earned you.'

Reluctantly obeying, my jaw dropped as the beauty of my surroundings slowly engulfed me.

Now that we were in the air, it was as if I were sitting on a soft, swaying cushion. And below us, the majesty of the mountains and trails gave a true bird's eye view. 'This is…incredible,' I murmured, delight replacing terror.

'Told you,' Jasper said smugly.

I glanced up, saw his smile and the easy confidence with which he operated the glider and ventured a smile of my own.

'Want to go higher?'

At my nod, he sent us soaring higher, then, before I could catch my breath, his lips pressed close to my ears. 'Look to your left.'

I looked and gasped out loud. 'Oh, my God.'

A flock of grey-winged geese on their migration path flew in perfect V-formation about fifty metres away. Caught on a warm thermal, their wings barely moved, the only movement the graceful undulation of their necks. Totally entranced, I stared until my eyes watered, until my smile threatened to split my face.

When Jasper alerted me that he was changing direction, I felt a moment's sadness, then intense joy that I'd experienced this once-in-a-lifetime moment. My heart slamming against my chest, I wondered if that was a harbinger of my relationship with Jasper. Was he destined to blaze through my life like a comet, then fade away once this trip was over? Because really, once the last few teething issues in our contract were ironed out, there would be no need for further day-to-day contact.

And as we glided towards our designated landing spot, the ground rushing up at us, my breath was snatched from my lungs. Because I knew the seventy-minute flight would've been right up there with the most intensely exhilarating thing I'd ever done had I not felt another thunderbolt of emotion the moment we stepped back onto *terra firma*.

Despite suspecting this was coming, I stood shell-shocked and completely willing for Jasper to believe, as he laughingly loosened my harness and pulled it off, that it was the flight that held me tongue-tied. While all the time, the sonic boom of revelation ripped my life apart.

I was in love with Jasper Mortimer.

I struggled to hold myself together as he trailed a finger down my cheek, his eyes caressing my face. 'You should feel this free every day, Wren. Let the baggage go. It suits you.'

I must have given a satisfactory response, because his teeth flashed in another devastating smile before he took my hand and walked me back to our SUV.

In the car, I grabbed my laptop and attempted to make notes about the experience, even though my focus was shot to pieces. Thankfully, it kept Jasper from engaging me in conversation, gave me the reprieve to contain the uncontainable.

My heart had handed itself over to my family's worst

enemy and I knew deep in my bones that it was irretrievable. Did I even want it back? In a different world, had there been a chance with Jasper, would I have taken it? While my soul wanted to scream *yes*, my head forced me to face reality.

We'd gone from regular sex sessions for the sake of peaceful contract negotiations to a week in a desert paradise already counting down to its conclusion.

None of it reeked of permanence or commitment. And even if it did, did either of us have the tools to sustain it in the long term?

Shaken by the glimpse of the desolate future that awaited me, I was relieved when, on arriving at the resort, Jasper was handed a note that made him frown.

'I need to make a call to London.'

The tightness in his voice temporarily prised me from my inner turmoil. 'Is everything all right?'

His lips firmed. 'It's Gemma. She's been trying to reach me. So has my aunt.' He anticipated my next question with a shake of his head. 'I can't tell you why because I have no idea.' When he raised his gaze from the note, I caught a glimpse of apprehension.

'Go deal with it. I'll be fine.'

He gave a brisk nod and strode away, tension vibrating off him.

As quickly as my relief arrived, it evaporated. I was in love with Jasper. And whatever permutation I came up with showed our liaison as heart-wrenchingly temporary. My mother's stark condemnation and Perry's possible reaction aside, Jasper had initiated this thing between us out of frustration over my reluctance to sign on to his deal. Would we even be together otherwise?

If you want to know, ask him.

For the first time in my life, I shied away from my rational inner voice. Every inch of my soul recoiled against receiving another rejection. And yet, when the voice retreated under the relentless force of the shower I took when I returned to the suite, I mourned its silence.

My senses were still in turmoil when Jasper stalked into the *riad* half an hour later. His hair stood in haphazard spikes, as if he'd repeatedly run his fingers through it.

'Is everything okay?'

'No,' he growled. 'I need to head back to London.'

My heart lurched. Was this over already?

Dear God, I'm not ready!

The need to stop the damning words from spilling out kept my lips firmly shut as he paced to the liquor cabinet. His jaw remained set as he splashed a finger of cognac into a glass, then glanced over at me, one eyebrow raised. When I refused the silent offer of a drink, he picked his up and swallowed it in one gulp. Setting it down with suppressed force, he faced me.

'There's a board meeting tomorrow morning that requires my presence.'

I frowned. 'You didn't know it was happening?'

Granite-jawed, he answered, 'Hell, no. But I have no intention of missing it.'

Questions crowded my brain but his forbidding demeanour dried them all up. And really, wasn't this short, sharp shock of a break exactly what I needed?

No, my senses screamed. *Take whatever you can get.*

And then what? My chest squeezed painfully as desolation took hold. When Jasper crossed over to me, slid his hands into my hair, it was all I could do not to melt against him as he fused his lips to mine. To do everything my instinct warned me would only intensify the impending anguish.

'I'm sorry, sweetheart, but this is unavoidable.'

I forced a nod. 'It's fine. But I think I'll stay, make sure everything is in place before I leave.'

He took a long moment to reply and when he did it was with a curt nod. 'Okay. I'll send the plane back for you in a couple of days. And I'll take you out to dinner when you get back to London.'

One small step, Wren. That's all it takes.

The words that fell from my lips seared my insides raw and bloody. 'No. I don't think that's a great idea.'

A frown clenched his forehead. 'Why not?' he growled.

'What are we doing, Jasper?' I blurted before I could stop myself.

To his credit he didn't give me a flippant answer. And even when his hands dropped, his gaze remained fixed on mine. 'Do we need to label it? As long as it feels good, why question it?'

'But that's the problem. How long would it feel good for?'

I was aware I was worsening the mood when his eyes shadowed. 'Wren—'

'That ride this morning? It felt exhilarating. But it ended.'

He shrugged. 'So we'll choose the next adventure. And the one after that.'

'That's all life is to you? A series of thrilling rides?' If so, how long before I was a stale experience he needed to replace with a more stimulating one?

He paced away from me. 'This is so not the time to be dealing with this, Wren.'

A part of me felt sympathy for him. Whatever reason had triggered the unscheduled board meeting, it'd rattled him. But the grounded part of me stressed this was exactly the moment to end this, before I lost even more of myself. 'Is there ever a right time?'

His eyes narrowed, my answer obviously incensing him. 'Nice try, sweetheart, attempting to slot me into some ordinary box you usually reserve for past lovers.' His phone beeped and his jaw gritted after a furious glance at it. 'I need to leave for the airport. But trust me on this...this isn't over.'

'Isn't it?'

With strides powered by frustration, he returned to me, dragged me against his body and stole another hard, tongue-stroking kiss. 'Fuck no, it isn't.'

Self-preservation insisted I didn't prolong this moment, so I pursed my lips, remained in the living room as he stalked to the bedroom. Five minutes later, his suitcase was at the door. Another kiss and he was gone.

And for the next twenty-four hours, I remained in suspended animation of heartache, anguish and mind-shredding debate as to whether I'd done the right thing.

Then it all ceased to matter as all hell broke loose.

* * *

'Let me get this straight. You called a board meeting to get us to vote for you to stage a hostile takeover of Bingham Industries?'

I stared at the man who'd had the audacity to claim a seat at the head of the conference table. The years had turned his hair white and his face weathered. But those piercing eyes and that cruel mouth were the same.

The roar in my ears was nothing compared to the tight vise around my chest. Wren would never forgive me for this. I'd left things in a precarious enough state in my rush to return to London. And taking her to Morocco would be seen by her as the perfect opportunity to get her out of the way in order for my family to stage this ambush. Hell, I'd feel the same in her shoes. Which was why I needed to end this debacle asap.

'You have balls of steel, I'll give you that,' Damian murmured from his place two seats over. Next to me, my cousin Gideon snorted and reclined deeper in his seat, his expression reeking of boredom. I knew it was deceptive because he wouldn't have attended this meeting at all if he were uninterested. But he knew what the instigator of this meeting had done to me. To my siblings. Just as I knew he was here to support me. Hell, maybe my family wasn't so dysfunctional after all.

'Big, fat ones. Trouble with big balls is, expose them like this and they're stupidly easy targets,' I tossed in.

Hugh Mortimer's gaze turned to ice, his gaze tracking his eldest son's, then Gideon's before meeting mine. With me, he lingered, as if trying to spot the weakness he'd condemned me for all those years ago.

I stared him down. *Look all you like, old man. I'm immune to you now.*

He blinked first, his gaze shifting to take in the other Mortimer board members. 'Have you all gone soft in my absence? Bingham is ripe for the plucking.'

'Along with a hundred or so other struggling companies. Why this one in particular?' I taunted.

'Because it's the lowest hanging fruit, that's why,' he answered, his voice booming across the room.

'So much hot temper, Hugh. Calm yourself before you suffer a stroke.' This from Aunt Flo, whose gaze threatened to turn my father into icicles.

To my left, my cousin Bryce sniggered. 'This is way more fun than the reality TV shows Savvie's addicted to,' he murmured.

I allowed searing jealousy to consume me for a moment before I shrugged it off. If I let my guard down, I'd walk away with nothing. Destroy for ever the possibility of having what Gideon, Damian and Bryce had with their new but thriving relationships. Hell, even my wild-child cousin, Graciela, had settled down and was insanely happy with her new man.

'I don't have time to sit around all day debating this. This company isn't in the habit of staging hostile takeovers. I, for one, don't intend to start now.' I glanced at Uncle Conrad, chairman of the board. 'Shall we put it to a vote?'

He glanced at my father, his expression apprehensive. 'Um…'

'I vote nay,' I snarled.

Gideon's hand barely left the armrest. 'It's a *fuck, nay* from me.'

'And from me,' Damian growled, his eyes shooting daggers at the man who'd sired us.

I lost interest after Aunt Flo, Bryce, Gem and Graciela also sided with me. Even if the remaining board members voted against me, I'd still win.

The second the votes were counted and confirmed as fourteen to six, I rose from the table.

All my calls to Wren so far had gone to voicemail. The moment I'd discovered what my father was up to, I'd tried reaching her in Marrakesh, only to discover she'd packed her bags and left without waiting for my plane. She was probably still in the air. Or blocking my calls.

Stomach hollow at the strong possibility it was the latter, I reached for my phone again. It would be easy to check which flights had left Marrakesh—

'Jasper, a word.'

I stiffened at my father's voice. Damian's eyes narrowed. But when his gaze flicked to me, I nodded. Ten seconds later, I was alone with my father for the first time in years.

He sauntered away from me, hands deep in his pockets as he looked out of the window for a full minute before turning to face me. 'I expected you to be the loudest dissenting voice and you didn't disappoint. Still grappling with that bleeding heart, son?' he sneered.

The bite of his condemnation was less…sharp than I'd expected. 'You say bleeding heart, I call it exercising good business sense. You still know what that is, don't you? Or are you so locked on this trifling obsession you can't see straight?'

He inhaled sharply. 'What did you say?'

'You heard me. When are you going to let this go?'

'Not for as long as I draw breath, that's for sure.'

I studied him for a handful of seconds. 'There's more to this than just business, isn't there? What really happened between you and Bingham?'

I didn't expect him to answer but, surprisingly, he responded. 'The upstart had the nerve to try to steal your mother from me.'

Shocked laughter barked from my throat. 'All of this because some guy made a pass at your wife?'

Volcanic rage built in his eyes. 'He disrespected me. No one disrespects me, boy. No one.'

My humour evaporated. 'I'm not a boy. And in case you haven't heard, George Bingham is dead. Don't you have better things to do than to wrestle with a ghost?'

His nostrils flared but the hard rejoinder I expected didn't arrive. Eyes eerily similar to mine considered me for several seconds, before a hard smile twisted his lips. 'I heard you were sleeping with her…the Bingham girl. I didn't think you would be so dense. Obviously, I was wrong.'

'I'd seriously watch it, old man.'

The flicker in his eyes said my warning had got through. 'Answer me this, son. Would you let it go if someone made advances on what you considered yours?'

He clearly knew which buttons to press because the answer was *hell, no*. Wren was mine. She'd been mine long before that first sizzling episode in her maze. But scent-marking her was one thing. Destroying countless lives over an overblown feud was another. 'No, I won't,' I answered my father. 'But neither would I use a bulldozer to squash a gnat.'

'Ah, ever the peacemaker, eh, son?'

A flash of pain and anger twisted inside me. Then curiously the ache eased, leaving in its place a feeling of…acceptance. Calm. Some things just weren't meant to be. 'You keep calling me son, and I really wish you'd stop.'

His eyes narrowed. 'Excuse me?'

'No, you're not excused. Stop calling me son because you haven't earned the right. You were simply a biological ingredient that helped form my existence. You made it clear your children were simply a means to an end. So do us all a favour, *Hugh*, and go back to wherever the hell you came from.'

I headed for the door, the urgency to get to Wren a nuclear force inside me.

'Come back here, Jasper. We're not done.'

I delivered the same corrosive smile his genes had helped me perfect and had the satisfaction of watching his eyes widen. 'Oh, yes, we are.' I turned away from him, then veered back to make the final, vital point. 'Stay away from Bingham's, too. Or so help me, I'll devote every single penny of my many billions to crushing you.'

Every second of my trip to Wren's house four harrowing days later felt like a light year. Unsurprisingly,

Hugh hadn't heeded my warning. And even without the weight of the Mortimer board behind him, he managed to cause an uproar that gripped the city. Every photo I saw of Wren looking anguished as the tabloids hounded her intensified my fury. Staying away from her until I resolved this disaster had felt like death by a million cuts.

My mouth dried as I turned into her street. While my trusted spies had confirmed she was home, gaining entry was another matter.

But I couldn't give up now. Striding to her front door, I leaned on the doorbell. My heart leapt as I heard faint steps and her voice ending a phone call.

Then, 'Fuck off, Jasper.'

'No, sweetheart. I'm not leaving.'

The door burst open. 'Who the hell do you think you are, coming here like this?'

'Let me in, Wren. Please.'

'Are you deaf? I said fuck off.'

God, she looked glorious. Fierce pride elevated her chin even as pain clouded her beautiful eyes. Unable to heed her request, I simply shook my head. 'No.'

Her face twisted as she tried to hang on to her composure. 'You cut me off. Wouldn't even take my calls. Now, my lawyers tell me I'm all out of options and I have forty-eight hours to accept your terms. So, I guess you've come to gloat?'

'No, I haven't. And I'm not the one threatening you. It's my father.'

She paled, her hand dropping from the door. 'What?'

'Let me in and I'll explain.'

Numbly, she stepped back, then flinched from me as I turned to her.

Gritting my teeth, I went down the hallway into her living room, relieved when she followed. Since there was no point beating about the bush, I launched into explanation. 'I didn't answer you because I was dealing with my father. The board backed me against him, Wren. Our contract is airtight. As for that farce of a takeover, it'll happen over my dead body.'

Her jaw sagged open. 'What are you saying?'

'I'm saying that before end of business today, the threat to your company will be over. And before I'm finished with him, Hugh will know that his lastborn son isn't weak. That like I've always done, I'll fight for those who matter to me. To the death if I have to.'

Her eyes grew into alluring saucers and I wanted to grab her, wrap her tight in my arms and never let go. But we'd been through the mill the last few days. I knew it would take more than a few declarations to make things right. Plus I had a feeling that, while I might have won this skirmish with my father, he would continue to be a nuisance for a while.

As those thoughts flashed through my head, the light died from her eyes. 'It's too late, Jasper. The Bingham board are seriously thinking of selling—'

'Fuck that. You won't be selling Bingham's. Not to someone who'll break it into little pieces and sell it, and certainly not to my father.'

Her chin went higher. 'It's not up to you, though, is it?'

I tried a different tack. 'Did I tell you Damian is married now?'

She frowned. 'What?'

I shook my head, the very thought still bewildering in the extreme. 'My hard-hearted, closed-off brother, whose only friend in the world is my certifiably psychotic cousin Gideon, is in love. With an actual red-blooded woman. Who apparently loves him back.'

Her confusion grew. 'Why are you telling me this?'

'Because he's proof that the unthinkable can happen. And they're not just in love, they're also in business together.'

'That's great, but were they locked in a family feud before they got together?'

'No, but fuck that, too,' I snarled. 'Tell me you don't want this to end, once and for all, Wren. That we haven't paid enough for the wrong decisions our parents made?'

She swallowed and that small hesitation sparked hope in my chest. Her gaze flicked to the phone she'd tossed onto the coffee table, and my instinct latched on to it.

'Who were you talking to just now?'

Her lips pursed for a second. 'Perry. Apparently he's allowed phone calls after the first four weeks.'

'What did you talk about?' I pushed, that blind hope still building.

She slicked her tongue over her bottom lip. 'He said he didn't hate me for sealing the deal with you. Or…for going out with you.' The relief in her voice was palpable.

'Good. What else?'

'He said he would support me in whatever decision I make about the company. And...'

'And what?'

'He knows he was the favourite child, that I got a raw deal when it came to our parents' love. He wants me to forgive him for taking advantage of it.'

'As he should.' I paused for a heartbeat before speaking the words that blazed from my soul. 'While you're giving your brother a chance, would you consider giving me one, too?'

Panic flared over her face before her gaze swept away. 'I told you, I'm not some lost cause you need to save. You can go ahead and bid for Bingham's if you want but I—'

'I love you. Does that count?'

Her jaw dropped and a visible tremble shook her body. 'What?'

'I love you, Wren. And you're far, far from a lost cause. You're fit to command armies and your indomitable spirit makes me fall harder for you every passing second.'

She inhaled. Right before her eyes narrowed into accusing slits. 'You refused to take my calls. You left me floundering in the dark for days, Jasper!'

'Because I was scrambling to stop Hugh from getting his hands on Bingham's. Between Gideon, Damian and I, we've been up round the clock for days, blocking every conceivable avenue Hugh might exploit.'

Several layers of anger drained away. 'You...have?'

'If it was just a question of money, it would've been easy. Between the three of us, we have enough to stop

Hugh financially. But before you got your lawyers to implement the freeze on the votes, he was busy trying to buy off your board members. And I was busy trying to put this together.'

Her gaze dropped to the document I held out. 'What is that?'

'A solution I'd love for you to consider when we're done taking care of what's more important. I love you, Wren,' I reiterated. Because I needed her to hear it. To know that the powerful emotion that had taken root inside me when I wasn't looking and fused itself to my very soul wasn't going away. 'I think I fell in love with you five years ago, at the intern's seminar.'

Green eyes grew shiny and I dared to go closer, to hope for an echo of what I felt. 'I don't... I can't...'

'Sweetheart, be brave. One last time. Let's defy the odds and shove our happiness in the faces of our doubters.'

A shocked gasp left her lips. 'Perry said something just like that.'

'And I'd kick his arse for stealing my thunder if I didn't wish with every fibre in my being that you would consider it.' Unable to bear being apart from her, I stepped closer, cupped her chin and nudged her gaze to mine. 'Please, Wren. You mean everything to me. I want to build a life with you. I want to see that smile every day, wait with bated breath for you to blow me away with your brilliant mind. And, sweet heaven, I want the privilege of fucking you every chance I get, even if some of those include you and a certain trench coat I've decided can stay. For now.'

Her laugh was music to my ears and manna to my soul. Too soon, it died away. 'Are you sure, Jasper? This upheaval…it feels like a lot.'

I nodded. 'I get it, and there will probably be a few more to come. But would you rather face it alone or with a seriously handsome dude who worships you?'

Again that smile threatened to make an appearance.

'Take the step,' I pleaded.

Her breath caught and her hand rose as if to touch me. I held my own breath until she did. Then I tugged her into my arms, groaning as my lips found hers. But far too soon, she pulled away.

'Wait. Tell me you didn't know what was happening when you left Morocco.'

I grimaced. 'All Gemma would tell me was that I was needed at the board meeting. I think she suspected I wouldn't attend if she told me Hugh was the one behind it. I didn't know, sweetheart. It killed me the way you found out. But hopefully, I can make it up to you.'

She glanced at the document, then her gaze returned to mine. 'I was terrified you'd betrayed me, Jasper.'

'Never. For as long as I live, I'll never let you down that way. Or in any other way. You're mine. I fight for what's mine. And you are right at the top of that list.'

Tears filled her eyes and neither of us cared when they drenched her cheeks. Because she was smiling through them, her arms encircling my neck. After another long, soul-stirring kiss, she whispered in my ear, 'Do you want to know when I fell in love with you?'

The electric shock that went through me held me

rigid. Then, pure happiness blazing through me, I said, 'Yes, I do.'

'When you took me into the sky with the promise to be the wind beneath my wings and laid the world at my feet.'

A knot in my throat hoarsened my words. 'You have my promise that I will do that for you every day, Wren.'

Fresh tears filled her eyes but she looked more beautiful than ever. 'Only if you let me do the same for you.'

'Deal.'

We kissed, long and deep and soul-sealing. 'I love you, Jasper.'

'My heart and soul and trust and body are yours. And if you can squeeze in a wedding before the launch, I swear to you that I'll find another fraction of love for you.'

Her laughter branded my soul and I vowed to wear it with pride. Because I was Wren's and she was mine.

'Challenge accepted.'

EPILOGUE

THERE WERE MOMENTS in the past three months when I was a little bit ashamed of the precious time I'd wasted fighting this feeling even though I recognised things had played out the way they were supposed to.

That pain and desolation made this all-encompassing bliss suffusing me now even more precious.

'You're smiling again, Wren. I swear if you don't get your act together, you'll blow this for me.'

'Sorry.' I laughed at my almost sister-in-law's mournful voice. 'I can't help it.'

Gemma Mortimer approached, tweaking the veil she'd tweaked a dozen times already. 'I know, but maybe just…pretend for five seconds? I really want to see Jasper's face.'

'Why?'

Gemma shrugged. 'Just…a little payback for all the tricks he pulled on me when we were kids.'

The woman who was fast becoming as precious to me as her brother stared at me with pleading eyes. Damn, those irresistible hazel Mortimer eyes. 'Three seconds, that's all I can give you.'

Gemma whooped. 'I knew you were awesome when you chose me as your maid of honour.'

My smile widened, my heart swelling at the closeness between the siblings these past few months. But my heart was even more grateful for the transformation within my own family.

As if summoned by my thoughts, my mother walked in as Gemma retreated.

Agnes wore a burnished orange lace dress that perfectly complemented the tan she'd cultivated in the pre-wedding week we'd been in Morocco. But her attire wasn't what interested me. The tentative smile that grew at my silent welcome was what touched my soul, the light kiss she dropped on my cheek before stepping back what drew tears to my eyes.

An open conversation with her on my return to London, and then with Perry after his successful stretch at rehab, had stopped the rot of our relationship. Full recovery was a long way off, but my mother's raw admission that she didn't want to lose her daughter, that she'd taken a wrong stance in order to please my father, had helped.

'You look beautiful, Wren.'

'Thank you, Mother.'

She stepped closer. 'I hope this doesn't make you cry and ruin your make-up, but thank you for healing our family.'

Swivelling to face her, I felt a small sob burst out of me. 'Oh, Mum!'

Her own eyes watered. 'You've never called me that before. I... I like it.'

I gripped her hand as she sniffed. Then after touching up my make-up, she looked into my eyes. 'Your brother is ready to walk you down the aisle. Are you ready, Wren?'

'The love of my life is waiting for me, Mum. I'm ready.'

I watched the woman twirling expertly on the dance floor, drawing smiles and laughter from family and guests alike. Silently I shook my head in wonder as she caught my gaze and blew me a kiss.

My wife. Wren Mortimer-Bingham was my wife.

'Jesus, don't let her catch you with that idiotic smile on your face, Jasper. She'll own you for life.'

'Don't listen to Gideon,' came the rejoinder from Damian. 'I catch him staring at Leonie like that at least a dozen times a minute.'

I mourned the disruption of my adoration and turned as Bryce joined us. 'Yeah, I say don't watch her like that because it creeps the rest of us out.'

I couldn't help the laughter that barked out of me or the now familiar warmth that infused me. I'd come to recognise it as a different kind of love. The sustaining kind that was always there but buried beneath the clutter of other emotions.

All it'd needed was the right woman to help us all buff off the hardened edges to rediscover the diamond-strong connection beneath.

And, sweet heaven, the shine of their love was blinding. For a silent moment we watched the women in our lives—Wren, Leonie, Neve and Savvie—dance some more.

'Are you ready to talk business or shall we wait for this sappiness to pass?' Damian muttered.

My gaze flicked from my brother to his wife, Neve, who looked up just then and sent him a secret smile. Then I gazed at my own wife. 'Don't hold your breath, Damian. This is a lifelong thing,' I replied.

He turned and watched me for a second. Then slapped me on the back. 'I'm proud of you, brother.'

The lump was still in my throat when I wove through the guests to my wife's side. Wrapped my arms around her, held her tight and just breathed her in as she threw her arms around my neck.

'I missed you,' I confessed. 'And I love you like mad, even though I still owe you big time letting Gem pull that prank at the wedding.'

Gemma had suddenly frozen halfway down the aisle, stared at me and mouthed *Sorry*. A heartless trick that'd nearly killed me until Wren stepped into view on her brother's arm, her smile incandescent.

Wren threw back her head and laughed now, and I shamelessly buried my face in her neck, basked in her joy and beauty.

'And how are you going to punish the love of your life?'

I kissed her long and deep, uncaring of who saw us. 'I'll come up with something, I'm sure. Right now, I'm a little stumped since you've blown me away with the success of this launch and I'm scrambling to see past your genius.' All around us, A-listers enjoyed the buzz and celebration of the opening of Mortimer Marrakesh.

And according to the data, we were fully booked for several months.

Wren's fingers brushed my cheek, her eyes shining with love. 'You're the genius. For urging me to take this wild ride with you. I love you, Jasper. So much.'

'Are you glad we joined forces?' The document I'd brought to her flat had been a merger proposal between Bingham and the Mortimer Group. Her agreement had stopped Hugh in his tracks. He'd left London soon after and I didn't miss him one little bit.

'Absolutely ecstatic. I couldn't be happier. With you. With our life. With our partnership.'

'Hmm, but I bet I could make you a tiny bit happier…'

Her eyes sparkled. 'Let me guess. Are you going to take me flying again?'

'Any time you want. But for now…' I looked over her shoulder, spotted a darkened doorway that led to a secret place '… I promise a different, way better type of flying. Come with me?'

Her smile threatened to burst my heart wide open. 'To the ends of for ever.'

* * * * *

LET'S TALK

Romance

For exclusive extracts, competitions and special offers, find us online:

- **f** MillsandBoon
- **𝕏** @MillsandBoon
- **📷** @MillsandBoonUK
- **♪** @MillsandBoonUK

Get in touch on 01413 063 232

For all the latest titles coming soon, visit
millsandboon.co.uk/nextmonth

MILLS & BOON

THE HEART OF ROMANCE

A ROMANCE FOR EVERY READER

MODERN
Prepare to be swept off your feet by sophisticated, sexy and seductive heroes, in some of the world's most glamourous and romantic locations, where power and passion collide.

HISTORICAL
Escape with historical heroes from time gone by. Whether your passion is for wicked Regency Rakes, muscled Vikings or rugged Highlanders, awaken the romance of the past.

MEDICAL
Set your pulse racing with dedicated, delectable doctors in the high-pressure world of medicine, where emotions run high and passion, comfort and love are the best medicine.

True Love
Celebrate true love with tender stories of heartfelt romance, from the rush of falling in love to the joy a new baby can bring, and a focus on the emotional heart of a relationship.

Desire
Indulge in secrets and scandal, intense drama and sizzling hot action with heroes who have it all: wealth, status, good looks…everything but the right woman.

HEROES
The excitement of a gripping thriller, with intense romance at its heart. Resourceful, true-to-life women and strong, fearless men face danger and desire - a killer combination!

To see which titles are coming soon, please visit

millsandboon.co.uk/nextmonth

JOIN US ON SOCIAL MEDIA!

Stay up to date with our latest releases, author news
and gossip, special offers and discounts, and all the
behind-the-scenes action from Mills & Boon...

 @millsandboon

 @millsandboonuk

 facebook.com/millsandboon

 @millsandboonuk

It might just be true love...

GET YOUR ROMANCE FIX!

Get the latest romance news, exclusive author interviews, story extracts and much more!